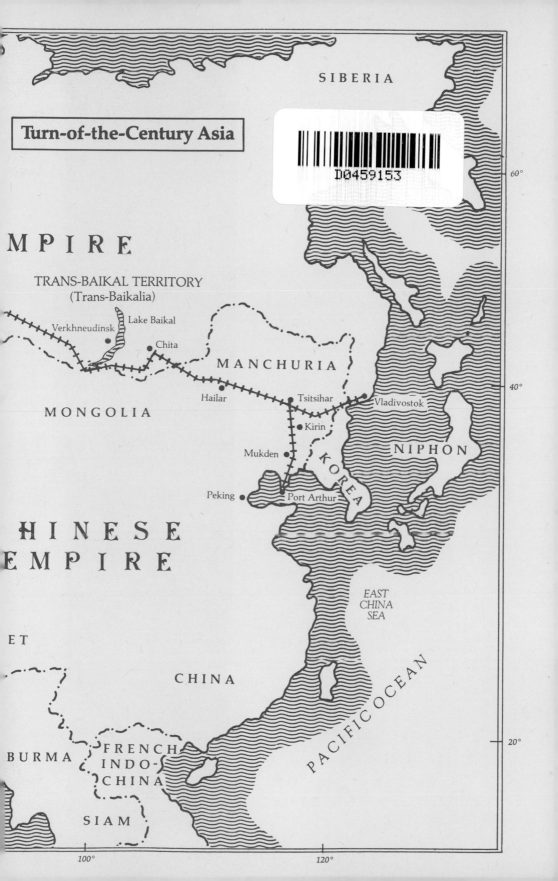

SIBERIA

Turn-of-the-Century Asia

60°

MPIRE

TRANS-BAIKAL TERRITORY
(Trans-Baikalia)

Verkhneudinsk Lake Baikal

Chita

MANCHURIA

40°

Hailar   Tsitsihar

MONGOLIA   Vladivostok

Kirin

NIPHON

Mukden

KOREA

Peking   Port Arthur

HINESE

EMPIRE

EAST
CHINA
SEA

ET

CHINA

20°

BURMA   FRENCH
INDO-
CHINA

PACIFIC OCEAN

SIAM

100°   120°

THE NAME OF HERO

THE NAME OF HERO

A NOVEL BY
RICHARD SELTZER

Published by **J. P. Tarcher, Inc.**
Los Angeles
DISTRIBUTED BY HOUGHTON MIFFLIN COMPANY,
BOSTON

Library of Congress Cataloging in Publication Data

Seltzer, Richard.
The name of hero.
1. Bulatovich, A. K. (Aleksandr Ksaver'evich),
1870– 1919– Fiction.   I. Title.
PS3569.E584N3   813'.54   81-50329
ISBN 0-87477-187-0   AACR2

Requests for such permissions should be addressed to:
J. P. Tarcher, Inc.
9110 Sunset Blvd.
Los Angeles, CA 90069
Library of Congress Catalog Card No.: 81–50329

Design by Tom Lewis, Design Quarter

MANUFACTURED IN THE UNITED STATES OF AMERICA

V 10 9 8 7 6 5 4 3 2 1
First Edition

To Bobby, Heather, and Michael

CONTENTS

THE LINE OF BULATOVICH

(DATES APPROXIMATE)

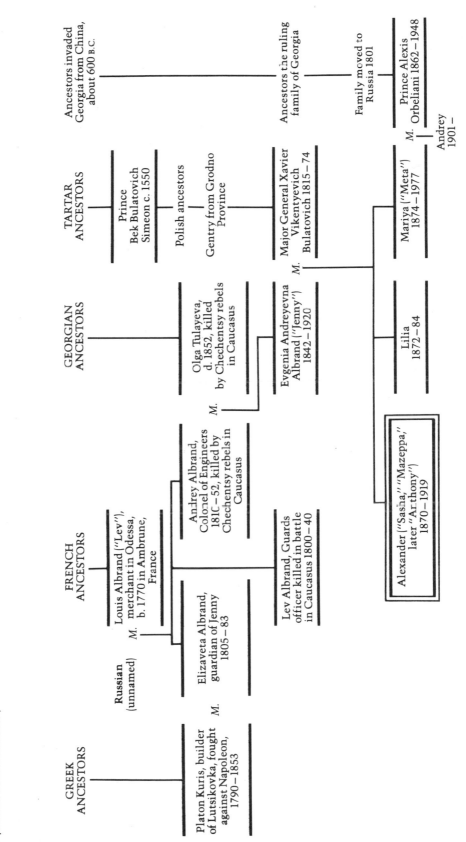

GREEK ANCESTORS

Platon Kuris, builder of Lutsikovka, fought against Napoleon, 1790–1853

Russian (unnamed)

FRENCH ANCESTORS

Louis Albrand ("Lev"), merchant in Odessa, b. 1770 in Ambrune, France

M.

Elizaveta Albrand, guardian of Jenny 1805–83

Andrey Albrand, Colonel of Engineers 1810–52, killed by Chechentsy rebels in Caucasus

Lev Albrand, Guards officer killed in battle in Caucasus 1800–40

GEORGIAN ANCESTORS

Olga Tulayeva, d. 1852, killed by Chechentsy rebels in Caucasus

M.

Evgenia Andreyevna Albrand ("Jenny") 1842–1920

TARTAR ANCESTORS

Prince Bek Bulatovich Simeon c. 1550

Polish ancestors

Gentry from Grodno Province

Major General Xavier Vikentyevich Bulatovich 1815–74

M.

Ancestors invaded Georgia from China, about 600 B.C.

Ancestors the ruling family of Georgia

Family moved to Russia 1801

Prince Alexis Orbeliani 1862–1948

M.

Andrey 1901–

Mariya ("Meta") 1874–1977

Lilia 1872–84

Alexander ("Sasha," "Mazeppa," later "Arthony") 1870–1919

CHARACTERS
(AGES AS OF 1900)

Alexander Xavierevich Bulatovich, also known as "Sasha" and "Mazeppa," 30—Staff-Rotmister (captain of cavalry) in His Majesty's Life-Guard Hussar Regiment; one of the finest horsemen and cavalrymen in Russia; after four years in Ethiopia on special assignments, now with the Hailar Detachment fighting in Manchuria.

The women in his life:

IN RUSSIA, Sonya Vassilchikova, 23—Daughter of Prince Vassilchikov, the colonel in command of Bulatovich's home regiment; she lives at family homes near Petersburg and at Kovno, near the Polish border; unofficially Bulatovich's fiancée.

IN ETHIOPIA, Asalafetch, 36—Wealthy Ethiopian woman, four times divorced, between husbands; well experienced at using her sensuality to achieve her practical ends.

IN CHINA, Chinese Sonya, 17—Chinese orphan raised from infancy by Russian priest in Hailar, Manchuria; now homeless, in love with Bulatovich and determined to marry Strakhov.

His family:

Jenny (Evgenia Andreyevna Bulatovicha), 58—His mother; widow of Major General Xavier Bulatovich; ancestry: French, Georgian, and Russian; spends winters in Petersburg, summers at family estate, Lutsikovka in the Ukraine.

Meta (Mariya Xavierevna Bulatovicha), 26—His sister; has just married a Georgian prince, Alexis Orbeliani.

His superiors in Manchuria:

General Nikolai A. Orlov, 58—Good-natured commander of the Hailar Detachment who encourages Bulatovich's independence and daring.

Colonel Kupferman, 64—Commander of the cavalry regiment (3rd Verkhneudinsk Mounted Cossack Regiment); waiting for retirement; a creature of habit concerned with his personal comforts; he enjoys intimidating his subordinates.

General Paul K. von Rennenkampf, 46—Ambitious, decisive officer who takes over some of Orlov's responsibilities toward the end of the campaign.

His would-be rival:

Major Strakhov, 31—Assistant commander of the cavalry regiment; ambitious son of a cabinetmaker; no previous combat experience; anxious to make a name for himself, but continually upstaged by Bulatovich; in love with Chinese Sonya.

His devoted followers (known as the "Mazeppy"):

Alexei Starodubov, also known as "Old Blockhead" and "the Old Thief," 54—A huge white-haired Cossack volunteer.

Pyotr Zabelin, 17—An Old Believer from near Lake Baikal; joined for the excitement.

Trofim Zabelin, 25—Brother of Pyotr; a would-be priest; joined to fight for a holy cause.

Login Zabelin, 30—Brother of Pyotr and Trofim; joined to protect his foolish brothers.

Yakov Shemelin, 25—Trans-Baikal Cossack; fine horseman; taught himself how to read; very sensitive about his name.

Alexei Butorin, 40—Trans-Baikal Cossack; self-styled expert on the local terrain and customs; has a glib tongue and a superstitious imagination; rather unpredictable.

Mihail Laperdin, 32—Formerly a medical student in Kiev; has lived in Trans-Baikal for ten years; avowed atheist.

Filimon Sofronov, 30—Formerly theology student, then mendicant pilgrim, then unskilled laborer, before joining up for this campaign.

Ivan Aksyonov, 17—Married just one week before being called up.

His friend:

Captain Smolyannikov, 50—Russian mercenary formerly employed by Russo-Chinese Railway as "railway guard"; has lived in China for nearly twenty years; married to invalid Chinese woman.

RAILROADS AND RELIGION

1

Eastern Siberia, July 20, 1900

End of the line, sir."

Bulatovich woke up, only he wasn't sure he was awake. "What's the meaning of this? Where are we?" he asked, his eyes still out of focus, his glasses awry, sweat soaking his brow, his beard. "Must be a hundred degrees in here," he thought.

"Chita, sir. End of the line."

"Chita? What Chita?" The compartment was empty. The train had indeed stopped. The corridor was clogged with baggage and short-tempered travelers.

Bulatovich quickly assessed the situation, opened wide the window, and leaped feet-first onto the platform.

Hundreds of soldiers were milling about on the platform and in the dirt street. Many were lugging heavy bags of gear and shouting questions above the din of the steam brakes and the train whistle. Obscured by the dust kicked up by these recent arrivals, Bulatovich could see lines of soldiers and recruits, snaking back and forth through the streets.

Bulatovich stretched his limbs. The muscles were stiff after a week in one train or another. From Petersburg to Moscow and then eastward on the Trans-Siberian Railway, thousands of miles to this little wooden town in the middle of nowhere.

Despite the heat, Bulatovich was wearing the white and red dress uniform of a Hussar Guards officer. The Guards stripe on his high collar and sleeves was red, indicating the 2nd Guards Division. His close-cropped hair was beginning to recede at the temples, but that was covered by a red cap with a black leather visor in front. His dark eyes seemed extremely large, perhaps magnified by the thick lenses of his wire-rimmed glasses.

His head was by nature square, with a full firm jaw and a thrust-forward chin. But a black, bushy beard and mustache upset the natural balance and harmony of his face, as if he were not content to look the way he had been born to look or to be the kind of person he had been born to be. He was short, five feet four inches; but there was an intensity about him, as if he gained in energy from being compressed into so compact a package.

He strode up to a young lieutenant who was shuffling through papers on a clipboard.

"What's the meaning of this?"

The lieutenant immediately jumped to attention and saluted. He noted the newcomer's rank and the Guards stripes on his collar and sleeves. "Lieutenant Sidorov, sir. At your service, sir."

"Why have we stopped?"

"This is the end of the line, sir. Chita, sir. Capital of Trans-Baikal Territory."

"I was under the impression that the rail line was completed to the Chinese border and beyond."

"More or less, sir. The whole Chinese section of the railway was due to open soon, east to Vladivostok and south from Harbin to Port Arthur. That's the way it was, sir. But now this is the end of the line."

Something about that phrase was particularly irritating. "Look, Lieutenant, how far are we from the border?"

"Two hundred thirty miles, sir," Sidorov saluted again sharply, as if he were trying to make a good impression.

"Where can I get a fast horse? I have to get through to Port Arthur."

"Begging your pardon, sir, but it can't be done, sir."

"But it must be done, Lieutenant."

"Begging your pardon, sir, but the Chinese are at war with us. They control all of Manchuria. And Port Arthur is at the other end of Manchuria, over eleven hundred miles from here."

"I'm not asking for a geography lesson, Lieutenant. I need a horse."

"They're fanatics, sir. They're tearing up tracks, burning stations, wrecking the whole Chinese section of the railway. They're wrecking everything Russian, killing missionaries and Chinese converts. 'Kill the foreign devils,' they say. Cross the border and you're as good as dead, the papers say."

"I have orders."

"Orders have been changed, sir, nearly all of them have. What did you say your name was, sir?"

"Mine are no ordinary orders. I am to report to the commander-in-chief of our operations in the Far East, Vice-Admiral Alexeyev, in Port Arthur. That's from the Chief of Staff, with the concurrence of the Tsar himself."

"But what did you say your name was, sir?"

"Staff-Rotmister Alexander Xavierevich Bulatovich of His Majesty's Life Guard Hussar Regiment. You won't find that on your clipboard."

"Begging your pardon, sir, here are your new orders. You've been reassigned to the Hailar Detachment."

"The what?" he asked, taking the papers from the lieutenant.

"The detachment we're putting together here at Chita to march on the Manchurian city of Hailar and regain control of the western section of the Russo-Chinese Railway."

"There must be some mistake. Who's in charge here?"

"General Orlov and his superior, General Matsievsky, head of the Cossack forces in Trans-Baikal."

"Where can I find this Matsievsky?"

"That's him over there in the armchair."

Dozens of officers and clerks were sitting at field tables set up in the dirt street and apparently were processing conscripts, Cossacks, volunteers, and soldiers newly transferred from other units.

In normal times, the town of Chita would probably

hold little more than ten thousand inhabitants. But an additional ten or twenty thousand had just arrived for the mobilization. The temperature was well over ninety degrees. Shouting and scuffles erupted now and again in the long, increasingly impatient lines and in the crowded shops on either side of the street.

Bulatovich strode up to the general's armchair from behind. "Your Excellency, Staff-Rotmister Bulatovich reporting. Apparently there has been some mistake. I have orders to Port Arthur. . . ."

"Bulatovich?" Another officer with the epaulets of a general jumped to his feet and squinted in his direction. "Did I hear you say 'Bulatovich'?"

"Yes, Your Excellency."

"Welcome! Welcome, Bulatovich!" The man rushed at Bulatovich, clasped him, slapped him on the back as if he were an old friend. "I'm General Orlov. I've heard of your exploits in the steeplechase at Krasnoye Selo in front of the Tsar himself. Two years or was it three in a row you won it? And an African explorer, too, I hear. When your orders came through reassigning you to my detachment, I was simply delighted. It isn't every day we get a celebrity."

General Orlov was a heavy man in his late fifties, with white hair, bushy sideburns, and chin whiskers caked with sweat and dust kicked up by milling crowds and an intermittent refreshing breeze. His sweat-soaked shirt was open to the waist. He squinted often, although he did not wear glasses; and he seemed more inclined to use his hands—touching, holding, squeezing—rather than his eyes.

While he was talking, Orlov guided Bulatovich along the street, behind the rows of tables, past surly-looking Cossacks who reluctantly made way for them.

"We're short on officers—on everything—especially officers with experience. Had to import some, so to speak, from the Kazan and Orenburg military districts. And you—what a find! What good fortune that you had to pass through Chita, and we could get those orders of yours changed.

"Your rank was a bit of a problem. I wanted to give you a command, if I could; put your experience to the best use. But 'staff-rotmister'—that's captain of cavalry; in our Cossack ranks that's about the same as 'esaul.' We have half a dozen or more of those, all commanding cavalry squadrons. And a Colonel Kupferman and a Major Strakhov as commander and assistant commander of the mounted regiment. Best I could give you was second assistant commander. But we'll find ways to use your talents, you can be sure of that. Now and again we can put together special handpicked units for reconnaissance and attack, 'flying detachments.' We won't let such foolish things as protocol get in our way. We'll put you in the thick of things, have no fear."

Just off to their left, a store window shattered as a Cossack fell through it. Two officers rushed to the scene. General Orlov and Bulatovich simply stepped around the broken glass and continued, "Let me introduce you to Colonel Kupferman. He can help you find accommodations of one sort or another.

"Mobilization caught us a bit off guard. Everything is going well, remarkably well. Not German style, mind you, but with typical Russian peculiarities. Our lists were rather incomplete, and there was no way to tell how many men would actually answer our summons. We called up every man of working age in all of Trans-Baikal—every farmer, thief, miner, and doctor. There's about twenty-five thousand of them altogether, spread out over an area bigger than France.

"As it turned out, far more of them showed up than we need. The ones we don't want we have to send home, at their own expense. There is simply no money left—not a single kopeck— to take care of them. That has led to some minor confusion and considerable crowding, while we straighten things out.

"As for the troops we're winding up with, we've got a fair number of ex-convicts out here in Siberia, and aborigines too, mostly nomad Buryat tribesmen. It's a motley group. Discipline might be a problem at times. But a fair number of them are true Cossacks, raised and trained as fighters, even though their fathers—if they know who they were—were probably banished here as criminals or heretics or politicals. The Cossacks supply their own uniforms and weapons, whatever they can afford. I don't think you'll find two belts the same size and color among the whole lot of them. But they're crack shots, I can tell you.

"A fair number of them know the territory well, have been coming and going for years in the Mongolian part of Manchuria, trading and herding. Lots of intermarriage with the Mongolians and Mongolian-like aborigines. Aside from our boys wearing white tunics and the Chinese wearing black or blue, it would be hard to tell some of our troops from the enemy.

"As for the Buryats, it's best to leave them be—let them keep their native robes. We don't have supplies enough to uniform them, and they'd resent it. It'll be hard enough keeping them in line and getting some use out of them. Why aggravate them unnecessarily? We'll just let them handle the transport. It'll all work out in the end. But some of these new garrison officers, with all their spit and polish and inexperience, don't seem to understand. . . .

"Pardon me for burdening you with all my headaches," he said, coming to a stop. "I guess I got a bit carried away. So good to have someone aboard with real combat experience, and in Africa, no less, where the armies are probably even more irregular than this one. Last time I saw action myself was over twenty years ago, against the Turks.

"But I forget. You must be exhausted, sitting up day after day in a crowded railway compartment. Better rest up now. There won't be much time later.

"Tomorrow we leave for Abagaitui, a little station on the Chinese border. That will be our staging point. Our first goal is Hailar, the district capital, about a hundred miles from there. Then we'll push on toward the rail junction at Harbin and hope to link up with other Russian armies advancing into Manchuria from the north and east. There's no telling what kind of opposition we'll meet. We must be prepared for every eventuality.

"Colonel Kupferman," he signaled to someone nearby, "I'd like you to meet your new second assistant commander, Staff-Rotmister Bulatovich, one of the finest horsemen in Russia. You remember my telling you about him? See what you can do about finding him some place to rest up and spend the night."

Colonel Kupferman was older than Orlov and, long overdue for promotion, was soon to be retired. He was heavier than Orlov, especially about the face, which was clean-shaven, with heavy jowls and a triple chin, accentuated by a stiff posture. Every piece of metal and leather in his uniform was highly polished. (He probably kept his orderly up half the night every night, polishing.)

Judging from his rank, the man beside Kupferman, Major Strakhov, must have been at least thirty, Bulatovich's age. But Strakhov looked no more than twenty-five, while Bulatovich could have passed for forty. Strakhov's eyes were clear and blue, hair blond. His first wrinkle was just taking shape on his forehead. He was nearly half a foot taller than Bulatovich. From the whiteness and smoothness of Strakhov's beardless skin, he looked more like a doctor or a lawyer, a professional accustomed to working indoors, rather than a soldier. Like Kupferman, he kept his uniform in impeccable condition.

"I'm afraid there's not much to be had in the way of accommodations," began Kupferman, as soon as Orlov had left. "For myself, I brought along my own—a large springless carriage, a tarantass, that I've fitted up with all the comforts of home. For the rest of the officers, there's only one hotel in town—small, rather shabby, and filled to three times its normal capacity. You might be able to prevail on one of the local residents to put you up, but only the most obstinate of them have not already done so to the fullest extent they deem possible. Best that you make the acquaintance of a number of our officers in hopes that one will be willing to let you share his space."

And what about the enlisted men?" asked Bulatovich.

"There's a campsite of sorts on the south side of town, where enlisted men have pitched their tents and unprocessed recruits sleep out in the open. I haven't been there myself, but . . ."

"Thank you, sir," said Bulatovich, abruptly saluting and taking his leave.

He proceeded directly to the baggage car, picked up his gear, then, in the nearest open space, pitched his tent.

Kupferman, Strakhov, and the other officers looked on in disbelief.

His was not a regular army issue tent. Rather it was a smallish affair, with a multitude of pockets and other useful contrivances. From the outside, the patchwork of irregular stitching and the bulges aroused curiosity. On the inside was displayed a potpourri of gear, arranged for ready access—like the wares of an efficient Gypsy. There was a pocket for his maps, a pocket for binoculars, a loop for his saber, a pocket for beginning Chinese grammar and phrase books, and straps for photographic gear and surveying gear. The tent held and displayed all his essential baggage except his clothes. And tucked into the sides, near the peak, were a photo of the Tsar, Nicholas II, and an icon of Christ.

As soon as his tent was set up, Bulatovich kneeled before the icon and prayed reverently. Then, with the flaps open to let in any breeze, he stretched out, fully dressed, on his back, with his hands behind his head.

✿ ✿ ✿

He shut his eyes, but he couldn't shut off the thoughts and images that kept racing through his mind.

Port Arthur was the key to Russia's position in China. Although it was not much farther south than Vladivostok, the currents made it a warm-water port, free of ice and open to shipping year round. Its acquisition had been a major diplomatic coup.

The Japanese had gone to war with China in 1895, had won decisively, and had thereby gained control of Port Arthur. But the Western Powers had intervened, rushing to the aid of poor defenseless China, applying diplomatic pressure to force Japan to return Port Arthur to China.

No sooner had Japan pulled out than those same friendly Powers—Germany, France, Russia, and Britain—forced China to give them trade and territorial concessions in payment for their goodwill.

At that time, construction of the Trans-Siberian Railway, begun in 1892, was rapidly advancing. Between the tracks running southeast from Lake Baikal and the tracks running northwest from Vladivostok lay that awkward little bulge in the North of China known as Manchuria. The terrain was rugged along the northern, Russian side of the Amur River. It would be far more direct and inexpensive to go straight through Manchuria.

In 1896 Russian coercion and diplomacy resulted in permission to do just that, under the auspices of an ostensibly private company, the Russo-Chinese Railway, with the Russian government as the main shareholder. Then the diplomats scored again, obtaining for Russia without a shot what Japan had fought and won a war for: control of Port Arthur and the Liaotung Peninsula, at the southern end of Manchuria, in the form of a "lease."

With the new acquisition, the project had expanded in scope, with a connecting rail line to run south from Harbin to Port Arthur.

The company had the right to protect its interests with a private army of "railway guards," made up, for the most part, of former Russian soldiers. In some cases, entire companies of Cossacks volunteered for this high-paying mercenary duty and stayed together, with Chinese officers placed in titular command over them.

A thousand miles of railway on Chinese soil, over a hundred thousand Chinese coolies employed in the construction that was already just months away from completion—it was a major step toward economic and eventual political domination of the area. And Manchuria would be the jumping-off point for gaining control of Korea, with its even more advantageous ports.

Port Arthur was headquarters, the decision-making center for all Russian activities in the Far East. It would be supported and defended at all costs. If Bulatovich could get there, he would probably have an opportunity to play an important role in history-making events.

If the situation there was under control, he might be sent to join the Allied expedition to save the diplomats held hostage in their legations in Peking.

News of trouble with the religious and antiforeign Chinese fanatics known as "Boxers" had been appearing in the Western press for some months. By the time Bulatovich first heard of it, on his return from Ethiopia in May of 1900, the situation was already critical. Then it had sounded as if the old Manchu dynasty were about to fall. These religious fanatics (*i he ch'uan*— "Harmonious Fists"—they called themselves; "Boxers" Western reporters called them) would certainly vent their wrath on the decrepit and corrupt central government that had repeatedly backed down before the military threats and bribery of the Western Powers. The government had already given Western merchants and missionaries special privileges, relinquishing control of customs duties and governmental authority in major port areas, opening up the country to the opium trade and to the

27

disruptive influence of Western goods and technology and beliefs. Only the jealous watchfulness of the vulture nations—Britain, France, Germany, and Russia (with the United States tempted but still aloof)—prevented one or another of them from seizing control of what remained of the vast Chinese Empire. It seemed that the partition of China depended only on these governments arriving at some mutually agreeable set of boundaries.

But now these spontaneous anti-Western, anti-Christian outbreaks. Christian missionaries and their Chinese converts were murdered here and there throughout the Empire. Westerners and those who dealt with them, including government officials, were treated first with disrespect, then with disdain, then with open hostility. At first, official word from above urged cautious and selective suppression of such outbreaks, trying to soothe the anger of the Western Powers and at the same time quiet this potentially explosive popular movement. Then gradually and subtly, the Dowager Empress or her ministers (who could say who, if anyone, really "ruled" in China?) had manipulated public opinion, or perhaps it had changed unprompted. One way or the other, the full energy of hatred had focused on the foreigners rather than on the government officials who had collaborated with them. Since June 20 all the foreigners connected with the legations in Peking and a sizable number of Chinese converts were besieged in the sector of the city that had been set aside for them, held hostage by a huge and volatile mob of fanatics, with the tacit assent or covert connivance of the weak central government. The same sort of trouble was echoing throughout China, with mobs attacking foreigners, especially missionaries, and destroying foreign property, especially railroads. Rumor had it, too, that provincial governors and military leaders, at least in Manchuria, had come out openly in favor of the fanatics and were using their regular armies not to quell the riots, but rather to attack foreign military targets.

Religion—that was the key. Bulatovich's friend Colonel Molchanov had emphasized that back in early June when they had first discussed the situation in China.

"Nationalism is nonsense," he had said. "The newspapers keep using the word, but it means nothing in China. Religion's the key. Religion and railroads, that's what people understand. Their basic beliefs are threatened—the meaning of their lives— by these missionaries with their strange notions and by these great iron monsters. Where it used to take weeks to go from one city to another, now it takes hours. Their markets are flooded with cheap machine-made Western goods. Their economy is in chaos. Most of them can't make sense out of these outward changes, can see no meaning in lives that depend on these goods and machines. Some of them have adopted the religions of the West in an effort to understand. I've heard that in just a few decades, Catholics, Protestants, and, to a far lesser degree, Ortho- dox missionaries have won hundreds of thousands, if not mil- lions, of apparently devout converts.

"Now there's this new religious fanaticism, a sort of wild revival of old pagan beliefs and superstitions, of secret societies. Apparently the Boxers believe that by saying the right words, the right incantations, they can make themselves superhumanly powerful—immune to bullets and able to take on Western armies and machines single-handed. The papers say that believers claim the Boxers who die must not have learned the right words.

"Basically, facts don't matter. It's what people want to believe that they believe, and what they believe governs what they do. These materialists and socialists have the world all backward. They put the emphasis in the wrong place, on things. Sure, things affect the way we think; but, to a large extent, we see what we want to see, we make ourselves what we want to make our- selves—at least that's what I want to believe. Only I can't say why I want to.

"It all comes down to religion, I tell you, that and railroads or technology and change as threats to religion—to the meaning of life, not to money and goods."

Religion. Bulatovich said another prayer, silently, a simple one: "Lord Jesus Christ, Son of God, have mercy upon me." He repeated it again and again.

He felt somewhat guilty for letting personal ambition play so large a part in his motivations. While he was remembering the words of his friend Colonel Molchanov he had been nursing the hurt to his personal pride and ambition of this reassignment to the Hailar Detachment. Port Arthur and these troubles in China had seemed like a perfect opportunity for him to start his career afresh after his failure in Ethiopia.

He had believed that Russia should help Ethiopia maintain its independent and expansionist role in Africa, competing with Britain for territory in the heart of the continent. But his efforts on behalf of Ethiopia had been frustrated somewhere in the maze of ministries in Petersburg, or perhaps his dispatches had never been forwarded from Addis Ababa.

If only he could have had a chance to explain his beliefs and observations directly to the Tsar himself. Bulatovich wondered to what extent Nicholas II even knew what was going on, any more than the Dowager Empress in Peking, separated as she was from her people by hordes of palace eunuchs.

Now he was in Chita, in eastern Siberia. Port Arthur had seemed to hold possibilities for a fresh start. He had delved into his Chinese phrase books and a Chinese grammar during the early part of the train trip before the lack of sound sleep had undermined his concentration. Once again it seemed the train of his career had been sidetracked or derailed. This was, perhaps, "the end of the line"—stuck in the middle of nowhere, with an objective that no one had ever heard of or was ever likely to hear of.

He felt some moral twinge for having such thoughts, for considering a disastrous situation—the massacre of defenseless Christians—as an opportunity for personal advancement. He reminded himself that he hadn't made it happen, that he in fact wanted to help resolve it, that someone must do the job, and that it was the very sort of job his experience and training suited him for: dealing with an unpredictable and superstitious enemy.

He would probably see no action at all, marching through the relatively uninhabited Mongolian section of Manchuria with this overly friendly, disarming, and apparently well-meaning general. As for the regimental commander, Kupferman, if that wasn't his way of being openly hostile, then he was the sort of man who was concerned about his own comforts and totally insensitive to the needs of others. Then there was that spit-and-polish, boy-faced assistant commander, what was his name?

"Strakhov . . ." Bulatovich heard hushed voices outside his tent. Maybe they had been talking before and he had just now become aware of it. Maybe he had drifted off to sleep. Maybe he was dreaming now. "I don't know what we're going to do with this new man. This flamboyant contraption of his—it's not a tent, it's an affront."

The voice was Kupferman's. "It's one thing for a regimental commander like myself to indulge himself a bit, to show a little eccentricity. After all, I'm getting on in years. I've earned my little comforts. But a mere cavalry captain, even if he is from one of the most prestigious regiments in the Russian army—it's an act of insubordination for him to flaunt a Gypsy thing like that. It's his job to set an example of orderliness, decorum, and discipline for these unruly and, I'm sure, untrustworthy troops of ours."

"Perhaps we should bring the matter to the attention of General Orlov," Strakhov suggested in a far more subdued, almost inaudible whisper.

"I already have. Described it in great detail, as well as I could from what I've seen. And do you know what he said? He said, 'Sounds marvelous. I wish I had one myself.'

"This Bulatovich is going to be a problem," Kupferman continued, a little too loud for a whisper, as if he wanted to be overheard. "Mark my words. You saw the way the general treated him, and that business about the steeplechase and Africa and whatnot. He's too much of a celebrity for our little operation. Upsets the command structure, the protocol, to have a cavalry captain that buddy-buddy with the general. Dangerous, disruptive influence."

"Yes, sir," agreed Strakhov, quietly. "There's something very peculiar about this Bulatovich. Did you notice the earring?"

"What earring?"

"He has a gold ring in his left ear, like a Gypsy."

"Peculiar, yes. What's he doing here, anyway? Orlov corraled him here, but he must have volunteered for Manchuria in the first place. What's he after? He has more than enough feathers in his cap. If he were simply ambitious, he would stay put in Petersburg for a while. Only sensible thing to do. Cultivate acquaintances, make himself known in important places, play regimental politics. That's how to get ahead in this army. A little foreign duty looks good on the record, but you have to stay put for a while in your own regiment to make something of it.

"All this chasing about from one end of the world to the other—it reeks of scandal," concluded Kupferman. "Maybe it's not what he's looking for but what he's running from that counts. Some nasty business he'd like people to forget about, so he stays away. Or that he'd like to forget himself, so he keeps on the go. A woman, I'd wager. Some nasty business with a woman."

In the background, a long train clattered by, perhaps already on its four-thousand-mile way back west to Moscow, or perhaps heading toward some turning point in the east.

2

B ulatovich was on the train again, in that stifling compartment.

Where was he going?

He needed sleep. Day after day he had been sitting up like this, eight people crowded into a space intended for six.

They had passed through European Russia, crossed the Urals. They must be near Omsk.

Hadn't he been here before?

While inside all was crammed, outside was all the space a man could want. A vast sea of flat, empty, treeless land stretched to the horizon and beyond.

A man needed space to breathe, to rest, to sleep.

How many thousands and tens of thousands had come this way before? They wanted land. They wanted freedom from oppressive laws and taxes, freeedom from serfdom. Even now, forty years after the end of serfdom, peasants still fled eastward to this open space. They didn't want to stay forever in the same place. They didn't want to be tied to the meager strips of land that had been farmed by their fathers and their fathers' fathers for centuries. They wanted to get away from the land where their ancestors were buried, away from their own past, to start fresh. A new life.

Religious men had passed this way, too, Orthodox monks and sectarians—*raskolniki*—people whose beliefs differed from the official doctrine of the day. Some sought solitude. Some sought religious freedom. Some were banished here. Some chose the frontier because of the very difficulties they would encounter there and deliberately pushed themselves to the limits of their endurance. Maybe they were trying to block out the world from their minds so they could find some peace within themselves. It was said that suffering helped purify the soul. They were mortifying the flesh in this life, perhaps to gain merit in the next. Perhaps they wanted to atone for some real or imagined sin.

Why was he here?

Now he was steaming through rich agricultural land. Now through huge forests of pine, fir, and silver birch. Now through vast coal fields. He passed a collection of wooden houses called "Irkutsk," ferried across Lake Baikal, that "Holy Sea of Siberia," into the virgin forests of Trans-Baikal, where the trunks of fir trees were as wide as peasants' huts.

He left the forests behind. Up ahead . . . that litt6le town . . . Did someone say that was Chita?

What was he doing here? After all his brilliant service, why was he being exiled to Siberia? What had he done?

He heard the train's clatter again in the distance. . . . He wasn't on it. No, he was on the ground. In his tent. Sleeping. At last.

He slept restlessly, one dream following another at a dizzying pace. The warm sensuous hands of Asalafetch, the innocent smile of Sonya, his mother's frown, his father's grave. He'd open his eyes from one dream, or think that he had opened his eyes, and see his mother standing there beside him in the moonlight, her thin lips pursed, her chin thrust out.

"You heard me, don't pretend you didn't. Look at me when I talk to you. And wipe that silly grin off your face. What are you trying to prove? I told you to be home by supper, and here you are asleep in the field in the middle of the night. You're a sinful disobedient little boy, Sasha, and a plague to your poor mother."

Bulatovich cringed, waiting to be beaten, hoping he would be beaten; but he never was, because there was no father to do the beating, because his mother was so helpless or pretended she was so helpless. If she had just beaten him, he could have gotten mad at her or felt self-righteous that the punishment was more severe than he merited. But no, she would just look at him, her lips pursed, her eyes full of disappointment and weariness, and the guilt would weigh on him. There would be no way to get rid of the guilt.

He awoke for a moment beneath the stifling heat of his odd little tent. He glimpsed the icon of Christ and the photo of the Tsar, then felt that he was waking again, not quite, still unable to move, waking perhaps into another dream.

"Why do you pray?" he asked his mother. She was kneeling in front of an icon of Christ as she always did before going up to bed.

She glared up at him, then squeezed her eyes shut, trying to concentrate again on her prayer.

He had just taken and passed the final exam in geography, his worst subject. Proud of himself, he would soon be out on his own, away from this despotic mother of his. But despite himself, he would miss her. He would miss the simple pattern of rewards and punishments, the certainty of her disapproval when he broke her petty rules. Without knowing why, he had an urge to provoke her, to arouse her martyred wrath.

"Why do you pray?" he persisted.

She opened her eyes, pursed her lips, and heaved a sigh of disappointment. "Have I raised a little heathen? Don't you believe in God?"

"No," he surprised himself with his answer. He observed all the forms of religion, including prayer. But since the death of his sister Lilia, he had avoided thinking rationally about the subject.

He was fourteen when Lilia had died of typhoid. They had argued often. He teased her; she retaliated. Through their running battles they grew close, testing themselves against one another, anticipating one another's responses. Then there was silence, emptiness, no response. He had dreamed that he was standing in front of a mirror, showing off his strength, and suddenly the mirror was gone and he was standing before an endless dark chasm.

For days he had prayed to God to bring her back or to wake him, for he must be dreaming a terrible dream. Then he had asked for an explanation—why her? why now? why? He had asked for a sign, any sign that there truly was a God. But silence was the only answer.

So he had cursed God and all of creation. He had cursed Father, Son, and Holy Ghost. He had cursed the Church and the priests and all believers. And he had dared God to strike him dead for such blasphemy, as he knelt, trembling, beside his bed, cursing God innocently, in the humble posture of prayer; saying he didn't believe in God, but fully expecting at any moment to be struck by a bolt of lightning.

There was no lightning. But he continued his childhood ritual of evening prayers, never asking himself, as he asked his mother now, "Why do you pray? Do you expect that God is going to give you something? that He's going to do something for you?"

"No," she answered. He was shocked by her seriousness. He had expected her to attack him verbally, as she had so often with far less provocation. But instead, she suddenly sank into self-reflection, as if the question had awakened old memories. For a moment she looked old and defenseless. He had never thought of her as old before. He had never seen her with her guard down like this. He was used to her using her diminutive size and the presumed frailty of her sex as a weapon. He was sure she could make herself look even smaller and more frail than she actually was. She manipulated people by making them pity her. She was well practiced at assuming the look of a martyr, and she did so with finesse and authority. But now the muscles of her face were relaxed, hung more loosely than he had ever seen before. She was an active, dynamic woman in her early fifties. But for the moment, the energy was gone from her face. She just looked old.

"Then why do you pray?" he persisted.

"I suppose . . . because I'm weak . . . because I'll die."

"But I remember when we were in Switzerland, at Father's grave." He didn't know why he kept up this line of questioning. She was clearly shaken. He didn't want to hurt her. At least he didn't think he did. "You were crying uncontrollably. You brought Meta and me back there to visit the grave, years after he died. You asked some Catholic priest to say a prayer at his grave, because Father had been Catholic and would have wanted it that way. And the priest refused. He said Father wasn't Catholic enough because he had married an Orthodox woman and let the children be raised Orthodox. You cried and told him that his prayers weren't worth anything, that prayers hadn't kept Father alive, that no prayers were worth anything. And yet every night you still pray. Can you tell me why?"

"I really don't know," she admitted, bewildered as he had never seen her before. "Whatever happens to me, I suppose I'll still want to pray . . . to talk to God. . . . I can't imagine living without praying. I suppose even animals pray."

They were both silent for a while, and then she continued. "An old priest once told me, actually it was twice, I think; not the same words, but the same drift. When Anatole, the man I was betrothed to, died, just a week before the wedding, and then again when your father died, I went on a pilgrimage to a monastery outside Kharkov. I was numb, empty. My aunt forced me to go the first time.

"The priest asked me what was wrong. I answered, 'Death.'

" 'Is that all?' he asked.

"That caught my attention. I answered indignantly, 'Of course. That's certainly enough. More than enough. Far too much. The fact of death.'

" 'Yes, it is just a fact.'

"He must have wanted me to understand, because he went on to explain:

" 'Facts you find in the outside world. They can be proved and disproved. They can change. They can be changed.

" 'Faith you find, if you find it at all, inside yourself, beyond change and so beyond proof, beyond reason. For reason sees only change and difference; it can only deal with distinctions—separating, combining, shuffling to arrive at "understanding."

" 'Of facts there are many. There is no end to their number. Of faith there is one.

" 'The truth of facts we call *pravda*.

" 'The truth of faith we call *istina*.

" 'Reason cannot see one unless it changes; and then it is no longer one, but many different states.

" 'To reason one is nothing. To faith one is everything.

" 'To seek this one within yourself is to pray."

"I didn't know what he meant then, and I don't think I do now either. But I did pray. I shut my eyes and shut out the world and repeated words not for what they meant but for how they helped me to shut out the world, helped me to stop thinking and reasoning.

"It was peaceful, I remember, when I finally got deep into prayer. And I remember the sensations of church—the smell of incense, the feel of a priest's hands on my head as a child, the tones, not the words, of chanting. When I came out of it, Anatole was still dead, your father was still dead, and there were all the day-to-day things that had to be done, and I did them.

"Why do I pray? A nonbeliever might call it wishful thinking. I pray for strength or patience. I believe the Lord gives me strength or patience and so I act strong or patient; but then it's not just wishful anymore, because I've changed. Whether I've changed myself or the Lord had a hand in it doesn't much matter. The Lord helps those who help themselves. I do believe that. Maybe that reservoir of strength within ourselves we draw on at times of need is God's strength. Maybe prayer is like dropping a bucket into a deep well within ourselves, hoping to bring up some of the water of life."

☨ ☨ ☨

In his sleep Bulatovich jumped, waking up on a horse that was rearing and neighing at the first signs of dawn.

He was riding now across the desert. Genghis Khan was leading his Mongolian and Tatar hordes against Russia. Bulatovich was leading the last army of defense.

If he failed, all of Russia would be overrun. He stood for order; they, for the destruction of order.

At the head of the onrushing horde, seated on a white horse very like his own, with sword raised, racing at him, he saw— himself.

He awoke with a start, with the dream still fresh in his mind, wondering what to make of it. He remembered his mother saying, "Yes, you have Polish blood in you, on your father's side. From Grodno Province. Polish gentry. The family of Bulatovich is entered in the ninth book of nobility. But you're Tatar, too, if you go back far enough. A Tatar prince, Bek Bulatovich Simeon, was adviser to Ivan the Terrible."

After he first heard of his Tatar blood, he had stood for an hour in front of a mirror, looking for Tatar traits. He had noticed that when he squinted defiantly, his face took on a slanty-eyed look. So he had decided that his defiant streak was "the Tatar in him." Whenever he stood up to his mother and defied her, before she had a chance to manipulate him with her martyred look and her disappointed sighs, he would squint like that—it gave him strength to think of himself as a Tatar Bulatovich as opposed to a French Albrand, his mother's family.

"Squinting again?" she would say. "Have you been wearing your glasses like the doctor told you? You'll ruin your eyes if you don't. Even when you go riding and hunting, you have to wear those glasses. God gives you only one set of eyes, remember. Someday you'll think back and know your poor mother was right."

He awoke again. (He didn't remember having fallen back to sleep.) His eyes were sore, the corners of the eyes, near the bridge of the nose. He had an inflammation of the tear ducts or glands—different specialists called it different names and gave him different drops that temporarily soothed the irritation.

The problem would go away for years. Then it would come back mildly, like now, as a minor irritation, or severely, like some nine months before on his third trip to Ethiopia, when a jungle fever had aggravated the eye problem to the point that he was sure he was going blind. That time Asalafetch had nursed him while the disease ran its course.

For her, touch was far more important than sight. While she nursed him, she caressed him. Her hands learned his body, learned its rhythm. He became an extension of her and she of him. He loved her and hated her as he loved and hated himself.

Sight and reason had little to do with their relationship. She communicated with him at another level, awakening feelings, needs, and strengths in him that he had never known he had.

To an eye of logic that coldly appreciates a Grecian harmony of curves and the charms of tightly corseted ladies, she was too fleshy—her breasts too large, her waist too thick, her hips too broad. He would have difficulty recognizing her on a crowded street of Lekamte, Andrachi, or Addis Ababa.

But he knew her by touch and feel and hold. With her gentle groping touch, she opened him, like peeling back his skin and gently touching the bare exposed nerves; like peeling back her own skin and bringing her nerve ends into touch with his so that her sensations were his and his hers and neither of them knew where one ended and the other began, nor cared, sensed only, in the dark boundless realm of touch together.

His visual rational mind had quickly forgotten her individual features. He tried to reconstruct an image of her from general characteristics. She was in her midthirties, about five or six years older than he was. She was "Oromo," as they call themselves, or "Galla," as the ruling Amharas call them. Dark but not Negroid, with dark intricately braided hair. She was tall. His eyes were at the level of her lips. He had only to shut his eyes to recall her lips, her long tongue on his eyelids, soothing. Lying down in the dark even now, he could feel her absence—as if she had been there but moments before, beside him, on top of him, beneath him, around him. He had an urge to reach out quickly and pull her back close to him. Often he woke up in the middle of the night, reaching, grabbing at nothing.

She would have laughed had she seen him reaching out for her in his tent here in Siberia. To her and her people, Ethiopia was the center of the world, just as to the Chinese China was the center and to the Europeans Europe. So the strange ways of the rest of the world were "quaint." She found professions of romantic love, the kinds of words that young Russian ladies expected from their suitors, from men who had never touched their naked flesh, "very quaint" and "amusing."

"Do your European women touch themselves often?" she had asked. He hadn't known how to answer. "All this talk of 'love.' All this sighing and dying and saving oneself for the one 'true love'—so silly," she laughed. "And do men really go off and fight and kill one another over a woman—not for her property, but for her 'love'?"

Her passion required no justification. It arose of its own accord, without excuses, without regrets, without limits. And her touch made him as abandoned as she was, drew him into her world of sensation. But at the climax, he would sigh sincerely, "I love you; I'll always love you." He couldn't help himself. He could no more stop himself from saying that than from doing anything that their mutual sensations dictated. She took him out of control of himself. And when he said it, she would laugh if she were already sliding down the hill; or if not, she would tell him to shut up and would hold him harder, concentrating on her sensations, giving a final push, hoping the next push would be the final one.

Sometimes she blamed him for disturbing her sensations by talking at such critical moments. She didn't lecture him, but sometimes she responded bitterly to his tender words and grew cold quickly, rolling aside to be alone. He would reach for her, needing her next to him, and she would push him off or, sometimes, she would relent.

One night—he must have been drunk or very tired to be tricked like that—as he said, "I love you; I'll always love you," she broke out laughing. It was her laugh, but from far behind him. Then another laugh, not hers, but from the person he was holding, from this person he was sure was she, whom he loved dearly and tenderly, and only for her could his body respond so completely.

Then he felt two sets of hands, two bodies—her hands were on his back, then around him, grasping his chest, and her body pressed warmly against his back, but she was beneath him, too, and there were two of her laughing, but only one had her low-pitched voice, and they rolled together in the dark, all three of them, and he didn't know which of her was which or when, but all three of them were one in sensation, touch-groping through the night.

The other woman disappeared before dawn. He never saw her, and Asalafetch never told him her name. She just laughed whenever he asked and sighed softly in Russian, "I love you; I'll always love you." And she laughed again.

He had never let himself get this close to a woman before— or was it that no woman had ever let him get this close to her? When they were alone together, she took him to a realm beyond shame and self-consciousness. But when he walked with her in daylight, in public, he was once again Alexander Xavierevich

Bulatovich, on his third trip to Ethiopia, a Russian cavalry officer on special assignment to Ethiopia at the request of Emperor Menelik II. Bulatovich was a man with status and position to uphold, a man with a European, Victorian code of ethics. In that frame of mind, he couldn't help but wonder "what kind of woman" she was, how many other men she had been with, how many of the men they passed on the street while strolling together had been with her too. He wondered if there was any man for miles around she hadn't been with already or wouldn't be with if the fancy struck her. He felt foolish and small and laughable to be seen with such a woman in public. But he also felt ashamed for having such thoughts, for in her culture her behavior was acceptable, and she was a woman with social status of her own, though she seemed to pay little heed to it, wearing her role comfortably, like the loosely draped togalike shamma that she could let drop to her feet with a slight shrug of the shoulder. She had what was considered a small fortune. She had been married and divorced four times to men of noble or near-noble rank. She was between husbands and in no particular hurry to find another.

Despite such rational considerations, if they were in public and her hand touched his, the sensation was disgusting, repulsive. He felt that all eyes were on him, unless he pressed his eyes shut, squeezed her hand, and, squinting defiantly, strode up the street in self-made semidarkness. Then he'd explain to her that his eyes were bothering him again, and she'd kiss his eyelids and touch them with her soothing tongue, standing there in public. For a moment at least, it would be as if they were alone in the dark.

He rarely wore glasses when he was with her—that was partly why his visual memory of her was hazy. "Why do you need to see?" she would ask. She preferred the darkness. Sight was distracting. Thoughts got in the way of sensation. Darkness seemed to liberate the potential for touch and taste and smell and feel.

His first memory of her was of touch—at a welcoming dinner at the provincial residence of Ras (Prince) Tasamma. That was on his third trip when he already knew and loved her country.

He had first arrived in Ethiopia about three years before. At that time the only wars in the offing were in Africa, in China, and perhaps in the Balkans—in relatively backward nations and in colonies. Russia, which had no colonies, had been at peace for over twenty years.

Ethiopia offered an otherwise idle Russian cavalry officer a unique field of action. Like Japan, Ethiopia was an exception to the general rule that rapid introduction of technology destroys native cultures. Menelik II, princeling ruler of the little feudal state of Shoa, claiming descent from Menelik I, legendary son of Solomon and the Queen of Sheba, had effectively manipulated the Western Powers contending for dominance in Central Africa. He had bought arms from the French. When the Italians, entering the race for colonies rather late, declared that Ethiopia was in their "sphere of influence," Menelik negotiated with them, posed as their friend, signed agreements with them—all in exchange for modern rifles and ammunition that he used effectively to intimidate other feudal lords to join forces with him, to coerce or defeat rivals, and to become Emperor of Ethiopia. He then turned on the Italians themselves and defeated them resoundingly at the Battle of Adowa in 1896.

When news of that battle reached Russia, there was a popular outpouring of sympathy and support for this ancient Christian nation set upon by modern imperialist Italy. Ethiopia was the only Christian nation in Black Africa, a nation with an ancient variety of Christianity, dating back to far before the split between Orthodoxy and Roman Catholicism, with reverence for the early traditions of the Church and none of the accretions and changes and philosophizing of the West. Perhaps the fact that Italy was a member of the Triple Alliance with Germany and Austria and against Russia and France had something to do with those sentiments. But primarily, it was a feeling of a common bond of religion with this distant and little-known people.

Money was raised and volunteers were recruited for a Russian Red Cross medical mission to go to Ethiopia and care for the Ethiopian wounded. Bulatovich, with the permission of his regiment, had been one of those volunteers.

On that his first trip, he had seen how readily the ruling ethnic group—the Amharas—assimilated Western technology and ideas and how they treated the peoples they had conquered with respect, allowing them to keep much of their culture, religion, and social forms intact. And by way of the Amharas the technology of the West was gradually filtering through to these previously isolated African tribes, with positive rather than disruptive effect. Or at least that was what Bulatovich believed—that Ethiopia had a special role to play, softening the impact of railroads and technology on native cultures.

In 1897 Russia sent its first diplomatic mission to Ethiopia, sending Bulatovich, who was now considered an expert in the language and the country, ahead to prepare the way. That trip had provided him an opportunity to accompany an Ethiopian army on an expedition to conquer lands previously little known or never seen before by Europeans.

He had proven so helpful on that expedition that Menelik had personally requested that he come back to Ethiopia a third time. This time he was to inspect the recently conquered northwestern region of the country and advise on what measures should be taken to fortify the frontier and strengthen the allegiance of the tribes in the border area. The British might otherwise be tempted to expand into that area south and east from the Sudan, because it would be the most convenient route for a railway from Cairo in British Egypt to Mombasa in British East Africa. Perhaps Menelik actually wanted the advice. Then again, perhaps all he really needed was the presence of a Russian "military adviser" in the area, to make an impression on British diplomats and perhaps on his own not always trustworthy princes and generals.

On this trip, wherever Bulatovich went, word was sent ahead by runners, and elaborate preparations were made for his arrival. At the residence of Ras Tasamma, Asalafetch, at her own request, had been given the honor of washing the feet of the distinguished foreign guest and feeding him, dropping tiny morsels of food into his mouth.

He had grown used to such lavishly sensual treatment in Ethiopia. The first time it had happened, on his first trip three years before, he had been shocked and had instinctively withdrawn his foot. But quick to sense and respect the customs of others, he had let the young woman proceed, despite the embarrassment of feeling sexually aroused in public. After a dozen such welcoming banquets around the country, he had grown accustomed to the sensations and had come to appreciate them. As his initial distaste for highly spiced food gradually developed into an appreciation (and his bouts with diarrhea became less frequent), he had found that after a long journey, the sensual touch of a young girl's hands on his bare feet was both soothing and invigorating, that it helped awaken his sense of taste and added to his enjoyment of the meal that followed, without arousing any specifically sexual expectations.

It was a common procedure, one that he enjoyed but took for granted, when Asalafetch's hands first stroked his feet. But his stomach tightened and as at first he instinctively withdrew his foot, losing his train of thought in midsentence. He looked down. There was nothing unusual about her looks, except that she was somewhat older and more confident than the women who had done this for him in the past. Nor was there anything unusual about what she had done. But it was as if no one had ever done this to him before. He cringed with shame for having insulted his host by such a reaction. He apologized profusely, and the meal began. But he remained aroused, and the memory of her touch continued to arouse him. His mind wandered. He would lose the drift of the conversation, forget a word or phrase of Amharic that he knew.

Probably it was the first stage of the fever that made him react so strangely, he had told himself in retrospect. A few days later, the fever struck him down, leaving him weak and sweating, with his eyes, his tear ducts burning. She was sent to him as a nurse. In the darkness, he recognized her touch. In his fevered state, her hands were like fresh water from a deep well, bringing new strength.

LOVE, DEATH, LIFE, AND OTHER MINOR MATTERS

3

The grass beside his head was cool and moist.

As a boy, back when everyone called him "Sasha," he had loved to play in the grass, rolling down the steep hill behind the servants' house, or sliding down it on a big piece of waxed cardboard. This makeshift toboggan went fastest with two or three others and a running start. Usually it was just he and the servant boys, but sometimes Masha would jump out of nowhere and hop aboard at the last minute. They always yelled at her for that, but her momentum made those the best rides of all.

She was the daughter of one of the maids and was old enough to be doing maid's work herself. In fact, that's what she was supposed to be doing. But though as tall as a woman and with the shape of a woman, she was still a child inside and loved playing tomboy games. In contrast, his sisters had to be ladylike and practice the piano and listen to their French and German governess.

He had known her from earliest childhood, but mostly he had just ignored her. She was merely one of the gang of servant and peasant children he played with.

It was the summer after Aunt Elizaveta died, when he was thirteen and Masha was fifteen that he first paid attention to her.

Somehow it felt different and good when he was the last one aboard the "toboggan" and she jumped on behind him, wrapping her arms and legs about him to hold tight.

The other boys started reacting to her differently, too. Instead of yelling at her, they welcomed her. They let her ride in the middle so they could hold her. In fact, they surreptitiously helped her finish her chores and kept a watch out while she sneaked away to join them. They got conspiratorial about it, not only because she was supposed to be working, but also because holding Masha or being held by her aroused pleasurable yet uncomfortable new sensations in them.

The game kept up for a few weeks. Then one day, when the other boys were busy, Sasha managed to get Masha to ride with him alone. She sat down first and he jumped on behind, reaching round and holding her chest, her newly formed breasts, boldly, as he had never done when the others were around. When they reached the bottom they fell in a giggling tangle.

They kissed. Dry lips pressed together expectantly, patiently, not really knowing what to expect. His eyes wandered to her leg, exposed to nearly her hip. (Would she wear underwear on a day as hot as this?) Curious, he reached for her. She slapped his hand, pushed him away and straightened her dress. She took one last look at him, but didn't meet his eyes. Still curious, still hoping, he wasn't looking at her eyes. She blushed deep red and ran away. That was the last time Masha played children's games with the boys. "It's not fitting," was all the explanation she would give.

That was also the summer his mother, Jenny, began her endless lectures about learning one's proper place in society.

"Yes, all men are equal in the eyes of God," she admitted. "But, pity though it is, men don't see with the eyes of God. Frail mortals that we are, we cringe at the sight of a dirty, ragged shirt, at the sound of a peasant's ungrammatical speech. And you are known by the company you keep.

"It's high time that you appreciated your status in society and started to take pains to preserve it. Not that you should be getting uppity notions and trying to climb where you don't belong, but just that you should know your place and keep to it.

"Some would say that I rose above my proper station when I married your father the general. An orphan I was, dependent on the charity of my aunt. But she was a wealthy woman and treated me like the daughter she never had; and my father, God rest his soul, was a colonel of engineers in the army and would have risen higher had it not been for his untimely death. And my grandfather—his father—was a wealthy merchant.

"You should know your place—know that you are a member of a proud family—of two proud families: your father's and my own."

His mother's grandfather, Louis Albrand, had been a merchant from Ambrune, France, trading in Russia's newly acquired Black Sea ports. For many years the entire Black Sea coast had been controlled by Turks as part of the Ottoman Empire. Gradually the Russian state, which had originated as the small principality of Moscow, had expanded southward, coming into frequent conflict with the Turks, trying time and again to get access to warm-water ports on the Black Sea. Finally in 1774 the armies of Catherine the Great had succeeded in conquering a strip of coast near the mouths of the Dnieper and the Dniester, rivers that could carry goods from deep within the heartland of Russia to seaports like Kherson and from there to Western Europe. Recognizing the opportunities for trade that were opening up, merchants from Greece, Italy, France, and Germany soon gravitated to the area.

Many times in the 1780s and early 1790s, Louis Albrand voyaged between France and the new Russian Black Sea ports, first in his own ship, then with his own small merchant fleet. When the Revolution and the Reign of Terror made it dangerous for a wealthy merchant to return to France, he decided to stay permanently in Russia. Eventually, he settled in Odessa, a small port town built in 1794 by a pair of French engineers. A French nobleman and royalist, Armand, Duc de Richelieu, was appointed as the first governor of the district, and under the encouragement of Catherine the Great, the émigré population of the new town grew rapidly.

Business thrived as war raged in Europe off and on for two decades. Louis bought more ships and sheep and pastureland as well (the demand for wool for uniforms was heavy), and somehow he found time to marry a Russian and sire seven children.

His son Andrey, Jenny's father, went to expensive schools,

and, as colonel of engineers, took part in building the Military-Georgia Road—part of another Russian expansion movement, this time into the Caucasus, where fiercely independent mountain tribesmen resisted for decades, raiding forts and scouting parties, destroying bridges, blocking roads. While in Georgia with that interminable project (forever interrupted by sabotage and raids), Andrey had married a Georgian, Olga Tulayeva, Jenny's mother. It was in 1852, two years before the Crimean War, when Chechentsy tribesmen suddenly attacked their home, killing the mother and father and leaving ten-year-old Jenny with her little brother and sister, cowering in the darkness.

"You take all this for granted," Jenny would tell Sasha time and again. "This fine estate, with all the furniture and trimmings of luxury. Why, all you have to complain of are the lessons your tutor gives you and the sound of your sisters practicing scales on the piano.

"When I was your age, I lived in a log hut in the wilderness, some mountain pass in the Caucasus. We kept moving from one hut to another, each more cold and uncomfortable than the one before. No piano, no tutors. Just lugging water from the well and doing other chores. Do you have any idea what it's like in the dead of winter trying to break up the ice in a deep well?

"We weren't poor, mind you, but conditions were primitive out there in the Caucasus. The other married officers had left their wives behind in Russia. They stayed in barracks at one fort or another as the road moved along. But Mother was a Georgian girl Father had met there. He had learned the language. He loved those mountains and the Georgian people, and he preferred to live in the countryside, romantic fool that he was."

The orphans were divided up among relatives. Madame Kuris, Andrey's sister, had taken Jenny in and raised her at Lutsikovka, an estate in Kharkov Province in the Ukraine.

The master of the house, Platon Kuris, was a son of a Greek merchant in Odessa. He had joined the Russian army as an officer of the Guard during the wars with Napoleon and had marched all the way to Paris. Like many of the wealthy in Russia, imitating the nobility, his parents had seen to it that he had a French education, with genuine French émigré tutors. He had been raised to think of French as the only truly civilized language and

Voltaire as the greatest of modern writers. Arriving with the conquering army in France itself, Kuris was dazzled by the wonders of Paris and Versailles and became a rabid Francophile. On returning to Russia, he had bought a piece of wilderness in the Ukraine and supervised the construction of a vast mansion with elaborately structured gardens in the style of Versailles. It was an impressive sight, but few ever saw it—far from any neighbor, off in the woods alone, a private dream.

While visiting his parents in Odessa, he had met seventeen-year-old Elizaveta Albrand, Jenny's aunt. He dazzled her with his flawless French and his tales of Napoleon and Paris. Soon he married her and carried her off to his palace in the woods.

But the young girl's dream soon turned to nightmare, for the great admirer of the French philosophers, the great lover of Republican France and republican principles, ruled his young wife like an autocrat. She cringed when he entered the room. She dared not speak in his presence for fear that he would correct her French or mock her accent. And she dared not walk in his presence for fear that he would lecture her again on the proper way a "true lady" should walk. Fifteen years her elder, he assumed that her mind was a blank slate. He was determined to shape "Madame Kuris" to his ideal notion of a graceful and educated woman, just as he had shaped this corner of the wilderness into a French palace. He gave her books to read and quizzed her relentlessly on her assignments. At first she tried hard to live up to his expectations, but she became so intimidated in his presence, especially when he knitted his huge bushy brows and glared at her, that even when she knew the answer he wanted to hear, she often couldn't bring herself to say it, or stuttered it or expressed it poorly. He never yelled at her. He just sighed softly and leaned back in his chair, taking a deep breath. She would rather have been beaten than have to endure that sigh and look of disappointment.

Once Madame Kuris had tried to run away. Leaving at night, she ran and walked twenty miles along the desolate wilderness road before he caught up with her in a coach and took her back to Lutsikovka. He then sat down opposite her in the vast drawing room, sighing deeply, his bushy brows knit in deep concern.

After that incident, he had stopped the lessons. And she came

51

to miss them as part of the relatively idyllic early stage of their marriage. Instead of trying to form her mind, now he set out with equal fervor to make himself a *philosophe*. He ordered books, hundreds and thousands of French books, from Moscow, Petersburg, and even directly from Paris. And for long hours every day, he immersed himself in these impressive volumes. His library became a sacred shrine. Neither servants nor wife dared enter there except by specific invitation. And while he read, the house must be perfectly silent.

Then in the evening at supper, he would read aloud passages that had struck his fancy, or some of his own writings in the philosophic vein. Madame Kuris had to learn to smile just the right way and say just the right words at appropriate intervals or she would incur again the awful silence, the heavy breathing of his disappointment.

He aged quickly, and as he grew old, even that ritual came to an end. He took up residence in the library, eating his meals there, reading all night, and sleeping all day. Madame Kuris saw to such mundane matters as running the house and estate. So long as the house remained quiet and the food arrived regularly, he was quite pleased.

This blissful state was interrupted briefly when the house began to collapse about them. It had been built of unbaked brick. In his rush to make his dream a reality, Kuris had used the materials at hand. It would have taken too long to have baked bricks shipped in from Kharkov or to build his own little factory to bake them. One stormy spring, the magnificent palace, with its thirty rooms reverted to mud, as if a magic spell had been withdrawn.

They managed to save most of the books. Platon retired with them to an apartment in Kharkov, while Madame Kuris set about the work of rebuilding.

As Platon had gradually withdrawn into his books, Madame Kuris had assumed an increasing share of the responsibility for managing the estate. In that silent house, her will had grown strong. She had come in certain ways to resemble the man she so hated and loved. His dream of a palace in the wilderness was now her dream, tempered somewhat by a strong sense of practicality. Through all the years she had developed into a good manager, commanding respect and obedience from her serfs and from the merchants she dealt with. Under her able management, Lutsikovka, her husband's private dream, his expensive toy, had become a productive and valuable estate. Platon would have been proud of her, had he noticed.

So Madame Kuris oversaw the rebuilding of the house, on a less grand scale and following an architect's drawings. The new house lacked some of the extravagant charm of the original, which Platon had designed himself, such as a room without doors and an elegant staircase that led nowhere. But it was nonetheless impressive, and to the delight of Platon, the new library was twice the size of the old one.

Old Platon died a year or two after Jenny came to live at Lutsikovka. But even after his death, his spirit continued to reign there. The library was sacred ground. One entered there only with the utmost respect. If one borrowed a book, it must be put back exactly as the master had left it. Since he had rarely been seen those last few years, it was sometimes hard to believe that he wasn't still there, poring over his books all through the night. And a portrait of him that hung in the hall had eyes that seemed to follow you as you walked by.

Madame Kuris, also known as Aunt Elizaveta, was now the autocrat. She ruled the household with a benevolent, somewhat enlightened despotism. She hired a French governess for her orphaned niece and, in general, treated Jenny as she would have treated her own daughter, had she had a daughter. She listened to Jenny recite her lessons every day, listened to her say her prayers morning and night. If the child made a mistake or seemed insufficiently devout and sincere, Aunt Elizaveta sighed deeply, leaned back in her chair, and stared into the distance. Whenever her aunt did that, little Jenny pursed her lips and cringed, silently resolving never again to be so ungrateful as to displease Auntie. But try as she would to please her aunt, there were always those moments when her aunt sighed deeply, in disappointment.

Jenny couldn't help but dream of escape from this tyranny of kindness. Some dashing young man (like those she had read about in French novels she found buried behind the impressive philosophic works in the library) would carry her away to a new and dazzling life.

For a while, it seemed that her dream would become a reality. She met such a man—Anatole, son of a nearby landowner—and he did fall in love with her. They were going to get married. He would take her to Paris for their honeymoon. They would live in Petersburg.

It rained heavily that spring. Several weeks before the wedding was scheduled to take place, the two of them got drenched while riding. He left her at Lutsikovka and laughed merrily as he went riding off in the rain toward his father's estate. He caught a severe cold. It turned to pneumonia. He died.

For seven more long years, Jenny remained, unmarried, in her aunt's house, under her aunt's firm but quiet control. As the estate grew richer and the aunt grew older, distant relatives began to visit the matriarch with ever-increasing frequency, solicitously asking about her health, bringing her little gifts, doing her little favors. They snubbed the little orphan niece, the charity case who should be eternally grateful for everything she had received and who certainly shouldn't expect anything more. They implied that Jenny was trying to please the old woman just to get a part of the inheritance. Every time she did her aunt a service, the everyday household tasks she had learned were her duty to perform, the other relatives would glare at her and whisper among themselves.

As Aunt Elizaveta's wealth increased, local officials and neighbors started visiting frequently, not expecting immediate reward but responding to the natural magnetism of wealth. April 24, her nameday, became a major social occasion in the province. Everyone who was anyone—all the major landowners, the wealthier merchants, government officials, and military officers—came to pay homage to her and also to see one another. It was at such an event that Jenny first met Xavier Vikentyevich Bulatovich.

This Bulatovich was a Pole by descent. His ancestors were gentry from Grodno Province on the Polish border, territory that had changed hands frequently in the wars between Poland and Russia and the various partitions of Poland. He had graduated from the Academy of Engineering in Petersburg and had served his Tsar well, earning the medals of Stanislav, Vladimir, and Anna—for service in the Caucasus, quelling the uprisings there, and, later, in the Crimean War. He was a widower, a distinguished gentleman, and Jenny was flattered that he took an interest in her. Also, he was a general. His wife would have the title *generalsha*—quite a contrast to the prospect of becoming an old maid as the ward and nurse of an aging despot.

He was fifty and she twenty-five, the same age as his daughter by his first wife.

But it was religion, not age, that posed a problem.

While Old Platon was alive, Aunt Elizaveta had tried hard not to believe in God, in deference to her husband's philosophy. But she never quite succeeded, and after his death, with a sigh of relief, she gave up trying not to believe and allowed herself that one indulgence: fervent belief and devotion to all the outward forms of Orthodoxy.

Even though her own father, the merchant from France, had been Roman Catholic, she was frantically concerned that if Jenny should have children, she raise them as Orthodox. To calm her aunt, Jenny promised to do so, though she never mentioned it to the general, who up until his death was somewhat indifferent to questions of religion.

As Jenny often told her children afterward, "I could never see any essential difference between Russian Orthodoxy and Roman Catholicism. I suppose that's due to some deficiency in my education, my religious training, my understanding. Maybe that's the effect of that free-thinking uncle of mine. The difference is all a matter of outward forms and bureaucracy, as far as I can tell. They have a Pope in Rome, and we have a Holy Synod in Petersburg and a Patriarch in Istanbul. A few words in the creed and politics. It's the same God, I presume. But what a 'true believer' won't do for a few words or a ritual gesture. It makes me sick to think of all the hundreds and thousands of Old Believers executed by the state because they crossed themselves with two fingers instead of three and because they said "Alleluia" two times instead of three at the Eucharist—so ridiculous. Just two hundred years ago. And it was the Church that had changed its mind, not the Old Believers. The Church had switched from two to three for some political reason and expected all the peasants suddenly to start doing the same. Let them go ahead, I'd say. It's a comfort to them to cross themselves the way they always have, the way their ancestors did. So why force this petty innovation on them? What difference does it make? It's certainly not worth killing people over. Thank goodness they don't kill people anymore for that. But they still make life very uncomfortable for Old Believers and all the other sectarians or *raskolniki* who don't follow the official line precisely. If you are a Russian, you are supposed to belong to the Russian Orthodox Church. If you believe anything else, you are subject to all kinds of legal penalties. At the slightest provocation: 'Off to Siberia with them.' 'Fine them.' 'Take away their legal rights as citizens.' With the new laws, if your father were alive—a Pole and a Roman Catholic—he wouldn't be allowed to hold any official position; and he and others like him served the Tsar so well. Religion has nothing to do with reason, I'm afraid.

"Not that there's no difference among sects. Some are flagrantly fanatical. Take the Skoptsy, for instance—castrating themselves for Christ. Lord only knows how many thousands of those poor demented creatures there are in Russia today. But within reasonable limits, beliefs should be a private, personal matter.

"I wonder why I keep coming back to 'reason'—echoes of old Platon Kuris, and it's hard to imagine a more unreasonable man."

The general was charmed by Jenny's wit and vivacity. She made him feel young again. With her faultless French and her gentle upbringing, she could make a fine general's wife. Of course, at his age, he was set in his ways, but she was young and malleable. She would learn to adjust. And she would bear him a son.

In 1866, five years after the emancipation of the serfs, the orphan married the general and went off to live with him. But there was no time for a honeymoon. Maneuvers were coming up soon, and they'd have to postpone it for a while. Maybe next year. And he was always gone, at least during the day. It seemed she hardly knew him when she first discovered she was pregnant. Then for eight straight years, she was always pregnant or just getting over the last pregnancy. Two sons died within a year of their birth. Then came Sasha in 1870, Lilia in 1872, and in 1874 the youngest, Mariya—"Meta" they called her. She was born in Austria shortly before the general's death in Switzerland, at the end of a traumatic race across Europe from one health spa to another.

It had been another rainy spring, and the general had caught cold on maneuvers, a cold that wouldn't go away, that painfully racked his lungs with every cough. The doctors had advised that he try a warmer climate. So, leaving the children behind, he and his pregnant wife had set out on a sad parody of the honeymoon they had postponed too long.

Returning to Russia as a widow, Jenny had taken up residence once again with her aunt at Lutsikovka, bringing along Sasha, Lilia and newborn Meta.

By now Aunt Elizaveta was bedridden but still regal. Her incense-filled room became sacrosanct. As her eyes failed, she loved to hold and kiss and touch the icons, to inhale the incense. The feel, the smell, the taste of religion—in her own way she reveled in it all.

Every morning the young children made a pilgrimage to that room to say their prayers and to kiss the hand of their generous aunt and benefactress. Inside that room, Jenny was once again the meek, obedient little orphan girl. But outside that room, Jenny ruled as her aunt had ruled before her. Somehow the disappointments she had endured had tempered her will, had made her strong; and, unconsciously, she had learned something of her aunt's techniques. Small as she was, little more than five feet tall, she learned to use her apparent helplessness as a weapon now that she was a widow with an estate to manage and three young children to raise. When her rambunctious little son disturbed the books in the library or ran noisily about the house, she wouldn't yell and she wouldn't beat him. She would just look at him, her lips pursed, her eyes blank and weary, and she would heave a little sigh of disappointment.

Somehow she coped with all that needed to be done. Then finally in 1883 the old aunt died, and Jenny found herself with three half-grown children she hardly knew, with a son who at thirteen was still a little savage, with no playmates but the servants' children and the children from the peasant village of Markovka. There was no social life to speak of, but what else was she to expect? The nearest town was forty miles away, and that millionaire sugar-beet grower, Khritoninka, had bought up all the other estates in the district. For herself, she hadn't really noticed and didn't really care. But her children would need opportunities to socialize with people of their own class.

The governess seemed to have the girls well under control for the moment, but Sasha was another matter. Jenny lectured him, "You must learn to keep your distance from the peasants and their children. You must learn to treat them with cordial condescension.

"Remember, the huntsman and the coachman are your servants, not your equals. And their children are servants' children.

"It was one thing for you to run around with them and make playmates of them when you were an ignorant child. But now you have reached an age when that is no longer appropriate. It is time you began to show some discretion, to act the part of a gentleman."

"But Hrisko is my friend."

"The huntsman? A friend? Fooey and nonsense."

"And Masha . . ."

"The daughter of a scrubwoman? What's become of you? What have I let you become? You simply grew too fast. Where did the time go? Lord only knows. I should have realized before. Keeping you isolated out here in the wilds with no one but these urchins to consort with. It's high time you got a proper education, time I took you to civilized society where you can be with your equals and profit from examples of behavior appropriate to your station."

"What do you mean, Mother?"

"I'm going to take you to Petersburg and make a proper gentleman of you. Lord grant that it's not too late already, that you can be cured of your ragamuffin ways. I had hoped to set aside some more money. Petersburg is so expensive, and especially schools, proper schools for the girls, too. It will all be so expensive, and I had hoped to put it off for just another year. The crops have been poor and the tenants have been cheating me, I know they have. That new overseer isn't to be trusted either. Trust in God, yes, but man is another matter.

"It's the worst of times, really, but you force me to it. And Masha—I've seen you with her. What have I been thinking? And you at the threshold of manhood, the threshold of sin, with peasant servant girls all about, smiling sweetly, and playing games with the young master.

"Enough of that. I'll have no son of mine mix his blood with peasant stock.

"And you with your notions that everyone's equal in the eyes of God—equal indeed! You might even get notions of marrying such a girl. Enough of that. Petersburg it is. Petersburg will cure you."

Was that why they left for Petersburg then, not later, not the next year? and Lilia caught typhoid a few months later? and died?

Was he why?

More than her looks—her long black tresses, her dark eyes with their glimmer of playfulness—he remembered Lilia's patient stumbling practice at the piano. She wanted to do so well, and she did so poorly.

Her sister Meta, two years younger than she, was a genius at the piano and made it seem easy. But Lilia showed no jealousy. She just plodded ahead persistently with her practice, thoroughly convinced that hard work and merit would have their reward in the end.

Chopin, in particular, she would practice over and over again. She had trouble with timing, racing ahead, then slowing for a difficult phrase, then racing ahead again. And there were those times, agonizing for the listener, when she stopped in the middle of a phrase she had played hundreds of times, and hunted, it seemed an eternity, for the next note, or she'd give up and start again.

Her death was a mistake like that—stopping in midexpectation. But this time there was no chance to start over again.

When they were little, they fought often and they were inseparable. As they grew older they found equally petty things to argue over and keep them close.

In the year before she died, she had become his confidante. He needed someone to tell of his adventures and his misdemeanors, someone to complain to about his mother's quiet self-sacrificing tyranny. Those heavy sighs of disappointment of hers were really beginning to hurt. He needed to unburden himself of guilt, needed to be reassured that he was not alone, that he was not altogether in the wrong, that his mother was often unfair.

After Lilia died (was there anything he could have done to stop it? to keep her safe and happy at Lutsikovka, to keep her from that accidental meeting with death?), no one could take her place, no one could relieve his growing burden of guilt.

And ever after he could never stand the sound of Chopin.

The death of his Aunt Elizaveta had been no surprise. She had been dying—of cancer, they said—for as long as he could remember. The shock was to see her laid out on the dining-room table instead of in her bed.

He had never seen her in the dining room before. That was what made her look so dead—it was so unlike her to be there like that. That couldn't be her at all lying there.

For the last few months Aunt Elizaveta had hardly moved. Only the pungent smell of incense, right under her nose, could revive her long enough for his mother to force her to eat something. It was as if she kept sinking deeper and deeper within herself, until nothing could pull her out and they called her "dead."

With Lilia it was different. No sinking. No gradual decline and emaciation. Just suddenly she wasn't there anymore.

For the longest while after the doctor said it was over, Sasha kept expecting her to prove him wrong, finally to breathe the next breath, finally to find that next note.

Only when he saw her laid out on a dining-room table, like Aunt Elizaveta, did he believe that that was all. There was nothing more.

Months later, his sister Meta forgot for a moment. Hearing steps in the hallway, she called out cheerfully, "Lilia! Is that you, Lilia?"

But it wasn't Lilia. It was Sasha. And seeing him she broke out crying.

He ran up to her and shook her, and shouted harshly, "When will you face the facts? You can't bring her back. No matter what you want to believe and how hard you want to believe it, you still have to face the facts."

His own words frightened him, and he awoke to the sound of oxen and carts and harsh shouting. The detachment was getting ready to move to the border.

BETWEEN PROVING AND BELIEVING

4

Ongun Station, Manchuria, about seventy miles from the Russian border, July 30, 1900

He must die. It's a matter of discipline," said Strakhov, loudly slapping his side to swat a mosquito. He had swung without thinking, out of boredom and annoyance. The loud crack surprised, aroused, and embarrassed him. Quickly, he regained his equanimity and assumed a stern look, as if he had slapped his side intentionally to emphasize his words.

He and other key officers had gathered in General Orlov's tent, expecting to receive final assignments and the order to begin fighting what for most of them would be the first battle of their lives.

Nearly ten thousand Chinese, well-armed soldiers, had taken up position on the plateau overlooking Ongun Station. The Russians, including about two thousand infantry, nine hundred cavalry, and a company of railway guards, were lined up behind a row of sandy hillocks, awaiting the order to attack. Instead of giving that order, Orlov kept bringing up matters of seemingly minor importance—for instance, this theft by a fifty-four-year-old Cossack volunteer named Starodubov.

"Major Strakhov is right, General," added Colonel Kupferman, wiping the sweat from his brow.

Inside the tent, the midsummer heat was stifling. There was no place to sit.

"We cannot tolerate robbery in our midst," Kupferman continued. His unseemly girth obviously contributed to his physical discomfort and general testiness. A friend now, but a man to beware of, noted Strakhov. "They know no shoe polish. They have no idea what it means to salute. Such minor lapses of discipline we must live with. There is no time to whip these ruffians into reliable soldiers. But crime we must deal with—swiftly and severely, or we'll find ourselves completely at the mercy of these cutthroats."

"And you, Alexander Xavierevich?" asked Orlov, turning to Bulatovich. "What would you do with the thief?"

Bulatovich squinted, adjusting his red cap and his glasses before replying, "I would exercise discretion, Your Excellency." He was shorter than the other officers, built like a jockey. But that red cap, distinctive of that exclusive cavalry regiment he came from, made him stand out from the crowd; and that way he squinted when he emphasized a point—Strakhov read it as a sign of defiance.

"Discretion?" asked Orlov, leaning back in his chair. He was the only one seated.

"Yes, Your Excellency," explained Bulatovich. "Had I been present when the man was apprehended, I would have confronted him privately, threatened him with severe punishment, and then set him free to prove himself in battle."

"Prove himself?" asked Strakhov. "But he has already proven himself a common thief."

"Indeed, Major Strakhov," replied Bulatovich. "And there are hundreds of thieves in this irregular army we are blessed with. That we know. But we do not know how many brave fighting men we have. Starodubov may well prove to be such a brave man."

"But leniency?" persisted Strakhov, annoyed at finding himself opposed by a subordinate over such a simple, clear-cut matter of discipline. The issue was trivial, but he had spoken up, and he would lose face in front of his new commanding general if he didn't defend his position. "For a thief in time of war you would recommend leniency?"

"I recommend not leniency, but discretion. Let the man's guilt be used as a goad to urge him to heroic feats. Let him try to earn his freedom."

"You would let a blatant criminal go free?" persisted Strakhov. "You would have a man like that at your side, at your back in the thick of battle?"

"And would you rather rely on a man who has nothing to gain by risking his life, another conscript, ducking bullets and serving out his time? No, give me a man with a touch of guilt, with a need to prove himself—that's the stuff heroes are made of."

"But we don't need heroes; we need discipline," insisted Strakhov.

"In a military academy or on garrison duty at Orenburg," Orlov interjected, "indeed, Major Strakhov, you would be correct. There is no need for heroism on the training field or in the classroom. But here in Manchuria, Staff-Rotmister Bulatovich is correct. One brave man on the field of battle can inspire dozens to feats they would never ordinarily attempt. An execution at this point would only breed distrust and despondency. Remember, officers, the men know you and trust you no better than you know and trust them. They're waiting for you to prove yourselves in combat and in cases such as this."

"Of course," added Strakhov, exasperated enough to pursue his point even in opposition to the commanding general. "What will leniency in a case like this tell them? What will that do to discipline?"

"It's a question of discretion, not leniency," repeated Bulatovich. "The man must be confronted. Apparently, there is no doubt regarding his guilt. Let him know that he has been found guilty. But suspend sentencing until he has had an opportunity to earn his life."

"He'll simply desert," objected Strakhov.

"Then he'll simply be shot as a deserter," concluded Bulatovich.

At the time of the officers' meeting, Bulatovich had not yet met the thief—Alexei Starodubov. They first met minutes later when Bulatovich went to release him.

Bulatovich had had no intention of defending this man, had known nothing about him. Nor was he being generous and humane. His arguments were based on his knowledge of human behavior. It seemed a waste to execute a man who could prove useful.

Bulatovich had grown accustomed to judging and controlling men in Ethiopia. When hiring bearers for expeditions into the wilds, he knew that probably several would die and several more would desert and that, if he lost control of these men, all their lives would be in danger. He had learned how to control men with the tone of his voice, the expression of his face, and his posture. Whenever possible, he influenced them by example. And he always hired more men than he needed so that the bearers would know they weren't indispensable, that others were anxiously waiting to pick up their burdens and their higher wages. The extras were also vital when minor disasters accumulated to thin out the ranks. Having dealt with that kind of situation, he was fully confident he could cope with one Trans-Baikal Cossack.

Most Cossacks had a tradition of military service to the Tsar that went back many generations, but in Trans-Baikal many were just second generation, sons of serfs from the imperial silver mines at Nerchinsk. Starodubov in particular was so old that as a boy he himself may have been a serf in the mines. On receiving their freedom in the emancipation of 1861, these former serfs had been given large tracts of land to be held communally.

Although all Cossacks had an obligation of twenty years of military service, these seemed to have spent little time on active duty; and what training they had had, they had conducted themselves. They had probably spent more time hunting, herding, and farming than going through military exercises. They were wilderness settlers first and soldiers second. If they bothered to salute, they did so with a swagger and a mocking smile. But, purportedly, they were fine horsemen, good marksmen, and fearless fighters.

Bulatovich didn't expect this man to be subservient like an enlisted man to an officer or like a peasant to a wealthy landowner. But he assumed that fear of death would make tractable even the most independent and insubordinate frontiersman.

He planned to dominate the man with voice and gesture, to make him cringe, make him realize that in the eyes of the military he was as good as dead. Then would come the surprise of reprieve, the chance to prove himself in battle. But he found a huge hulk of a man, who didn't behave at all as expected, who just sat calmly, cross-legged, oblivious to his chains.

Momentarily taken aback, Bulatovich recomposed his features, assumed the harsh attitude he had planned. But again Starodubov surprised him, looking up at him with a huge innocent smile, as if delighted at recognizing a long-lost friend. Disconcertingly, Bulatovich felt a reciprocal surge of friendliness. Something about this man—the long white hair and beard, the dark leathery skin, the pale gentle eyes—reminded him of the huntsman Old Hrisko, his childhood friend back at Lutsikovka.

He tried to suppress these feelings and get down to business as planned. "Starodubov. That means 'Old Oak.' I should call you 'Old Blockhead.' Stealing money from an officer."

"No, sir; not me, sir."

"Then you deny the charge?"

"What need have I for money?"

"Do you deny that you stole? Must we go through the formalities and call witnesses? It will go worse for you, I promise."

"But I would never steal money, sir. The man who says I did lies. A dagger's all I took, sir. A fine antique dagger, with carved ivory hilt."

"But why did you do such a thing? What were you trying to prove?"

The peasant smiled up at him as if genuinely pleased that Bulatovich had asked the question. "I've asked myself that too, sir." He leaned back and stared up into the sky. "When I was a young man, I was very strong. People kept picking fights with me. They'd insult me and heckle me until I had no choice but to fight them or do something that would awe them and shut them up. They say that once I even lifted a horse. I must have been drunk. I don't remember it myself. Maybe I did, maybe I didn't.

"Then one day I asked myself, 'What am I trying to prove?' I was tired of bashing heads and taking bruises. Why should I care what strangers think? Why should I have to be the strongest man for miles around?

"I learned to back down from useless fights. I didn't walk so tall anymore. I kept to myself. When they'd chase after me and try to provoke me, I'd just sit and carve, holding the knife hard and the wood hard. I came to love carving with these big rough hands of mine. I learned when to hold back, when to push and how to use these muscles of mine to make beautiful objects. Yes, beautiful. I took pride in what I made with these hands.

"I grew older. I had two fine sons. We'd go off into the pasture together, high above Lake Baikal. I'd stand tall and laugh and show off my strength as I had as a young man. It felt good showing off for my sons. And they'd show off for me. They'd wrestle together and they'd wrestle with me. Then I'd sit and carve by the firelight. The tiredness of my muscles felt good. I felt alive.

"My sons are gone now. Both gone. One dead of typhus. The other conscripted for military duty thousands of miles from here. I'll not be seeing him again, not in this life." He crossed himself automatically. "He was a fighter, that Pasha. The day his brother died, we wrestled. I shamed him into it, spanked him like a child. No son of mine would sit about and sulk. He fought back like the devil himself. I thought he'd kill me. Afterward, we got drunk together. In the morning we were off in the fields with the herds as always.

"When I lost the last of my sons, when Pasha went away, I lost the urge to carve, I lost the urge to do anything. I just sat and my wife just scolded. Then I asked myself, 'What am I trying to prove?' And I left.

"The army needed men for this Manchurian business. I joined."

"But why did you steal the dagger?" persisted Bulatovich, bewildered by this unkempt peasant giant with his long white hair and his rambling tales.

"That wasn't the first. I've stolen before, dozens of times. I love beautiful carved objects. I've lost the urge to carve, but I love the feel of fine carving. It was too easy. I was lucky, too lucky. Luck can be dangerous, you know. It makes a man careless. I got careless. I don't know what I was trying to prove. I'm just a foolish old man."

"Wipe that silly grin off your face," snapped Bulatovich.

The man smiled still more, but not a grin of defiance. He wore a look of relief, as if he had just unburdened himself to a kindred spirit.

Bulatovich didn't know what to make of this man. He wished now that he had never gotten involved in this business. He took off his glasses and wiped the lenses on his tunic. Then he smiled condescendingly, hoping Starodubov would cower in his chains, that his eyes would flee from contact. But again, the peasant smiled back, innocently.

"You are a fool," said Bulatovich in disgust. But as he left, almost as an afterthought, he turned to the guard. "Take off his chains. Here's the general's order." And to Starodubov: "You'll come with me. You're now under my command."

The incident with the old thief upset Bulatovich's carefully cultivated calm. He had deliberately remained aloof from both officers and men, spending much of his time riding alone in the surrounding countryside, checking maps supplied by the railway company, making additions and changes based on what he could tell with field glasses and surveying gear, trying to distract himself from personal worries—Sonya, the derailment of his career—mostly just staring at the horizon in solitude.

His immediate superiors, Kupferman and Strakhov, couldn't understand why this Guards officer had asked for assignment to Manchuria. He made no effort to explain his presence. And he seemed to avoid them deliberately. Neither of them had ever before experienced the humiliation of being snubbed by a subordinate. They responded to his standoffishness in kind, saying no more to him than they had to in the performance of their duties, leaving him, as "second assistant commander of the mounted regiment," with no clear authority or responsibilities—a position that had suited his purposes fine, until it turned out that they were actually going to see action.

Apparently, the Chinese governor and the military commander at Hailar had come out in favor of the antiforeign outbreak, and on their own authority or based on covert orders from Peking, they were going to use all the regular troops at their disposal to prevent the Russians from regaining control of the almost completed railway.

It could well turn out to be a farce—there was no telling with troops that had never seen battle before whether they would turn and run at the first shot. The Russians were better trained, even if undisciplined, and had more experience with their weapons. The Chinese outnumbered them three to one. The Russians needed a victory now to give them confidence, for they would then have to march deeper into Manchuria to Hailar and beyond, with long and precarious supply lines and no idea how many more armies the enemy had waiting for them.

The Old Thief intruded on his consciousness.

"Will the battle be starting soon, sir?" asked Starodubov, following Bulatovich through the camp like a stray dog.

"Within the hour," Bulatovich answered curtly, without bothering to turn his head.

"Is it your first, sir?"

"No."

"It is for me, sir. And old fool that I am, I feel a bit funny about the belly."

"Hungry?"

"Scared, sir."

Bulatovich stopped and glared at him. "Would you rather be back in the guardhouse?"

"No, sir, no. I'm most grateful, sir." They resumed walking. "Will I be riding a horse, sir? Will I carry a saber?"

"Yes."

"I've never used a saber before, never so much as held one. I was in the infantry battalion, you see, sir. And I'm just a poor peasant. I could never afford anything so fine as a saber."

"We'll equip you."

"Have you ever used a saber, sir?"

"Of course."

"Against a man, I mean. Not just for practice, but real combat. Have you, sir?"

Bulatovich hesitated, then grunted, "No. I used a rifle and pistols."

"It must be most peculiar—to kill a man with a saber, at such close quarters. I think I'm more scared of that than of what might happen to me. All that blood. Like slaughtering sheep. Have you ever been wounded, sir?"

"No."

"And where did you fight your battles?"

"Africa."

"And were there many battles?"

"Yes. Skirmishes I'd call them."

"Many battles and never wounded. You must be very lucky, sir. Hope it hasn't made you careless," he added with a nervous laugh.

Bulatovich didn't respond.

"Will we be in the front line?"

Still no answer.

"Do you command a squadron, sir?"

"No."

"A troop."

"No."

"Then what do you do, sir?"

"I am second assistant commander of the regiment."

"What does that mean, sir?"

"It means I have no troops to command at all. None but you, Blockhead. We'll watch the battle from the hillside. If there's an emergency, I may be called on to lead some of the reserves."

"Oh, I see, sir."

"What do you see?" Bulatovich confronted him.

They were just passing the bakery at Ongun Station. Many men were eating and milling about. They all stopped to stare at the little Guards officer in the red cap and the white-bearded peasant giant who followed him.

"What do you see?" repeated Bulatovich.

"Nothing, sir, nothing," Starodubov hunched his massive shoulders submissively.

They started up the sandy hillside.

"I should have some troops to command," Bulatovich thought aloud. "That's what I'm trained for. It's an oversight, I'm sure—I'm going now to see the regimental commander." His own words surprised him. He started striding so fast that Starodubov had to jog to keep up.

🦅 🦅 🦅

Colonel Kupferman took another look at Bulatovich. A fine time to ask for a command. Just half an hour before a battle. What kind of army did he think this was?

Kupferman was used to treating subordinates abruptly, quashing all signs of individual pride and independence. But he didn't know what to make of this little man with his Guards-officer self-assurance.

Kupferman had sensed trouble as soon as he had seen the man's odd Gypsy tent. For himself, he had no tent at all, but rather a spacious carriage, his tarantass. He was getting on in years, and he was used to certain comforts. His feather mattress from home fit neatly into the carriage; he exercised his prerogative as commander and brought it along. He would have brought his favorite chair, perhaps even his wife, but there was no room for them.

It seemed this Bulatovich was exercising the prerogatives of a regimental commander without having the rank or command. His Gypsy tent interrupted the rows of uniform tents that the regulation-conscious officers from Kazan and Orenburg had struggled to convince their irregular troops to erect in orderly fashion. Its flamboyance was better suited for the jungles of Africa or for the chaotic encampment of railway guards, civilian camp followers, and Chinese Christian refugees on the outskirts of the bivouac.

"Well, what do you expect me to do?" Kupferman asked Bulatovich impatiently.

Men on horseback were rushing by and jostling one another, trying to find their units. Less than half an hour to go, and these men still hadn't formed up and seemed to have no notion of where they were supposed to be.

A young officer with a smile on his face ambled by, in no particular hurry.

"You there!" Kupferman lashed out. Startled, the officer stumbled to a stop. "Yes, you! Where are your men, and why aren't you with them? I asked you a question, Lieutenant. I expect an answer."

Regaining his composure, the officer snapped to attention and saluted smartly. "Lieutenant Grotten reporting, sir. My men are already in position, sir. I'll be rejoining them in a minute. I command one of the troops of Krasnostanov's squadron."

"You used to command," barked Kupferman, delighting to see the young man cringe. He didn't really know how to deal with Bulatovich. He wanted to put him in his place but wasn't really sure what that place was or how far his own authority actually extended—Bulatovich coming from such an elite regiment and the general holding him in such special favor. It was a relief to be able to single out this other foolish young officer and revel in exercising power over him.

"But, sir . . ." the young officer protested.

"Don't 'but' me. I'll brook no more insubordination. One more word from you and I'll have you in the guardhouse. Meet the new commander of your troop—Staff-Rotmister Bulatovich. You'll be serving under him. Take him to his troop, on the double, Lieutenant."

With that, Kupferman saluted sharply and turned his back before his subordinates had time to return the salute.

👑 👑 👑

"I tried to be conscientious," Grotten explained to Bulatovich and to himself, nervous, overanxious, trying to absorb the shock of this sudden setback to his career. "Ever since I arrived at Chita and was given my command, I have tried my best to get acquainted with my men—all twenty of them. I believe that a good commander should know his men."

Bulatovich nodded assent, and they continued to pick their way through the confused crowds, toward the rallying point for Krasnostanov's squadron.

"This was my first command," explained Grotten, trying to restrain his anger, trying to be logical, to make the best of the situation. "I interviewed each of my men individually before we left Chita. An old sergeant had warned me not to pursue the questioning too far. 'Here in Siberia,' he said, 'it isn't healthy to ask too much about a man's past.' Apparently, a lot of the men are criminals or sons of criminals who were banished here. So I asked just enough to satisfy my sense of a commander's responsibility but not enough to satisfy my personal curiosity."

"Commendable," noted Bulatovich.

Grotten smiled nervously, anxious to get any kind of approval. "That's my troop, I mean your troop, our troop, just

71

ahead, sir." They stopped twenty paces away. "Before I introduce you to them and we go riding off into battle, I feel I should pass on to you what I know about some of these men."

"Please do, Lieutenant, I appreciate your help."

Grotten cautiously assessed his new commander. It probably wouldn't hurt to curry favor with this standoffish but apparently influential new man. "There weren't enough able-bodied Cossacks available so they filled out the ranks with whomever they could get. All the men in this troop are from along the Uda and Selenga rivers near Lake Baikal and the town of Verkhneudinsk, a mountainous, heavily wooded area. They are mostly hunters, a few farmers and sheepherders, four or five Cossacks, and a couple who seem too well educated to be native to this area—probably banished or running from the law for political or religious reasons.

"The three in the front row are the Zabelin brothers. Pyotr's the young one with the dirty-looking fuzz on his face. He's been trying to grow a beard since he joined up in Chita three weeks ago. He's about seventeen, says he joined for the excitement. The one crossing himself is his brother Trofim. He's no more than twenty-five. He was probably born with a wrinkled brow and a frown on his face. A very serious type. With all the horsing around these last few weeks, I've never seen him smile. He says he joined to fight for a holy cause. The one with the beard is Login, the eldest, about thirty or so. He's the leader of them, the head of the family actually, since their father is dead. He joined just so he could protect his foolish brothers.

"If you look closely when Trofim crosses himself, you'll see he does it with two fingers, instead of the Orthodox three. They're Old Believers," announced Grotten, proud of his powers of observation and deduction. "The two fingers symbolize Christ's human-divine dual nature. While Old Believers suffer severe penalties and restrictions back in European Russia, out here in the wilderness quite a few of them have prospered. There are scores of Old Believer families along the Uda and the Selenga who openly practice their heretical faith, unmolested by the authorities. Some have been there for many generations and are among the leading families of the district.

"Over there to the left, that swarthy one with the long, lean face, the one who's smoking his pipe so calmly, showing off how unconcerned he is—that's Butorin, one of the Cossacks, a self-styled expert on the local terrain and customs. He's about forty. From the look of him there's probably more Mongolian blood than Russian in his veins. He's a slippery character. Never seems to answer a question straight; at least not for me. Ask him about himself and he'll answer with anecdotes about the local Buryat tribesmen and a lecture on how to ride a camel.

"The one off to the right, brushing his horse, is another Cossack—Shemelin, Yakov Shemelin. He's about twenty-five, I'd say. A fine horseman and very bright. Taught himself to read, I hear, with very little guidance. Most of these men are completely illiterate and quite content to stay that way, but not Shemelin. He'd have probably done all right by himself if he'd ever had a chance to go to school. Always thinking. He had as many questions for me as I had for him.

"One thing's peculiar about him, though—he doesn't like to be called 'Yakov,' even though that's the name on his papers. He prefers 'Ivan.' Yakov's a fine old biblical name, but he seems to think it sounds too Jewish. I don't know what he has personally against the Jews. Aside from now, I don't think he's ever been very far from his village; and most Cossacks would never allow a Jew to settle on their land. Maybe things are a bit looser here in Trans-Baikal. Anyway, his nose is straight. He's generous to a fault. His father was a Cossack before him. I don't know why he'd think anyone would mistake him for a Jew just because of the name Yakov.

"That young one beside him, playing with the pendant around his neck—that's Aksyonov, another seventeen-year-old. He was married just a week before he was called up. He carries his wife's picture around his neck and worships it like an icon.

"The two educated ones are in the back. Notice, their skin is lighter than the rest and doesn't have the leathery texture that most natives here have by the time they're thirty. I'd say they're both at least thirty. The one on the left, clean-shaven with the wire-rimmed glasses—that's Laperdin. He dropped those glasses once and I picked them up. The lenses are very thin and not very powerful. He can probably see quite well without them. Not too many people from around here would be so fastidious as to wear glasses if they didn't absolutely need to. Has to be somebody who was used to doing a lot of reading. And he talks like an educated man, using long words when little ones would do just as well. Sofronov, the one on the right, talks that way too, only he has a tone in his voice sometimes that's just like a priest delivering a sermon."

As Grotten went through the formalities of calling the troop of twenty men to attention and informing them that Bulatovich was their new commander, Bulatovich quickly scanned the ranks. It was a motley group. As in all Cossack units each man had to provide his own "uniform" and equipment. There was no uniformity at all in what they wore, except their white tunics and the *ichigi* they wore on their feet—heelless, soft substitutes for the boots they couldn't afford. None of them wore spurs. They each carried instead a *nagaika*, a heavy whip. Their rifles were slung across their backs with the sling coming across the right shoulder, opposite of how it was done in the regular army. Each also had a pistol and a sword. The horses were smallish and of questionable quality.

The boy called Pyotr seemed to pay no attention to what Grotten said. Pyotr and his horse moved nervously. Login looked Bulatovich straight in the eye, not a look of malice, but of calm assessment. Butorin grinned rather foolishly. Bulatovich remembered him as the soldier who had fallen through the window in a fight back at Chita. He looked none the worse for it. Sofronov seemed to be mumbling a prayer to himself. The sunlight reflected off Laperdin's fastidious glasses, making it difficult to tell where he was looking or what he was thinking.

A cannon shot from the left flank interrupted Grotten's introduction. Commands were shouted and repeated. The cavalry mounted. With a loud shout, "Urah!" the charge began.

⚜ ⚜ ⚜

Orlov checked his watch: one-fifty. The cavalry had started on time. When they reached the plateau, that would signal the advance of the infantry battalions.

He crossed himself. His orderly and his adjutants quickly did likewise.

The night before, he had led all the troops in prayers and hymns. He had done everything he could to prepare for this battle. Now it was in the hands of God.

The bivouac was set up near a little pond on the south side of the Hailar River, sheltered from the Chinese by a row of sandy hills. Orlov had placed the 4th Battalion on the hilltop on the left flank with the six-cannon artillery battery to their right and the 6th Battalion to the right of them. Several companies guarded the railway station and its bakery in the valley off to the right, and on the far right flank the cavalry regiment was now rapidly approaching a comparable body of cavalry on the Chinese left flank.

Orlov had been anxious, perhaps too anxious to begin the campaign. Rather than wait until all his troops had assembled and organized, he had crossed the border into Manchuria with only two foot battalions and one company of mounted railway guards. A few squadrons of the cavalry regiment had caught up with them a few days later. When they first encountered the enemy here at Ongun, Orlov had insisted on waiting until the final squadrons arrived and had had time to rest and refresh themselves and their horses. But even now his detachment was far from complete: two more foot battalions under Colonel Vorobyev were still organizing back at Abagaitui, and three companies of mounted railway guards under Captain Smolyannikov were taking the northern route to Hailar by way of Staro Tsurukhaitui.

For the upcoming battle the Russians numbered two thousand foot, one thousand mounted. The Chinese were about ten thousand strong, armed with Mauser and Winchester rifles, and camouflaged in shallow one-man foxholes on a plateau about half a mile away.

For several hours the Chinese had been firing continuously. But at that distance, most of their bullets fell harmlessly in the sand in front of the Russian positions.

During the long wait, Russian soldiers had amused themselves by making fun of Chinese marksmanship, strolling about, eating fresh bread, and drinking tea, sheltered by the hills, or taking needless chances by standing unprotected on the hilltops, while bullets whistled by overhead or kicked up the sand in front of them. It was rumored that ammunition was scarce in the

Chinese army and that target practice was prohibited. Many of the soldiers facing them now may never have fired a rifle before. Besides, the range was too far for even the best sharpshooters to be accurate—or so the Russians figured, too inexperienced themselves to admit fear, cavalierly ignoring the fact that the rumor might be wrong, that these Chinese soldiers might know how to shoot, that in any case a stray bullet could accidentally hit and kill. Only a few worried enough to risk ridicule by staying under cover, lying on their bellies in the hot sand.

The Battle of Ongun was an important test of strength, thought Orlov, crossing himself again, and trying to think of the words he would use to describe this moment in his memoirs. There were very few fanatical Boxer types in this western section of Manchuria. The people here, for the most part, were Mongolian, speaking a different language, having a different culture than their Chinese masters. As a subject people their loyalty to the central government was questionable. Their allegiance was a question of which side had the stronger armies, or which side they believed was stronger. Right now they apparently believed in the strength of the Chinese. This battle would confirm or confound that belief. If the Russians, God forbid, lost this battle, the campaign could turn out to be a long and bitter one. On the other hand, if the Russians won, the war in this region could be over very quickly, and they all could go back to their normal business.

The cavalry reached the plateau. The cannon opened fire. The foot soldiers began their stumbling, enthusiastic race down the sandy hillsides.

The battle had begun.

☙ ☙ ☙

At the first shout of "Urah!" Starodubov jumped on a horse. It had been many years since he had last ridden a horse, and then it had been bareback—saddles were a luxury. He didn't know what to do with the stirrups. They seemed too small, too short. He let his legs hang free and clung to the horse's neck as the frightened beast raced along with the throng.

Starodubov would have crossed himself, but he needed both hands to keep his wrestler's grip on the horse's neck. His thighs, crotch, and behind ached from the jouncing he was getting.

Off to his left, horses collided. A man lost his balance and fell, screaming, beneath onrushing hooves. Starodubov leaned the other way, pulling his horse with him and riding into a flurry of kicks as a rider on that side tried to stave him off and avoid collision.

His eyes stung from the dust, the heat. He prayed loudly but couldn't hear himself. The clatter of the hooves, everyone yelling, in the distance heavy gunfire.

Just ahead, he spotted Bulatovich—his bright red cap still visible in the dust of a thousand horses. Bulatovich rode high, hardly touching his saddle at all.

☨ ☨ ☨

Grotten had raced to the front, proud of the speed of his mount, proud of his skill at maneuvering through the press of other riders, proud of his own bravery. When he reached the crest of the plateau, he could see the Chinese cavalry scattering and galloping off without a fight, the Chinese infantry scurrying out of their shallow foxholes and away from the oncoming Russian horses.

Shots whistled by. The Chinese were all around them. Grotten's horse stumbled, righted itself. (Had that been a rock or a man his horse had struck?)

In the distance, the Russian infantry was running across the valley, shooting wildly in their excitement at the complete rout of the enemy.

Grotten tried to turn, tried to stop, but to avoid collision he had to keep going, racing beyond the enemy now, away from them. He felt foolish at his helplessness. He wondered where his troop was—Bulatovich's troop. In the excitement of his first battle, Grotten had completely forgotten about his men. Irresponsible. Foolish. How could he find them now?

Gradually, he and those around him slowed and jockeyed to avoid collision. Units were hopelessly dissolved in other units.

Overanxious officers added to the confusion with their shouted commands. Individuals managed to turn and begin the charge back again at the enemy. Grotten slowly picked his way through the crowd, anxiously trying to remember what his men looked like and to recognize them through the masks of sweat and dust.

Suddenly, he spotted a red cap. Bulatovich. And gathered around him—nearly all the men of the troop. They were just now turning and charging back at the enemy. Grotten followed close behind.

⚜ ⚜ ⚜

The battlefield broke up into dozens of individual skirmishes, separated by clusters of dry brush and clouds of dust and smoke. Here and there, scattered across this patchwork battlefield were accidental islands of peace, with no enemy in sight.

When Bulatovich and his troop chanced on such an island, Starodubov stopped, tumbled down off his horse, and stood there shaking unsteadily, still feeling the agonizing motion of the horse and trying to sort out his other sensations. He could feel liquid dripping down his back.

Butorin and the rest of the troop burst out laughing at him. Butorin was the loudest of all, standing behind him, holding an empty canteen.

Then suddenly, they stopped and stared. He felt his back—soaked with water. He looked down at his trousers—soaked with blood. Through a rip in the cloth, he could see the raw bleeding flesh of his thigh. Yet somehow he had managed to stay on his horse and keep up with the rest.

This vision was interrupted by another, emerging from a cloud of dust—a huge Chinese in a blue robe, waving a black banner with a red border and leading a hundred or more Chinese, running, shouting, shooting wildly. Somehow this giant had managed to hold together and inspire his entire company in the midst of the general rout.

Bulatovich drew his pistol and carefully aimed. Others hesitated, on the brink of running for cover. But Starodubov, with only a dagger in his hand, rushed at the giant, churning his big bleeding legs.

78

Before the Chinese giant could decide how to react to this madman, Starodubov leaped and kicked him three times—in the crotch, in the belly, in the head. As the man fell, Starodubov grabbed his flag and waved it in triumph. Then Bulatovich, Grotten, and the rest raced forward, cheering all the while for Starodubov, who charged ahead recklessly, flag in hand, with a big grin on his face.

Fortunately for Starodubov and the rest of the Hailar Detachment, the rumor had been right—the Chinese, although well-armed, were untrained in the use of their weapons. They missed repeatedly, even at point-blank range.

"Why did you do it?" Bulatovich asked Starodubov after the enemy had scattered. "What were you trying to prove?" As he asked that, there was admiration in his eyes, magnified by the thick lenses of his glasses.

"I don't know, sir. I just wanted that flag. Did you see how it caught the light and the wind? It's a thing of beauty, sir."

"You Old Thief," laughed Bulatovich.

And Starodubov smiled—proud of the recognition.

He held his head high and lifted high the flag to the cheers of the troop and of Bulatovich himself.

☬ ☬ ☬

The cheers of the men were contagious. Grotten had wanted to perform heroic feats himself; but joining in the cheering, he felt not envy but rather exhilaration. And who had inspired these cheers, this feeling? Who had shown them all what they were capable of? A reckless, foolhardy old man. Look at him now—the enemy's flag in his hand, his right foot firmly planted on the chest of a giant—like a hero from a folk song.

Bulatovich, smiling broadly and laughing, mounted his horse, slung his rifle across his right shoulder like a Cossack, waved his red cap, and shouted to Starodubov, "To horse, you Old Thief! Let's finish what we've begun."

"But sir," objected Grotten, remembering his own irresponsible enthusiasm in the first charge. "They're sounding the muster call."

"No matter."

79

"But sir," he persisted, conscientiously. "It will soon be dark, and there's no telling how many of them may be out there hiding in the brush, just waiting for us. It's not my own safety I'm thinking of. We mustn't forget the men, sir."

Bulatovich raised his saber. "Go back if you like. I intend to pursue the enemy."

Grotten stared, speechless, bewildered by his new commander's recklessness. Trofim crossed himself. And Aksyonov glanced at the picture of his wife, clasped his precious pendant. But when Bulatovich went riding off eastward, with Starodubov somehow staying at his side, every one of them followed.

⚜ ⚜ ⚜

When Strakhov saw the cavalry routing the Chinese, he left Kupferman and led a reserve squadron into battle, afraid that victory would come too quickly and that he would miss an opportunity to demonstrate his abilities. At the crest of the plateau, a shot rang out beside him. To his left, sheltered by a bush, not five feet away, a Chinese soldier was aiming at him. Another shot. Strakhov froze but his horse, wounded, reared, toppling Strakhov toward the sniper. Two Cossacks quickly charged with sabers and literally hacked the sniper to pieces, severing head and arms. Covered with the victim's blood, Strakhov stood there on the battlefield and, in full sight of his men, loudly retched and vomited.

His first thought was that he should never have eaten right before going into battle. His second thought was that the jolt of falling had shaken the food loose.

He tried to regain his composure, borrowed a horse from one of his men, ordered his men to check every bush, every suspicious mound of sand for snipers. Then he noticed that his trousers were wet, soaked, stinking. He had no idea when it had happened, whether his men had noticed it. His body was betraying him. He was physically revolted by the sight of bloodshed. Fourteen years a soldier. His very first battle. And he couldn't stand the sight of blood. His whole career was at stake. The thought sent a chill down his spine. His mind had been prepared for battle, prepared to play the role of the fearless hero. His body had revolted.

Somehow he lived through the humiliating experience. He tried to cover the stain on his trousers unobtrusively. Keeping his distance from his men, he hoped to stave off their ridicule with harsh decisive commands, ordering them this way and that to flush out enemy stragglers. When the bugles sounded the muster call, he kept his men in the field, waiting until after dark to lead them back to the bivouac.

🛇 🛇 🛇

General Orlov didn't want to sleep that night. This was his first campaign, his first major battle. He was accustomed to paperwork and friendly camaraderie, commanding a small out-of-the-way garrison and helping his friend, Matsievsky, commander of the Cossack forces in Trans-Baikal, in the administrative duties of that underpopulated territory. The only other combat Orlov had seen was against the Turks some twenty-three years before. Then he'd been an underling, consigned to the reserves, had heard gunfire, had seen the wounded being carried to the rear. He had never seen the enemy.

Now he slouched in his canvas-backed folding chair, at the opening of his tent, balanced his vodka-filled cup on his paunch, and grinned up at the stars in calm content. His chief of staff, Colonel Volzhaninov, was stretched out on the sand beside him, bottle in hand. And young Matsievsky, General Matsievsky's son, Orlov's orderly, was curled up in a corner, asleep.

Orlov couldn't help but be proud of the day's events. His well-fed and well-prepared troops had completely routed the enemy. If he hadn't sounded the muster call, his men would have pursued the enemy long into the night. He was proud that they were so enthusiastic and daring that they needed to be restrained. He shut his eyes just to savor the memories.

Someone nudged him, gently, "Your Excellency . . ."

Orlov jumped up with a start, spilling the contents of his cup over his lap.

It was Sidorov, one of the staff adjutants. And behind Sidorov, standing at attention, with a deep gash over his left eye—a Cossack, wobbling slightly from fatigue.

"Sit down, man, sit down," ordered Orlov, automatically

81

offering his seat. "Grisha, run fetch Stankevich or Volf. If they're not at the medical tent, check Bodisko's."

Young Matsievsky, suddenly sober, rose and ran.

The frightened, exhausted Cossack collapsed in the general's chair.

Volzhaninov poured him a cup of vodka and refilled Orlov's cup.

Orlov asked Sidorov, "What is this business? Where has he been? The battle ended hours ago, but that wound is fresh."

"He says he was with Bulatovich, Your Excellency," replied Sidorov.

"Bulatovich?" asked Orlov. "Where is he?"

"About twenty miles from here," answered the Cossack.

"And how did he get there?"

"We rode past the Chinese, our whole troop. We chased the Chinese and just kept going."

"Didn't you hear the muster call?" asked Orlov.

"We heard, Your Excellency. And Lieutenant Grotten—that's our regular commander—he told Bulatovich we should go back, told him several times. But Bulatovich just kept going.

"Yes, Your Excellency. We were drunk with excitement. When Bulatovich said, 'I intend to pursue the enemy,' we didn't stop to think.

"It's hard to say why, Your Excellency. You see, we were nearly dead—I thought I was, anyway—and this old Cossack went running up bare-handed and grabbed the enemy flag. I've never felt anything like it, sir, like coming back from death it was. Luck like I'd never seen before, like nothing could touch us. It was like they say about the Boxers, that they get all worked up and get to thinking that nothing can touch them and they can do anything. We felt like that. I felt like that. We all felt that way together."

"You actually believed that?"

"It was in the muscles, not the head. We had this strength we'd never felt before. It had come back with us as we came back from near dead; it was there in our muscles ready to do something. And Bulatovich showed us what. He pointed his saber at the enemy—it was like a lightning rod, sir, and the lightning was in us. Only Grotten held back, God rest his soul. It's not for me to think ill of the man." He crossed himself, and Orlov automatically followed suit.

"Is he dead?"

After a hurried drink, the Cossack continued. "Wounded, yes. I saw him fall with his horse. By now, yes, probably dead. They're all probably dead. We all followed Bulatovich, even Grotten couldn't hold back for long, orders or no orders—the pull was too strong.

"It was soon dark. We followed the railbed. Moonlight reflected off the rails. There was something magical about it, about us being there in the dark and the enemy all around us unseen. All we could see were the tracks and our own shadows, cast by the moonlight, riding huge ahead of us.

"The darkness was part of it, sir. And the death we had seen that day. We were beyond fear, sir, if you know what I mean. Anything was possible.

"Time and again, we heard screams, then frantic running and riding. Bands of Chinese had seen us, riding high by the railbed, the moon behind us. We couldn't see them, but they could see us, and they ran like from the Devil himself.

"We saw campfires, hundreds of them, up ahead to the left. It must have been their main bivouac.

"Bulatovich didn't pause a moment. He pointed his saber, and we all followed, right into the midst of their bivouac.

"It was madness, Your Excellency. We must have all been mad. There must have been thousands of them, and there were only about twenty of us. I must admit, sir, that I felt strange riding toward those campfires—like I was a god or something or was being led by a god.

"Lord, forgive me for such thoughts," he added quickly and crossed himself.

"We galloped through, slashing left and right with our sabers, cutting down tents and people, whatever came in our path."

"How many men did you lose?" interrupted Orlov, anxiously.

"Not a one, not there, sir. No one fired a shot at us. They were shocked, sir. They screamed and ran. They're probably still running. And we rode right through to the other side and kept riding."

"Where were you going?"

"We followed the track, sir, to the next station."

"The next station?"

"Yes, Your Excellency, Urdingi Station, some twenty miles from here. That's when the shooting started, when Grotten and one or two of the others got hit. We stopped to water our horses at Urdingi Station, and a bunch of them, no telling how many in the dark, maybe they'd followed us all the way from the bivouac, they surrounded us there at the station house and opened fire. That's when Bulatovich sent me with the message."

"Message?" asked Orlov.

"Yes, Your Excellency, this message."

Orlov quickly grabbed and unfolded the dusty leather packet, took out a little scrap of brown paper, and read aloud, "Surrounded by the enemy. Out of ammunition. Horses exhausted."

"Good God!" exclaimed Orlov. Then he turned to Volzhaninov. "Ivan Semyonovich, saddle all the remaining squadrons of the cavalry regiment. Send them to rescue Bulatovich. This Cossack will guide you. And see to it that his cut gets bandaged. Without him, Bulatovich and the rest are lost—if they're still alive even now. What did you say your name is?"

"Shemelin, Your Excellency," the Cossack replied. "Yakov—I mean Ivan—Shemelin."

⚜ ⚜ ⚜

By order of Colonel Kupferman, no liquor was allowed in the cavalry regiment. And Strakhov strongly approved of this policy. Sobriety was necessary for discipline. But tonight Strakhov himself needed a drink.

At the fringes of the Russian bivouac, among the railway guards, Staff-Captain Bodisko was holding a party and all officers were welcome. Bodisko had personally captured an enemy flag, and his close friend Dr. Volf was providing the refreshments for the celebration. Volf was renowned for traveling with just one change of clothes to leave room in his trunk for cases of champagne.

The celebration lasted long into the night. Everyone, even Letsky the telegrapher and Zhemchuzhikov, a civilian railway construction engineer, had participated in the battle. And everyone but Strakhov had a tale he wanted to tell.

Dr. Volf himself arrived late. "I had a little business to take care of," he apologized.

"What was the score?" asked Bodisko, passing him a bottle of his own champagne.

"About ten dead and eighteen wounded."

"I told you so," said Bodisko, nudging Strakhov. "Those Chinese couldn't shoot worth a damn. They must have outnumbered us three or four to one. And that's all they could do." Bodisko laughed loudly, the nervous laugh of someone who has narrowly escaped danger, and others joined in.

Strakhov tried to laugh along, but his laugh sounded hollow. Maybe it was the champagne; maybe it was his stomach; but he failed to see the humor in the deaths of ten Russians.

When the laughter subsided, Volf added, "Before the night's out that number may well double or triple."

"What do you mean?" asked Bodisko.

"Bulatovich. That Guards officer from Petersburg who keeps to himself. Word is that he's still out there somewhere behind enemy lines with about twenty men."

"Trying to win the war by himself?" laughed Bodisko.

"Well, if that's what he's up to, he's not doing much of a job of it," commented Volf. "The general just sent most of the regiment out after him."

"The man's a fool," thought Strakhov. "He'll get the whole regiment killed. Imagine riding through the midst of the enemy in the middle of the night."

⚜ ⚜ ⚜

"Staff-Rotmister Bulatovich reporting, Your Excellency."

Orlov rubbed his eyes. It was dawn. He had just dozed off, or so it seemed. He wasn't sure whether he was asleep now or awake. He gripped the arms of his chair, pulled himself forward. "Is that really you?" He stood up, reached out, touched, then clasped the returning officer, even more warmly than when he had first met him just ten days before. "But so fast . . . it couldn't have been more than two hours ago . . ."

"They met us on the road not five miles from here."

"You gave us quite a scare," laughed Orlov, with relief. "What a message—'Surrounded, out of ammunition, send help.' And here you are—safe and sound."

"But Your Excellency," replied Bulatovich, smiling with the corners of his mouth and struggling to hold back signs of exhaustion, "I didn't ask for help. I just reported on the situation. Everything was under control."

"That's not the way the message sounded."

"Well, next time I'll write 'Surrounded. Out of ammunition. Nothing to worry about.'"

⚜ ⚜ ⚜

The story soon spread throughout the camp. Bodisko's tent shook with the laughter of drunken officers.

"To Bulatovich!" proposed Bodisko.

"To Bulatovich!" the tent resounded.

"No man's that brave," thought Strakhov, "not without cause. He must be bucking for rank. But it's got to be more than that. What's he trying to prove?"

5

Ongun Station, Manchuria, July 31, 1900

By the time Bulatovich lay down to sleep, the sun was already up and his closed tent was stifling. He couldn't sleep. He kept hearing the screams of that wounded soldier—what was his name?—the boy with the locket around his neck, just married. Was it just an echo in his mind from that nighttime ride through the midst of the enemy? Or, he asked himself, was the boy still screaming?

By noon the tightly shut little tent was an oven. Bulatovich shook and rolled as he had in the worst of his jungle fevers. He was on a train, racing through desolate wastelands—in Ethiopia, no, east of the Urals, no. He had no idea where he was going or why. The terrain was unfamiliar. His train was on the wrong track, or he was on the wrong train. He wanted to get off, but he wasn't sure how to get off or what he could do once he succeeded.

Voices around him talked about a great hero, a Russian soldier.

"He raced across that desert faster than the native couriers ever had. And on camelback no less."

"Wasn't he the one who guided that Ethiopian prince beyond Kaffa through uncharted lands?"

"I hear he could subdue hostile natives just by the tone of his voice and the power of his eye."

"He was the trusted adviser of the Emperor Menelik."

"They say that he spoke Amharic like a native and understood Oromo and many of the local dialects."

"He was a key figure in Russian involvement in Ethiopia."

"Russian involvement in Ethiopia?" someone laughed.

Bulatovich tried to interrupt them to let them know that he was the very man they had been talking about. But no one seemed to notice that he was there—no matter how loud he screamed.

He woke up screaming. Old Hrisko the huntsman was kneeling beside him, putting a cool cloth on his forehead. "It'll be all right, sir. A bit feverish. It's hellish hot out here on the desert."

"What are you doing here?" asked Bulatovich, annoyed not to be alone. But he fell back to sleep again before Hrisko could answer.

He was alone in the wilderness. He had been walking for days. He was following the course of a mighty river.

He knew he had been given a choice. Which stream would he follow to the end, mapping its course for the first time?

All the streams had looked the same near their source. He had chosen this one. And his spirits had risen as his stream was joined by many tributaries and rapidly grew to a mighty river. He would be known as a great explorer, a hero. Every schoolboy would know his name.

Then its twisting course led to a wasteland. No more tributaries appeared. It slowed. Little stagnant pools lay here and there.

Finally, exhausted, he collapsed beside an insignificant lake in the middle of the desert. And he lay there, pounding his head against the hot sand. Which stream should he have chosen? Which way led to glory?

"Is there no justice?" Bulatovich screamed.

"It's hellish hot out here on the desert," he heard, and didn't know if he was hearing it for the first or the second time. Maybe the whole dream had taken place during the time it took him to hear that sentence. He knew he was dreaming and he wanted to wake up, he had to wake up before the recurrent dream began, the dream of blindness. His tear ducts were inflamed, his eyes burning. He was going blind. He was awake, but he could see nothing. And he woke up, relieved that it had only been a dream. A large man was kneeling at his side.

"Who are you?" he asked tentatively, touching himself, reassuring himself that he was awake this time.

"Alexei Starodubov, sir. At your service."

"Yes . . . yes . . . I must have been talking in my sleep. You can go now. I'll be all right. I want to be alone. . . . No, wait. I'll walk with you." He wondered why he had changed his mind. It was unlike him to be indecisive. He wanted to lie down again, to be alone. But somehow he was ashamed to change his mind yet again, to be indecisive with this peasant giant. Somehow he instinctively cared what this man thought of him.

He had come out of his dream misanthropic and disillusioned. Reason told him that it didn't matter what people thought of you, that it was sheer foolhardiness to risk your life, to waste your life's energies for reputation and renown. People only cared about themselves, really. It was chance not merit, circumstances beyond a man's control that led to one man rather than another being called a "hero" or a "great man." And the people who did the talking didn't really know or care about the people whose reputations they made and destroyed. They were just trying to make their own reputations as reputation makers. Oromo warriors arguing over who deserved credit for killing an elephant, or reporters editorializing in the pages of a Petersburg newspaper—it made no difference. "Heroes" were the stuff of stories. It was the stories people needed, not the heroes themselves. They needed the stories so they could imagine themselves as heroes, so they could dream and admire and emulate and strive. They wanted to believe in the importance of being a "great man," in the importance of praise. They envied, and they wanted to be envied.

"What do men call you, sir?"

Bulatovich started, nearly stumbled. He was walking. It was about noon. A peasant giant with a long white beard was walking at his side—Starodubov, yes, the thief. Bulatovich must have been more tired than he had thought. The battle, yes. And the question. "What did you ask?"

"What do men call you?" repeated Starodubov.

"My full name is Alexander Xavierevich Bulatovich." He no more understood why he had answered than he understood why he was walking with this man through the Russian encampment.

"But your short name, sir. What do people call you?"

"My family calls me 'Sasha,' " he answered automatically.

"Yes, but you are a man of names, sir. I can see that at a glance. Tell me, you have a ring in your left ear. You are no Gypsy. Men in Petersburg do not wear earrings. Why would you wear one? And why only one?"

"In Ethiopia a gold earring is a sign of a great hunter. They gave me such an earring. It was a gift I could not refuse."

"And what did you hunt?"

"Elephants."

"Yes, you see, you are a man of names. 'Great hunter,' they call you in Africa. And what do they call you in Petersburg? Not the officers—officers know nothing of names. What do the common soldiers call you?"

"They call me 'Mazeppa.' "

"Mazeppa? What is this Mazeppa?"

"He was a Ukrainian."

"And you are from the Ukraine. But what manner of man was this Mazeppa?"

"He was a Cossack hetman, Prince of the Ukraine."

"And you are a hetman, a prince?"

"No. I suppose they think of me as someone who can control horses and men, a fighter like Mazeppa."

"And what became of this Mazeppa?"

"He rebelled against Tsar Peter the Great and lost at the Battle of Poltava."

"Are you a rebel, sir?"

"Not that I know of," replied Bulatovich, yawning and stretching.

"Yes, Mazeppa. Most strange this name. I must remember this Mazeppa."

Bulatovich laughed softly. He wished it could be that simple—a single name to sum up a past and a future.

He actually liked this Old Cossack, and some of those others who rode with him last night—the three brothers, the good horseman he had picked as a messenger, the one with the long roguish-looking face, the one who talked like a priest, even the one with the glasses. And the young boy with the locket who was wounded, who had screamed all night, but wasn't screaming now. He'd have to learn their names.

✿ ✿ ✿

Meanwhile other officers were inundated with the paperwork and decision making that inevitably follows a victorious battle. Volzhaninov, as chief of staff, was processing a multitude of requests for medals and citations—including one for Starodubov. The two staff adjutants, Sidorov and Kublitsky-Piottukh, were organizing a convoy to send the nineteen wounded, the prisoners, and the trophies back to Abagaitui on the Russian border. General Orlov and Colonel Kupferman visited the wounded as they were being transferred to two-wheeled ox-pulled carts.

"We have to do something about that Guards officer," insisted Kupferman.

"Would you suggest a medal?" offered Orlov, giving Kupferman a good-natured pat on the back. He was in an expansive fatherly mood. Victory felt so good.

"Good God, no!" exclaimed Kupferman, his puffy cheeks turning red in exasperation.

"Please watch your language, sir," replied Orlov, amused that it was so easy to aggravate this stuffed shirt.

Kupferman bit his upper lip, then continued, "Your Excellency, may I point out to you that this Guards officer went riding off recklessly into the midst of the enemy after the muster call was sounded. We had to send the whole regiment out to rescue him, and we were damned lucky that they weren't annihilated.

"He's a glory hunter, I tell you. A little self-appointed hero.

91

It was my mistake to give him a troop to command. I should have known better. He's a troublemaker. He's dangerous.

"Just look at these wounded. Here's Grotten, a young lieutenant. He was in Bulatovich's troop. He got his toes shot off. He'll never ride again, not in this army. He'll be lucky to get a desk job.

"And that one over there, the one with his hand on the pendant. He was with Bulatovich. Got a bullet in the bladder. There was nothing the doctors could do.

"Bulatovich is an insatiable glory hunter, I repeat. Such disobedience should not, must not go unpunished, not when it leads to this—brave Russian soldiers needlessly maimed and killed."

"Calm yourself, Colonel," ordered Orlov in an impatient whisper, his good mood rapidly evaporating. "These men can hear you. These brave and gallant men. They've sacrificed leg and eye and arm for God and Tsar. I'll not have you throwing doubts at them and tormenting their souls with notions that their suffering might be 'needless.' We've won a great victory, and they contributed to it. I hope that is some consolation for their personal loss.

"If you are ready to bring charges, to name names, then by all means do so, later, in private. But I'll not stand for another such public outburst.

"From what I can see, this Bulatovich is a brave soldier, an inspiration to his men and to the whole detachment. It's hard to assess the impact of that expedition of his last night, but it may well have put the fear of God into the enemy and may well save us many lives."

That afternoon, as Orlov and the other officers stood on a nearby hilltop, to the sound of bugles and drums, from all sides of the bivouac came stretchers with the eleven Russian dead. Followed by the rest of the troops, the stretcher bearers climbed the hill and placed the bodies around a wide rectangular pit, deep as a man is tall. There was no priest, so Orlov said a few appropriate words. A chorus of officers sang several hymns.

Because they didn't have enough material for making coffins, Orlov had decided that the bodies should be laid directly on the sand in the bottom of the pit and covered from above with a series of boards. One by one, the bodies were lowered into the pit and stretchers taken away, to be used again in future battles.

✿ ✿ ✿

Orlov ordered a minute of silence and looked down at the dead. They almost looked like they were sleeping in the shady pit, sheltered from the one-hundred-degree desert sun. But pale. And here and there—bloodstains. Brains protruded from the bandages around one man's shattered skull.

Orlov felt a bit queasy. He hadn't been prepared for that. He quickly glanced around to check the reactions of others.

Kupferman looked disgusted, as if someone had tried to serve him rancid meat.

Strakhov was unnaturally pale but seemed able to control himself.

Bulatovich had shut his eyes tightly, apparently in prayer.

Several of the younger officers backed away, involuntarily, as flies swarmed and feasted on the exposed brains.

Then Lieutenant Bloom fainted, nearly falling into the pit.

Officers clustered around to help him.

The tension and solemnity of the moment were broken.

✿ ✿ ✿

Most of the enlisted men stayed at a distance, near enough to perform their duty, but not so close that they could see the bottom of the pit.

The men of Bulatovich's troop stayed near him, at the edge of the pit. Starodubov knelt so low his beard brushed the sand. He prayed softly for his lost sons. Shemelin nervously adjusted the bandage over his left brow. He had a deep gash just half an inch from his eye where a bullet had grazed him on the ride back from Urdingi with the message. Only now did he realize how close he had come to death. Last night he had been propelled by nervous excitement. Now it was over, and he shivered with fear.

Trofim crossed himself again and again with two fingers and silently repeated the Lord's Prayer, using the Old Believer "Our

93

Father" instead of the Orthodox "Our God," a few other prayers, some vivid passages from Revelation, whatever he could remember—he had the will but not the memory of a priest.

Butorin smoked a pipe and grinned in amusement at the embarrassment of the fainting officer.

Laperdin took out a handkerchief, took off his glasses, and calmly polished the lenses.

Sofronov stationed himself near Bulatovich and prayed audibly, "Lord Jesus Christ, Son of God, have mercy upon us." His head was bowed reverently, his whole bearing had the look of a priest.

Sofronov's father had wanted him to be a priest, parading him proudly to church each Sunday and introducing him as the "priest-to-be." His father thought of the priesthood in terms of social status. With intelligence, tact, and a little politics, his son might one day become a bishop.

But the son rebelled, not against religion, but against the established Church, the pomp and status. His mother entertained pilgrims, the flocks of pilgrims who were forever wandering across Russia from one holy place to another. She gave them food, shelter, and alms. Pilgrims were always hanging about the kitchen—tired, hungry, in rags. The young boy was fascinated by their tales of far-off places and of feats of faith.

As he grew older, his sentiments took a reasoned form. At the Kazan Theological Academy, he studied Church history and found it an abomination that, from the time of Peter the Great, Russia had had no Patriarch. Since that time the Church had been controlled by a State-dominated "Holy Synod." The Church was little more than a department of the bureaucracy, an appendage of the government, a tool for controlling the masses. He disdained the Church hierarchy and bureaucracy—the men who grew fat on other men's faith. He defended mysticism and meditation as forms of personal religion that required no bureaucracy. And he revered holy humble men, particularly pilgrims.

Failing at the theological academy was a form of rebellion against the established Church. But despite himself, he was ashamed he was failing. One day he left school, put on peasant's garb and a false name and set off for Siberia as a pilgrim. For discipline he tried repeating the Jesus Prayer: "Lord Jesus Christ,

Son of God, have mercy upon me." He repeated it continually, day and night, aloud and silently, until the rhythm of his breath seemed to say the prayer for him.

After two months, he could no longer tolerate the life of a pilgrim. Not so much the hunger, the fatigue, or the physical pain of pushing himself beyond his endurance, but the rejection, the disdain that he met with all too frequently when he asked for alms. He felt not so much like a holy pilgrim, a man to be revered, as a petty beggar, a slouch, a fake, an able-bodied man too lazy to earn his daily bread.

Ashamed to return home, for ten years he went from one menial job to another, ten years of humiliation. Finally, with the outbreak of war he joined the army. It was a fresh start for him, and he intended to make the best of it.

He retained his respect for the simple mystical faith of mendicant pilgrims. He also realized that he was unsuited for that life. From deprivation he had acquired an appetite for the finer things and comforts of life that he had taken for granted as a child. He now had a keen awareness of and respect for social status and an appreciation for the physical advantages that came with an improvement in status. He immediately recognized that Bulatovich was an extraordinary individual and sensed that something might be gained by close association with him. As he prayed there, reverently by the graveside, he was thinking perhaps not so much of God as of Bulatovich, and hoping that he might be noticed and remembered.

Pyotr never noticed the officer fainting. He wept and couldn't take his eyes off Aksyonov, motionless down there with the other bodies. The two of them hadn't really spoken much to one another. It seemed natural that he and Aksyonov should become friends. They were both just seventeen. But making friends was a serious business, not to be entered into lightly. His brother Login often told him, "Choose your friends carefully. That's one way you have to control your destiny." So Pyotr had held back. And now Aksyonov was dead, and, standing before his open grave, Pyotr rehearsed in his mind all the things he might have said and done had he been more free and natural.

There had been nothing heroic about Aksyonov's death. It was dark, and they were watering their horses at Urdingi Station when shots started coming from everywhere. A bullet ripped off Grotten's toes.

They dropped to their bellies in the sand, firing at the flashes of light that flickered from the Chinese rifles in the dark. They ran out of ammunition, and lay there wondering how long it would take the Chinese to realize it and move in.

Then Aksyonov got hit, kneeling by the well—a bullet in the bladder. He let loose a horrifying scream and the shooting stopped.

He kept screaming. Bulatovich picked him up and slung him across the back of his horse and ordered everyone to mount.

Aksyonov screamed hideously all the way back. They encountered no resistance from the Chinese.

Pyotr realized now—Bulatovich had recognized immediately that the maddening screams of a dying man at night would hold at bay a superstitious enemy.

♕ ♕ ♕

The men of the grave detail began to cover the bodies with boards, some of which were too long. Orlov quietly cursed. Someone had forgotten to make sure they were the right length. It was an awkward moment. There was no saw at hand. Without the boards properly in place, they would be throwing dirt right in the faces of the dead soldiers—a sacrilege Orlov simply could not tolerate.

He glared at Chief of Staff Volzhaninov. Volzhaninov glared at Staff Adjutant Sidorov. Sidorov stared at his boottops.

A cough, then another cough. Feet began to shuffle nervously in the loose sand.

Then one of the soldiers near Bulatovich, a quiet, firm-looking man, pulled out a dagger, jumped into the pit, and quickly lopped off the ends of the boards. In this man's hands, the dagger was swifter than an ax. Orlov stared in awe, admiring the handiwork, relieved that the solution was so simple. He resolved then and there to promote the man to sergeant. Later he found out the man was Login Zabelin, from Bulatovich's troop.

After Login had finished his job and scrambled back among the living, the general threw in the first three shovelsful of dirt.

Other officers added a shovelful apiece. The men on grave detail finished up the task.

Later Orlov ordered a whole battalion to bury the dead Chinese and horses. In the wilderness heat, the smell of rotting meat was already becoming unbearable.

⚜ ⚜ ⚜

When they had lowered the bodies into the pit, Aksyonov's pendant had come out of his shirt. The chain was broken, and the picture of his new bride lay exposed on his chest.

Pyotr had been tempted to jump down and put it back in place but had hesitated to disturb the proceedings.

While chopping boards, Login, apparently sensing his brother's concern for Aksyonov, had quickly and unobtrusively pocketed the pendant. Later he gave it to Pyotr saying, "Remember. War is no game. It could just as well have been you lying there."

But looking at the pendant, all Pyotr could think about was the beautiful young girl whose face he saw. What was her name?

⚜ ⚜ ⚜

Bulatovich stayed, even after the grave detail and everyone else had left. He sat on a nearby rock and picked up a fistful of sand, sifting it carefully from one hand to the other, like a crude hourglass. Now and again his eyes wandered off to the east along the train tracks in the direction of Urdingi and Hailar. He found it hard to believe that he had acted so rashly and even harder to believe that his new troop had followed him blindly into danger even after the muster call. Madness—he couldn't rationally justify either his own behavior or the sudden devotion these men had shown to him. And luck—they should all be dead now, that's what reason said, not just one of them.

Then he suspended thought and just let the images race back through his head. He felt again, though faintly, that same exhilaration; and he needed more of it, almost like an addiction. Even without glitter or glory, whether it was the end of the line or the beginning, whether his name became renowned or he was buried here in total obscurity, he needed the challenge and the danger,

97

the feeling of being alive—the overwhelming knowledge that he feared nothing, that he'd dare do anything, that whether anyone knew it or not, he was a "hero."

The train track caught his eye again, running back as well as forward, back through all the turns of chance or fate, through the moments of adolescent indecision and the sudden surges of self-confidence that had made him the man he was, back to Petersburg and Sonya.

6

Bulatovich remembered Petersburg as gray stone buildings casting long gray shadows on gray snow.

The snow was white, dead white when it fell. It soon turned gray with the coming and going of carriages and people bundled up in brown and black and gray coats, hurrying to get out of the cold.

From early November to May it snowed. The Neva froze solid, gray, and became a roadway for carriages, sleighs, and pedestrians.

The sun stayed low on the horizon. For a month or more its rays would never reach many of the side streets and little alleys. Even the open parks near the cluster of gray palaces along the banks of the Neva got only a few hours of sunlight, on the rare days when the sun did shine.

Usually, if it didn't snow, it was dull, gray, and overcast; and cold gales blew in from the Gulf of Finland.

In the fall it rained. In the spring it rained.

It was even worse in the summer, when for a month or so there was hardly any night at all, when midnight was more like twilight, when those gray buildings and gray streets became unbearably hot. As soon as the heat came, epidemics of cholera struck the crowded tenements of the working-class districts and threatened to spread through the city. It wasn't unusual for several hundred people to die of it in a summer.

In the fall, winter, and spring, people died of pneumonia, lung diseases of all kinds, and typhoid. It was an unhealthy city any time of year. You had to boil the water before drinking it.

Back at Lutsikovka, the samovar had been the center of the house on cold winter days. The tea was warm and fragrant, but it was also part of the traditional family scene. When you came home cold and weary from a snowball fight, the uplift it gave you was almost religious.

Here in Petersburg, the samovar had no joy to it, or so it seemed to him. Here it was just a handy device for boiling filthy water, and the tea leaves were just a way to kill the taste of the water.

What could you expect of a city built on a swamp? Peter the Great had built this nightmare of a capital in the eighteenth century on land he had conquered from the Swedes. Peter believed in Europe, in European technology and European culture, and he would force those beliefs on the Russian people regardless of the cost in money and lives. Regardless of the resistance of the Russian people, regardless of the resistance of nature, he would change the "facts" to match his dream. He would force Russia to look West through this new window of his, rather than East to its origins. He would make this a European nation, despite all obstacles. Whatever the project, obstacles seemed to strengthen rather than discourage his interest.

The ponderous gray structures of bureaucracy rose high on pilings along the swampy Neva. People came to settle there because they had no choice, because they needed work of any kind, or because they dreamed of a better life than their ancestors had had in their little peasant villages. And despite the recurrent floods and disease, they stayed and multiplied.

In the summer, the Tsar, the nobles, and everyone else who could afford it evacuated the city and headed for their country estates. The Tsar usually went to his summer palaces at Tsarskoye Selo or Peterhof, ten or twenty miles away.

Others, like Sonya's family, went to estates in the nearby Baltic provinces. Bulatovich's family returned to Lutsikovka in the Ukraine.

His mother had inherited the property from her aunt. But while Aunt Elizaveta had always been considered a wealthy woman, there never seemed to be any money after Jenny took over. There was one summer when she rented the estate for a good price, and they took a trip to Germany, France, and Switzerland. That was when they had visited his father's grave. But most years she just complained about crops, prices, weather, the way her tenants and overseer cheated her. She claimed she got nothing from the estate, especially after a trade treaty with Germany lowered the price of grain. In addition, she had a substantial pension as the widow of a general, with extra sums for each of the major medals he had earned. But she always talked about how expensive everything was in Petersburg. If there was any money (and Sasha always thought there was), his mother kept it close.

He felt like a pauper and a country bumpkin at that fancy school she sent him to. Everyone at the Alexandrovsky Lycée was from the gentry. The poet Pushkin had graduated from there, as had numerous important government officials and diplomats.

On the one hand, his mother was very conscious of social status. She forever reminded him that he mustn't fraternize with coachmen and servants and their children as he always had at Lutsikovka. She sounded so impressed about the dinners she went to with princess so-and-so and colonel such-and-such. She kept telling him that success in this world depends on who you know, not what you know. But on the other hand, she held tight to her money, giving him just a few kopecks now and then to spend.

To save himself embarrassment, Sasha avoided his classmates with their often-expensive pastimes. He was always a loner.

His sharpest memory of school days was when he was at the preparatory school, right after they arrived in Petersburg, right after his sister Lilia died of typhoid. His grief had lasted for months. He had kept to himself, quietly, then somehow found himself in a running battle with the teacher, Lemm, a strict German disciplinarian. The battles were a relief, a distraction. He defied Lemm again and again, and Lemm, unlike God, punished him predictably, beating him and confining him in a small dark coffinlike closet. He suffered, but there was a pattern to the suffering, a justice or an injustice that could be assigned to this man Lemm. Lemm came to expect defiance and disobedience and punished Sasha often without cause. Sasha forgot the injustice of God and vented his anger on this, His mortal counterpart.

That year of lonely rebellion in a strange school in a strange city, more than the lack of money, made him a loner. The other students called him "the Ukrainian boy." He hadn't a drop of Ukrainian blood in him; he had a mixture of Polish, Russian, French, and Georgian ancestry. But he acted like an outsider, and all were quick to label him one.

He studied French, German, English, history, geography, and law while his mother politicked in the background to get him started in a career in government. With money tight, he would have to fend for himself. She wanted him to have a respectable position in a reasonably prestigious department, with a steady, secure income and opportunities for advancement.

On graduation in 1891, he was duly awarded the rank of "titular councillor," the lowest civil rank in Tsarist Russia, the starting point even for nobility in their climb for prominence in the government bureaucracy. He was offered a job in the offices of the Educational and Charitable Institutions of the Empress Mariya.

Where would he be now had he followed that path of least resistance? If he had been an extraordinary success, he could be head of some department. Perhaps he would have married Sonya or someone like her, and he would have a big house and a dozen children. Perhaps he would ride about town in a horseless carriage, smoking imported cigars. And in the evening, he would read novels and travel books, imagining himself in far-off places.

Instead, he had insisted on joining the army, and not just any regiment—His Majesty's Life-Guard Hussar Regiment.

In the Russian army, the true status of an officer often depended more on his regiment than on his rank. In particular, the two dozen Guards regiments headquartered near the Tsar's palaces in Petersburg and at nearby Tsarskoye Selo and Peterhof were like exclusive clubs that only a member of the gentry could join and only on the recommendation of influential friends and relatives. Bulatovich, fresh out of a lycée, never having attended a military academy, had been accepted into one of these ultra-exclusive regiments, and after a year's training as an enlisted man, had been promoted to the lowest officer rank—kornet. Then, in relatively rapid succession, he had risen to lieutenant and staff-rotmister.

His decision to join had come as a shock not only to his mother but also to himself.

"Are you out of your mind?" she had exclaimed when he first mentioned the possibility. "Do you realize the expenses? Why, the cost of the uniforms alone—the beaver hats and collars and trim and all the gold embroidery. The pay is next to nothing. They're all independently wealthy. There's no way you'd be able to keep up with the other officers. You'd be living beyond your means, cultivating expensive tastes, gambling, drinking—all the vices of the idle rich. And who would have to pay for it all? Who would come to the rescue when you got over your head in debt? Don't expect me to. We're not rich, you know. And the sooner you accept your lot in life, the better off you'll be."

"I told you that I'm going to join the regiment. That's all there is to it," he squinted to emphasize his point. But at the same time he was surprised to hear himself speak with such certainty. A few moments before, the regiment had been but one of several possibilities he was toying with. But now he had taken a stand like a hero in a play, like he had in his obstinate battles with Lemm in the preparatory school.

"And who do you think you are, young man, to speak to your mother like that?"

"I'm twenty-one. I can do what I want with my life. And I will."

"Will indeed. Do you think you can just decide you want to be an officer in a regiment as exclusive as that and that's all there is to it? There are hundreds of young men out there begging to get in, young men who have been preparing themselves since early childhood for just such an opportunity. And you, out of nowhere, decide that you're just going to jump in and beat them?"

"I've always wanted to be a soldier. Like Father." Once again, he was surprised to hear his own words. But he was proud of them: they helped strengthen his resolve.

His mother heaved a little sigh of disappointment, her eyes blank and weary, her lips pursed. "I never thought I'd raised such a rude and ungrateful son."

Sasha had to smile. His mother had played her trump card— the role of martyr—but she had played it too soon and with too little conviction. He had the upper hand. He really could join the regiment if he wanted to. And having won his point, how could he change his mind like a whimsical child? He must be a man now—firm, unbending, master of his own mind.

Recognizing defeat, Jenny struck out bitterly, "Go then. Join your regiment. We have relatives. Maybe I can twist a few arms and get you in. Maybe just to show you what a fool you are, I'll get you in. Even with those bad eyes of yours. Exceptions can be made for things like that. But getting in is the least of it. Staying in is the tough part. How well do you think you'll stack up against those cadets fresh out of military school? You don't even know how to salute properly. They could take you on only as a private, with the enlisted men. You'd have to learn all the rudiments with them and prove yourself before they would even think of making you an officer."

"Do it," Sasha smiled firmly. The obstacles seemed to make the object more worthy of attainment. "You get me in. I'll do the rest."

His mother was clearly impressed with his resolve. He had never stood up to her like this before. And he was proud to see that he had impressed her.

Thinking back now, Bulatovich couldn't help but wonder what he would have done with his life if his mother hadn't objected so strongly to his idle thoughts on a possible military career, if the conversation hadn't taken just that turn. How fragile the fabric of our lives; how arbitrary our "wants" and "needs"; how much depends on the pushes and pulls of others—especially when we suddenly decide to take a stand and determine our own destiny.

✾ ✾ ✾

With his jockeylike build and the ability as a horseman he had developed as a boy in the Ukraine, it was only natural that Bulatovich join a Hussar regiment. By definition a Hussar regiment consisted of the very best lightweight cavalrymen matched with the best light horses and trained to work closely together as a team; for only as a closely coordinated team all charging at the same speed and with uniform excellence could a cavalry regiment have maximum impact on the battlefield.

In all of Russia there were only two light cavalry regiments trained and maintained at the level of uniform excellence that earned the designation "Hussar." One was the Grodno Life-Guard Hussar Regiment, associated with Bulatovich's father's native province, near Poland. He chose instead His Majesty's Life-Guard Hussar Regiment.

His father had been a major general, but it was relatives on his mother's side who got him into that regiment. Jenny's father, the colonel of engineers who was killed in the Caucasus, had a brother Lev, who was also killed there on a separate occasion. In a skirmish with mountain rebels, he had lost his left arm and continued fighting with his right until he died. He had served in this very regiment, and his portrait hung in the reception hall of the regiment. Bulatovich had considered him a great hero, an inspiring example. Starodubov would have asked, "And what was he trying to prove?" Bulatovich wondered, "What was the point of such 'heroism'? Why did he do it? And why would I do the same if given a chance?"

The boy from the Ukraine was impressed with all the glitter and with himself for being part of it. He'd always thought of himself as a bit of an outcast. His learning to ride so well had been an act of rebellion. Rather than put up with his mother and deal with matters of petty household friction, more often than not he had run off alone or with the huntsman Old Hrisko and the coachman Mihailovo, hunting or riding. When his mother made him feel guilty for riding off on his own without permission, he all the more felt the need to get away—to the woods, to the fields, to push himself and his horse to their limits, testing his endurance, proving his ability as a horseman.

Here that determination and those abilities, which had been

a plague to his mother, had earned him a position of status and honor, with traditions and responsibilities closely related to the imperial throne—for not only was he a Hussar, but also he belonged to one of the two dozen imperial Guards regiments.

The enlisted men in these regiments were selected from regular army units around the Empire and proud of their elite status. Their officers drilled them day after day to improve the precision and uniformity of their difficult, highly disciplined maneuvers.

In peacetime, the official function of the Guards regiments stationed near Petersburg was largely ceremonial, parading on state occasions and standing guard at the Tsar's various palaces. The changing of the guard at the Winter Palace in Petersburg was a regular item on every tourist's itinerary.

The traditional, ceremonial aspect of their duties was part of the military-religious trappings of an imperial family that ruled by "divine right," with no legislature to curb its power. The Tsar was held in "holy" awe and revered by many, gentry as well as peasants. The Fundamental Laws of the Empire defined him as God's representative on earth. Allegiance to the Tsar was a matter of religious faith. "To the Emperor of All the Russians belongs supreme autocratic power. Submission to this power, not only from fear, but also as a matter of conscience, is commanded by God Himself."

A parade of the Guards was also a reminder of the might, splendor, and magnificence of the Russian Empire and its Tsar. That aura of greatness and divine invincibility was an important factor in holding together the vast assemblage of people called the "Russian Empire"—after centuries of conquest in Europe and Asia.

Such a reminder was particularly necessary in and around Petersburg, where there were far too many unskilled laborers and rootless displaced peasants, and far too many students and foreigners with radical notions, anxious to stir up trouble. When mobs gathered in the streets, like the year Bulatovich joined up, when widespread crop failures led to soaring food prices and famine, the Guards were used as an effective "show of force."

The barracks of His Majesty's Life-Guard Hussar Regiment were at Tsarskoye Selo, a town about fifteen miles from Petersburg that was the site of two imperial palaces, which served as the summer home of Tsar Alexander III. Mounted Guardsmen rode around and around the high iron fence of the park, day and night. Detachments of Guards infantry were posted at all the palace gates and inside the Imperial Park. Guardsmen were posted as sentries throughout the palaces themselves. And at the entrance to the private wing where the Tsar and Tsarina resided, four gigantic Blacks, called "Ethiopians," stood guard and opened and closed the doors for Their Majesties.

In the summer of 1892, just a year after graduating from the lycée, he was promoted to kornet, and Prince Vassilchikov, the colonel in command of his regiment, invited him to visit during the summer furlough at his estate at Kovno in the Baltic provinces, near Poland.

Bulatovich was reluctant to accept. He had looked forward to returning to Lutsikovka and perhaps visiting his cousin Sophia Sboromirsky in nearby Sumy. But his mother broke out in exasperation "You fool. Don't you realize that you get ahead in this world not by the things you do but by the people you know? The colonel's shown a liking to you—you, a newcomer, a nobody. That's an opportunity you can't afford to pass up."

When he didn't respond to logic, she sighed deeply and her chin quivered. "After all I've done for you. I thought you had learned. I was proud of you—my boy, the officer. And I spent the last bit of our savings to outfit you. This was your career, and you were serious about it. This was what you had chosen to do with your life. With that determination of yours, I knew you would be a success at it, and you would soon be able to pay your own way instead of depending on your poor widowed mother. But here you are, throwing away an opportunity like this. It's stubborn, that's what it is; it's your father in you, God rest his soul. Polish pride. He was just as stubbornly foolish, or he wouldn't have ended up as he did: just a regimental commander, relegated to the provinces . . . "

On and on she went, wearing down his resolve. It was too small an issue to make a stand on. Besides, he was curious to see the estate at Kovno, to see how Colonel Vassilchikov lived. Yet his mother's words added an element of guilt to the venture. He felt uneasy. What if Colonel Vassilchikov interpreted his acceptance as politicking?

Riding up to the estate, he was teasing the ends of his newgrown mustache and trying to make up his mind just what tone to take to demonstrate to himself, and perhaps to the colonel as well, that he was coming out of a sense of obligation and good will, that he was not just trying to get on the good side of his commanding officer, that he fully expected to rise in the ranks through merit and hard work and not through favoritism. Then he spotted a young girl in a white dress with a pink ribbon racing after a little black dog.

He pulled up short as she ran in front of his horse. She was stumbling through the muddy grass, running awkwardly.

Sonya, the colonel's daughter, had just turned fifteen, and her mother had decided that it was time for her to dress and act like a lady and stop running about with the servant children. Sonya found it difficult to maneuver in her tight new shoes and her new, all-too-fragile dress.

Her dog jumped into a mud puddle and started splashing about playfully. Sonya started to take off her shoes and go in after him, but they were so tight that she had trouble getting them off.

Then suddenly, this young Guards officer ran past her, scooped up the muddy little dog, "helped" her back to the dry ground of the roadway, lifted her up sidesaddle onto his horse, and gallantly led her home. She almost burst out laughing. But she restrained herself, just barely.

She found him strong, decisive, and attractive, even if he was just a bit shorter than she. She could see that he was proud of himself for "rescuing" her, for getting himself dirty to save her from getting dirty. So she acted helpless and grateful and thoroughly enjoyed her performance.

On succeeding days, Bulatovich and the colonel's daughter were together often, not riding and hunting as he would have preferred and as she would have, too, had she been willing to admit it, but sitting sedately on the porch or walking about the garden.

Her eyes seemed to hover between blue and green. When she was at her most coy and cautious with her long lashes partly shielding her pupils, they tended toward green. But at moments of excitement, enthusiasm, or bold playfulness, when she opened wide, they could flash bright blue. Her light brown hair hung straight and long, turning out a bit at the ends and gently framing her round face.

"Will you compete in the steeplechase?" she once asked, idly twirling a daisy near her turned-up nose.

Bulatovich hesitated. He hadn't even considered the possibility.

"It's always such a glorious event," she rambled on, delighted to have found another topic to fill out their pleasant and very "grown-up-like" conversation. She held her shoulders and her back straight and wouldn't let herself squirm about nervously. She was proud of the little snippets of information she knew about the regiment and Petersburg society. "I wouldn't miss the steeplechase myself, not for the world. Father takes me every year. There's the excitement of the race itself, and everyone's dressed in their very finest, with the Tsar himself and the royal family in attendance. If I were a man . . ." She caught herself up short, brushed her hair with the back of her hand, and continued, "It must be very dangerous for the riders. Very few who start the race ever finish. There were quite a few broken legs and arms this year. One man nearly died, I hear. I don't remember seeing you there," she raced ahead, hardly pausing for breath. "And if I had seen you, I'm sure I would have remembered." She hesitated a moment, not sure how flattering she wanted to sound. "You look so distinguished, so impressive on horseback. Have you ever been photographed on horseback?"

"No," replied Bulatovich, still thinking about the steeplechase.

"Well, you should be. You should make a point of it."

"Who can enter?"

"Enter what?"

"The steeplechase."

"Why everyone, everyone who is anyone; that is, all the officers in the Guards regiments."

"Then I will compete next year," he said with determination.

"How very nice," remarked Sonya, racing on to other topics, proud that she was such an accomplished conversationalist, that she could hold the attention of this handsome officer. "And do you fence?"

From that visit on, Sonya got along far better with her

mother, listening carefully to all her mother's advice on how a young lady should dress and fix her hair and comport herself. But her girlish energy and spontaneity didn't go away. They'd surface now and again at unexpected moments, maybe even amplified by the forced restraint. Sometimes, breaking into a sprint, she would race up the stairs at record speed, then suddenly remember, pull up short, quickly straighten her dress, brush back her hair with the back of her hand, then start up again with a more dignified gait.

Her father laughed, "Look at our little lady. She's learned so well, I'm sure if the house were on fire, she'd descend the stairs at that same dignified ladylike pace."

"Yes, isn't she charming," replied her proud mother, missing her husband's point, absorbed at the sight of her just-now-blossoming daughter. "A blue ribbon, I think," she added.

"A winner?" asked the colonel, not following her drift.

"Yes, she should definitely wear a blue ribbon. It would go better with her eyes. Remind me to tell her."

For Bulatovich it was a pleasant two weeks. Sonya was charming. But he thought nothing more of her until he described his visit to his mother. She insisted on a detailed account of his every moment. And he obliged, naively, answering her every question, with no idea that he should have anything to conceal.

"And on these long walks," she asked, "did you take any liberties?"

"Liberties? What do you mean?"

"Ah, from your look, you didn't. Fine. What a fine boy you are. She's probably pining for you now. In another year or two it will all develop naturally. Yes," she sighed, "young love. And the colonel's daughter, no less."

Bulatovich cringed, imagining the tales his mother would tell her friends, imagining that his fellow officers at the regiment would interpret his visit in the same light.

"Yes. When I first met Anatole . . ." Jenny trailed off into memories of her youth.

He wondered what Sonya must be thinking, what indignities she must be suffering for a few simple innocent conversations. He thought of writing her a letter of apology, then thought better of it.

She considered writing letters, too, but of a different kind. At night she hugged her pillow tightly, thinking of him. She'd obey him; she'd love to obey, if only he would command. She would run off with him to the far corners of the world. By night she wrote him letters telling of her undying love. And by day she tore the letters up. She didn't want to seem too anxious, too easy. She had learned that tactic from her reading—mainly French and English romantic novels and poetry. She would make him prove his devotion to her as she looked on. And she would act prim and proper and ladylike as she never had before.

The reaction he got at the regiment was unexpected. He had resolved not to say anything to arouse suspicions that there was anything between him and the colonel's daughter. He had rehearsed his lines silently to himself, over and over again, expecting he would have trouble quelling the curiosity of his fellow officers.

But no one showed the least interest in his visit to the colonel's estate. Some bragged of casual conquests; others were the subject of gossip. But Bulatovich remained an outsider—excluded, as he had been at school. He had made it into their regiment; he had become an officer. But he hadn't gone to a military academy, and he had spent a year training and fraternizing with the enlisted men. He was technically the officers' equal, but he wasn't one of them.

He found himself wishing they would prod him with questions. He gave them clues, but no one bothered to follow up on them. They ignored him.

Most of the social life of the regiment revolved around women. But at parties, both respectable and disreputable, he felt uncomfortable and self-conscious and tended to stand off to the side and watch while others danced or caroused.

All the junior officers seemed to deal with women simply as objects for a man's pleasure. Their talk made him feel like a child. He was ashamed to admit his relative innocence. At the same time, he felt morally indignant—sensing that there was something shallow and cruel in the attitudes they expressed.

Physically well-developed for his height, Bulatovich was the match of any man in the regiment as a horseman or a fencer. Others in his position would have talked and laughed their way into comradeship with the other junior officers. Bulatovich immersed himself in his duties, using his free time to practice for the fencing team and for the steeplechase. In the refectory, he tended to sit apart. But the more separate he made himself, the more he felt the need to belong to the crowd. And whether he sat apart or tagged along seemed to make no difference to anyone but him.

Once he found himself following along with half a dozen others on their way to a house of prostitution. One of them, a couple years younger than Bulatovich, was going to be "initiated" at the expense of the rest. Curious, yet ashamed of his innocence in this company, Bulatovich tried to disguise his own inexperience. No one paid enough attention to his awkward and inappropriate remarks to suspect him. He felt a need to prove himself to himself. He drank heavily and eventually found himself alone with a naked woman. He put his hand on her breast, and she started unbuttoning him mechanically, with a hollow drunken smile on her face.

Her hair was red, but the roots were black. Naked she looked young, vulnerable and beautiful. He was frightened and attracted, but he wasn't sure what was expected of him. She touched him and he lunged at her in what he thought was a show of manly passion, knocking her down on the floor, pulling his pants down, jumping on her.

Then suddenly, his strength and desire evaporated. He felt a cold moisture on his leg. He lay on her like so much dead weight. With difficulty, she pushed him aside. Only then did he notice that she was crying.

"Did I hurt you?" he asked.

She cried still more, lying there, naked, helpless, shameless—now he noticed that she was shameless, that she made no effort to cover her nakedness. He looked away and quickly, clumsily pulled on his pants, then rushed for the door, opened it, started out, then turned back quickly to throw money on the floor and ran out.

That night he couldn't sleep. He needed to talk to someone. So for the first time, he sat down and wrote a letter to Sonya. He wrote quickly, and the flow of his ideas was conversational, as if he were once again sitting with her on the porch back in Kovno.

After apologies for not writing sooner and other friendly banalities, he wrote:

> You'll probably think I'm terrible, and you'll be right. I wouldn't
> blame you if you never spoke to me again, but I need to tell some-
> one because it weighs on my conscience. Tonight I went to a house
> of ill repute. I'd been drinking with some friends—but that's no
> excuse. I wanted to take advantage of a poor young girl who had
> probably been forced by poverty into a life of sin. She was probably
> no older than you. And there's no telling how long she had been
> living that way. I certainly wasn't the first. She went about every-
> thing like she had done it many times before.
>
> I know you must be shocked that I would do such a thing, that
> I have such evil impulses. And I must admit that I often have these
> dreams and desires. I feel ashamed when I think that a man such
> as I dared to become the friend of someone so sweet and innocent
> as you.
>
> I pray the Lord to preserve me from such temptation. And this
> time, this one time, He was most kind to me and stopped me
> before it was too late. So instead of cruelly using the girl, I spoke
> to her at length and made her recognize the error of her ways.
> When I left her she was weeping in repentance. I gave her what
> little money I had with me. I intend to send her more when I can,
> to help free her from her shameful bondage.

That very night, just before dawn, he dropped the letter into
a mailbox. Then and only then could he sleep soundly, at ease
for having confessed and in full expectation that he would never
again hear from, never again see Sonya. She would now know
what a hateful person he was. But losing her (and he thought in
terms of "losing" her, as if she had in some sense been "his" until
now) was a necessary penance he must endure.

Much to his surprise, she replied by return mail, acknowl-
edging receipt of his letter but saying nothing about the contents.
She just rambled on in friendly, one might say "delightful," fashion about her everyday life. It was an animated, exuberant letter.
Even he could sense the overflowing emotion around and
between the words.

When his letter had arrived, Sonya had scanned it quickly
in her mother's presence. She blushed when she got to the part
about the prostitute and went running off to read it in private.

She had expected and hoped for polite expressions of affection from her dashing officer. But his confession about the prostitute excited her imagination. She had read surreptitiously about such things in novels. But to have a firsthand account from the man she loved—she was so curious that it never occurred to her to be jealous or distressed. She wanted to ask him for more details. What did the room look like? What color were the curtains? What was she wearing before she stripped?

Sonya slept naked that night, and with her hands she explored her own nakedness while she imagined herself totally at the mercy of a confident, experienced, and handsome older man like Bulatovich.

As the excitement and glitter of the regiment gradually wore off, leaving the monotonous routine of a peacetime soldier, Bulatovich busied himself learning the circuslike riding tricks of the Cossacks, then trained for and entered races and riding competitions of all kinds and made enough in prize money to make up partly for the tightfistedness of his mother.

He kept in touch with Sonya; and when he saw his mother, which was rarely now, he no longer minded her prying and pumping about Sonya. He made no secret of the fact that they were "in correspondence." At the regiment, he let it be known as well. But still no one there seemed particularly interested.

As Sonya had suggested, he entered the annual steeplechase at Krasnoye Selo. The first year he came in third, then two years in a row he won it. Sonya was so proud, seeing him photographed on horseback in the winner's circle in front of the Tsar.

For a year and a half, Bulatovich had been assigned to the fencing team of another regiment. By the time he returned to his own regiment, he was so accomplished a cavalryman that he was made assistant director and then director of the regimental training detachment.

"They call me Mazeppa," he bragged to Sonya.

"Are you some kind of rebel?" she asked.

"A rebel? No, I never thought of it that way. I think they call me that because I'm strict—I demand and get obedience."

"And what would you have me do, master?" she asked playfully, dropping to her knees and coyly bowing her head. She was nineteen now and far more confident of her ability to play the games of respectable flirtation and courtship. But she was impulsive and would sometimes assert herself and act unexpectedly, even against her own best interests, even if for no other reason than to prove that she could if she wanted to. When Bulatovich had first met her, her hair had hung straight and long, turning out a bit at the ends and gently framing her round face. But she never seemed satisfied with that natural beauty. She was forever changing her hair style, cutting it, curling it, teasing it, or tying it. She was very aware of her appearance and very imaginative at altering it. Sometimes, like now, when she had her hair tied back in a bun, she seemed to look her worst deliberately; yet with her eyes, her voice, and her gestures, she made herself seem all the more willful and sensuous.

Bulatovich laughed, as he usually did when he didn't know how else to react to her. This was one of his rare official visits at her parents' house just outside Petersburg. She only let him come here once or twice a year. Usually, they met secretly, in the summer riding in the woods, and in the winter rendezvousing at the house of a married friend of hers in Petersburg. She insisted that such secrecy was necessary so her parents wouldn't think that they were serious and take steps to keep them apart.

He didn't inquire too deeply into the question of why her parents should object. He presumed it had something to do with money. Unfamiliar with the ways of society and the subtle distinctions of status near the top, he simply took her word for it and did as she advised.

She often had him at a disadvantage, pretending that her knowledge of the sensitivities of society was beyond his comprehension.

When he laughed just now, she sensed his discomfort, jumped to her feet, took his hand, and led him on a walk through the garden. For early March, it was quite warm outside. And there was nowhere else they could be alone without the danger that someone would come walking in.

As they walked among the high hedges, well sheltered from probing eyes, she squeezed his hand warmly, then touched his palm and wrist lightly, sensuously, leaning gently against his arm and shoulder. "And now that you are such a brilliant success—director of the training detachment, finest horseman and finest fencer in the regiment—what new challenge will you take on?"

Bulatovich laughed again, nervously. What did she expect of him? Sometimes in their playful times in the woods she had made him pretend that they were running off together to be vagabonds in France or Italy. She seemed to love to fantasize. Did she want him to talk fantasy now?

She was hard to figure out. There had been moments, riding with her, when she thrilled him with her recklessness, jumping over high hedges and fences at full gallop. There had been moments too when she suddenly kissed him, even inserting her tongue deep into his mouth. Other times in public, even at the dinner table at her own house, when it appeared that no one was looking, she slyly slid her hand onto his lap and rubbed him high on the thigh. Once when he had shown her his Cossack riding tricks, *djigitovka*—doing handstands on the horse's back, then hanging low off the side of the horse and touching the ground with his palms, all while the horse was galloping—she had hugged him tight with one hand and with the other had fondled his crotch, just for a moment, then pushed off with her elbows before he had a chance to respond. Then she was instantly a very proper young lady, who had never been anything but a very proper young lady.

Once when they had arranged to meet by a pond on a hot summer day, she, incredible as it seemed, was swimming in the nude when he arrived. She had smiled seductively, let him get a quick glimpse of her full figure, then acted horrified that he should dare to try to look at her "in such a state." She had dressed quickly, while, at her insistence, his back was turned, and then had ridden off without saying a word, and without ever again alluding to or allowing him to allude to the incident.

Such behavior reminded him of the way Sonya played the piano. Like Lilia, her problem was one of rhythm, but Sonya didn't come to abrupt hunting halts; rather she sometimes got carried away. Her fingers would race ahead far faster than the established tempo, till they stumbled over themselves. Then after a false note or two, she would quickly and smoothly, as if nothing had gone wrong, return to a measured ladylike beat.

Bulatovich could remember numerous other occasions when she had unexpectedly taken the initiative and given him some physically provocative sign of endearment, only to fend him off when he responded and adroitly return their encounter to a calmer, more respectable tempo. Unwittingly, she had trained him to be cautious and slow to respond to her bold affectionate gestures.

But this time, when she sensed his hesitation, she dropped his hand, went walking on ahead, then turned abruptly. "Well, what are you going to do? Play soldier boy on a training field for the rest of your life? Or will you become a horse trader instead?"

Bulatovich flinched. He had wanted to turn Lutsikovka into a horse-breeding farm, to raise and train Thoroughbred racehorses. He had thought it could be a lucrative business, that he would soon earn enough to afford to get married. As it turned out, his mother had refused to relinquish control of the estate.

"Well, don't just stand there with your mouth open," Sonya lashed out suddenly. "What do you intend to do?"

Did she want him to try to kiss her? Or tell her some wild improbable tale of their future together? Instead he said what was uppermost on his mind. "I was thinking about Ethiopia."

"Ethiopia?" she grimaced.

He explained the situation, as best he knew it then, while she looked on, incredulous.

"A Red Cross mission is being organized to help the wounded from the Battle of Adowa. I was thinking of volunteering, with the permission of my regiment, of course."

"Adowa? What is Adowa?"

"Ethiopia, you see, is the only Christian nation in Black Africa. It became Christian back in the fourth century, long before Russia or even Italy. Ethiopia is an extraordinary place, from what little I know. Not far from the equator, it's a land of jungles, elephants, deserts, and high, forbidding mountains. There are vast territories near there that have never been seen by any European."

"But what is Adowa?"

"A town, a battle, a turning point in history, perhaps," he was beginning to get carried away with enthusiasm. "The Ethiopian Emperor, Menelik, has been competing with the Western Powers for dominance in Central Africa. First he bought arms from the French. You may have heard of the French poet Rimbaud?"

"Yes, of course," she answered, beginning to show signs of interest.

"He gave up writing poetry in his early twenties and became a gunrunner in Ethiopia, supplying Menelik. Later, when the Italians declared that Ethiopia was in their 'sphere of influence,' Menelik negotiated with them, posed as their friend, signed agreements with them—all in exchange for more modern rifles and ammunition. He then turned on the Italians and defeated them resoundingly at the Battle of Adowa.

"If you read the papers, you would know about the outpouring of sympathy here in Russia for these Ethiopians. The papers show them as poor helpless Christians armed only with spears."

"Rimbaud, you say? That vagabond bohemian, with his 'Drunken Boat' poem?" she asked.

"Yes, that's the one."

"And Pushkin's great-grandfather was an Ethiopian, wasn't he? There's something intriguing about that place," she admitted. "I think of it as somehow romantic, exotic, Oriental, even." She cuddled up to his shoulder and looked deep into his eyes, with a helpless pleading look. He expected her to say, "You aren't going to go, are you? You wouldn't leave me, would you?" Instead, she stroked him firmly with both hands and whispered, "I'll wait for you."

After several months, he hated Ethiopia, the recurring fever, the climatic extremes—the heat of the jungle, the unexpected cold at night on the plateaus, the thinness of the air at eight thousand feet above sea level, and the perpetual steaming fog by the low banks of a jungle river. He hated the constant nervous tension—having to stay alert, to watch what he said, to read motives into the gracious phrases of all the semifeudal princelings and governors and the Emperor himself. There were times when he longed to return to Petersburg and Sonya.

But when he got back, Sonya awakened his imagination, and he saw Ethiopia quite differently in the light of her words.

While he was gone on his first trip, she had made herself a student of Ethiopia, reading everything she could find about it, even going so far as to visit Professor Bolotov, an expert on Eastern languages Bulatovich had consulted, for advice and books that could help in learning Amharic. After his return, she was

Bulatovich's helpmate, listening attentively and bringing out the moral or romantic, nearly allegorical implications of the bare facts he reported; as his mother would put it, she had a knack for finding a trace of essential truth in mere facts. She encouraged him to write a book about his experiences, particularly what he had observed during his brief excursions into the hinterland after the medical mission had left.

Geographically, his main interest was the Omo River and the puzzle of its true course, whether it became a tributary of the Nile or ended in some lake to the south. But she was far more interested in what he could tell her about the Little Abay (the Blue Nile) and the Awash, two rivers that started quite near one another but had very different destinies.

The Little Abay begins at Lake Tana, gently meanders to the east and south before it runs west and north, gradually gaining strength and becoming the main tributary of the mighty Nile, the Blue Nile, contributing two thirds of the water of the Nile and carrying millions of tons of fertile soil to Egypt every year. Not far from the source of the Little Abay rises the powerful Awash River, which rushes dramatically in a torrent north and east to the desert, where it dries up and ends, never reaching the sea. Sonya found a sort of irony and tragedy in the fate of that powerful river with all of its energy and potential leading nowhere, ending unfulfilled, unimportant, unnoticed.

He described to her the geological oddities known as *ambas*—flat-topped, cliff-sided mountains. But it wasn't the geology she was interested in. She wanted to hear of the monasteries perched inaccessibly on top of those ambas and also of the princes, younger brothers of emperors, who reportedly had been kept confined all their lives in pleasure prisons on such ambas to avoid any conflict over dynastic succession. She imagined Samuel Johnson's *Rasselas*, translated from a "happy valley" to the top of an amba, thousands of feet above sea level.

He told her of the changes that were taking place, how Menelik's Amharas were conquering one tribe after another and helping introduce Western civilization to Central Africa. He saw Ethiopia as having a special destiny as a conduit for introducing the benefits of Western medicine, science, and technology to these people without totally destroying their native cultures. He saw change as inevitable, but wanted it to be positive rather than destructive, as was all too often the case in European colonies.

Sonya, however, couldn't accept the notion that the world must change. She wanted some romantic, unchanging ideal. And she seemed to find that ideal in the details he provided her about the Galla or Oromo people. Before being conquered by the Amharas, they had ruled themselves in a number of separate states, many of which had what Sonya called a "republican" form of government. Once every forty years the head of each family had a five-year term as a member of the *lube* or ruling council and judicial court. It was with her notions in mind that he wrote in his book that "the peaceful, free way of life that could have become the ideal for philosophers and writers of the eighteenth century, if they had known of it, was completely changed" by the recent conquest by the Amharas.

She wanted to find out more about such cultures. She wanted to help him record details of these unique social structures before they totally disappeared. She felt an urgency. It was important to gather information quickly so some record of this aspect of human potential and diversity would be preserved, to save a few little pieces of the gigantic puzzle of mankind's nature and destiny.

For her there was an urgency about everything. Their meetings, with few exceptions, were still secret and hurried. She made it appear that it must be that way. Maybe she actually believed so herself. The hurried words, the sudden kiss and departure—their innocent moments together had the intensity of a romantic intrigue.

When he was ordered to return to Ethiopia, selected to go ahead to prepare the way for Russia's first diplomatic mission to that country, he was primed and prepared to take full advantage of this fresh opportunity to record every precious detail he could of those unique and disappearing cultures in the hinterland. He left just a week before his book was published.

⚜ ⚜ ⚜

On this second trip, he accompanied the army of Ras Wolde Georgis on its expedition of conquest, south-southwest from Addis Ababa to Lake Rudolph. Bulatovich was the first European to traverse Kaffa, a little despotic kingdom that prior to its recent conquest by the Amharas had been completely closed to all outsiders for several centuries. Beyond Kaffa he passed through lands unknown even to Ethiopians. His ability to chart their course with compass and surveying gear had been essential to the mission's success. A few hundred out of their sixteen thousand men died along the way in skirmishes with natives and of disease and sunstroke. But the expedition established Ethiopia's claim to vast stretches of territory that might otherwise have been claimed by England or France in their insatiable quest for colonies.

Along the way, he named a newly discovered mountain range in honor of Tsar Nicholas II and rescued a little three-year-old boy, who had been emasculated and left for dead probably by some of the more vicious and trophy-hungry irregular volunteers who accompanied Wolde Georgis' army.

Bulatovich brought the boy, Vaska, back to Russia with him, and overcoming his mother's initial reluctance, left the boy with her at Lutsikovka.

Bulatovich had walked in the door at Lutsikovka carrying a solid gold saber and shield—a gift to him from Wolde Georgis. Georgis had himself received them from Emperor Menelik two years before as a reward for having conquered the kingdom of Kaffa.

In fact, Bulatovich had returned in such glory that it was hard for his mother to object to anything, even paying his bills, which were astronomical. In just 211 days he had spent over 5000 rubles out of his own pocket—five times his annual salary.

Back in Petersburg, Bulatovich received medals from both the Russian and Ethiopian governments. He was promoted to staff-rotmister. The Foreign Minister, Muraviev, was so impressed with his report on the military strength, political situation, and special destiny of Ethiopia that he had copies of it sent to Russian embassies in Paris, London, and Constantinople and to their diplomatic agent in Cairo.

Bulatovich was asked to deliver a paper at a meeting of the Russian Geographical Society, and his friend Colonel Molchanov set to work with him immediately, helping him prepare his notes and diary for publication as another book. While the first book had been an overview of Ethiopia and its people based on a relatively short visit, this was to be a work of scientific importance, recording ethnographic information about peoples never before observed by Europeans and other peoples who because of the incursions of the Amharas were now in a state of flux, their old customs and social forms eroding away.

He had hoped that Sonya would help him. But things didn't work out that way. The married friend whose house they used to meet at had moved to Moscow, and there was always one reason or another why meetings set up through their surreptitious correspondence were canceled or he was left waiting for her. He heard rumors that while he was gone she had received several proposals, that she had acquired a reputation for intelligence as well as good looks and was very popular and sought after at parties.

He saw her at a dinner at her parents' house and at a special reception arranged for him by the regiment, and she seemed to be beaming with pride and joy for him. But there was never any opportunity for them to talk in private. Before they had a chance to get reacquainted and to establish any kind of mutual understanding, the request came through from Menelik himself for Bulatovich to return again to Ethiopia and provide advice on defensive military measures in newly conquered territories that seemed threatened by the British.

That was the trip when he met Asalafetch—an experience he still couldn't deal with rationally, not now. Better that he look ahead, to the east, to Hailar, and get on with business at hand.

7

Hailar, Manchuria, August 1, 1900

Hailar, the administrative capital of the western district of Northern Manchuria and the first goal of the Hailar Detachment, was not very large. Perhaps it could hold five thousand civilian inhabitants.

But to eyes unaccustomed to Mongolian ways, it was unique—like a honeycomb or one huge house divided into many cells, made up of small houses with yards enclosed by rectangular walls. The straight rectangular clay walls that defined the city limits served as walls for the houses next to it, and the walls that defined yards were all interlinked. The rectilinear streets reinforced the overall pattern.

Somehow the city and the scattering of buildings around it blended harmoniously with the sloping fields in the wide green valley and the twisting bed of the Emingol River. Every tree, every bush, every outcropping of rocks seemed to play its part in creating the overall effect of balance and harmony.

Bulatovich carefully scanned the city with his binoculars. Butorin, who knew the territory and spoke the Mongolian language, stood beside him. A hundred Russian cavalry were waiting behind them at the base of this sandy hill, expecting to be called into action at any moment.

Bulatovich had never expected to get this far without a skirmish. Orlov had given him half a squadron and asked him to observe the enemy and note their position. Orlov had said that some twenty thousand Chinese troops and reservists were stationed at Hailar, that the terrain lent itself to defense, that reinforcements would probably be sent here from deeper in Manchuria, that this would be the site of the most important battle of the campaign.

Everything was still uncertain. Phone and telegraph lines were down. They had no idea if the Europeans at the legations in Peking had been slaughtered or saved. They had no idea how other Russian armies were faring elsewhere in Manchuria. For all they knew, the whole war might depend on the expected confrontation at Hailar.

They had left Ongun two days after the battle. Bulatovich had volunteered. He had gotten caught up in the excitement of battle. He had delighted in the enthusiasm and admiration of the men in his command. He wanted more. He needed more. He couldn't face the letdown that would come with inactivity. He had asked Orlov to let him scout ahead immediately with the same troop he had commanded before—men he felt he knew and could trust. Kupferman had looked too shocked to say a word. Strakhov had objected on the grounds that surely Bulatovich and his men needed more rest—it was only natural; they had only had one full night's sleep after their all-night "excursion." But Orlov was delighted at this show of enthusiasm. He gave Bulatovich the men he wanted plus about eight more.

They rode all day, following the railway, pausing to water their horses at Urdingi, then on to Hailar. Forty miles, and no sign of the enemy, no sign of anyone at all.

These Chinese were a mystery to Bulatovich. At Ongun they had amassed a sizable, apparently well-armed army. Orlov had shown bad judgment. Overanxious and perhaps overconfident, he had marched ahead with only half the infantry while the other half and the cavalry were still getting organized back at Abagaitui. And he had sent the troops who knew this territory best, the railway guards under Captain Smolyannikov, by a different route. If the Chinese had attacked right away, they would have had a tremendous advantage. Instead, they had waited; the Russian cavalry had arrived; and Orlov had taken the initiative. It was as if the Chinese didn't intend to fight at all, as if they only wanted to put on a show, to shadow box, to intimidate at a distance, to watch and wait, perhaps to harass, until the enemy got tired and went away.

Orlov had said that the Mongolians and the Trans-Baikal Cossacks looked very much alike. But Bulatovich hardly noticed the faces of the enemy. He saw instead the long pigtail on each of them. Butorin explained that it was a sign of submission to the Manchu dynasty, that all men in China wore it. Submission—that was what Bulatovich could not understand: passivity and submission.

After Urdingi the desert gradually gave way to cultivated fields and an occasional squat mud house that seemed like a natural feature of the landscape. The people and the livestock were gone.

A few miles away from Hailar they had spotted what looked like a town: a cluster of small, well-kept clay buildings with their rectangular walled-in yards and ornate gates.

"Nobody lives there," offered Butorin. "Nobody living, at least. Those are tombs. The Mongolians—all the Chinese, for that matter—are very particular about their dead. As much or more so than about their living. I wouldn't go poking about those tombs, sir, not without good reason. Even the loot that's probably there wouldn't be reason enough. Disturb those graves and these people will never rest till they tear you limb from limb, if the ghosts don't get you first."

The men had laughed a little nervously at the notion of ghosts. While they considered the Chinese as overly superstitious, they were not above having similar fears themselves.

Now Bulatovich and Butorin were on one of several sandy hilltops overlooking Hailar. Off to the south was a green hill topped with a carefully cultivated grove. To the north was another such hill with a grove. Still farther north they could see a mountain and, with binoculars, a huge stone statue of Buddha near its summit.

Bulatovich spotted some smoke several miles south of Hailar. He focused on it and saw the onion-shaped cupola of a Russian church and a handful of large wooden houses, with crude mud huts strewn haphazardly in between.

"What's that over there?" he asked, passing the binoculars to Butorin.

"The railway station and the Russian town, headquarters for construction in this area. Chinese laborers brought in from other parts of Manchuria live in those huts. When they got the chance, they probably looted their masters' houses, set a few fires, and took off."

"What's the station doing so far from the city?"

"It's the dead again, sir. They have a thing about the dead. They were afraid that the railway would disturb the spirits of their ancestors. They didn't care about the racket of the trains for themselves, that much. But they had to make sure it wouldn't disturb the sleep of the dead. They set up all kinds of experiments with sound. I think they figured about three miles was a safe distance, so the tracks had to be at least that far from any gravesite. The dead are part of the landscape, like rivers and rocks, only more important. If there were graves around, our engineers couldn't just draw straight lines across the plains. The railway had to twist and turn to avoid the dead."

Bulatovich took the binoculars and scanned the steep slopes on the far side of the river, the quiet, seemingly empty Mongolian city. "You've been here before. You've lived among these people. What do you make of it?" he asked.

"They've gone. That's all. The city's ours."

"But why?"

"I don't know, sir. I've never seen anything like this before. But I do know that the Chinese would rather wait than fight, unless you get them really riled up like these Boxers. Then again, it's probably superstition of some kind. There's always a spirit of this or a spirit of that they don't want to disturb; and good days and bad days. Looks like they figured this was really a bad day for them, which means it's a good day for us. If I've learned anything from the Chinese, it's don't argue with luck, sir."

"We'll soon find out," replied Bulatovich, signaling the others to join them on top of the hill. "Shemelin," he shouted, "take a few men and check out the city. Any trouble, we'll hear the shooting. Butorin, check the railway settlement. Sofronov, go with Butorin; find the Russian church. There could be Christians hiding there, Chinese Christian converts who could tell us what happened here. Laperdin, the arsenal, the prison. See if they left any munitions or prisoners. Login, take a few men up that mountain off to the left, the one with the Buddha. This could be a trap. You should be able to see for fifty miles or more from up there. Use my binoculars. Watch especially to the north, beyond the Hailar River. Any sign of life—a cloud of dust, a wisp of smoke—signal with three shots. Stay there until I send relief."

"And me, sir?" asked Starodubov. "What would you have me do, sir?"

"You and the others will dig trenches."

"Trenches, sir?"

"Yes, trenches. Fill your canteens at the well in that grove over there. Water your horses. And start digging. The trenches needn't be pretty—just deep enough to give us some cover in case of attack."

"But sir, the city is empty. There's nothing there but plunder, just waiting to be taken."

"Dig."

ꗃ ꗃ ꗃ

Bulatovich already trusted some of these men he had known for just a couple of days. Login—who at the funeral had been so quick to know what must be done and so quick to do it. Shemelin—who had served well as a messenger. Starodubov—Old Blockhead, the thief, who had turned out to be an inspiration in the midst of battle.

On the road to Hailar, Starodubov had called him "Mazeppa." It reminded him of his days back at the regiment when the enlisted men in the training detachment he commanded had called him that. Like most nicknames it was probably a combination of mockery and respect.

"You don't mind my calling you Mazeppa?" Starodubov had asked. "We were talking around the campfire last night—the men from Grotten's old troop—and I told them your name. You frightened them. They didn't know what to make of you. Now they can say, 'That's Mazeppa.' I hope you don't mind, sir."

Bulatovich had shrugged, preoccupied with the task at hand, the ride to Hailar, the absence of any sign of the enemy.

"You can't stop men from naming, sir. It's part of our nature. Adam named the beasts of the field and the birds of the air, and we've been naming ever since. If a name fits, many men use it. If not, it's forgotten. The name that fits is a true name. It tells something about the man who wears it, and it will stay with him no matter what he may wish or say or do—unless he makes himself into a new man.

"Take Shemelin, sir. The 'Jew,' I called him last night around the campfire. We were drinking. I was naming names. Login I called the 'Old Man' because he sounded like one—serious beyond his years. And Sofronov—the 'Priest,' because he's pompous like a priest even when he doesn't mean to be. Trofim would like the name of 'Priest,' judging from the way he prays so loudly and makes such a show of crossing himself. But I called him 'Father' instead—Trofim, the father of many sons. He has no wife and no children now, but he will. You can sense it in him. Because what a man wants to be isn't the same as what he is."

"But people change," Bulatovich overreacted to that remark. "You don't just have to accept your lot in life. You said so yourself—you can make yourself into a new man."

"I don't know, sir, not being educated. But it seems that even that's in a man from the beginning. You're either born with the spirit and the will to change yourself or you're not. Trofim just doesn't have it in him, sir."

"Fatalism. That comes from living too near the Chinese."

"I don't know what that word means, sir, but what I say is plain old peasant sense. You are what you are. You don't grow a birch from an acorn."

"But what about Shemelin? You were going to tell me about him. I know he's a fine horseman. What more can you say about him?"

"Shemelin's a strange case, sir. Everyone says he's generous to a fault. He keeps nothing for himself, always giving to friends. Yakov's his name, but he wants to be called 'Ivan.' I called him 'Jew' as a joke, but he got angry at me for it and started shouting,

'I am not a Jew!' Then later when he was even more drunk, he stood up on a rock, dropped his pants, and shouted, 'You see! I am not a Jew. I am not circumcised. I am not a Jew!'

"That wasn't a name I had thought much about. But it worked the best of all the names I made last night. For sure, none of the Mazeppy will forget it."

"Mazeppy?" Bulatovich asked.

"That's what I call us—the men who follow Mazeppa."

Shortly after that conversation, they had stopped at Urdingi to water their horses and relieve their own one-hundred-degree thirst. Butorin playfully doused Shemelin by the bucketful and shouted, "Hey, Jew!" Shemelin took off after him, the two of them weaving their horses in and out among the rest of the squadron, amid loud peals of laughter. Then Bulatovich grabbed Shemelin's reigns and brought the game to an abrupt stop.

When things had calmed down, he asked, "Why do they call you 'Jew'?"

"I do not understand, sir," replied Shemelin, sincerely confused. "My father was Ivan, son of Pyotr. His father was Pyotr, son of Ivan. And so it was in our family as long as anyone can remember. The eldest was Ivan or Pyotr. But my parents called me 'Yakov.'

"No one in our village was Yakov. My young brothers they named Pyotr and Ivan. But me, my mother insisted that I be 'Yakov.'

"I asked my mother, 'Why Yakov?'

" 'I wanted a son,' she said. 'I prayed for a son. And I had a dream that if you were a son, your name should be Yakov.'

"So Yakov I am. What can a man do against dreams?

"To the other children of the village it was just a name, a good Bible name. Odd, but not too strange.

"Then one day I fought with a boy, an 'Ivan' he was. We both liked the same girl. We argued. We wrestled. We insulted. He called me 'Jewish bastard,' and I hit him hard like I never hit anyone before. He remembered, remembered well, and others called me 'Jew,' 'Yakov the Jew.' It hurt, and they saw that it hurt.

"And here, too. They do not know me, but here, too, they call me 'Jew.' Why, I do not understand.

"Sometimes I wonder, do they sense what I do not know? Am I really Jew, Jewish bastard?"

Bulatovich laughed, "So you need a father. Starodubov needs a son. We all have needs, thank God. Where would we be without our needs to pull us on? Ah, Yakov, you should be proud of that name. Men will remember you for it."

"I'd rather be forgotten, thank you."

Bulatovich mused, "And so many men risk their lives for their names to be remembered. How foolish, when all they have to do is change their name to 'Yakov.' "

"But it is not easy to change a name. That is my trouble. A name sticks to a man. It is like a shadow. And as much as I try, I cannot make my shadow change shape."

"If you change, your shadow will change with you."

"But how can I change, sir? How can I become Ivan?"

Bulatovich laughed again, then quickly sobered, seeing that Shemelin was quite sincere in his confusion. "Why don't you read?"

"Read what, sir?"

"I don't know. Read anything. Improve your mind. Make yourself an educated man. Take charge of your destiny." At that, Bulatovich shook his head and spurred his horse. Here he was in the middle of a wasteland in China, lecturing some Cossack on the merits of education. As if his words could have any effect on this man.

👑 👑 👑

Sofronov was the first scout to return. A Chinese girl was sitting behind him riding astride, not bothering to hold on, arms akimbo.

"Found her in the basement of the church, sir," he reported, "behind a heap of bodies."

About seventeen or eighteen, the Chinese girl was very attractive, spoke perfect Russian. She said her name was "Sonya." There was something about the way she looked at Bulatovich and he looked back that made him uncomfortable. From a distance, with her complexion, her slanted eyes, her straight black hair, she looked very Chinese. Up close, it was hard to pay attention to anything but her lively dark eyes and the musical, alto, rapid, but never breathless rhythm of her voice.

The name evoked painful memories for Bulatovich. She was an inch shorter than Bulatovich and had a beauty that seemed to require no effort and no adornment. As he realized he was staring at her, he noticed that her pupils were slightly out of line with one another. His own eyes automatically danced back and forth trying to line up with them and were quickly caught in her spell. He forced himself to turn and walk away.

He would have preferred not to talk to her, not to think of her. She hadn't eaten much of anything for three days. He had Sofronov get some food for her, while he inspected the trenches. Then he couldn't in good conscience delay any longer. None of the other scouts had signaled. Apparently the city actually was deserted. And this young, too-attractive girl might have some clue as to what had happened.

By the time Bulatovich approached her again, she was already talking to Starodubov, who was asking, "Sonya? How did you get a name like that?"

"That's the name the priest gave me. Father Ioann." The words poured out as if she desperately needed to talk. "They say that when I was a newborn baby my real father was about to bash my brains against a rock, when Father Ioann stopped him and took me away. You shouldn't blame my real father. I don't. It happens all the time. Girl babies are considered just a trouble and a bother if there's already a son in the house. They must have a son. It's a great sin against filial piety not to have a son to continue the line and do honor to the ancestors. But an extra daughter is just an extra mouth to feed. It's a disagreeable task, I'm sure, killing babies, and they don't much like doing it. But many do what they feel they must do. Most smother them. Father's more a breaker and a smasher, a blacksmith by trade, near the main intersection in town, at least he was before everyone left."

"You know this man, your father?" asked Starodubov in disbelief.

"Yes, he's a fine man at heart. I have hopes that one day he will convert. Father Ioann thought so, too, God rest his soul." Seeing the pained expression on Starodubov's face, she rushed

131

on. "You must understand that they believe death is not death. It's just starting over again in another form, or so they say. An extra girl is a mistake, so why should you suffer and she suffer? Just erase the mistake as soon as possible and free the soul to start over again somewhere else, perhaps as a man. It's hard for a Christian to understand, I know, but they consider it a kindness and one that is difficult to do, just as it is difficult to accept one's own death no matter what one believes. They love their children as much as anyone else does and a mother sometimes goes frantic when her husband kills their newborn. But many husbands consider it their painful duty.

"You see, they think of death and life as two parts of one whole—yin and yang. You don't have one opposite without the other. Death is quite natural, really," she rambled.

"It's not that foreign an idea. You believe in Christ and the Resurrection and the Life Everlasting. They believe in lots of resurrections, over and over again, until the soul finally reaches perfection and can be freed from earth. When you think about it, it's not that hard to convert the Chinese. The morality of Confucius is similar to the morality of Jesus. All you have to do is convince them that they need to be resurrected only once. They're glad to hear that.

"Of course, not all Christians believe what they say they believe. I know that from my reading," she added proudly. "Father Ioann had a fine library. Religious works, but literature, too— Pushkin, Gogol, Dostoevsky, Tolstoy. I think of that story 'Three Deaths' by Tolstoy, where the rich lady, who says she is a Christian, can't accept the fact of her own death, but the peasant, who is more pagan than Christian, and the tree, which, of course, can't think at all, simply die, like they lived, like a part of nature. The way that peasant dies strikes me as particularly Chinese.

"When I think of all those people dying," tears started to appear in her eyes, "my friends, Chinese and Christian, Father Ioann. It's so hard to die well, no matter what you believe and how hard you want to believe it." She started shaking. "All the blood . . . the blood was cold when I woke up. . . ." She squatted there on the sand and stared at her hands.

Sofronov offered in a soft solicitous voice, "I wouldn't trouble her further, sir. She was hiding in that basement with those bodies for three days, with nothing to eat and drink but wafers and wine, and not much of that. She doesn't have much notion of what went on outside."

🛆 🛆 🛆

Soon Laperdin reported back. The arsenal was empty. The prison was empty.

Butorin returned to say he had found large stores of grain and food in the railway settlement. A row of Russian houses and a large supply of oats had been burned. The remaining Russian houses had been looted and vandalized. But strangely, the other storehouses were intact and full.

Shemelin didn't return right away, but he sent back the men who were with him to say that the city was quiet.

There had been no signal from Login on the mountain.

So Bulatovich sent a messenger back to Orlov with news that the city had been taken without a shot. Then Bulatovich had his men move their bivouac to the shady shelter of the half-constructed railway station and set up listening posts around the periphery as a precaution. He had the girl taken to a nearby house and posted guards for her protection. With the exception of the Mazeppy, these hundred men were new to him. He didn't know them very well, but they were men and had gone too long without women.

While others celebrated the "conquest" of Hailar, Butorin took other precautionary measures. He spread grains of rice in a circle around the bivouac. "When the Chinese get luck like this, they become a bit uneasy about it. Rather than celebrate and call attention to their good fortune, they spread rice at the city gates as a sacrifice, lest the spirits turn on them with a balancing portion of bad luck."

It was nightfall by the time Shemelin found his way to the new bivouac, walking, leading his horse; a large box was tied to the saddle. Everyone gathered around him, staring at the box. They had all assumed that rich plunder was ready for the taking in the abandoned dwellings of Hailar. But no one, not even Starodubov or Butorin, had dared disobey Bulatovich's orders and go looting. And here Shemelin had the audacity to dawdle about the city all day, making them all worry and wonder what had become of him; then, to come straggling back with a box full of plunder.

"Yakov," said Bulatovich, softly but firmly.

Shemelin cringed, "Yes, sir?"

"What do you have in that box?"

"I only took Russian goods, sir; things that had been stolen from Russians."

"I never expected you of all people to go looting. And here you've brought back more than you can ever hope to take away with you. Butorin, untie that box. Lift it down from his horse. What does he have there?"

Shemelin shrank with shame and put up no resistance.

"Books?" grunted Butorin in disbelief. "It's nothing but books, sir." He tossed them aside one by one.

"Do you like books, Yakov?" asked Bulatovich.

"Yes, sir," replied Shemelin, shamefacedly gathering up and brushing off the books as Butorin tossed them aside.

"And what do you intend to do with these books?"

"I'll read them, sir. Like you said, sir."

"And can you really read?" asked Bulatovich.

"Yes, sir. Often I have read the Bible, and the Almanac too. The Almanac of 1896."

"Yes," Bulatovich grinned indulgently, "the year of the coronation of Tsar Nicholas—a good year."

Starodubov picked up a few books and carefully brushed off the bindings, apparently admiring the handiwork. Pyotr, too, picked up a book and stared at it with the wonder of an illiterate.

"They're in Russian, sir," explained Shemelin. "Fine books. Fine bindings, sir. It was like a gift from heaven. I wanted to read, to learn, like you said, sir. And there they were—books and more books. I guess I lost my head, sir."

Bulatovich looked at a few titles, all by Tolstoy. He was familiar with them, had enjoyed reading them, surreptitiously, when he should have been doing his schoolwork. But holding them in his hands now, he felt a physical repulsion. Maybe it had something to do with what that Chinese Sonya had said about Tolstoy and death. He threw them down in disgust. "Heretics and fiction writers. They'll weigh down your horse and weigh down your mind. There's no room for foolishness like that in a soldier's saddlebag. All you need are facts and more facts."

"Not all books are evil, sir," offered Sofronov meekly, with bowed shoulders. "Here are the thoughts and meditations of Ioann Sergiev of the Kronstadt Cathedral."

"Worthy, perhaps," conceded Bulatovich, amused by Sofronov's self-demeaning posture and by this evidence of his erudition. He took the book in his hand, hefted it, then tossed it aside, "Heavy, far too heavy."

"Then here's a slim volume packed with wisdom and holiness. It's about a true Russian hero, a *podvizhnik*, a selfless pilgrim suffering for Christ and striving to know Him."

"And what's his name?"

"He has no name, sir."

"A hero without a name?"

"The author of the book is the hero of the book. No one knows who he was, nor does it matter. That we don't know his name is but a sign of his selfless devotion to Christ."

Bulatovich didn't know how to reply to that. The concept seemed both foreign and familiar, something his mother might have heard and repeated without believing. He took the book and looked at it quickly. The title was *The Way of the Pilgrim*. Impulsively, he tossed it to Shemelin. "Take that one, Yakov, and be glad of it. We'll have no more looting—understand?"

"Yes, sir, thank you, sir, yes, sir," jabbered Shemelin, anxiously grabbing the little book and slipping it inside his shirt.

When the commotion died down, Pyotr quietly put aside a few small volumes for himself. Maybe one day he would learn to read, and these would be valuable to him. Books were hard to come by in Trans-Baikal. Login could advise him, when Login came down from the mountain. Login knew so many things.

✥ ✥ ✥

Bulatovich's request had fit in well with Orlov's plans. Someone had to scout ahead, and Bulatovich already knew the terrain as far as Urdingi. The cavalry regiment would rest for another day, then proceed to Urdingi, where they would wait for word from Bulatovich on the enemy position.

Orlov had left two reserve battalions under Colonel Vorobyev in Abagaitui. He now ordered them to advance at once with a large transport of provisions. Orlov himself, with the main body of troops, would follow the cavalry at a leisurely pace, giving the reinforcements time to catch up. He wanted his army at full strength for the upcoming battle for the city of Hailar.

That evening, August 1, at supper back at Ongun, Bodisko's railway guards were singing to the officers—a medley of hymns, military songs, and bawdy ballads—when a messenger, out of breath, exhausted, interrupted the proceedings.

The crowd fell silent. Without a word's being said, everyone knew he must be from Bulatovich.

Orlov hurried forward and with good-natured concern quickly took and opened the dispatch.

"Good God!" whispered Kupferman, loudly and bitterly. "What mess has he gotten into this time?"

Strakhov pressed forward anxiously, trying to see for himself as the commander strained and squinted by the candlelight to decipher the hurried scrawl.

Then Orlov's bushy brows leaped high in amazement. "Bulatovich is in Hailar. The Chinese—soldier and civilian alike—have abandoned the city. The supplies are intact. Hailar has been taken without a shot!"

Strakhov did not join in the cheers and applause that followed. He didn't know if what he felt was intuition or simply envy. Something was wrong. He told himself, "I hope to God I'm not near him when his luck finally turns. Lord only knows what hell could break loose."

🦅 🦅 🦅

At dawn Bulatovich heard three rapid shots from the mountain. Sentries came galloping back from their listening posts.

The Chinese had returned. They were swarming, on foot and horseback, from the north, east, and west toward the railway settlement. The Russians quickly mounted and instinctively started off toward the south before the Chinese could plug that last route of escape.

"Halt!" shouted Bulatovich, shooting the horse out from under the lead Russian rider. Bewildered, they halted immediately. "To the hill! We'll hold out there and wait for reinforcements."

He galloped northwest toward the sandy hill where they had dug trenches. But no one followed him.

He turned. His horse reared high. Then he drew his saber and charged, alone, against the several dozen Chinese foot soldiers who stood directly between him and the hill.

There was a moment's hesitation. Then Starodubov grabbed hold of Chinese Sonya, lifted her onto his saddle, and shouted, "Mazeppa!" The station sheds shook with his voice. Off he rode, awkwardly as ever, because of his size and the extra weight of the girl, but with determination, spurring his poor horse to a frenzy in pursuit of Bulatovich. Next followed Shemelin, then young Pyotr Zabelin with a loud, "Urah!" then the rest. Not a one of them rode to safety in the south.

Somehow they all reached the entrenchments, surprising the Chinese with their audacity and riding past them without a scratch.

But Butorin, who had been on sentry duty, hadn't returned from his listening post, and Login Zabelin and the two scouts who had gone with him to the mountain were now cut off completely by the Chinese army.

As the Chinese closed in around the sandy hilltop and the barrage became intense, Bulatovich sent Shemelin through enemy lines with a new message for Orlov: "Chinese returned. Surrounded. This time we're in trouble."

⚜ ⚜ ⚜

Quickly, Shemelin picked two horses and tied them loosely by their reins to either side of his own horse—No Name, he called him now, after the hero of that book he hadn't read yet, and because he hadn't given his horse a name before.

He lengthened the left stirrup of No Name and mounted, keeping most of his weight on that stirrup, pressing his body flush against the horse's left side. At his request, half a dozen riders started out with him, guiding his three horses and riding due west.

When the Chinese spotted them, the Russians broke into a gallop and, at a shout from Shemelin, scattered, momentarily distracting the Chinese. A hundred yards later, first one, then the

137

other riderless horse broke its loose bonds and ran off at random, creating a further diversion. Shemelin just held tight, not daring to look around for fear he would attract attention.

He heard cannon to the left, cannon—no, thunder—to the right. No Name panicked, nearly threw him, and raced wildly, leaving the road, veering north.

Heavy, driving rain turned the dusty ground to mud and slowed the horse so Shemelin, swinging up and into the saddle, could regain control.

They were near the Mongolian graveyard. Shemelin dismounted, took off his shirt, and used it to shield his horse's eyes from the flash of lightning. He then guided the horse inside the walled garden of one of those houselike tombs. As quickly as it had started, the rain stopped. The distant rumble of thunder was soon replaced by the sound of approaching horses.

He hadn't lost them—they were still after him. He whispered to No Name, "Quiet, boy. Quiet. I'll treat you like a king when we get back. The finest oats around. And sugar—fat lumps of sugar. Just quiet, boy. Still and quiet. Or we'll never get there."

It was hard to tell if the horses were really getting closer or if his hearing was becoming more acute as his fear mounted.

Then it was quiet—the stillness of a grave.

Shemelin shivered, remembering he was standing in a graveyard and remembering what Butorin had said about ghosts. Images of the recent funeral—the man with the smashed brains, Aksyonov's face with its agonized grimace. Involuntarily, he touched the wound above his left eye. The bandage had fallen off and the scab was gone, too. It was bleeding again.

He wanted to pray but, standing in this ancestral shrine, he didn't really know who his ancestors were. Should he pray to the Christian God or to the God of Abraham and Isaac? If he prayed to the wrong one, if he were wrong about his ancestors, would the other God, the right one, be offended and punish him?

The little book—the one Bulatovich had let him have—was still inside his shirt. It was a holy book. He held it in his hand.

He wished he knew some incantation to ward off ghosts. He wished at least he had some rice in his pocket to do like Butorin and spread it in a circle around himself.

He kneeled and repeated the Lord's Prayer over and over.

Frightened, superstitious, reverent, he blanked out everything from his mind but the prayer.

By the time he became aware of his surroundings again, both his legs were numb. He shook them and slapped them to start the blood flowing again. He stood up shakily. He had no idea how much time had passed.

It was still quiet. No sign of the Chinese.

He hurriedly led No Name out of the garden, accidentally overturning and breaking a delicate vase. He crossed himself quickly, trembling, then mounted his horse awkwardly, the lengthened left stirrup taking him by surprise. No Name reared and nearly threw him. Shemelin yanked at the reins and whipped him viciously with his *nagaika*, more to punish than to control—angry at the horse for his own distracted mistakes.

After a few moments, both rider and horse settled down. Instinctively, Shemelin sought a shortcut across the rough wasteland, away from the main road, that would get him to Urdingi quickly and make up for lost time. The horse galloped, stumbled, galloped, lost a shoe, and hobbled on as best it could. All the while, Shemelin could think only of Bulatovich, the Mazeppy, and the others; their lives were in danger and his dallying had placed them in still greater danger. He had to make up for it.

👑 👑 👑

The evening of that day, August 2, 1900, Orlov was at Urdingi with the main body of troops, fighting off swarms of gnats with smoke pots, then choking on the heavy smoke. The troops and their horses had used up the little fresh water that had been there. The bread was stale. Colonel Vorobyev and the supplies from Abagaitui were at least two days behind them. Hailar with its vast supplies was still two days of marching ahead.

By day they sweltered in the one-hundred-degree sun. At night the temperature dropped to fifty degrees, and they huddled close to campfires to keep warm.

There were the usual dysentery and fleas to contend with.

Dr. Stankevich had just reported a severe case of typhus, and Orlov was contemplating what measures he should take if that deadly disease should start spreading. Then Shemelin arrived with the second message from Bulatovich.

"Ivan Semyonovich," Orlov ordered his friend and Chief of staff Volzhaninov, "load the carts with as many men as will fit. We leave for Hailar within the hour."

Based on the first message from Bulatovich—that Hailar had been taken without a shot—Orlov had sent Strakhov ahead with most of the cavalry. If Shemelin had taken the main road to Urdingi, he could have met Strakhov halfway and quickly led him to the rescue of Bulatovich. As it was, Strakhov had no notion that there was danger ahead and any need for urgency. He would be proceeding at a walk, with his guard down.

Shemelin felt responsible for all the lives that were now in jeopardy. He kept muttering aloud to himself that everything would turn out for the best.

As for his horse, No Name was ruined and would have to be destroyed. But Shemelin was spared the pain of having to do it himself because he had to head back to Hailar, on a fresh mount, with Orlov and the main body of troops.

❁ ❁ ❁

"You should be court-martialed!" yelled Strakhov, confronting Bulatovich on the sandy hilltop overlooking Hailar. "You had us riding into a trap." The sunset reflected off Bulatovich's glasses, concealing his eyes. "Abandoned city?" continued Strakhov, nervously running his fingers through his blond hair and leaving it in wild, uncharacteristic disarray. "Indeed. Is that what your reconnaissance told you? Brilliant. Absolutely brilliant."

Rather than make excuses and apologies, as might have been expected, Bulatovich made no response at all. In the background, rifles were loaded and readied. They expected an attack at any moment.

"You could have at least sent a second messenger to give us some warning that the enemy had returned in force."

"I did, sir," replied Bulatovich, standing at attention, his face and beard pasted with a patchwork of sweaty dust.

"Well, I don't see how he could have missed us. There's only one road from here to Ongun."

"He's probably dead, sir."

Strakhov hadn't considered that possibility. He shivered, then grimaced in reaction to his shiver. The enemy might attack at any moment. He tried to prepare himself for battle. He must maintain control of his body this time; he must perform well; no, not just well—heroically. If he must die (they were heavily outnumbered and surrounded), then he wanted to die heroically, he told himself. Should Orlov and the rest of the army come upon his corpse lying here on the battlefield, what would they think if his clothes were stinking of excrement? He looked hurriedly around, spotting the ditch they had dug as a latrine. He must be sure to relieve himself before the battle began.

Turning again to Bulatovich, he gestured grandly, "You had just a hundred men against at least two thousand of the enemy. If you had had any military sense," he lectured, "you would have retreated while you had the opportunity. Then you would have met us on the road, and we'd all be safely out of here. But no, not the great Bulatovich, not the little hero with the dirty red cap. No, you had to make a stand on a barren hilltop. . . ."

He was interrupted from behind. "Sergeant Folimonov reporting, sir. The cannon are ready. It's a beautiful position, sir. Couldn't ask for better. Whatever side they come from, we have a good angle. My compliments to Staff-Rotmister Bulatovich . . ."

"Fine, Sergeant, fine," Strakhov cut him off. "Load grapeshot, and stand by for further orders."

They had arrived a few hours before, but Strakhov still hadn't inspected the entrenchments and thoroughly assessed the situation. Was he being just? Was he making the right decisions? Strakhov was a deliberate man. He believed in careful planning. Under normal circumstances, his every move was premeditated. He distrusted his instincts because he had no control over them. Now he couldn't tell if he was being rational or was just taking out his frustrations on Bulatovich.

Strakhov shook himself, kicked the sand. This was no time to think about niceties of motivation.

But he needed time. How could he act if he hadn't thought it all out in advance?

He had been caught off guard when that first message had arrived saying that Hailar had been taken. He had felt there was something wrong, almost diabolical, about the luck of this Bulatovich. Strakhov was still puzzling over the problem and trying to find a rational basis for his feelings when Orlov ordered him to proceed at once to Hailar with a few hundred men, to prepare things for the arrival of the main body of troops a few days later.

All that night, riding through the moonlit wasteland, Strakhov had been distracted. Was it simply physical exhaustion? How else to explain this inability to sort out and understand his own motivations, this failure to plan and follow through with his plans, these doubts left over from his first, so embarrassing, combat experience. He must take better care of his body or it would betray him again in a crisis. Rational thinking was possible only if the body was sound.

Now, without thinking, forgetting for a moment the hundreds of soldiers dashing about and readying their weapons, the nervous neighing of the horses in the background, forgetting even Bulatovich, who was standing right in front of him, Strakhov took out a pocketknife and began cleaning his fingernails. His mother had always insisted that he keep his fingernails clean. His father talked only about the big things, the things that required planning—what are you going to do with your life? His mother insisted on the details—clean fingernails and polished buttons.

His father had wanted him to be a cabinetmaker. His father was the finest cabinetmaker for many miles around the city of Orenburg, near the Ural Mountains. His family had been cabinetmakers for three generations. Strakhov, as the only son, was expected to follow the family tradition.

Strakhov rebelled: he wanted to choose his destiny, not simply inherit. For long hours his father and he would argue at the dinner table over what he should do with his life. The arguments were heated, even bitter at times. But then his father, for all he had argued to the contrary, went to great lengths to ensure the boy success in his chosen career—the military. He had bought his son's way into an exclusive military academy normally reserved for the gentry and had outfitted him in style.

Thinking back, Strakhov had the uncomfortable feeling that those arguments had not been so straightforward. He suspected that his father, too, as a boy, had not wanted simply to follow in his father's footsteps but had not rebelled and somehow regretted it; and while playing devil's advocate, hoped all along that his son would have enough spirit to stand up for himself and strike out on his own path. It was rather disconcerting now for Strakhov to think that his great act of independence might well have been orchestrated by his father.

Ironically, Strakhov's success at his "chosen" profession probably had more to do with his mother than his father. It was his fastidious attention to details of dress—forever, at odd moments, cleaning his fingernails, polishing his buttons, buffing his boots—and it was the way he insisted on obedience from those in his command, his respect for his superiors, and his sensitivity for matters of protocol that endeared him to his instructors and superiors.

What was he to do now? What good were clean fingernails on a battlefield? He threw the pocketknife in the sand, then noticed Bulatovich, still standing there in front of him at attention. "Dismissed," he muttered, angry at himself.

How could he be so distracted at a time like this? It was as bad as this morning at dawn, when they were suddenly set upon by hundreds of Chinese. He had been careless, not sending scouts out as far ahead as he would have if he had expected danger. And yet he had sensed danger when that message had come saying the city had been taken without a shot. He knew something must be wrong. It was just too easy. Everything Bulatovich did seemed too easy. It smelled of luck, luck about to turn sour. He should have followed his instincts and been cautious. Instead, he had discounted his intuition as mere envy, had done nothing about it but brood, and had ambled right into a trap.

A soldier since his teens, this campaign was Strakhov's first opportunity to demonstrate his leadership in combat. There would soon be an opening in his home regiment for a lieutenant colonel. If he distinguished himself here, he stood an excellent chance for promotion when he returned. Because of the shortage of officers in the Hailar Detachment, he was already acting assistant commander of a cavalry regiment 899 sabers strong, a job that would normally be filled by a lieutenant colonel.

What had he done with this opportunity? First Ongun and then the near disaster of this morning. Thank God the Chinese had been poor shots. Despite his carelessness nearly all of his men had made it to this desolate hilltop with its patchwork of trenches that Bulatovich's men had dug.

And any moment now, the next crisis would come, the next test . . .

Bulatovich was still standing there. Hadn't he heard that he was dismissed? Or had Strakhov only thought the command, forgotten to say it?

Horses whinnied wildly and pulled at their reins. Seconds later, gunfire and a deafening shout. The Chinese came swarming in from all sides. Instantly, Bulatovich dropped to the ground and crawled to the nearest trench. And while everyone's attention was focused on the enemy, Strakhov quickly scrambled to the latrine ditch and relieved himself.

The roar of gunfire became fierce. The enemy sprinted forward recklessly, firing without aiming as they ran. When the black robes and streaming pigtails were less than a hundred feet away, Strakhov stood in the midst of the encampment, his troops on their bellies in the trenches around him. He raised his sword and bellowed above the din, "Fire the cannon now! Now! I tell you, now!"

The Russian cannon rang out, spraying grapeshot through the crowd of onrushing Chinese. With the third round, the Chinese turned in panic and ran back beyond the Emingol River, taking up positions on the high right bank. The timing had been perfect. The surprised Russian troops in the trenches, even Bulatovich, turned and looked up at their commander with newfound respect and appreciation.

For the main body of troops with Orlov the bumpy ride in the squeaky, two-wheeled, ox-pulled carts seemed interminable. Where the desert first became spotted with cultivated fields, they came upon a tall, slender Trans-Baikal Cossack with a long, rather foolish-looking face. He was afoot and on the point of collapse. "Butorin" he called himself, and Shemelin confirmed that he was one of Bulatovich's men, a sentry who hadn't returned from his listening post, who had been cut off by the sudden attack.

A few hours later they reached the hilltop, with its trenches and its cluster of tents, horses, ammunition boxes, cannon, and vehicles. In the distance, on the near bank of the Emingol, Russian sharpshooters were spread out in a long thin line—their white shirts brightly reflecting the sun. Off to the right, large gray eagles circled round and round the grove and the temple.

Strakhov reported, "Six dead, four missing, Your Excellency. We've kept our casualties down, no thanks to the misinformation that brought us here, and no thanks to a certain Guards officer who decided to make a stand on this hilltop, when he could just as easily have withdrawn."

Orlov quickly noted Strakhov's biased tone, and reacted instinctively, coming to the defense of his protégé. "You seem to have the situation well under control, Major Strakhov. You should be commended for choosing such a fine position," he went on, as if he hadn't heard what Strakhov had just said. "These hills command the valley and the western approaches. You saved many a Russian life by securing these hills."

Orlov soon spotted Bulatovich, recognizing him from a distance by his red service cap, and rushed up to him, embracing him and loudly congratulating him in front of his men.

8

Hailar, Manchuria, August 3, 1900

The night after Hailar was taken, Butorin rested his limbs on the soft mattress and feather pillows in Kupferman's spacious tarantass and drank and ate. "I haven't feasted like this for years," Butorin said, "not since my brother's wedding, God curse his soul."

Kupferman and Strakhov didn't know what to make of him or how much to believe of what he said. He seemed to have quite a capacity for invention, but he was willing to talk; and he did, apparently, know a few things about Bulatovich, enough at least to prompt them to break their own rules and serve him vodka. They treated him like a hero, listening again and again to his escape story and inquiring, in passing, about Bulatovich.

"They say that you are one of his favorites," said Strakhov, deliberately flattering him, trying to lead him on.

"Yes," said Butorin proudly, "me and Starodubov and Shemelin and Login Zabelin, whatever's become of him. We haven't seen him now for two days, not since he was sent up that mountain to stand lookout."

"And why is he so brave?" asked Strakhov, somewhat annoyed by all the digressions.

"He knows what he's about, that Login. He's young, no more than thirty, but he acts like one with many years of experience. Cool courage he has, not hot daring. Hot comes and goes. One day a hero, next day a coward. Cool you can count on."

"Yes, I'm sure this man Login you speak of is a brave man. But Bulatovich, tell us about Bulatovich."

"He, too, is brave. But such bravery I've never seen before. Like hot, like scalding hot, but always it's there. Once I asked him, I said, 'Why do you do these things? For me, I have no family, no yesterday, no tomorrow. Besides, I'm crazy. Sometimes I do things not for women or drink or money; I don't know why. But you with your fine education and your fancy regiment, you have much to live for. Why are you so brave?'

"And he laughed and said to me, 'Oh, I'm not really brave. An Ethiopian general once told me, "You're bold and daring, but true bravery comes only with experience." Yes, Alyosha—he calls me Alyosha—'I need more experience.'

"And I told him, 'General, you say? And he expects bravery greater than yours? Much I pity his enemies.' "

"Indeed," noted Strakhov, pouring him another drink. "Bulatovich is a fine soldier, as you are, too . . . Alyosha. And we want to know more about our fine soldiers. Come visit us often. We'll drink a little, talk a little. You'll tell us about yourself, about Bulatovich."

"Yes," added Kupferman, "ask Bulatovich about his women. I am very curious."

Butorin laughed, "Always I enjoy talking about women." He proposed a toast. "To women and to Mazeppy!"

"Mazeppy?" asked Kupferman. "What is this Mazeppy?"

"Bulatovich is Mazeppa. Starodubov names him 'Mazeppa,' " explained Butorin, pouring himself more vodka. "So men of Bulatovich are 'Mazeppy.' "

"Mazeppa? They call him Mazeppa?" asked Kupferman.

"The Battle of Poltava," interjected Strakhov. "Ukrainian and Swede against Peter the Great. Mazeppa was a traitor, a rebel, a Ukrainian nationalist."

"You don't have to explain, Major." Kupferman's voice was frosty. "Pushkin and Byron both wrote long poems about him. Mazeppa had a weakness for women. Like I said before, this man's a puzzle—why he's here, why he takes the risks he takes—and the answer is surely a woman."

Butorin watched warily, drinking with abandon the fine vodka they offered him, but weighing his words carefully before speaking them. He was no fool. He knew they were no friends of Bulatovich. But he could hold his liquor, and he saw no reason to pass up free drinks, so long as he kept his wits about him. "You make too much of this name," he said. "We like the sound, that's all. Besides, it's Starodubov's doing. And who can take Starodubov's names seriously? He calls a spendthrift 'Jew' and a celibate 'Father.' "

"But there's got to be a reason," insisted Kupferman, "a reason for the name, a reason for his unnatural bravery. And I believe that some scandal regarding a woman is at the bottom of it."

"Ah, no, sir," suggested Butorin cautiously. "Women he may have and trouble, too. But that's no answer to his fearlessness in battle."

"Then what is the answer?" asked Kupferman.

"It's witchcraft," answered Butorin, taking a long slow swallow and savoring the surprise on their faces. "Some deviltry he picked up in Africa."

"Witchcraft?" asked Kupferman in disbelief.

"At first I thought he was crazy, the risks he takes," explained Butorin, almost convincing himself as he spun his tale. "But it's not natural, I tell you. Any ordinary man would be dead ten times over. Bullets turn around in midair to miss him. I've seen it with my own eyes. That's not bravery—that's witchcraft."

☗ ☗ ☗

Meanwhile the other Mazeppy sat by a nearby campfire. A new set of scouts had just returned from the mountain, where they had been unable to find any trace of Login or the men who had gone with him to stand lookout. Butorin, who had stood guard at a listening post in that vicinity, might have some clue as to their fate or whereabouts, but no one, aside from Strakhov and Kupferman, had had a chance to talk to him since he arrived.

"Hey, Jew!" Sofronov shouted, to break the tension.

Shemelin jumped to his feet, fists clenched.

Everyone but Shemelin broke out laughing. Baiting Shemelin had quickly become a standing joke among them. This time it took their minds off Login and the other two scouts who had been stranded up on the mountain. Too quickly, the laughter died down. Shemelin stood there a moment longer, rather pointlessly. Everyone was staring through the dark toward the mountain.

Just then, Butorin finally emerged from the tarantass, a broad grin on his long roguish face.

"Where is my brother?" asked Pyotr anxiously.

"What happened out there?" asked Bulatovich.

"How did you get away alive?" asked Starodubov.

Butorin strode dramatically to the campfire. The fire's light cast shifting upward shadows, giving his features a hellish look. Everyone stared at him expectantly. He chuckled inwardly at the effect his silence had on the crowd. Then he launched into his tale.

"I was standing lookout near the foot of the mountain. Hundreds of Chinese must have slipped by, without me seeing them or them seeing me, when the night was at its darkest, before the moon rose. They must have been getting ready for their surprise attack on you back here at Hailar. I heard them before I saw them, jabbering away in whispers. I couldn't make out the words, but I could tell they were all around me. I dropped to my belly and crawled, as quietly as I could, to a nearby ditch. When I reached the ditch, there was a group of them not more than ten paces away. Slowly and quietly, I burrowed my way into the ditch, scraping away sand and soft dirt at the bottom to make it deeper. The moon was due to rise any minute. I covered myself with whatever I could lay my hands on quickly—straw, sand, and, I was lucky, there was some fresh horse manure right there; I used that too.

"You laugh? You think I'm some sort of fool? Well, think again. Who would look closely at a pile of horse manure? I couldn't have hoped for better camouflage.

"I lay there motionless, through the chills of night. At dawn I heard shots in the distance, hundreds of them, but I didn't dare move. The Chinese had set up a campsite not more than twenty paces from where I lay.

"All day, through the scalding midday sun, I lay there, without food, without water. And I was close enough to hear their every word, to hear the water they spilt carelessly on the ground, to hear the food sizzling over the campfire.

"Once a horse nudged me. I thought that any moment he'd be trampling my back. But I was lucky. The horse just dumped some fresh manure on my back and trotted off.

"That night it got cold again. I couldn't hear any voices, couldn't hear the crackle of the campfire anymore. I was crazy with hunger and thirst, so I dared to raise my eyes. The ashes of the campfire still glowed, but there was no sign of the Chinese. I raised my head farther and spotted in the distance the grove and the temple on the hilltop outlined in the moonlight. I crawled toward it, figuring that was the direction where you would be, if you were still alive.

"I spotted a Chinese sentry, crawled away to avoid him, and came upon another, and another. I figured I must be inside a chain of sentry posts. My strength was giving out. I had no choice but to kill one of them, quietly, and make a run for it. I took out my knife and crept slowly, making no more noise than the breeze blowing that night. After half an hour, I was halfway to him; then I slowed still more, stopping often. Finally, when I was within three paces and could not risk getting any nearer, I jumped. With one hand I covered his mouth and with the other I drove the knife into his throat from behind, being sure to avoid the heavy knots of his pigtail. Quickly, I drove the blade clear round, cutting the windpipe. When his head ripped off in my hands, I knew he couldn't scream.

"Then I crept, crawled, staggered to my feet, half running, half falling, losing all sense of direction. It was then that I saw Login."

Pyotr jumped. "You saw my brother?"

Butorin restrained a laugh. He hadn't had this much attention in years, and he loved attention. He had invented that detail for effect and now wanted to play it for all it was worth.

"Don't just sit there!" shouted Pyotr. "You said you saw my brother. Where? Where is he?"

"There," Butorin pointed, and everyone looked in that direction as if they expected to see him appear at any moment.

"Where?" asked Pyotr, exasperated.

"There. There I tell you. In the moon."

"What?"

"Maybe it was having held that head in my hands that did it. That and the full moon. The moon was just behind the hill with the grove and the temple, where I was heading. And suddenly the moon had the face of Login. I swear it. I saw Login's head floating there in the sky, his severed head. The eyes were open wide, like they had no eyelids. And the mouth seemed about to open. But I didn't wait to hear what he might say. I just ran in the other direction, until I stumbled on Orlov and his troops."

"If that's a joke," said Sofronov, "it's in very bad taste."

No one else said a word. They just sat, staring at the fire or the moon or at their own feet and hands, as quiet as they had been on their way back from Urdingi, when Aksyonov was dying and screaming.

Bulatovich remembered something Molchanov had told him. "It's what people want to believe that they believe, and what they believe governs what they do. They'd rather believe in ghosts and supernatural powers than in the finality of death."

※ ※ ※

The first light of dawn revealed dozens of large gray eagles, soaring around and around the grove and the nearby temple. General Orlov was in a jubilant mood. The Chinese army had withdrawn during the night. The detachment celebrated and prepared to move to more comfortable quarters in the city—all except the Mazeppy, who moved about listlessly, staring now and again at the eagles.

The bodies of men and horses had all been quickly buried the day before, to avoid the rotting stench they had had to put up with at Ongun.

There had been no fighting in the grove. The Chinese apparently had avoided it out of religious respect. But the scavenger birds spoke of death.

Finally, Bulatovich ordered, "Starodubov, Shemelin, Butorin, come quickly. It's probably just the carcass of a horse."

As they got close, their horses became restless, perhaps sensing their riders' concern, perhaps sensing something their riders could not yet see.

The temple was empty.

Butorin walked boldly ahead. He was proud of the story he had told, proud of the superstitious fears he seemed to have aroused in his comrades. He was so proud of himself that he nearly tripped.

A pair of binoculars, lenses smashed, lay in the middle of the path. He bent down to pick them up and saw three headless bodies—Russian soldiers without heads. He fell to his knees laughing hysterically.

The heads were nowhere in sight.

🏛 🏛 🏛

The Mazeppy held a special funeral that night. Bulatovich had agreed that everything should be in accord with the wishes of Login's brothers. They wanted cremation, not burial for their brother, harking back to the early days of the Old Believers, in the seventeenth century. Back then, believing the changes in ritual that were being forced on them by the Church hierarchy and the State were the work of the Anti-Christ and that the end of the world was at hand, tens of thousands of them had burned themselves to death, gathering in their local churches and setting fire to the buildings, chanting psalms and prayers and passages from Revelation as the flames closed in on them.

" 'Then I saw thrones, and seated on them were those to whom judgment was committed,' " intoned Trofim, reciting with authority the few passages he knew from Revelation.

Several campfires cast conflicting shadows across the Mazeppy, across the sandy hilltop, across the headless corpses, across Trofim himself—arms outstretched, beard thrust forward, reciting the story of the Apocalypse like a prophet intoning the dread words for the first time. The full moon hung fire-orange on the horizon.

" 'Also, I saw the souls of those who had been beheaded . . .' " Trofim continued staring wildly at Butorin.

Butorin stared back, startled that the precise words of the Bible so matched the present situation. An eerie coincidence.

Trofim changed his voice to distinguish his own improvisations from the exact words of Revelation, to avoid any confusion that might make him subject to the curse called down upon anyone who should alter or add to the words of that Holy Writ. "Praise be to the Lord our God, who gives us signs of the End," he improvised. "Praise to the Lord, the giver of dreams that speak Truth, who makes prophets even of liars to confuse the godless. For the Lord God is with us and in us and verily all things, even suffering and death, come from the Lord.

"I saw the souls of those who had been beheaded," Trofim quoted again, "for their testimony to Jesus and for the word of God and who had not worshiped the beast or its image and had not received its mark on their foreheads or their hands.

"Praise to your martyred brother!" he improvised again. "He died in a holy cause, fighting heathen who slaughter innocent Christians and missionaries. Praise to him, for it is written that such as he—beheaded in a holy war for Christ—will come to life and reign with Christ a thousand years.

"The rest of the dead will not come to life until the thousand years are ended," he continued in his somber quotation voice. "This is the first resurrection. Blessed and holy is he who shares in the first resurrection! Over such the second death has no power, but they shall be priests of God and of Christ, and they shall reign with him a thousand years." Trofim fell silent, as if in a trance.

Starodubov stood close to Pyotr and watched him carefully, looking for some sign of emotion. The young boy stood stock still, the little wisps of would-be beard reflecting in the firelight. He had asked no questions and shed no tears. Only a deep furrow was forming over his left brow. "Do you share your brother Trofim's beliefs?" asked Starodubov softly.

"God didn't do this," muttered Pyotr. "I pray to God that God did not do this. How could I revenge my brother's death if God did it?"

"But what would vengeance prove?" asked Starodubov.

"An eye for an eye, a head for a head—only I'll pay them back ten times over; for Login was ten times better than any of them." Pyotr kicked the sand. It scattered and sizzled across a campfire.

Starodubov would have liked to have grabbed the boy and spanked some sense into him—make him mad at him rather than mad at the world. That's what he had done with his second son when the first had died. The son had fought back, and they had had a bruising tussle, and afterward they got drunk together.

He might have started such a fight even now; but Sofronov drew near, solemnly expressing his condolences to Pyotr and adding softly but in all seriousness, with a priestly tone that outdid even Trofim's solemnity, "Pan-Mongolism! That's the word for it. The End is coming and coming from the East. In this very land the Anti-Christ, the true Anti-Christ will appear. And soon, perhaps even now. And all true believers must join together—Orthodox and Old Believer, Catholic and Protestant, even the Jews. All must join together to fight the Anti-Christ in these the Final Days."

In the silence, Sofronov's softly spoken words carried. Not just Pyotr and Starodubov, but also all the Mazeppy turned to him. Sofronov, apparently recognizing that he had an audience, raised his arms and raised his voice. "Pan-Mongolism! The modern prophet Solovyov coined the word. 'Pan-Mongolism!' he said. 'Although the name is wild, I find some consolation in the sound, a mystical premonition of the glorious providence of God.' Kill these Mongolian hordes. It's the will of God, I tell you. In the name of God we should kill the beasts who have done this outrage!"

He fell silent, and silence reigned for a moment, until Pyotr whispered, "Revenge!" And others repeated aloud "Revenge!" and Trofim picked it up as if it were part of a litany, "Revenge! And again I say, revenge!" And the Mazeppy, even Bulatovich, caught by the spell of the moment, echoed, "Revenge!"

Trofim grabbed a burning log from the fire and cast it at his brother's corpse. Fire leaped up from all sides, enveloping the body, rising high into the night.

"May his soul be released now to heaven," intoned Trofim. "Praise be to the Lord!"

It had been arranged beforehand—the kindling carefully stacked around Login's body. (The other two would be buried.) But the ceremony had been so long, and then the sudden gesture, the sudden flame came as a shock. None but Trofim and Pyotr had ever witnessed the burning of a human body.

Butorin started shaking uncontrollably. It finally dawned on him that for him, at least, this funeral wasn't an end, but a beginning. He had always mocked the superstitions of others, but he had some of his own as well; and he had just discovered a new one. Planting a body in the ground seemed final—let it rot and be forgotten. But fire was another matter. Watching the flames, he thought he saw the spirit being released from the body to wander and to haunt. Even now, as in the lie he had so glibly told, the moon seemed to take on the shape of Login's missing head.

At dawn, Trofim gathered the ashes and cast them to the wind, down by the river. And the Mazeppy dispersed—all but Pyotr and Laperdin.

Pyotr stood and stared at the rising sun and the clouds that kept covering it and uncovering it, until his eyes hurt. He wanted to be alone. He thought he was alone. Then he noticed the reflection of Laperdin's glasses and saw him standing nearby, with a cynical smile, showing his bright white teeth.

"Do you really believe in the resurrection of the dead?" Laperdin chuckled.

Not only the words, but also the fact he spoke at all came as a shock to Pyotr. They had never spoken to one another before. Laperdin was usually withdrawn, and Pyotr shy and reluctant to speak unless spoken to.

"If you really believe in the resurrection," Laperdin continued mockingly, "then why all this talk of revenge? Why should you be so angry if your brother will come to life and reign with Christ for a thousand years? You should be happy, if that's what you believe. You should thank the men who made a martyr of him and thank them again for lopping off his head and making him one of the specially chosen."

"Godless wretch," muttered Pyotr, both angry and bewildered at having his basic beliefs questioned and challenged at a time like this.

"I suppose you still think you believe in God," persisted Laperdin. "A common ailment. So often we think we believe long after we've stopped believing. Or does anyone ever believe? Or is it a matter of wanting to believe or not wanting to believe?"

"Get out of here, you bastard," muttered Pyotr, turning away.

"Maybe you do believe in God. Maybe you are that naive, accepting things on little or no evidence."

"Faith it's called, you heathen," Pyotr answered without looking. He should have simply walked away from this nuisance, but despite himself, he felt the need to have the last word, as if what this educated cynic said and believed made some difference.

"Faith. Yes, faith. I have faith in death and suffering, those I've seen. God I have not. Either God doesn't exist, or He's irrelevant, or He's malevolent."

"Why spew your venom at me? Leave me in peace, I pray you."

"I prayed, too. I prayed for peace and for joy and for happiness, when I wasn't much older than you. I prayed for the well-being of those I loved. . . ."

Pyotr turned back to look at him. The sun was behind the clouds again, and Laperdin's dark eyes were clearly visible through the lenses of his glasses. There was no hint of mockery now.

"Yes, I prayed," he continued, "until I learned better, until I learned that the only way to survive in this world, the only way to remain sane is to stop yourself from loving, stop yourself from caring, stop yourself from hoping and praying that the impossible will happen. The dead are dead, and that's the end of it."

Pyotr put his hands to his head and shouted, "Why me? Why can't you leave me alone?"

"Curiosity, I suppose," smiled Laperdin. "Perhaps a touch of sympathy, too. I'm not entirely devoid of it. Maybe you remind me of myself ten or fifteen years ago. So vulnerable. So wide open to all the injustice of life, of chance. I just wanted to give you a little advice—seal up that heart of yours before the world rips it to shreds.

"You cover your ears. You don't dare to listen to me, but you don't run away either. You should know better than to show such weakness. It just lures the wolves closer. So I'll tell you a little story to give you an idea of who I am, so you'll know that I know what I'm talking about.

"I come from Kiev. For a price, the Cossacks let me settle in Trans-Baikal with no questions asked. I've been here maybe ten years now.

"I was a medical student, the pride of my parents, until I met Natalya. They had nothing against her personally, and nothing against her family either. Her father and my father were both businessmen. We were a little better off, but not that much. My parents just didn't want me to marry so soon, they said. They wanted me to finish my studies first. And they let it be known that they hoped that once I was a doctor, I'd be in a position to make a more fashionable match—someone from a family that could provide a richer dowry and better social contacts.

"We were both young and impulsive. We ran off to Kharkov and lived together. We said we were man and wife, but our love was our only bond, that and our poverty; for breaking off all contact with our families and friends, the only work I could get was in a factory. If I had let on that I was educated, sooner or later it would have come out who we were and that we were living together illegally. No one pays much attention to the poor and illiterate. We wanted it that way—just the two of us, in our pathetic little freedom.

"We had a child, a beautiful baby girl—'Natalya' we called her, the image of her mother—the jet-black hair, so much for such a tiny baby, and the green eyes—I'm sure they would have stayed green.

"One day the baby died. The mother went hysterical. Her parents, who had been looking for her, were scandalized to find her living in sin—the shame of it, what people would say seemed to bother them more than the death of the child. They took her away.

"Since I wasn't married to her, I had no rights. They wouldn't tell me where they had sent her, but I found her months later, in an insane asylum. Outside of the immediate family, no visitors were allowed. So I got a job as an orderly.

"She didn't recognize me. She just sat there, hour after hour, knitting baby clothes.

"She had been knitting baby clothes back then when someone had knocked at the door. She had left the room for a moment, and when she came back, the baby wasn't breathing—simply struck dead, without cause, without reason.

"Now she wouldn't leave her chair, she wouldn't leave her

knitting without an hysterical fight—they were trying to kill her baby.

"As an orderly, it was my job to force-feed her as she sat there and to clean up her messes and get her out of that chair into her bed and strap her there each night. She would curse me when she saw me coming, calling me 'murderer,' 'baby killer,' and she'd claw at me and bite me as I dragged her to the bed."

"Why did you stay?" asked Pyotr.

"I don't know."

"Why did you leave?" asked Pyotr.

"She died."

"Oh."

"I killed her with my own hands."

Pyotr stared, repelled, yet fascinated by this strange man and his wild tale. Despite himself, he felt an impulse to befriend this man, but held back, as he had held back in the case of Aksyonov.

Login had always said, "Pick your friends carefully—that's one way to control your destiny." And he had said, "Pick your friends carefully or one day you may hate the person you become."

But a man needed friends. Login had been a friend as well as a brother. Now Pyotr had no friends, just acquaintances.

There was something compelling about this educated man with his cynical talk and his sentimental past. It was flattering to have been singled out by him both for the confession and even for the provocative questioning that had come before.

Pyotr had always lived in his brother's shadow. Even the one time when Pyotr had tried to break free of the family and had joined the army for the excitement of battle, Login had joined too, just to watch over him and protect him. And despite himself, Pyotr had welcomed his brother's support and friendship.

Trofim was another matter, caught up in himself and his notions of religion. Pyotr and he were no closer than acquaintances from the same village.

Login's death left a gap, and now here was this Laperdin, singling him out to give him advice.

How could he pick and choose who would influence him? It wasn't by choice that he was assigned to this particular troop, that he had met men like Bulatovich and Starodubov and now this Laperdin.

Where was the choice? Where was the freedom? Whom could he ask now that Login was gone? What would become of him now that, despite himself, he was one of the Mazeppy?

CROSS-PURPOSES

9

Hailar, Manchuria, August 5, 1900

At Login's funeral, when the flames suddenly consumed the headless body, Shemelin took off his hat, bowed his head respectfully, and shivered, despite the heat of the fire. "Ashes," he thought, "ashes to ashes." And he remembered the vase he had accidentally broken at the shrine. Did it contain ashes? What was a man when he was reduced to ashes? Where did the spirit go? Where were the spirits of all those ancestors in ashes? Can you stuff a spirit into a vase? What size vase would it take to hold his own spirit? Question after question with no answers. He was a simple peasant. How was he expected to have answers? Who could blame him for his ignorance? Who could blame him for disrespect for the dead when he had no idea what remained of the dead after death?

He should have slept. He was exhausted. But the wound over his left eye itched and sometimes ached, and besides, he needed to talk to Bulatovich about ancestors. After that ride to Urdingi, Shemelin was convinced that Bulatovich knew everything.

Shemelin found Bulatovich sitting outside his odd little tent, awkwardly struggling to pull off his boots. His red regimental cap was crumpled in the dust beside him.

Shemelin stared first at the tent, with all its pockets and contrivances, then at Bulatovich, who looked so small and vulnerable sitting there. It was hard for Shemelin to think of Bulatovich as the mere clumsy mortal that he appeared to be in such a setting.

"Don't just stand there," snapped Bulatovich. "Give me a hand."

Shemelin got down and, after some struggle, managed to pry the boots off. The legs and feet were badly swollen from long hours of standing.

"Well, what do you want?" Bulatovich snapped again, wearily.

"I've been thinking, sir," Shemelin started slowly.

"And what have you been thinking?"

"Sir, have you ever wondered who your father really is?" When Bulatovich didn't answer right away, Shemelin continued "Often I have wondered. I look at Mother scrubbing clothes like her mother and like her mother's mother. I look at Father plowing another man's fields and reaping another man's harvest, year after year. And I ask 'How can anything new come from these people? Even with a name that's not like my father's name, or his father's, or his father's father's name, even with a name like Yakov, how can I be but what my father is?' And people look at me and say 'You have your mother's nose, your father's eyes . . .' But I don't smell with my mother's nose. I don't see with my father's eyes. The village isn't home to me. The plow feels strange to my touch. But can this be if Father is my father and Mother is my mother? Elm does not grow from acorn. Who can say? Maybe I am a Jewish bastard. Sometimes I wish I were a Jewish bastard. Then I'd be a strange new mixture, with a strange new future, not just the plower of another man's fields."

He felt he had expressed himself clearly. He was proud of his turn of phrase. But Bulatovich answered angrily, wearily, irrelevantly, "Why didn't you follow the main road like I told you?"

"But . . . you didn't . . . sir . . ."

"Well, why should I have to tell you every step? Anyone with a little common sense would have realized that troops might already be on their way. All you had to do was follow the main road, and you would have met the cavalry and warned them. As it was, they rode into an ambush."

"I'm sorry, sir . . ."

"Sorry, we're all sorry. I'm sorry. I'm tired. Just get out of here and let me sleep."

Shemelin wandered off through the camp in the half light of a cloudy dawn. He wanted to be alone, but there were people all about—cleaning their weapons, drinking and singing, tending to their horses. Why couldn't anyone sleep? Not watching where he was going, Shemelin tripped on the ashes of a campfire, regained his balance, and nearly bumped against a young soldier—no older than sixteen—brushing his horse.

"You fool!" shouted Shemelin. "Can't you see that that horse has scratches and cuts all up and down his side? Take him to the vet and have him taken care of. Don't just brush him. You're torturing the poor beast."

The boy dropped the brush and stood there staring after Shemelin, who continued on his way, muttering over and over, "If you just had some common sense . . . a fine way to treat a horse."

Shemelin was just beginning to wonder why he was saying those things, whether he was talking about someone else or himself, when a little beggar boy, no more than six or seven years old, tugged at his pant leg. White but slant-eyed, the boy was of mixed ancestry, Shemelin quickly guessed. Probably the casual offspring of some Russian railway worker. Maybe the result of a rape. Shemelin shook him off and continued on his aimless way. The child followed, but Shemelin ignored him.

An officer came riding by. The boy tugged at his pant leg. The officer kicked him aside and rode off.

Shemelin watched, silently, as the boy picked himself up, blood pouring from his forehead, and ran off without a whimper. For a moment, Shemelin considered following him, offering to help. He thought better of it, took a step or two in the opposite direction, then changed his mind again—but the boy was gone, and there was no way he could wipe away the guilt. He kept seeing that young boy's bloody face everywhere. But the boy himself he couldn't find. Maybe he had never seen him at all. Maybe it was just a dream. He hoped so. He prayed so.

He returned to his tent, poured himself a cup of water, then another; but instead of drinking the second cup, he sat there staring at his reflection. The scar over his left eye was pulling

163

the skin tight and giving it a slant-eyed Asian look, like the young boy.

He threw the cup on the ground. The water splashed on the little book Bulatovich had let him keep—*The Way of the Pilgrim.* Quickly, he picked up the book, brushed it off. The damage was slight.

He heard footsteps, looked up, and nearly bumped noses with Sofronov. This was either an extraordinary night or an extraordinary dream. "Ah, Yakov," Sofronov began. "I'm glad that I found you." And he proceeded to crawl into Shemelin's tent, uninvited, making himself comfortable like an old friend. Shemelin stared in disbelief. Before now Sofronov had never said a civil word to him.

"I wanted to apologize," Sofronov continued. "You see, I was only joking those times when I called you 'Jew' and jeered at you. We were all joking, really. You know as well as I that things are a bit lax out in Trans-Baikal. Nowhere else would Cossacks allow Jews to settle on their territory, but in Trans-Baikal they do, openly, for a price—over five hundred Jews, I've heard, and probably hundreds more who keep their religion a secret officially, and, for a price, no one asks. Yes, we in Trans-Baikal are open-minded about these things. We don't go chasing down the Jews and beating them up every time the crops fail or something else goes wrong, like they do back in the Ukraine and Poland and such. When we called you 'Jew,' it was all in fun. I don't believe any of us are really anti-Semitic."

"Anti-Semitic?" Shemelin had never heard the word before.

"After all, you know, there's no philosophic ground for anti-Semitism. In fact, I have great respect for your people and your beliefs."

"My people?"

"Yes, the Hebrew people. Your belief in one God, your expectation of the Messiah, your interpretation of history as the revelation of God's will. It occurred to me at Login's funeral. I don't approve of cremation, do you? I never knew that there were sects of Old Believers who did such things. In some higher philosophic sense, perhaps they're right. But I must admit I find the burning of human flesh repulsive. And I had to speak to you."

"About the burning?"

"No, about your religion and your people. Trofim's words reminded me of the noble role the Hebrew people will play in the final battle with the Anti-Christ. So I wanted to apologize for making fun of your noble ancestry and beliefs."

"But I am a Christian."

"Marvelous. Was it your father who converted?"

"My father didn't convert."

"Then you, you, Yakov, saw the light." Sofronov was delighted, almost as if he had performed the miraculous conversion himself.

"But I am not a Jew!" protested Shemelin.

"Of course not," Sofronov readily agreed. "In the eyes of God and even in the eyes of the law, once you have converted you are a Christian and not a Jew, and none of the legal restrictions against Jews apply to you, even back in European Russia. Why, you could live outside the Pale of Settlement; you could buy farmland; you could get an education without worrying about the quota on Jews."

"I never was a Jew!"

"The Lord be praised—you have been reborn in Christ."

Shemelin stared in amazement as Sofronov sank deep in prayer, then emerged and asked "Was there a priest in your village?"

"No," replied Shemelin. "Our village is small. But I learned to read. Few in our village can read, but I have read the Bible."

"My God!" exclaimed Sofronov, in all seriousness. "A natural—you read the Bible and the Bible itself converted you—the Word of God without the intermediary of human interpreters. How beautiful and yet how dangerous. It's so easy to misinterpret, to misconstrue God's Truth, to fall into the sin of heresy. But then again, you have a pure Russian soul—Hebrew blood, but a Russian soul, the simple soul of the Russian peasant. Far be it from me to tell you how to interpret God's Word. My mind's so filled with philosophies and heresies, I've been so trained in sophisticated argument, I'm lost in a maze of logic. I'd give anything to achieve the pure, simple faith of the Russian peasant. That's the meaning of that book, you know."

"The Bible?"

"No, that little book you have in your hand, the one I picked out for you, thinking it might help convert you."

"How many times do I have to tell you? I don't need converting. I never needed converting."

"Indeed. Such fervor. So natural. I envy you that naive faith."

"Will you stop listening to yourself and start listening to
me? Who are you?"

"What do you mean?"

"I mean what I say. But you, I have no idea what you say or
what you mean or who you are." Suddenly Shemelin struck
Sofronov on the shoulder.

"What?" asked Sofronov, falling over.

Shemelin quickly helped him back to his sitting position.
"Then you really are there. I had to be sure. I can't believe my
eyes or my ears anymore, but maybe I can trust my hands."

"Are you mad?"

"I don't know. I've been acting strangely and seeing strange
things."

"What things?"

"A beggar boy struck by an officer."

"Not so strange."

"But the boy vanished."

"What do you mean?"

"I saw it. An officer—he looked familiar, but I don't know
his name—kicked a beggar boy in the face and rode off. The boy's
face was bloody. He looked at me. He was asking for help. I turned
away, then changed my mind, turned back, but he was gone. He
had vanished. Or maybe it was a dream."

"What do you feel about this boy?"

"Regret. I should have helped."

"Then it doesn't matter if the boy was real or a vision. He
served a purpose in the spiritual history of your life. He awakened
your awareness of your obligations to your fellow man."

"But he could be out there now—bleeding, cold, hungry."

"How beautiful."

"Beautiful?"

"Your pity—so natural, so Russian. That a Jew could so make
himself a simple Russian Christian, by an act of will."

"I am not a Jew!" yelled Shemelin, throwing the little book
at Sofronov, who ducked, caught the book, and nearly lost his
balance again.

"Certainly, certainly," said Sofronov. "But you need not worry about the boy. He may be suffering, but the suffering is not a punishment from God."

"I should hope not."

"God, the Christian God, the Orthodox God does not take an eye for an eye and a tooth for a tooth."

"Then why does he let such children suffer?"

"It is a test," answered Sofronov.

"A test?"

"Yes. We are here on earth to be tested by God. The hardest tests of suffering force us to use our inner resources of strength, or so I've heard. If we were never put to the test, we would never know what we are capable of, and we could never achieve saintliness."

"What does 'saintliness' have to do with it? He was a mere boy. He never asked to become a saint. Why do you make him suffer?"

"But I didn't make him suffer. You did. You turned your back on him."

Shemelin stared for a moment. His eyes went out of focus as he let the words sink in. Then he quickly turned, crawled out of his tent, and started running wildly, looking again for the boy.

⚜ ⚜ ⚜

"What audacity!" Kupferman said aloud as he awoke. He had had the strangest dream—that he was riding through camp, and a dog, some mongrel, had jumped up and bit his pant leg. He kicked it in the head, and the head became that of a young boy. "Probably a beggar, probably deserved it," he told himself in his dream. But some soldier saw him do it and looked at him, shocked, as if he had never seen violence and cruelty before.

How dare a soldier, a mere enlisted man, question his authority? The military depended on order and discipline. A military camp was no place for stray mongrels, beggar boys, and self-righteous young peasants who hadn't learned yet that the world is governed by violence, that order means violence, that a good beating is the best way to teach a boy or a dog good habits.

A wife was a different matter. He would never hit his wife,

167

any more than he would argue with her or take her opinions seriously. But his boys he had beaten often enough with switch and belt. So why shouldn't he kick a disorderly beggar boy who dared lay a hand on an officer?

Sleep. He needed sleep. He wished he could sleep.

It annoyed him having to be away from home so long. He missed his wife, his favorite chair, his quiet comfortable daily routine. He was a creature of habit, and he enjoyed his habits.

Twenty years earlier, Kupferman would have been delighted by an opportunity for combat. Then he was ambitious and sometimes even enthusiastic, like Strakhov was now.

But Kupferman had lingered at the rank of lieutenant colonel for too many years. He had been passed over for promotion far too many times. He had played the game of military politics as well as he could play it. He had risen as far as he could rise without better connections. He had no future in the army, and he knew it. He envied successful young men like Strakhov and Bulatovich, especially men like Bulatovich who had the connections it took to go far, if he just knew how to use them.

Kupferman was largely reconciled to his own relatively inferior fate. He had given up worrying over that years ago and was now concerned mostly about his present comfort and his future pension.

Domestic tranquillity was perhaps more important to him than anything else. He had come to that conclusion ten years earlier when he first discovered that his wife, Anna, was having an affair with one of his subordinates—a mere boy and she a mature woman. She and her lover were in the process of disrobing one another in the stable when he saw them. He didn't interrupt. He simply watched while they went about their business.

He never said a word about it, nor did she; but he sensed that she knew that he knew. After a year, when the young man was transferred to another post, and after a brief period of sullen fretting, she became quite warm toward him. He interpreted this warmth as her gratitude for his not having made a scene and disgraced her, or even killed her in a rage, as a typical, undisciplined husband might. She seemed grateful to him for having preserved their sacred domestic tranquillity.

He made a point of venting his frustrations on his subordinates rather than on his wife. Everyone has frustrations. Some people are orderly about the way they deal with them; others just thrash about irrationally. Such lack of self-control had ruined many a marriage, Kupferman felt; and he was determined that his marriage would not suffer that fate.

He treated Anna with utmost consideration. They lived in one of the finest houses in Kazan, near the theological academy. They entertained and were entertained by the most important officials and the wealthiest citizens of that provincial city.

Even when she acted ungrateful and irrational, he never criticized her. When, not long after their marriage, she grew listless and the house began to look disorderly, he hired additional servants without saying a word.

When they had their first child, Anna insisted that she would nurse the child herself. But when it became clear to him that she wasn't equal to the task, that the strain of trying to feed the child, her sore breasts, and the child's interminable crying were disturbing their precious domestic tranquillity, he immediately, without saying a word, hired a wet nurse. He was sure Anna must be grateful to be relieved of such a burden. She cried for a few days, but it meant nothing. She stayed in bed for weeks, but she needed the rest.

He never argued with her. Whatever she said, however foolish, he smiled and agreed. He never discussed anything controversial with her. He never involved her in any decisionmaking. Why should she trouble herself with the complexities of household finance? He gave her a substantial allowance, so she could buy whatever frivolities she cared to. The housekeeper saw to all the necessities.

After her brief spurt of exceptional tenderness and warmth, she had grown listless again. But he didn't say a word. And when she began to put on weight and lose the youthful figure she had tried hard and long to preserve, when she didn't seem to care what she looked like anymore, even in public, that didn't bother him either. Their marriage was firm and strong. He reasoned that now she no longer felt the need to be attractive to other men.

For him, that was one of the happiest periods of his married life. She was so comfortable and predictable. She had become so accustomed to his habits, and she had become so much a creature of habit herself that she took care of little obstacles and annoyances for him automatically, almost before he became aware of them.

Both of their sons (he had hoped to have more but had never expressed his disappointment to Anna) were away at school now. They were relatively well behaved, for children. Someday they would probably be a credit to the family name. But it was so nice when they were away, and the house was quiet. He could imagine Anna now, sitting by the fire, reading as she did every night, and occasionally glancing at his well-worn chair. He longed to sit in that chair.

He had tried to bring along to Manchuria as much familiar furniture as he could, stuffing it all into his tarantass. Why should he, a regimental commander, sleep in a tent? He had even brought along the mattress from his bed at home. He wondered how Anna liked the new one. She still occasionally liked something new. She had been quite unpredictable at first, forever moving furniture about, buying a new this or a new that, always excited about the newness of things, before he had quietly calmed her down.

On duty as well as at home, Kupferman preferred the comfort of the familiar. He liked to see the same orderlies, the same clerks, the same subordinates day after day. The men in his command were promoted only rarely. Mostly, he promoted the men he wanted to get rid of—like his wife's lover.

The young man had looked so shocked each time he got an undeserved promotion or letter of commendation. And when he was suddenly transferred to a promising post a thousand miles away, his head was so swelled from all his rapid advancement that he probably actually believed that he deserved it, that he had a brilliant career ahead of himself in the army. Why should he hang about this desolate garrison town romancing a middle-aged woman of fading charms? Rapid success had transformed a quiet, retiring, sensitive young man, who didn't know what to do with his life and probably needed mothering, into an egotistical dandy who liked to lord it over his subordinates—so recently his equals—and who probably longed to demonstrate his sexual prowess to a new set of ladies, far from the watchful eyes of his present mistress.

Kupferman was quite proud of himself for having arranged things so neatly and quietly and kindly. No one could fault him for his actions. But the young man was most certainly ruined by now, the victim of his own weakness, suffering the just punishment for his sins.

People were so weak-willed, so easily tempted and corrupted, especially young people and disorderly people, people who hadn't properly cultivated habits, people whose habits had developed by chance or who had very few habits. Kupferman's father had been such a disorderly man. A businessman of sorts, he had fled his native East Prussia to escape his creditors, and then had moved time and again in Russia, always promising more than he could deliver, always moving eastward, just beyond the reach of his creditors. His father had lied so often and so flagrantly that no one, not even he himself, had known when he was telling the truth. Kupferman always wondered what his true surname was. Heaven forbid, his father might even have been a Jew.

"Ah, but he could make you love him with that tongue of his," Kupferman's mother had told him, remembering with no bitterness. "I never knew how many names or how many wives he had had, nor did I care. He made me feel like I was at the center of the world, that I mattered to him and that that was all that mattered in the world. I'd have done anything for him, and I did—running off with him. If only he hadn't been so prone to drunkenness, he wouldn't have fallen under that coach; he'd be with us still today, spinning his tales of people and places, making them far more real than if you'd seen them yourself. The world's never seemed quite as real to me since he's been gone, since he can't tell me about it anymore."

Kupferman had built his life as the antithesis to his father's, helped considerably by his mother's family contacts and the money left to him by her father. Kupferman had shaped his own destiny by deliberately cultivating orderly habits.

He had chosen a secure profession, had married Anna when he was in his midforties and she in her midthirties—a quiet dependable woman, attractive but past the peak of her youthful beauty, a docile girl who had taken care of an invalid aunt while her less attractive sisters flirted and married. He was proud of his choice of a wife and of the respectful way he treated her, proud of the stable household in which he had raised his sons, proud of how docile and predictable they were.

He now looked forward to a quiet and comfortable retirement and looked forward to the day when he would be surrounded by grateful, obedient, and admiring grandchildren.

But here he was in Manchuria, far from wife and children, plagued with fleas, diarrhea, insomnia, dreams. "What audacity!" he repeated, suddenly remembering his dream of the dog or the beggar boy and that insolent soldier with his accusing look. It was only a dream, of course, but he was as upset as if it had actually happened.

"Where are my boots?" he yelled.

"Here, sir," replied Iosef, his orderly.

"And what are you doing with them?"

"Cleaning them, sir, as you ordered."

"But you cleaned them last night. Why clean them again?"

"But you were riding, sir. You just got back an hour ago. Remember? You couldn't sleep. And when you got back, you threw me your boots and told me to clean them. There was blood all over one of them. A nasty stain to get out."

"Liar!" bellowed Kupferman, leaping from the tarantass and kicking Iosef to the ground.

Iosef didn't resist. He knew his master's temper. It would pass. All things pass.

Kupferman quickly undid his belt and started beating Iosef as he had many times before. "You liar. You thief. You Jew. Why do I keep a Jew as an orderly? I should know better. I give you a chance. And what do you do? You lie to me. For all I know you wear my boots and my coat and ride through camp kicking beggar boys. You Jew. You dirty thieving Jew."

His anger had nearly run its course when he saw a vision. It seemed like part of his dream come back to haunt him—that same peasant soldier was staring at him in outraged innocence. Kupferman hit again and again, far harder than he had ever hit Iosef before. Iosef crumpled and squirmed with each blow.

Shemelin stood staring. It was like the dream—no, he had actually seen it. It had actually happened. He was almost sure that this same officer had kicked the beggar boy, and here he was kicking someone else, someone he called "Jew."

For five heavy blows Shemelin stood there as if paralyzed—repulsed, feeling he shouldn't interfere with an officer, wanting to turn away and forget it, but also wanting to grab away the belt and beat the officer.

Then Sofronov spotted him and caught up with him. "I want to apologize again, Yakov," he said, clearly upset, trying to make up for the hasty words that had sent Shemelin off so abruptly. "I expressed myself poorly. I wanted to explain the great Christian doctrine of self-sacrifice and suffering."

Suddenly, Shemelin saw Christ on the Cross, suffering. (Christ was a Jew, wasn't he?) He felt a surge of strength, like he had felt on the way to Urdingi, only far stronger. He pushed Sofronov aside and strode defiantly up to Kupferman. Iosef looked up in surprise. Kupferman halted his next swing halfway, and grumbled menacingly.

"What do you want, soldier?"

Shemelin stared him in the eye and said loudly and firmly, "I am a Jew, Jew by birth. If you must beat a Jew, beat me."

۞ ۞ ۞

An hour later, Starodubov woke Bulatovich in his tent.

"Sir," he repeated, "his back is just bruises and raw flesh."

"What?" asked Bulatovich, barely awake, automatically groping for his glasses among the shadows of his tent.

"Like I said, sir, Colonel Kupferman whipped him, whipped him himself."

"Whipped who?"

"Shemelin, sir."

"And why would he whip Shemelin?"

"Because he asked to be whipped."

"He *what*?"

"He says he was a Jew. He really believes he was a Jew; that if the Jews of this world must suffer for mankind, then he wanted to be a Jew; and now he has taken on the suffering of the world, he's a Christian, a true Christian. Sofronov explains it so well, but it makes no sense when I say it. I guess I use the wrong words."

Too tired to argue, Bulatovich pulled on his boots, leaving them untied. (His feet were still sore and swollen.) Then he followed Starodubov to the hospital tent.

Bulatovich was more shocked by the way his men were acting than by the ugly wounds on Shemelin's back. He had seen whip wounds before, but never before had he heard the word "Jew" pronounced with such respect, even reverence.

Sofronov tried to explain. "Physically, sir, I don't think he was ever a Jew. I mean, I don't think any of his ancestors were. At first, when he kept denying it so loudly, I thought he was. But now when he says he was, I don't. You see, sir, he made himself a Jew of his own free will. He saw a man suffering, a Jew, one of the downtrodden of the earth, and he wanted to take that suffering on himself, like Christ. Christ, before he became Christ, first had to be a Jew and suffer."

Bulatovich could make no sense out of Sofronov's words. He also couldn't understand why so many men had gathered outside the hospital tent, why they walked and talked so softly, and why they stared at Shemelin in silent awe.

Shemelin himself was a puzzle, too. "My body is weak, but my soul is strong," he said, and his eyes burned with enthusiasm, as if he had made some great discovery. "Remember, sir, on the way to Urdingi, we felt this surge of strength, like nothing could touch us. That's how I felt, anyway. We had been nearly dead, and then everything worked like magic—Starodubov grabbing the flag and standing there like that. Suddenly, we had this strength we'd never felt before, and it was in our muscles ready to do something, and you showed us the way, racing toward Urdingi. I felt something like that, sir. Great waves of restless energy. Then I saw Christ, or thought I saw him, and I knew what I must do. Every stroke of the whip just made me stronger.

"I feel I've been reborn, sir, as a Jew, and by taking on that man's suffering I became a true Christian. Jew by birth and Christian by religion," he added.

To Bulatovich the words were nonsense. He kept remembering Molchanov's words about people believing what they want to believe, but he couldn't understand why anyone would want to believe what Shemelin seemed to believe. And he could get no rational explanation for why Kupferman had whipped this man or why Shemelin held no grudge against Kupferman for having done it.

Bulatovich got the disquieting feeling, from the way Shemelin looked up at him in awe and thanked him without saying what for, that he was somehow responsible for this man's erratic behavior; maybe by something he had said inadvertently, when he was taking off his boots, exhausted after that long crazy funeral of Login's. Was everyone going crazy? He wondered why Kupferman would have so brutally beaten one of his men unless it were meant as an attack on him—a gross insult and a warning.

He had a rather low opinion of that overaged regimental commander who rode about the battlefield in a tarantass with feather pillows and mattress. Strakhov, too, he didn't trust since that meeting before the Battle of Ongun when they had argued about the Old Thief, Starodubov. Strakhov seemed too concerned about his own status and authority. He reacted as if he considered Bulatovich a threat of some kind. And Kupferman and Strakhov were close. All those officers brought in from Orenburg and Kazan were close, like back in Petersburg with officers from the same military academy. Envy, thought Bulatovich, remembering how his victories in the steeplechase and at fencing had aroused a certain hostility, how some of the other junior officers, insecurely grouped in closed cliques, had apparently seen his success as a threat to their own advancement.

He wondered what Kupferman and Strakhov would try next and how he should defend himself and his men. How dare they whip his men?

When he arrived at Orlov's tent, Strakhov was already there.

"Ah, Alexander Xavierevich!" Orlov greeted Bulatovich warmly. "We were just talking about you."

"Yes?" replied Bulatovich, angry but cautious, wanting to see the drift of things before having his say.

"I wanted to give you a squadron and send you out again to scout ahead. But Major Strakhov here was most helpful. He wanted to make sure that we didn't make a mistake of protocol that could leave a number of our other officers insulted, and we certainly wouldn't want that. You see, he pointed out that you're only a staff-rotmister and that the regular squadron commanders have the Cossack rank of esaul. They're at least your equals in rank, technically speaking; and it might be bad for morale if I give you a squadron and make one of them subordinate to you."

"Indeed," interjected Bulatovich, trying to assess the situation and work out a plan of defense. If Strakhov hadn't been there and if Orlov simply asked him "Do you want to take a squadron and scout ahead?" Bulatovich would simply have answered "I appreciate your confidence in me, Your Excellency. But my men and I need a rest. Why don't you send someone else instead. Perhaps Bodisko, or Strakhov, even. He knows his soldiering, even if he did learn most of it from books. He performs well under fire. After the way he took charge in that last battle, all the men respect him. And I believe he's anxious for more combat experience." But here was Strakhov actively trying to limit his command authority, trying to keep him out of combat. So Bulatovich offered, "I don't need a full squadron, Your Excellency. A troop will do fine—the men I know and who know me."

"The Mazeppy?" asked Orlov. "Yes, the name has spread. Everyone knows you now. Certainly, take the Mazeppy. But that's not enough. We have no idea what size force you might encounter. Better that you be prepared to put up a fight."

"But Your Excellency," interrupted Strakhov, "what about protocol and morale?"

"Yes, Major, you're quite right about protocol, but there are ways to get around such difficulties. Have you never heard of a 'flying detachment'? Alexander Xavierevich, pick any two hundred men and the best horses in the regiment. That will be your 'flying detachment'—a new and separate unit. The squadron commanders can continue to go about their business." With that, Orlov went walking off to talk to his adjutants about other matters.

For a few moments, Bulatovich and Strakhov stood there, alone and silent. Strakhov seemed to be staring at Bulatovich's untied shoes, at his slept-in uniform and his crumpled red cap. Bulatovich was trying to decide if he should say anything at all or leave matters where they stood. He had never gotten along with superiors who used discipline and protocol to hide their incompetence and protect their authority, officers who considered competent subordinates not as assets but as threats. Strakhov was his own age, apparently alert, active, intelligent, ambitious. Bulatovich wouldn't ordinarily have classed him with a superannuated, self-satisfied incompetent like Kupferman. But maybe this was Strakhov's way of trying to curry favor with a superior. Things were so much simpler in Ethiopia, where his status as a Russian military adviser was unique and beyond the realm of traditional protocol, or envy and competition.

Fortunately, here in Manchuria Orlov acted as a buffer. Another patrol—yes, he must keep on the move, away from this petty game of military politics.

Bulatovich turned to go.

"Are you satisfied?" asked Strakhov.

Bulatovich turned again and stared back. "That's a question I should ask you."

"What do you want? Rank? Glory? Do you have to make general like your father did? Or do you just want everyone to call you 'hero'?"

"And what do you have against me?"

"You nearly got me killed. Why didn't you send your second messenger by the main road?"

"Is that why you had him beaten?"

"I don't know what you're talking about."

"Kupferman himself whipped that man today."

"Nonsense. Why should a colonel dirty his hands in such a matter?"

"And why should you meddle in my assignments?"

"The general asked me for advice. I gave it."

Bulatovich turned again. He'd said enough, too much. Why drag it on and further aggravate this envious man?

But Strakhov added, "And stay away from that Chinese girl."

"What?"

"You know who I mean. The one your men found in the church. Sophiya or Sonya she calls herself. The convert."

"I've said no more than two words to her."

"Then leave it that way. Go off on your patrol and forget about her."

177

"Why should she be your concern?"

"She is. Believe me. Leave it at that."

"But why mention her to me?"

"Because she talks about you."

"About me?"

"Stop playing games with me. I've had enough. She calls you her 'savior.' She talks like you were some kind of god. Stay away, I tell you! Stay away!"

Bulatovich paused a moment, somewhat confused by this outburst, then turned and walked away quickly, surprised, amused, and rather flattered to have aroused jealousy over a girl he had hardly spoken to.

10

Hailar, Manchuria, August 1900

Chinese Sonya "loved" Bulatovich with all the passion of a headstrong, inexperienced teenager. When the Chinese had attacked at dawn, and Bulatovich had gone charging at them single-handed, when Starodubov had lifted her up onto his saddle and charged after him shouting, "Mazeppa!" she was convinced that Bulatovich was a "hero," the great man she had been waiting for all her short life. When she first saw Strakhov, she decided, with equal abandon, that he was the man she wanted to marry.

She saw no contradiction in "loving" one man passionately and marrying another. Perhaps she had picked up such notions from reading French novels—the missionary's library had been quite diverse. But it felt natural to her—as natural as yin and yang—to be attracted to opposites at once, to need both men in different ways, to love and revere the one for his strength and apparent inaccessibility, and to care for the other perhaps because of his very weakness, his vulnerability to her charms.

She took Strakhov totally by surprise. He had been courting a girl back in Orenburg, slowly, respectfully, for three years. But he had never had much success with women. He was never really sure how to act.

Sonya walked boldly up to him, a total stranger, and said, "Sir, you are a handsome man and a kind man, I can see from your eyes. You look at me, a stranger accosting you like this, and you try to think the best, not the worst of me. You ask yourself not, 'What does she want of me?' but 'What can I do for her? What does she need of me?' Some men would look at me lewdly and say coarse things, but that doesn't even cross your mind until I mention it. But I want it to cross your mind, for you should know about me, not merely guess.

"I am a virgin. I was raised here in Hailar by a Russian missionary. That's why I speak Russian so well. And I speak so fast, not because I'm frightened, which I am, but because that's just the way I am. I know what I want and I come right out and say it. You like my Petersburg accent? You find it amusing, perhaps even attractive in someone so—Chinese? I want it to be attractive. I want to attract you to me. But remember—I am a lady. I just turned seventeen. My benefactor, Father Ioann, who raised me from infancy, was killed by the Boxers.

"I have no family, no money, nowhere to go in the world. But you must remember—I am a lady. I need you. I want you. I can tell from your eyes that you can be a kind, considerate man, if you want to. I can tell that you find me attractive, but wouldn't take advantage of me. Are you married?"

He was so enthralled with her sweet singsong voice and her lively, lovely face that it took him a moment to realize that she had asked him a question. She was wearing a white Cossack tunic with a black belt, a long black skirt, and a little black cap with a visor. She stood there, arms akimbo, waiting for his answer. "Ah . . . yes . . . I mean, no. No, I'm not married."

"Good. Then you are the man."

"The man?"

"The man I will marry."

"What do you mean?"

"No matter, we can talk about it again in a day or two."

"Marriage?" he asked in bewilderment.

"Yes, of course. Don't look so serious. It's only natural. I'm a young girl without family, without protector. I don't just want a husband—I need one; for if I don't find a husband now, men will find me and force me and use me, and I'll never have a husband, at least no one as kind and decent as you. Besides, I've reached the age. My body is ready; I am ready to be a wife, and a good one. You'll never regret it, I promise." With that she stood on her tiptoes and quickly kissed him on the lips, with a little flick of the tongue, then ran away before he had a chance to realize what had happened.

That night, after dark, she came to his tent, bringing a few clothes, her only possessions, tied up in a tablecloth. She lay down beside him on the ground and said softly, "Remember, I am a lady. I am the woman you are going to marry. Treat me with respect, and I will learn to love you. Yes, from your eyes I see that I could learn to love you very quickly. But I talk too much. Everyone says that I talk too much. And I want to know you, and I want you to know how much I want to know you. Talk to me, please. Tell me about yourself. Where do you come from? What is your family like? What will our life be like after the war? No, don't argue with me. I'm not going to touch you or seduce you. I don't have diseases. I'm a virgin. I didn't come here to your tent to have physical love with you. You could force me if you like— I won't scream. When it's over, I'll get up and leave and you'll never see me again. Because that would mean you're not the man I think you are, that you're not the man I want to marry. Better to find that out now than later. Yes, you're tempted. You're calculating the risks. There are none, I assure you. No disease. No screaming 'rape.' And I just go away—you have no obligation to me; you needn't pay me; you needn't even feed me."

She had left the tent flap open. The light of a distant campfire reflected brightly in her eyes as she stared into his, searching them, a bit sadly.

"If you like, I'll make it easy for you," she continued. "I'll take my clothes off and spread my legs. Is that what you want?"

Still he didn't answer. Tears began to form in her eyes. They too caught the fire's reflection. And she began to undo her belt and pull off her tunic.

He reached for her. She must have thought he meant to grab

her and pull her toward him. She started to fall, sobbing in his direction. But he pushed her aside, gently, and helped her put her clothes back in order.

It gave him a strange exhilarating feeling and strength of will to consider of her feelings instead of just his own at a time like this, when she was so tempting and so vulnerable.

"Please," he requested softly, "please don't tempt me further. What can you expect of a man? No, don't answer," he insisted, covering her mouth. "If you start talking again, I'll never get a chance to ask you. Are you hungry?"

She nodded quickly, giggled, hugged him, then rolled away and up into a sitting position, with legs crossed—happy and waiting. She was indeed very hungry.

♔ ♔ ♔

Two days later he told her that he had submitted a request to General Orlov for permission to marry her. She looked up at him, with delighted doubting eyes, stood on her tiptoes and kissed him as she had when they first met—their first kiss since that time.

They slept together in the same tent, ate from the same plate, talked endlessly. She even let him talk, playfully tying a gag around her mouth to prevent herself from interrupting him and running off with her own thoughts.

She was direct and candid. He was candid in return. He even told her about his first battle experience, at Ongun, complete with all the embarrassing details. She laughed and he laughed with her—it seemed so long ago. Even the Battle of Hailar, where he had outwardly acted the part of a hero. They laughed together at how he had dashed off to the latrine ditch at the moment of attack. It was such a relief for him to talk to someone about these experiences, someone noncritical, someone who was delighted with who he was now and who he had been before.

He told her how his father had probably tricked him into becoming a soldier, getting him to rebel, to think he was rebelling when he was really doing just what his father had wanted him to do. He told her about Olga, the girl he had been courting back in Orenburg, and how awkward he had been, tripping on the top step the first time he tried to kiss her. Telling about himself, about his motives and concerns when he was back in Orenburg, his ambition to advance in the army, his sensitivity to what people thought of him, he felt he was talking about somebody else, and he told her so.

"Of course," she said, "before you were just Major Strakhov. Now you are my man."

She made him feel like he was her "man" the way she listened to him and looked at him, focused on him and him alone.

Then she started asking about Bulatovich. It seemed natural at first because he had brought up the subject himself, telling about their brief confrontation over the fate of the thief. But then she kept asking about him again and again. Whatever Strakhov did, she wanted to know what Bulatovich was doing. She said she had never really spoken to Bulatovich directly, had only seen him from a distance. But Strakhov wondered. This was one area in which he didn't dare be candid—not because he was afraid she would see he was jealous, but because he was afraid his fears would be confirmed. He knew that she had spent a night at Bulatovich's camp before he had met her. He didn't dare ask her where she had slept that night or if she had made the same offer to someone else before making it to him.

The thought of losing her made him feel empty and alone, a feeling he had never felt before in his life. He had never known before that there was an alternative, so he had never missed the close friendship of a woman. But knowing Sonya, living with her for a few days—there was no way he could go back to his old way of life. He needed her. The more she asked about Bulatovich, the more he knew he had to marry her, and the more he hated that vainglorious Guardsman.

When he told her he had asked for permission to marry her, she didn't know whether to believe him. She felt that he would marry her eventually, but despite her abundant self-confidence, she found it hard to believe that she had actually made that deep and lasting an impression on Strakhov in such a short time. Perhaps he had asked only halfheartedly in hopes of being refused, so he could use the refusal as an excuse. She didn't care; he was so kind, gentle, and considerate, sooner or later he would marry her.

One night as he covered her and brushed the hair from her eyes, she reached up and clasped her hands behind his neck. For a long minute, they stared at each other. Then she said, "You have shown that you respect me and that you care for me. That is enough. You do not need to prove it further by sleeping alone. I want you now. Take me now. You are my man. Someday you will be my husband. Not another word now." She kissed him before he had a chance to object. After they had kissed, he didn't want to object.

It was his first time. But he had already admitted his inexperience to her so he wasn't self-conscious about it. She was helpful, holding him, helping him, guiding him, as best she could, in her own frightened and curious inexperience. Time and again, he tried and failed to open her, and they broke out laughing and hugged and kissed and rolled. Finally, he lit a candle so they could see more clearly. She was beautiful in the flickering light. He lost himself completely in those deep dark eyes, caressing her gently, hugging her ever so tightly, and before they had time to set about things in the practical manner he had intended, before he even had time to kiss her deeply with his tongue, as she had taught him, she was his completely, and there was no need to be practical, ever, completely his, not Bulatovich's, just his.

👑 👑 👑

Would there never be time to rest? Bulatovich wondered. Time to look into unfinished business—like Shemelin and Kupferman, like Strakhov and this Chinese Sonya. Bulatovich would have liked to write a letter to his own Sonya, the woman who had been his Sonya. But now he was committed to leading another patrol—immediately. Already, Pyotr and Starodubov had gathered the Mazeppy, Bodisko's railway guards, and another hundred troops quickly chosen to fill out the "flying detachment."

They set out in late afternoon, following the railway eastward. Trofim prayed loudly, calling down the wrath of God on these "pagan headhunters," quoting again from Revelations.

Pyotr rode beside Bulatovich. They both seemed overexcited and needed to talk. Bulatovich talked about Ethiopia and about Vaska, the Ethiopian boy he had brought back to Russia. Pyotr spoke of his mother and his sisters, their pastureland overlooking Lake Baikal.

"What about your father?" asked Bulatovich.

"Yes, Father." The furrow that was forming over Pyotr's left brow grew deeper. "He's dead."

"Oh yes, I'm sorry. Grotten told me."

"It happened two years ago. A hunting accident. He got caught in another hunter's trap. Lost a foot. Probably bled to death before the wolves got to him. I wanted to kill those wolves," he added somberly. "Mother wouldn't let me out of her sight. I was fifteen. She was afraid I'd get myself killed too. Trofim just prayed. But Login slipped away. He came back a week later with the heads of two dozen wolves. No one's seen a wolf in those parts since."

And so the conversation ended, both men restless.

They overtook the main forces of the retreating Chinese about ten miles east, near Dzhaimete, the next station on the railway. Bulatovich was tempted to attack with his small force and try to confuse and scatter the Chinese by surprise. But he thought better of it: too risky. His men were too tired.

"Starodubov . . ." he began, thinking of ordering them to turn back. But already, Pyotr was racing across the plain, and Starodubov, awkward horseman that he was, urged his horse onward, protectively close behind. Trofim shouted "Revenge!" and the rest of the "flying detachment," including Bulatovich, joined in the charge.

Their attack was ineffectual. The rear guard of the Chinese put up a hard fight for hours and repulsed each repeated cavalry charge.

Butorin vanished in the midst of the fighting, then reappeared at dusk, horseless, saber in hand, slashing wildly at the gusting wind and laughing insanely. The Chinese who had fought so hard and long scattered at the sight of this strange apparition.

Butorin laughed again, this time the laugh of a sane man. "What fools! They're more afraid of ghosts and demons than living men. That's the trick: not bravery, just make them think you're possessed."

He ate heartily and joined in the small talk around the campfire. All of the Mazeppy looked at him, not knowing how to react. Then Sofronov asked, cautiously, "Where did you go? After the second charge, you disappeared. We thought you were dead or captured."

"I had some unfinished business to take care of."

"Unfinished business?"

"Yes, with my brother."

"I didn't know you had a brother. Is he here in the detachment?"

"No, he's dead."

"Oh. I'm sorry. Were you able to find the body?"

"What body?"

"Your brother's body. On the battlefield."

"What would his body be doing here? He died years ago."

"But you said . . ."

"Yes, you see we were never close. The closest we ever got was when he hit me. And he didn't do that often, not after I'd grown to full size and could fight back. So when he disappeared into the desert one day, it didn't bother me much. That was just a few days after he got married. I've never eaten so well as I did at that wedding. Her folks knew how to do a feast."

"But your business . . ."

"Yes, my brother's wife."

"You saw her?"

"Not for years. She was young, and he was gone; so I had her and left her like I would any other woman. So I had some unfinished business with that dead brother of mine."

"You mean you felt guilty and had to atone in some way?"

"Guilty? No. I wanted him to know. I wanted to tell him myself what I'd done to his wife. And I did."

"You did?"

"Yes, today." Suddenly he noticed the silence around him and laughed to see he had so many listeners. "Yes," he added, looking them each in the eye, "I talk to the dead. And they listen when I talk. That's one of the advantages of being haunted—you can take care of unfinished business."

Whether he was a liar or a madman or some sort of holy fool, the Mazeppy quietly decided to avoid him. The sight of Butorin called to mind disturbing memories of the funeral fire, the missing heads, and the unknown realm beyond death.

The next day the flying detachment continued its pursuit,

harassing the enemy past Yakeshi and Mien-tu-ho all the way to Khorgo Station, about fifty-five miles east of Hailar. They returned to Hailar that night. They had inflicted no significant damage on the enemy. They had learned nothing of any importance. They had been reduced to the role of pests. Their need for vengeance was still unsatisfied.

⚜ ⚜ ⚜

At Hailar, the army had nearly doubled in size. At the beginning of the campaign, back at Chita, Orlov had divided his forces. Under Captain Smolyannikov, three of the four companies of railway guards had crossed the Chinese border at Staro Tsurukhaitui to follow the road that ran north of the Hailar River. Meanwhile Orlov with two foot battalions, the cavalry regiment, the artillery battery, and Bodisko's railway guard company had set out from Abagaitui along the southern route. Two reserve foot battalions, under Colonel Vorobyev, had set out along Orlov's route just after the Battle of Ongun, with a large transport of supplies. Both Smolyannikov and Vorobyev had caught up with Orlov at Hailar, bringing the forces up to full strength.

Now that the Russians had taken control of Hailar, the Mongolian inhabitants were returning from all directions, setting up their shops and businesses and selling to the Russians as if nothing had ever happened. What with the additional troops and these returning Mongolians, Orlov was inundated with administrative problems and paperwork.

Provisions were now abundant. The storehouses contained more than 360 tons of flour, oats, millet, vermicelli, soap, and candles; over 3000 chests of tea; and large quantities of skins and tobacco. The transport from Abagaitui had brought cattle for fresh meat. Each man could now receive 2 pounds of meat a day.

But what were they to do with the captured supplies that they couldn't immediately use? Who could they give them to? Could Orlov, in good conscience, refuse to feed the hungry Chinese, particularly the Chinese Christians and the former railway laborers, some of whom had lost all their wordly goods? What about the Russian railway construction engineers and officials whose houses had been ransacked by the Chinese? Many of their valuables were now among the baggage of the Russian soldiers who had, contrary to orders and despite a respectable effort at policing, managed to loot the homes of the Chinese looters. Should Orlov try to confiscate these valuables and return them to their rightful owners? If so, how could he determine who was the rightful owner of the what?

Then, too, there were medical problems, multiplied by the increase of troops with no additional medical personnel or medical supplies. Already, as was all too common in war, more men had died of typhus and dysentery than of battle wounds. There were far too few doctors, and the ones they had were not trained for the kind of work they had to do. For the most part, they were civilian doctors from Trans-Baikal, conscripted for the campaign regardless of their specialties. One was a psychiatrist and three were obstetricians. The few doctors experienced in surgery had never had to deal with the kind of surgery most often required in the field—amputation. All but Stankevich and Volf were unused to working in a tent, coping with unsanitary conditions, and improvising to make up for the scarcity of supplies. They had run out of anesthetics, quinine, and even castor oil. They had to get a man drunk and lull him to sleep before cutting off his leg.

They also had to learn to cope with the questions of religion and esthetics that kept complicating their already difficult task. For instance, what to do with a man's leg after cutting it off? Throw it in a trash heap for the dogs to get at, or give it a solemn burial? And when the man insists on keeping the amputated limb because he's convinced that when he's dead he has to be buried with all his parts—otherwise, when Judgment Day comes and the dead are resurrected, he'll be left behind in his grave or be forced to hobble one-legged throughout eternity—how do you tell such a man that it'll rot, smell, and breed disease?

Orlov had his hands full with administrative problems, but still he somehow found time to indulge in his one weakness: his memoirs. The rapid success of his detachment had given him a sense of his own importance. Now and then he pushed aside the unfinished administrative business and feverishly jotted down notes for an autobiographical account of this campaign.

He, the garrison officer, the pen-pusher, the harried husband with three daughters and four granddaughters, but no sons or grandsons, was leading a substantial army to repeated victory against overwhelming odds. He felt compelled to record these historic events. He would write a simple, direct account, giving full credit to the enlisted men who were responsible for the success—men like Starodubov and Butorin. He'd just as soon forget the officers, all except Bulatovich.

A fine young man, that Bulatovich. Orlov wished he had had a son like that—a model soldier, not one of those garrison disciplinarians but a man with initiative and courage, a man able to inspire his men to feats of bravery.

Such was his frame of mind when Strakhov found him.

"Your Excellency, have you had an opportunity to consider my requests?"

"Yes, yes," mumbled Orlov, with a twinge of guilt, quickly pushing his historical notes off to the side of the table and shuffling through the large stack of petitions. "And what was it you were requesting? There are so many . . ."

"There were three petitions, Your Excellency." He stepped forward, apparently to help look for them. Then he hesitated.

Orlov didn't know whether to be pleased or aggravated at the young man's tact, at his not wanting to show up a superior. Had he helped Orlov and found the petitions, Strakhov would have made Orlov feel like a half-blind, fumbling old man. By not helping, he made Orlov acutely aware of his own foolish vanity. The general needed glasses but hated to admit the fact, just as he hated to admit that he was nearly sixty. Moments like this made him painfully aware of his own inadequacies.

"First, Your Excellency, I was asking for food, on behalf of the Chinese Christians."

"But they are being fed. I asked Volzhaninov to take care of that. I remember."

"Yes, Your Excellency. But only on a day-to-day basis. The Chinese are a proud people. They do not like to be treated as beggars."

"Yes, yes. I'll think it over. We have more than enough food. And your second request?"

"Also for the Chinese Christians. Many of them have lost all they owned simply because they were Christian and because they were friendly to Russians. Surely, we should make some effort at restitution."

"I've been thinking about that. You aren't the only one who has made such requests. And the third?"

"A personal matter, Your Excellency. I ask permission to be married."

"That Chinese girl I've seen you with?"

"Yes, Your Excellency."

Orlov laughed. "Then that's why you're so interested in all this Chinese Christian business. You work fast, my boy. We've only been here a few days. Congratulations that you've won her. But why marry her?"

"That's what I want, what she wants. She's a Christian."

"Christian or not—just sweet-talk her a bit. Remember, this is wartime, lad. All the niceties of peacetime Russia don't apply."

"But we want to get married," Strakhov insisted, surprised at this resistance.

Orlov laughed again, "I said that myself once; I hate to say how long ago."

Strakhov took heart, "Indeed, Your Excellency?"

"Yes, and I've regretted it ever since. I don't want you to make the same mistake. You hardly know the girl."

"But . . ."

"Listen to me, Major. This is an order. You will not marry this girl until the end of the campaign. If you take my advice, you shouldn't make her any promises until then, either. Blame it all on me. If you feel the same at the end of the campaign, then you can go ahead with my blessing. Be sure to invite me to the wedding. But if I were you, I'd just enjoy myself and avoid making promises I might regret later."

"But Your Excellency, she's a lady."

"Yes," Orlov chuckled, remembering an incident from his youth, "they all start that way."

Unable to dissemble his anger, Strakhov abruptly turned and started to leave, then turned again to say, "There was something else I wanted to mention, Your Excellency."

"Yes, what else would the Chinese Christians like?"

"It's another matter entirely. Captain Smolyannikov arrived yesterday with three companies of railway guards. He is Bulatovich's superior in rank, and he and his men know this terrain and its people thoroughly. If you have further need of a flying detachment, they would be a natural choice."

"Is Bulatovich back already?"

"Yes, Your Excellency. He is waiting to see you . . ."

"Alexander Xavierevich!" shouted Orlov, jubilantly. "Come in! Come in!" Bulatovich quickly entered. Orlov ran up and patted him on the back and shook his hand. "Good to see you, son. Did you put a scare into those Chinese?"

"No. Their rear guard held strong."

"You don't say? Any casualties?"

"Just three wounded, but not badly. We were lucky."

"You're always lucky, thank God," Orlov laughed. "We need more like you. By the way, I was just talking to Major Strakhov here, and he reminded me that we have one more officer like you, a new man, just arrived here. I've known him off and on for years—Captain Smolyannikov of the railway guards. From now on his railway guards will serve as our flying detachment with Smolyannikov in charge. I think you could learn something from him. He's lived here for years and he knows the land and the people. He's even married to one of them—a Chinese." He turned to Strakhov. "It can work, Major. Chinese are women like any other. Just don't rush into it." Turning back to Bulatovich, "He's set on marrying one himself—some girl he met just a couple days ago. Imagine? No, I guess you can't. You're still a bachelor. You've got more sense than us married men. Anyway, you're welcome to go along with Smolyannikov, if you like. In fact, I think you should, yes, do; that's an order. He's a savvy old fighter. You don't meet his sort often.

"But what I really wanted to talk to you about was my book. You see, I'm writing my memoirs of this campaign . . ."

Strakhov left with mixed feelings, glad to see Bulatovich temporarily held in check, uneasy about how or whether to tell Sonya that they would have to postpone getting married.

Bulatovich stood before Orlov, alternately knocking his dusty red cap against his knee and polishing his glasses on his shirt, while Orlov debated aloud with himself the pros and cons of first-person historical narrative. When Orlov was satisfied that the "discussion" had run its course (he was delighted to have found such an intent and discerning listener), Bulatovich excused himself, hurriedly, explaining that he had to introduce himself to his new commander, Captain Smolyannikov.

A CLASH OF CULTURES

11

Hailar, Manchuria, August 6, 1900

Captain Smolyannikov was stretched out on the ground in front of his tent. He had found a comfortable rise in the earth that provided support for his graying head and support for his muscular shoulders. He looked like he had lain there for years and was in no hurry to move on.

Staff-Captain Bodisko was sitting on a stool just inside the tent, and Dr. Volf had settled down on the box of champagne he had brought along.

Bulatovich stood near them. He had just introduced himself to his new commander and, much to his discomfort, found himself invited to join in the conversation with these men he hardly knew and had no desire to be with.

"You should have seen old Kupferman," said Bodisko, taking a swig of champagne and passing the bottle to Volf. "He went sneaking up to the hospital tent. Maybe the crowd made him nervous. Maybe he was afraid the man he had beaten had died and there might be repercussions. Maybe he felt bad about what he had done. Who knows? Maybe he even has a soul."

"To the eternal soul of man," proposed Volf. "And to his all-too-corruptible flesh."

"Well, there were about fifty people gathered outside Shemelin's tent," Bodisko continued. "I was there myself."

"So were half the wounded," added Volf, "nearly all the ones who could walk. Business was light at the doctor's office. To Shemelin!" he proposed.

"It seems they think this Shemelin's some kind of saint," said Bodisko. "They wanted to touch him or look at him or pray near him. Others, like me, were gathered around just curious to see what was happening. As far as I could tell, there weren't any miracles. Nobody got a leg put back on; nobody even got rid of their diarrhea or lice. But what Shemelin did with Kupferman was worth seeing."

Bodisko stood up to act out the motions. "Imagine, as soon as Kupferman arrives, the crowd parts, like he has some kind of disease they don't want to be near. When he's a hundred feet away, there's no one between him and Shemelin. Their eyes meet. 'Welcome, sir, welcome. I hoped that we would meet again,' says Shemelin. Kupferman stares cautiously. For a moment it looks like he wants to beat Shemelin again and put an end to him. 'I wanted to thank you for this blessing,' says Shemelin. 'You were God's agent.'

"Well, from the look in Kupferman's face, he doesn't know if he's being made fun of or what. He stares all around him as if daring anyone to laugh at him. Then he turns fast and runs away—yes, runs. And Shemelin shouts after him, 'Don't go, sir. Please, come back!' "

"Shemelin's one of your men, isn't he?" Smolyannikov asked Bulatovich.

"Yes, but I can't make any sense out of this business."

"To nonsense!" proposed Bodisko.

"It's this damned heat, the climate," suggested Volf.

"No, it's the country and the people with the pigtails," said Bodisko, "the graves and the ghosts all over the place. Something in the air makes men mad."

"Yes," agreed Volf. "All this Boxer madness—you wouldn't see anarchy like that in Petersburg."

"Things aren't always as different as they seem," noted Smolyannikov.

"That proves my point," Volf drunkenly insisted. "Who could be madder than you?" Turning to Bulatovich he explained "This tough old mercenary's been in China for nearly twenty years now, and it's gone to his head. Do you realize he spends all of his money on his wife's doctor bills? It's been years since he's even seen her. He can't afford to go to Petersburg to see her because all his money goes to pay the fancy doctors who keep her alive there. Filthy doctors," he added, and took another swig. "Should have let her die here with her folks in China."

"You never met her," said Smolyannikov, staring at the ground. "If you had, you wouldn't talk that way."

"You don't even know if she's dead or alive," Volf persisted. "All you know is they keep sending the bills."

"And as long as I pay them, she's alive to me. That's a cheap price to pay. It's easy to buy someone's death, but how often can you buy a life?"

They fell silent, passing the bottles around. Volf seemed to have an infinite supply of champagne. Tired of standing, Bulatovich sat stiffly on the ground and nursed a bottle by himself. His mind wandered back to Petersburg and to Sonya. He remembered a scene in the woods when she had sat with her head cuddled close to his shoulder, her hand idly caressing his thigh while he bragged to her about elephant hunting. If he had her there now, he wouldn't talk, and she wouldn't push him away. He'd know how to bend her and control her; he'd know how to move her from flirtation to passion. He remembered her, too, as she had stood, ever so briefly, naked beside the pond—her hair dripping wet, her eyes flashing blue, her half-smile an invitation and a challenge. She seemed to say, "Hold me close—I dare you."

When he looked up it was twilight. Bodisko and Volf were asleep. His eyes met Smolyannikov's. He got the impression that Smolyannikov had been looking at him for some time, not critical or angry, just curious.

"They were wrong, you know, about my wife. It's not the Chinese influence, it's the Russian in me that insists on trying to keep her alive. 'It's against nature,' she'd say, if she could talk.

195

That's what her eyes told me when I sent her there. To her, death is part of life and life is part of death. When the time comes to die, you should accept it and flow with it. She respects and loves nature."

"That's what aggravates me most about the Chinese," answered Bulatovich, surprised by the vehemence of his own words. "Their passivity, their acceptance, their fatalism, their unwillingness to take on obstacles."

Smolyannikov chuckled and scratched his graying mustache. He was about 50, nearly as old as Starodubov. No taller than Bulatovich, he was far more heavy set; still very muscular around the shoulders, but a bit flabby—or "relaxed," as he called it—about the waist.

"Yes, you want a challenge. You'd like to meet the enemy head on. A man of action. But don't underestimate this enemy of ours. Sure, they bend and flow, and they may lose the war. But they will win the peace.

"In the thirteenth century Genghis Khan comes rushing down with his Tatar and Mongolian hordes and conquers their country. But life goes on. The fields still get planted and harvested, and in a generation or two the conquerors are just as Chinese as the conquered. They aren't foreign oppressors anymore. They're just another Chinese dynasty. In the seventeenth century, the Manchus come down from Manchuria and conquer China, and they too are absorbed.

"Sure, we Russians are different. When those same Tatar and Mongolian hordes came our way, we fought and lost, and fought and lost again; and we rebelled whenever we had the chance, just to get stomped down again."

"But Russia rose again," objected Bulatovich.

"Yes, after centuries of being reduced to poverty, having had our civilization completely shattered. But I know how you feel; I feel it myself sometimes still—the pride that comes from fighting against all odds, not giving in. Sometimes I think it's a national trait. While the Chinese flow with nature, we Russians go against it. Why, most of Russia would be uninhabited if people just sought to live in harmony with nature. No human being can live in harmony with winters like ours. It takes determination to meet the challenge of nature like that—the kind of stubborn force of will that out of a swamp builds a city like Petersburg. It seems that fighting obstacles and fighting nature makes us strong, or forces us to discover our inner reserves of strength.

"But equal strength comes from the opposite direction. The Chinese love and respect nature and find strength from their knowledge of it. They seek the *tao*, the path of least resistance. They try to get the greatest result from the least effort. They respect quiet and peace and fragility. Their perfect action or *wu-wei* is motion without friction, totally effortless, but effective.

"No, I can see from the expression on your face that you wouldn't make a very good Buddhist monk. Nor would I, for that matter, much as I respect their beliefs and ways. Death more than anything I simply can't accept. I can't just let someone I care for die and presume that she'll come to life again in some new form as man or beast. And I need a challenge every now and then, too, a wall to pound my head against, just to reassure myself that I'm real and alive.

"But what brings you to China? Did you expect to find some great new challenge here? You had to have volunteered for this duty. There's no one else from your regiment or even from Petersburg in the whole Hailar Detachment. Are you looking for something impossible to perform for the honor and the glory of it? For the name of 'hero'?"

Bulatovich shrugged and took a deep swallow of champagne, finally stretching out on the ground, though it was uncomfortable. It didn't yield to his back nor did his back to it. He was tired and hungry. The champagne went to his head quickly and his thoughts were muddled. He wished he didn't need obstacles and challenges to define himself. He wished he were self-defined— a man of unyielding honor, an uncompromising hero out of Corneille or Racine, who knew who he was, who could stake his life and honor on what he believed, and who held his honor far more dear than life itself. He would like to be able to say, like Luther, "Here I stand. This is who I am. I can act no other way."

✿ ✿ ✿

In a few days, Smolyannikov and Bulatovich became close friends. They repeatedly tested one another's skills. Sometimes they ventured dangerously far, as much as a hundred miles from headquarters in Hailar. Both were excellent horsemen, highly respected by their men. But their styles differed.

Bulatovich was aggressive and determined. Smolyannikov, his elder by some twenty years, approached even the most dangerous situations almost casually, alert but unhurried, ready yet relaxed. Bulatovich pursued; Smolyannikov reconnoitered. Bulatovich sought conflict, Smolyannikov avoided it. Chewing tobacco, Smolyannikov rode at a casual pace, lingering where the shade was cool, the water clear, or the view pleasing. He knew the land well. He could let an enemy patrol slip out of sight for hours while he and his men rested, then with little effort catch up with them later.

For Bulatovich, it was a week without responsibility—almost a vacation. This new flying detachment was made up entirely of railway guards. The Mazeppy had been left behind in Hailar to dream dreams of severed heads and vengeance. Bulatovich had had nothing to say about it. With no men to command, he rode beside Smolyannikov, Bodisko, and Volf, shared their casual camaraderie, and occasionally tested his skills and daring in competition with Smolyannikov.

For the first time since his early days in the army, Bulatovich felt gregarious. He wanted to be one of the group, not the leader, just a comrade-in-arms. Smolyannikov welcomed him, and whomever Smolyannikov welcomed was accepted by all.

Today Smolyannikov had challenged Bulatovich to a race, making a game of their reconnaissance assignments. Leaving behind the flying detachment, just the two of them had ridden completely around the enemy army. The adventure had begun frivolously, but the information they had gathered could prove valuable.

The race had been exhilarating, not simply a short gallop, but a thirty-mile trek over rough terrain—the type of endurance race at which Bulatovich excelled, riding high with his weight on the stirrups rather than the saddle, pacing himself, getting the most from his mount without exhausting it. After a mile their paths diverged. Smolyannikov took a longer but perhaps easier route, taking advantage of his knowledge of the terrain. Bulatovich charged straight ahead. At sunset he found Smolyannikov waiting for him on a hilltop, with a Chinese prisoner tied across his saddle.

"How did you do it?" laughed Bulatovich.

"I just flowed with the land," Smolyannikov laughed back. "It's a trick an old Buddhist monk taught me."

Shots rang out from below. The valley was swarming with Chinese troops. Horsemen were racing up the hillside. Smolyannikov laughed and turned, threading his way among the boulders and brush, over ravines, up another hill, with Bulatovich struggling to keep up. Soon they had lost their pursuers and once again had an excellent view of the army in the valley.

"Ah! General P'ao," remarked Smolyannikov.

"Where?" asked Bulatovich, scanning the multitude of troops with his binoculars. "The one on the white horse with a parasol?"

"Most high-ranking Chinese officers ride white horses and carry parasols so their troops can see them and rally around them in the confusion of battle. But that's General P'ao, all right. I served under him for several years. He was in charge of the railway guards in this area. I've heard that when the war started, Sheu, the *dzyan-dzyan* or governor-general of Tsitsihar, capital of Northern Manchuria, respectfully suggested that dear old P'ao kill himself because he had accepted the patronage of the Russians. But he didn't do it like most of their other generals would. He said he'd rather die fighting us. He's a tough character, with Western notions of war that he picked up from us. With him in charge, you're liable to get that head-on decisive battle you've been itching for."

"How many men do you think he has?"

"Our friend here says about seven thousand."

As Smolyannikov had gathered from the prisoner's frightened chatter, the first Chinese commander, Chuan-do, had, like Orlov, divided his twelve-thousand-man army. The main force had proceeded along the southern route and encountered Orlov at Ongun. Chuan-do had died in that battle. The other two thousand troops had started out on the northern route toward Staro-Tsurukhaitui. If they had continued on that road, they would have met with Smolyannikov's railway guards. But when word arrived of the disaster at Ongun, they had turned back toward

Hailar and chanced on Bulatovich. After the Battle of Hailar, the remnants of the Chinese army had gradually broken apart and vanished into the wasteland. P'ao was bringing a new, apparently better-trained army to strike the Russians at Hailar once again.

Bulatovich and Smolyannikov paused to rest in a rocky ravine. They had to wait until dark to get by the enemy and back to their flying detachment.

They stretched out on the ground, Bulatovich resting his head on his saddlebag; Smolyannikov, his on a smooth rock. Smolyannikov took a swig from his canteen and passed it to Bulatovich. "You are ambitious, Sasha," he said. "But you are no Napoleon."

"Napoleon?" laughed Bulatovich.

"Not for power, not for money do you strive. What fate could give you would not be enough. You must push yourself to the limit, take one step beyond the impossible and know that you did it. It does my heart good to see the way you ride, the way you push yourself. It makes me feel young again."

It warmed Bulatovich to hear such praise from a man he respected. He had never seen himself in that light before. He opened up to Smolyannikov and told the story of his life, as simply as he could, not bragging, but not holding back either, like talking aloud to himself. He told about life at Lutsikovka and his battles with his mother, about his sister's death and the teacher Lemm; how he had chosen his career and made himself the best rider and fencer in the regiment; how he had gone to Ethiopia three times, had ridden camelback at record speed across hundreds of miles of desert, had seen lands and peoples that no European had ever seen before, and had become a trusted adviser of the Emperor Menelik. Bulatovich rambled on for over an hour and ended quite satisfied with himself—proud of who he was, the challenges he had met, and what he had accomplished.

Smolyannikov let him bask in his glory silently for a few moments, then asked, "When this war is over, what will you do next? The steeplechase again? Africa again? Where will you find a challenge strong enough?"

"I suppose . . ." Bulatovich started to reply, then realized, uncomfortably, that he had no answer.

12

Hailar, Manchuria, August 13, 1900

While Bulatovich, Smolyannikov, and the railway guards scouted to the east, back at Hailar Chinese Sonya took care of war victims. She found orphans cowering in alleyways or begging on the street and led them around, door-to-door—talking fast and persuasively, trying to find them permanent homes or at least collecting alms and leaving the householder with a feeling of guilt she might be able to capitalize on another day when she had a new orphan to offer.

For a week she was very successful, placing three dozen children. Each day, more Chinese families returned to Hailar from the surrounding countryside, where they had taken refuge. She would try to catch them as they were moving in—between that moment of despair when they saw what had been destroyed and stolen, and that moment of thankfulness when they realized that much still remained, that the house was still intact, that they had been lucky.

"Lucky, indeed," she would begin. "But many have not been so fortunate as you. . . ." And within an hour they would find themselves the proud parents of a hungry, frightened little child.

As the town filled and the flow of new returnees dropped, she tried to seek out friends and neighbors of the orphans' parents. But as everyone tried to go back to their usual business in the old town or in the Russian railway settlement, they fell into their old patterns of life and became more cautious and far more reluctant to take on new burdens. And it didn't take long for the old habits and defenses to reassert themselves.

The supply of prospective parents dwindled. But there were still children who needed homes. One boy in particular had won Sonya's heart. She called him Mitya. He had the light complexion of a Russian and the dark, slanted eyes of a Chinese. He had light brown hair and an ugly scar on his forehead from a recent wound. Because of his Russian looks, the Chinese were reluctant to take him, and the Russians rejected him because of his Chinese looks.

She was trying to find a home for Mitya the day she first spoke to Pyotr.

"The boy!" he shouted, running up to her. "That wound on his face—was he kicked?"

"He doesn't remember," Sonya answered for him.

"But you speak Russian?" he asked, seeing her face as she turned toward him, suddenly realizing that she was Chinese, even though she was wearing a Cossack tunic. It had been foolish of him to come running up shouting in Russian like that. She laughed. He blushed, remembering that this was the survivor, the pretty convert found at the church. Then he asked, "Are you his mother?"

She laughed again, "I just turned seventeen."

He looked at her more closely and blushed again; she was beautiful.

"Why are you so interested in the boy?" she asked, searching his eyes and smiling.

"I . . . you see . . . you believe in God, don't you? The Russian God, I mean."

"I didn't know He was Russian," she laughed.

"I mean . . . you are Orthodox, aren't you?"

"Yes."

"I'm not Orthodox myself. I mean I'm true Orthodox—'Old Believers' they call us." And he quickly crossed himself with two fingers. She was so beautiful.

"But the boy," she asked sweetly. "Why are you so interested in the boy?"

"I meant to tell you that. You see, it has to do with God. This soldier, Yakov Shemelin, had an experience. He felt the closeness of God. He saw Christ Himself. You can tell from his eyes."

"Yes, you can tell much from a man's eyes," she replied, still studying his eyes and smiling warmly.

Pyotr couldn't look at her and think at the same time. Those dark eyes . . . he looked down and tried to explain. "This boy or a boy just like him was part of Shemelin's experience. And he looked everywhere for the boy, afraid that it had all been just a dream."

As he spoke, she reached out, took hold of the locket hanging around his neck, and opened it before he had a chance to stop her.

"What's her name?" she asked sweetly.

"Nadyezhda."

"Your wife?"

"I'm not married."

"Ah, your sweetheart—a young man in love. It shows all over your face."

"My friend . . . Aksyonov . . ." he tried to explain, haltingly, embarrassed. It occurred to him that he didn't even know Aksyonov's first name.

"Yes?" she asked.

"He died . . . killed in the first battle," he struggled to say, trying to tell her that Nadyezhda wasn't his "sweetheart," that he had no "sweetheart." "We were with Bulatovich . . ."

"Bulatovich?"

"Yes."

"Then you know him?"

"I am one of the Mazeppy."

"Now I remember. You were there that day—when Sofronov rescued me."

"And you're the one that Major Strakhov . . ."

"Yes," she blushed. "I am Strakhov's Sonya. Strakhov is my man." She seemed to read his eyes. "You wonder about such a woman as me. What a bold, shameless girl, you think, living in sin and making no secret of it. I make no excuses. I am who I am, and I do what I do. Strakhov is a kind man, rather shy, but very responsible and loyal and considerate. He will make a fine husband. Yes, I intend to marry him; and sooner or later, he will marry me. He loves me already—his eyes tell me, not his voice; and eyes don't often lie. And I will love him; I'm sure I will. And I'll make him a good wife. That's it. Now you know all about me and don't have to wonder and doubt. I like you." Pyotr looked at his shoes. Sonya repeated, "Yes, I like you. You're a kind, loving soul. No wonder Nadyezhda loves you. She's a very lucky woman." Pyotr was too flattered and too confused to set her straight. "And your Bulatovich, his sweetheart is very lucky, too."

"Bulatovich? I didn't know he had a 'sweetheart.' "

"But he must. So great a hero as he must have a true love. That's the kind of man he is—brave, unselfish, kind. At least, I'm sure that's the kind of man he is."

"Yes," confirmed Pyotr, enthusiastically. "He is a great hero. It's a privilege to serve under him."

"I can well imagine. If only I were a man."

Pyotr found it very difficult to imagine her as a man.

"Do you think that he—Bulatovich—might want to adopt a boy?"

"But he already has."

"He has?"

"Vaska."

"Really? When? Tell me about it, please."

Pyotr looked down so he could gather his thoughts. She waited. The silence made him even more nervous. "We were talking, on the way to Khorgo Station. The Chinese had chopped off my brother's head. We never found the head," he tried to explain.

"How horrible."

"We were going to get revenge."

"Did you?"

"No. Not yet. But we will," he promised. He had been brooding on that thought for the last week of forced inactivity. Before this brief meeting with Sonya he would have said that revenge was the most important thing in his life. But it was hard to think of anything so harsh as revenge watching her animated eyes, except insofar as talking of revenge could impress her. He felt important repeating, "We will."

"I'm sure you will."

He felt a tingle of excitement, then returned to his train of thought. "We rode, we talked. I told about my father—my other brother Trofim, my ten sisters, my mother, my father's death. He told me about Ethiopia and about Vaska."

"Yes, yes," she urged. "What did he tell you?"

"Vaska's a little African boy. He found him . . ." Pyotr couldn't tell the whole story. He was embarrassed to have brought it up. The boy had been mutilated. Tribal enemies had emasculated him, taking his genitals as a trophy, like the end of an elephant's trunk, Bulatovich had said, to demonstrate their own manhood and bravery. "He had been left for dead," Pyotr continued. "Bulatovich took care of his wounds. He was only about three years old."

"Where is he now?"

"Back at the family estate in the Ukraine with Bulatovich's mother."

"What a beautiful story!" she suddenly exclaimed and gave Pyotr a quick hug and a kiss on the cheek. "Thank you for telling me. I knew he was a great hero—I just knew it."

The little boy, Mitya, stared wide-eyed and curious—apparently listening to every unintelligible sound. Silent, he seemed to ask for help and sympathy, leaving himself open to all the pains of rejection.

Pyotr wished that he could dare to look at Sonya with such open eyes. But he didn't dare risk rejection from her. It was easier to charge recklessly into battle, perhaps to impress her (and himself) with the ardor of his revenge.

If only he hadn't worn that locket. If only she hadn't seen it. Now he didn't know how to tell her that Nadyezhda wasn't his "sweetheart' without seeming utterly foolish. And if Sonya knew he wasn't spoken for, would she look at him that way, talk to him that way? After all, she was going to marry Strakhov, and she worshiped Bulatovich. How could he ever possibly compete with the likes of Bulatovich? He, Pyotr, a nobody, a nothing, a raw recruit, a peasant, couldn't hope to be anything but her friend.

Bugles sounded. Pyotr quickly turned, ready to run to the mustering point.

"What's it mean?" asked Sonya, clutching little Mitya protectively.

"Probably another battle."

"Be careful!" she shouted.

Pyotr had turned and started running. He stopped and looked back at her. She was talking to him and him alone. He felt a surge of pride and shouted back in a voice deeper than normal (the sound of it surprised him), "I must revenge the death of my brother!" Then he ran on, heroically, he thought.

⚜ ⚜ ⚜

Word had come from Smolyannikov that a Chinese army under General P'ao was approaching Hailar from the east. The flying detachment of railway guards was already skirmishing with the vanguard of P'ao's army at Yakeshi, about twenty miles from Hailar, trying to slow the enemy advance until Orlov could arrive with the rest of the Russian forces.

Strakhov viewed the upcoming battle as an opportunity. He had to look out for his own interests. The war wouldn't last forever—probably no longer than another month. Reports a week or two weeks old indicated that not just here but everywhere in Manchuria, Russian troops were advancing rapidly. Also, the international forces had nearly reached Peking to relieve the siege of the legations, if they weren't there already. Chinese resistance was ineffectual. For all he knew, this could be the last major battle of the campaign. He knew he had to take advantage of it. Advancement came painfully and slowly in peacetime. He had to think of his future and Sonya. He had responsibilities.

The timing was perfect. Kupferman's strange, and probably temporary, disability had left Strakhov in command of the cavalry regiment. Kupferman would suddenly break out in a sweat. His hand would start trembling. He had no fever, and Dr. Stankevich insisted that he was physically sound. But Kupferman was convinced that he was in no condition to command a cavalry regiment in battle. He would stay to the rear with Orlov and the adjutants, leaving the command and the glory to Strakhov. Barring the unexpected, this battle should bring Strakhov a promotion, or, at the very least, a medal with a glowing report to go in his permanent record. But the unexpected struck three times, and despite his foresight and bravery, he gained nothing from the battle.

Reports indicated that there was no water on the road to Yakeshi, so Strakhov carted along abundant water in barrels. He had his men trot along at a good pace, then wait and rest while the infantry caught up. When they arrived at Yakeshi, the cavalry was fresh and rested, while the infantry, whose officers had been in too much of a hurry to worry about water, were exhausted and thirsty. So Strakhov's cavalry took the initiative.

Smolyannikov's railway guards had successfully harassed and slowed the enemy for nearly a day. Now the railway guards were involved in a heated skirmish and in danger of being surrounded.

First, Strakhov's cavalry provided cover so the railway guards could withdraw and find refuge with the newly arrived army. Then Strakhov himself charged at the head of his troops, hoping to rout the enemy swiftly and decisively before other units could get involved and share the glory.

But the Chinese didn't run. They held their ground and shot far more accurately than they had in previous battles. The cavalry came to a standstill and became involved in a futile melee. This was Strakhov's first surprise—the fighting ability of these Chinese under P'ao. Soon Sidorov came racing up with orders from Orlov to withdraw and take up position with the rest of the army.

Orlov posted the railway guards, under Smolyannikov, on the left flank; the cavalry in the center; and the infantry on the right flank. Orlov held two foot battalions in reserve. At Strakhov's suggestion, a mounted reserve of two squadrons was posted behind the foot reserve, for use in the unlikely eventuality of an emergency. Strakhov gave Bulatovich the dubious honor of commanding that mounted reserve. Strakhov didn't want any competition for the name of "hero."

Unlike in previous encounters, this time the Chinese didn't wait but rather attacked first. Russian sharpshooters picked off the Chinese on white horses and carrying parasols, presuming those were the high-ranking officers. But this Chinese army, evidently better trained and experienced than the others, didn't give way. For several hours the outcome of the battle remained uncertain.

Strakhov found himself penned in by the Russian infantry on either side of him and the enemy in front. Orlov himself was directing this battle from a hillside a good fifteen-minute ride away, making it difficult to coordinate activities, to send messengers back and forth asking Orlov for permission to do this and that. Strakhov wanted to withdraw suddenly from the center, pulling the enemy in, then turn and attack while the Russian flanks turned and enveloped the enemy. This was the tactic that the Greeks had used against the Persians at the Battle of Marathon, and Hannibal against the Romans at Cannae. But Orlov didn't seem to understand the reference or the intent of the message. He sent back the order, "Hold the center at all costs." Sidorov delivered this order with urgency and emphasis, as if Orlov thought Strakhov were about to retreat.

Then the unexpected struck again—a torrential thunderstorm, with heavy rain and hail, bringing darkness, reducing visibility to less than a hundred paces. Horses sank ankle deep in mud, panicked at the thunder and hail, and slipped and fell. Strakhov ordered his men to dismount and meet the enemy on foot; but they couldn't see the enemy anymore, and after all the turning and splashing and falling, with rifle fire sounding on all sides, they couldn't be sure in which direction they should aim.

The third surprise—Bulatovich—Strakhov learned about later. In the sudden darkness of the thunderstorm, Orlov ordered the reserve foot battalions to the right flank. Somehow Bulatovich appeared at their head, leading them out of the mud, over firm rocky ground to the designated position. With this added strength, the right flank advanced in an enveloping movement. The Chinese retreated toward the Russian left, threatening to overrun and surround the railway guards. Again Bulatovich emerged from the darkness, this time leading the mounted reserves to the left flank and extricating the railway guards from danger.

As victory seemed assured and the Russians pursued the enemy in a confused rush, Bulatovich rode about gathering

Mazeppy and railway guards. At one point, chasing down some enemy stragglers, in full sight of Orlov and Kupferman, Bulatovich and the Mazeppy were suddenly fired upon from point-blank range by half a dozen Chinese hiding in the underbrush. Orlov flinched, anticipating disaster. But volley after volley missed completely as the Mazeppy chased down their assailants, killing every one of them, and rode away without so much as a scratch.

🦅 🦅 🦅

At nightfall, when the battle was over and other Russians were pitching tents, Bulatovich, on his own initiative, ignoring orders, slipped away, leading a makeshift detachment of Mazeppy and railway guards in pursuit of the Chinese.

The battle had lasted all day. Pyotr was exhausted.

He could tell from the looks on their faces that Bulatovich, Starodubov, Trofim, and the rest were still at a fever pitch of excitement, as they had been on their ride to Urdingi. After a week of frustrating, indecisive skirmishes and then another week of forced idleness, the Mazeppy were finally getting their chance for revenge. They were like hungry wolves racing to the kill.

Maybe they felt they owed it to Pyotr to revenge the death of his brother. Or maybe it was just this energy they had found in themselves in the heat of battle, and they had to use it before they could rest.

Pyotr himself didn't feel the need for revenge anymore. He knew he had felt it just yesterday—this tension that had built up like a spring pushed tight. Sonya had made him forget it for a moment, but it was there still, pressing against his innards, demanding release.

Well, it had sprung today, and he was left with a vague feeling of remorse and guilt, the feeling that when this force, this need in him was released through his muscles and his saber, he had not been himself; he had been someone else who was capable of the most bloodthirsty cruelty. This notion was rather unsettling.

Login's death had triggered the process that ended today, but what was this elemental need that had made him want to slaughter wantonly, that seemed to feed on blood? He called it "revenge" for lack of a better name. But was it always a part of him, some-

209

times sated and sometimes repressed, like hunger or thirst or sexual desire, but always there in his innards, ready to be tightened and released by the right set of circumstances?

He remembered vividly the first time his saber had sunk into the skull of one of the Chinese. The warmth of the blood gushing onto his hand had been a baptism. He had jumped from his horse and run at them slashing left and right, no longer content to shoot from a distance, needing to feel the shock of impact quiver from their bleeding flesh, through the saber to the muscles of his hand and arm. He remembered clearly that he had done those things, but why he had acted that way both eluded and frightened him.

He had wanted to impress Sonya; but that seemed so long ago and so childish, to think that a young girl or anyone could be impressed with killing. He was sick of death. He just wanted to be alone, to sleep, to try to forget; sleep and tell himself that the battle was a bad dream, that the Devil was just a superstition, not a force that lurked within him, waiting to be released.

Thinking of the Devil, he turned and saw Laperdin riding beside him. Since the fiery funeral, Laperdin had left him alone to his brooding, but here he was again, singling him out to harass him with moral questions.

" 'Blessed are those who mourn, for they shall be comforted,' " Laperdin intoned. "Have you been comforted today?"

"Stop," replied Pyotr, softly but firmly, staring straight ahead.

" 'Blessed are the merciful, for they shall obtain mercy.' Were you merciful today, Pyotr? 'Blessed are the peacemakers, for they shall be called sons of God.' Are you a son of God? Are you going to make peace with the Chinese?"

"What are you trying to do?" Pyotr finally looked him in the eye.

"You interest me, boy. You have spirit and potential. You aren't one of the 'poor in spirit' or the 'meek.' You don't want to 'inherit the earth.' I saw you out there today, hacking away with your saber. You are, or you could be, a man of action."

"You have no idea who I am."

"On the contrary, *you* have no idea who you are. You think you are a Christian, but you act like a noble heathen. 'You have heard it said "An eye for an eye and a tooth for a tooth." But I say to you "Do not resist one who is evil. But if anyone strikes you on the right cheek, turn to him the other also . . . ." ' And here you are bent on avenging your brother's death. How noble! How un-Christian.

"Shemelin has the true Christian spirit—the spirit of the willing victim. He has faith that whatever happens is the will of God. All the mad acts of man and nature somehow fulfill God's plan. The chaos of the world is just apparent. If we suffer seemingly for no reason, that's because God is testing us. He believes this world makes sense, even if the sense isn't apparent.

"But you don't believe the world makes sense. You believe in revenge. You believe that man and nature are unjust, and that the only way to find justice is to assert it yourself. If you had lived in the days of Jesus, you would have sided not with Jesus but with Barabbas—with the rebels. You would have attacked Rome and the puppets of Rome with acts of terror. You would have attacked the state to avenge the injustice of life. You would have attacked Roman justice because it was just a hoax. You would have dared confront the meaninglessness of life and have shocked others into recognizing it. You would have made your own justice and your own injustice rather than accept whatever the world gave you.

"You have potential, Pyotr. That's why I talk to you like this. You'd make a fine anarchist."

Pyotr was tired, confused. At first Laperdin's words just irritated him. Pyotr had never given much thought to what he believed or didn't believe and why. He had simply accepted the labels his parents had given him: "Christian" and "Old Believer." But today's experience had shaken him up. He needed some explanation for who he was and how he could have done the things he had done. He needed some label for himself to relieve the guilt of all that killing, to restore his self-respect.

At such a moment of weakness, he couldn't help but be flattered that someone, apparently intelligent and educated, was paying so much attention to his character. Might this godless man have some special insight? What would his own mother think? What would Sonya think, if she knew he had the impulses of a revolutionary?

After about an hour they came upon the main body of the Chinese army, thousands strong, in the midst of setting up their bivouac. They caught the weary enemy unprepared, and charged at the center. Panic spread from the center outward, until the whole Chinese army was fleeing. Bulatovich and his detachment pursued, trampling them and slashing at them with sword and nagaika. Since most of the Chinese had abandoned their weapons in their flight, it became more of a massacre than a skirmish. The pursuit continued ten miles, to the next station and dawn.

As for Pyotr, he hovered in the background, watching, wondering, trying to make sense of what he felt and of what Laperdin had said. Pyotr presumed that the others, all but Laperdin, were still going through what he had gone through earlier in the day, were still letting loose this inner force. He pitied them and yet feared them too, realizing the intensity of the need that drove them, an impetus that seemed indiscriminate, as if they could lash out at anyone or anything that dared stand in their way.

13

Yakeshi, Manchuria, August 23, 1900

He's bewitched," insisted Kupferman, pounding his fist on feather mattress in his tarantass. "I saw it with my own eyes."

"But the Chinese are such bad shots," explained Strakhov, edging his way toward the exit. Kupferman had become increasingly unpredictable, lashing out at subordinates for no particular reason. Strakhov was adroit at humoring him, but these days that was a risky business; better to avoid him, to cut short their meetings.

"The Chinese don't shoot that badly. Especially that army we just met under General P'ao," Kupferman continued, not letting the subject drop. "Bulatovich is bewitched and that whole bunch of them, what do they call themselves? Mazeppy—they're bewitched, too. They were no farther away from those rifles than you are from me. Even somebody who had never held a rifle before couldn't miss at that distance. There's no earthly way that that many men firing from that close range could miss so many targets. They could have hit the Mazeppy over the head with the barrels, they were that close. No, it was witchcraft. Like Butorin told us, the bullets stopped in midair."

Strakhov was tempted to agree and further stir up Kupferman's distrust of Bulatovich. But the less said to this rather unbalanced commander, the better. He tried to take the matter lightly. "I didn't know you were superstitious, sir."

"It's not superstition," Kupferman replied angrily, making Strakhov cringe. "It's common sense. That Bulatovich is dangerous. It's as clear as can be. He even parades around under the name 'Mazeppa'—the label of an outright rebel. As for the Mazeppy, I have reliable reports that two of them were talking openly about anarchism while riding to Yakeshi. This Jew of his—this Yakov Shemelin—you see how he's stirred up the men with his radical religious beliefs. Just another aspect of the same thing. This Bulatovich is using a witchcraft he picked up in Africa, and he's fomenting rebellion in the guise of leader of some wild new religious cult. Witchcraft and hypnotism—yes, hypnotism, I'm sure—he has an unnatural effect on people. He must be stopped."

Strakhov didn't know what to reply. It all sounded so ludicrous, and Kupferman had been acting so strangely since the Shemelin business. His eyes were shifting nervously and now he had started to sweat, even though the night was cool. On the other hand, Kupferman's accusations led Strakhov to remember Sonya's enthusiastic questions about Bulatovich; she made no secret of the fact that she considered him little less than a god. Hypnotism, yes, perhaps hypnotism.

👑 👑 👑

"Did you learn that trick in Africa?" Smolyannikov asked. Bulatovich had just caught a horsefly in midair.

"No, in the Ukraine."

"Then what did you learn in Africa?" slipping, as he often did, from light to serious. They were lying in a grassy ravine on a mountainside, fighting off flies, mosquitoes, and annoying little black gnats, waiting until nightfall, when they could slip back to their own encampment. The night before, they had crept to within fifty paces of the enemy bivouac, where they could hear snippets of conversation as well as see the preparations the enemy was making.

Bulatovich was once again in command of the flying detachment, but he and Smolyannikov continued to treat one another as equals and friendly rivals. This new Chinese army, under General Chou Mien, had taken up position in the Greater Hsing-An Mountains, about a hundred miles east of Hailar. Rather than advance and meet the Russians on the plains, these troops were digging in and fortifying themselves on the mountaintops, taking advantage of the piles of abandoned railway ties and the huge log cabins that had served as warehouses for the railway construction crews. The mountains were heavily wooded, and the valleys that separated them were swampy and bug-infested.

"No more and no less than you could learn here," Bulatovich finally replied.

Smolyannikov laughed, but his eyes remained serious. "And what was that, my wise friend?"

"Maybe I'd call it 'the power of nature.' "

"Strange," replied Smolyannikov. "Sounds a bit Chinese. But then you probably take it differently, as something negative, something to be fought against and overcome. The way you look at life reminds me of a passage from Ecclesiastes. 'Whatever your hand finds to do, do it with your might; for there is no work nor thought nor knowledge nor wisdom in Sheol, to which you are going.' Or maybe I'm just projecting my own beliefs on you. Tell me what you mean by 'the power of nature.' "

Bulatovich looked at his friend quietly. Bulatovich wanted to impress him, to spin some elaborate philosophy justifying his random words; but lying here in the lush mountainside greenery, those words had stirred memories. "It probably doesn't make any sense. I'm not sure what it means at all. But it was on my third trip that it struck me. I had a long bout with fever that time and was troubled by dreams. I remember that I returned to the scene of my first elephant hunt two or three years before. But I don't remember if I actually returned or if I dreamed that I did. The essence is the same: I recognized the power of the jungle, the relentless force of nature, annihilating all that man ever does.

"Dadyazmach—that's governor-general in Amharic—Gabro Egziabeer of Lekamte was my host—an Oromo in the service of the Amharic Emperor. There were a thousand of us on the hunt. For the Oromo, an elephant hunt is serious business—like war—

not because elephants pose any threat to the villages, not for meat, not for ivory, but because the Oromo have elevated killing to a cult. There are still some tribes where a youth doesn't have the right to get married until he's killed an elephant, a lion, or a man. Having killed one of them, he greases his head with oil, wears bracelets, rings, an earring, and returns home with songs. A man can become a hero only by killing, and only a hero is a true man.

"Of the thousand men, four hundred were on horse and armed with three small spears each. The other six hundred were on foot, half with small spears, the rest with four-yard-long spears with yard-long metal blades. They call these long spears *djambi*. They throw them from the tops of trees when elephants pass under. The force of the fall of the djambi is so great that sometimes it pierces all the way through an elephant. Only I, my servants, and several soldiers of the *dadyzamach*, who could afford them, had guns.

"After a week, we spotted a huge herd—more than a hundred elephants, big and small, all red from the clay of the stream bed. Djambi bearers quickly climbed the trees by the stream. The grass was set on fire all around in a circle, and those of us on horseback quickly crossed the stream to frighten the elephants from fleeing in that direction. They panicked and scattered. In the forest, the djambi bearers struck at them; at the edge of the forest, the spear bearers on foot and my servants with guns. And as the elephants broke out farther, those of us on horseback surrounded them and struck them with whatever we could.

"The elephants pulled spears out of their bodies with their trunks and hurled them at us. If an elephant charged after one hunter, others would try to distract the animal away. I saw one elephant, no more than twenty paces from me, grab an Oromo from the saddle with his trunk and hurl him at the ground. Another elephant threw a large broken branch at another Oromo and broke his arm.

"When an elephant fell, it was considered the catch of the first hunter who had wounded it. That hunter would rush up to lop off the tail, the end of the trunk, and the ears as trophies of his triumph.

"All around, the grass blazed with a crackling sound; in the woods there were shooting and cries of terror and triumph and the bellow and screech of the panic-stricken elephants, throwing themselves now at one man, now at another. At moments of desperation, the elephants would pick up sand and grass with their trunks and throw it at the sky. The Oromo believe that's the elephants' way of praying to God.

"My mother would like to have seen that. She, too, believes that animals, even elephants, pray. No matter what God does to us, still for some reason, we pray.

"The stream was red with blood. We had killed forty-one elephants that day. I killed three myself and my servants, two. Five men were killed that day: three crushed by elephants and two hit by stray bullets. The dead men got little attention. It was a day of triumph.

"That night the elders gathered and sorted out the disputes about who had first wounded what elephant. The Oromo would use anything, including bribery and trickery, to prove their right to an elephant.

"No one disputed my elephants, since I was the only one with an elephant gun. So I didn't wait for the end of the disputes. I just left with my trophies.

"For the people of Lekamte, it was a great and memorable day, a day when boys became men, a day to sing of for months or years to come. For me, it was a day of unusual excitement, good sport, an exotic challenge. My life didn't depend on it, although I could have died there, and my life didn't change because of it. I was an outsider with no sense of its importance aside from the danger and the struggle and the hunt. I've always enjoyed hunting, and how could I have passed up an opportunity to hunt the biggest animal in the world?

"It wasn't until I returned there in dream or in fact that I got some inkling of the meaning of the event. Actually, maybe it's only now in the telling of it that the pieces are coming together.

"Sometimes I wonder what our lives would be like if we never talked about them. So often we change the way we think or act because of what we say. With our words, with the names we give to others and to ourselves, we change the way we see the world; we change what we believe, what we want to believe, and that changes how we act. Or so it seems . . ."

"Well, what did you see? What did you learn?" insisted Smolyannikov, swatting a mosquito that had been casually biting Bulatovich's cheek.

Disoriented, Bulatovich hit back, and they wrestled until Smolyannikov pinned him and slapped him again, playfully. "Wake up, Sasha, come out of it. So we haven't slept for a day or two. That's no excuse to stop in the middle of a story. What did you learn in Ethiopia? Out with it, now."

Bulatovich shook himself, brushed the bugs from his face, picked up his glasses (fortunately, intact), and fanned himself with his red cap.

"I learned something about myself."

"Well, what? Damn you."

"An Ethiopian general, Wolde Georgis—you remind me of him a bit, the same build—he said, 'You're a devil. I don't know how you ever got out alive.' We were on our way back from Lake Rudolph. The Emperor had ordered him to march to the south-southwest as far as Lake Rudolph and conquer all the land between, and he was doing that with an army sixteen thousand strong, ten thousand of them armed with rifles, the rest with spears. We were going through territory, first jungles, then desolate dry wasteland, that no European had ever seen before, that wasn't on any map, that even the Ethiopians had never seen before.

"Whenever I got a chance, I would set up my surveying equipment on a hilltop to make measurements for scientific purposes and so I could chart our course to our destination and back. One time when I was taking such measurements, my servants and I were suddenly surrounded by hostile natives, spears at the ready. There were only five of us, dozens of them. I was unarmed, having removed my saber and revolver to take my measurements. I had to act fast. I stared at the nearest native and shouted 'khalio!' which means 'peace!' I walked toward him with just my compass in my hand. I concentrated my full attention on him, and he answered 'khalio!' When I got within five paces of him, I beckoned to him. He looked at me indecisively, like he didn't know what to make of me. Apparently, the others were waiting to see what he would do. I kept my eyes on him. He came out of the bushes, walked up to me, and said, 'komoru,' which means 'king.'

I stretched out my hand, and he kissed it. Then I squatted and signaled him to do likewise. I took his spear and showed him that I wanted them all to lay down their weapons. Then I called to the other natives who were nearest to him and signaled them to come near. About twenty of them squatted near me. I showed them my compass, let them listen to my watch. Then I called to one of my servants and ordered him to take my place in the ceremony of hand kissing, while I quickly got my weapons. Then shouting 'khalio!' several times, we started to leave. We hadn't gone a hundred paces when suddenly we heard the loud shrieks of hunting horns and war cries. We were surrounded again. This time the natives were attacking in earnest. We opened fire and fought our way out and back to the main bivouac. One of my servants was wounded in the arm by a stone, and a mule was killed. The rest of us escaped without a scratch.

"That was when Wolde Georgis called me a 'devil.' 'I don't know why your servants didn't just scatter and leave you there. It must have looked like you were as good as dead. But they stayed. I don't understand this hold you have on them.' I was flattered with those words. I was proud of the way I had stared down those hostile natives and gained time."

"Stared them down?"

"But that's not the point. Wolde Georgis added, 'Don't let this success swell your head. This bravery of yours isn't true courage. It's just the daring of youth and inexperience. Only when you have retreated and been wounded will you understand danger; and then this daring of yours will change to the conscious courage of a battle-hardened warrior.'

"He was right, you know. It reminds me of something my mother once said about istina and pravda, the truth of faith and the truth of fact. True courage, I suppose, comes from the depths of your being; you do what you have to do because you are who you are.

"So what did I learn? I learned that I had learned nothing, that that was my failing. I was cursed with good luck, and I have been ever since. I've been sick with one fever or another; but I've never been wounded."

"Damn it, man, will you get to the point of the story? What happened when you went back to the scene of the hunt?"

"Yes, yes, I was in fever. I had moments there when I was both awake and asleep, moments when I was lost and alone in the jungle at night and I saw people and places that I had known back in the regiment in Petersburg or back in the Ukraine—right there in the midst of the jungle. When I went into a fever, I'd relive those times, like I am now."

Bulatovich fanned himself again with his cap, then continued. "The hunt. Yes. I was on other hunts like that later, invited along as a courtesy by local governors. Sometimes the trail went cold; we never caught up with the elephant herd. But at other times there was that same pomp, danger, and excitement, sharing in the joy of victory. There were several times when I should have been killed—once my gun jammed and I came within inches of being trampled—but always I was the lucky one. I'd thank the Lord that I'd lived to laugh about it; it was all a game to me, fine sport.

"But when I returned, if I really did return—you have to imagine what the scene had looked like when I left it—the damage from the fire and the desperate battle of a hundred elephants. Where there had been jungle, there was nothing left standing more than knee-high for a mile around. And when I returned, two, not more than three years later, it was jungle again, as if nothing had ever happened there.

"I remembered the spot clearly—the fork in the stream, the little waterfall, the boulder hollowed to the shape of a bowl by the flowing water. I expected that the battle would have left its mark, even if an ugly one, a scar. But nothing."

"Yes," said Smolyannikov, nodding in agreement. "The Preacher says it in Ecclesiastes: 'A generation goes, and a generation comes, but the earth remains forever. The sun rises and the sun goes down and hastens to the place where it rises. All streams run to the sea, but the sea is not full; to the place where the streams flow, there they flow again.'"

"You accept it. I could not." Bulatovich continued. "The jungle frightened me. I took out a machete and started chopping wildly in the undergrowth. I didn't know why; I simply had to, until I fell from exhaustion and slept there on the jungle floor. When I awoke, drenched by a sudden rain, fresh growth had already sprouted where I had chopped.

"The growth was too easy, the growth of weeds. There was no struggle to it. How could it be worth anything, this growth and regrowth? A man's life is a struggle, and it can mean something; I'm sure it can—it must. But mankind? This perpetual re-creation, one generation after another, one war after another—how can it mean anything, this repetition?

"I think I know now why the Oromo fight the elephant. It's like Shemelin says life is: a test. If you don't go to fight the elephant, you never face the test, you never live.

"It isn't a matter of breathing or not breathing; it's a matter of living or never living at all, like true courage. But how can I speak of it? I've never experienced it. I'm just imagining it. That elephant hunt wasn't my test. It was just a game for me. I went through the motions. I wasn't running to face the test of life, to meet the challenge of elephant and nature. But the Oromo do. They respect the elephant they kill. They watch it pray to the same God they pray to. They honor the trophies they take home with them. Next year there will be new elephants and new men to hunt them and new jungle growth to hunt them in; and the Oromo are unafraid because they have met their challenge and they know it."

"But have they solved anything?" asked Smolyannikov, leaning back with his arms crossed behind his head, staring through the underbrush at the orange glow of sunset. "If I were going to remake the world," he laughed, "I really wouldn't know how to do it. Or if everything keeps changing, how can anything mean anything? If everything keeps repeating, like in Ecclesiastes, what's the point of that either? Somehow you want to make a mark in the world, but it's hard to accept that millions before you have been making their marks, and millions after you will too—and how could you ever expect to recognize your mark among all the rest? It's hard to accept the fact that you're just a man, that nature won't make any exceptions in your case. Just a man, not a god—maybe that's the test."

"Just a man?" asked Bulatovich. "It's not so easy to be a 'man', at least not in the sense the Oromo would use the word. You aren't a 'man' simply because of the body you're born with. 'Man' is a name to be earned, like 'hero.' Maybe we're born with the potential, but only through actions, through meeting challenges can you earn your name. Maybe that's what we're here for—to become whatever we have it in us to become."

⚜ ⚜ ⚜

August 24 had been a day of triumph. Even Strakhov had to feel it. Although only a few would be labeled "heroes," they were all winners in the Battle of the Greater Hsing-An Mountains. And the victory had been resounding and complete.

Sonya greeted Strakhov warmly when he returned, affectionately checking every inch of his body to make sure there were no wounds or scratches that needed attending to. When she looked at him with those open curious eyes of hers, how could he refuse to give her a complete account of the battle? And when she asked so anxiously about Bulatovich, how could he hold back any of the details that were sure to delight her? He loved to see that flash of joy in her eyes. He'd have done almost anything to make her look at him that way.

Strakhov told her, "We arrived at the mountains in the midst of a heavy rain. As you know, the troops had brought along all their transport. It was a motley assemblage—not a sight you'd soon forget—wagons and carts of all shapes and sizes, pulled by horses, mules, and camels, carrying all the 'souvenirs' the troops had acquired in Hailar, everything from vases to sofas.

"Bulatovich had a huge waterproof tent waiting for us, something he had managed to appropriate from the Chinese. There on tables he had spread out detailed maps and scouting reports, showing the disposition of the enemy troops, fortifications, gun emplacements, elevations, natural obstacles—everything needed for a campaign. I have to give the man credit for being thorough.

"The Chinese were prepared for a frontal attack. With a frontal assault, we'd be running through swamp and over a stretch of open ground, well in range of their mountain guns. But this detailed intelligence made it possible to hit them from three or four angles at once; even a fool like Orlov could see that.

"Orlov gave the obvious orders, then turned directly to Bulatovich. 'Take four squadrons, your Mazeppy, and some railway guards. I want you to circle wide around the enemy, crossing the mountains some twenty miles south of here and blocking the road to Tsitsihar where it's bordered on either side with swamp. In all it will probably be a ride of sixty miles over rough terrain. You'll leave at dawn. I'll count on your being at that road by noon of the next day.

" 'Meanwhile, our main forces will attack from front and sides, making full use of artillery. If our attack is successful—and we have every reason to believe it will be, God willing—the Chinese will have to retreat along this road, running right into your hands. With the right timing, we could trap and completely annihilate the enemy. If you should go astray or for any other reason fail to reach that road on time, the enemy could slip away, and the war in this sector could drag on until winter. We're counting on you.' "

"What did he do?" asked Sonya anxiously.

"Wait. First imagine Orlov in all his pomposity. He's just given Bulatovich this choice plum of an opportunity—admittedly not a simple task, but who wouldn't jump at a chance like that, especially now that the war is winding down? Well, Orlov turns to the rest of us, like we were a pack of medal-grubbing swine, and says, 'Now remember, all of you. Here we do not look at war as a pastime or as a means for achieving personal ends, but as a sacred cause.' Can you believe that Orlov is actually that naive?"

Strakhov didn't wait for an answer. He knew she wanted to hear more about Bulatovich, but Strakhov had to make his point. "Just imagine—he had just received reports that the Allies had taken Peking and that the Russians had taken the main rail junction at Harbin. The outcome of the war was a foregone conclusion. Even the outcome of this battle was a foregone conclusion. The Chinese had committed all their resources on the false assumption of a frontal attack. And regardless of their superior position and even with a frontal attack, their poor marksmanship would once again decide the day in our favor. There are only a few enemy strongholds left now; and they aren't so much obstacles as prizes to be taken by the first Russian detachment to arrive. The question isn't who will win the war, but what Russian officers will get credit for capturing such major cities as Tsitsihar, Kirin, and Mukden. Let's face it, that's how you get ahead in this army—by building your reputation when you get the chance.

The war may have started like a holy crusade, but it will certainly end as a race for rank and recognition. If Orlov is really that naive, he could be a real impediment to the ambitious men in his command."

"But Bulatovich? Is he all right?"

"Of course. He arrived at the road ahead of schedule, fought off an unexpected detachment of Chinese reinforcements from Tsitsihar, then turned and cut off the retreat of the army just beaten by Orlov. With the exception of a handful of soldiers who slipped away to hide in forest and swamp, the entire Chinese army was killed or captured. Bulatovich came through without a scratch—your typical shining hero. It must have been the pinnacle of his career."

"And the Mazeppy?"

"You're interested in them, too, now? Well, don't fret yourself. In the whole battle only three Russians died."

♔ ♔ ♔

Bulatovich remembered the battle somewhat differently. At first from a distance, it seemed like a celebration with loud fireworks. Then the retreating Chinese appeared, closely pursued by Bodisko's and Smolyannikov's railway guards streaming down the middle of the road, forcing the Chinese into the swamps on either side of the road.

Eventually, Bodisko himself appeared. And Dr. Volf. But no Smolyannikov.

While others celebrated, Bulatovich and the Mazeppy rode up and down that road, long into the moonlit night.

No one found Smolyannikov, but Butorin found his lifeless form—face disfigured—hard, unmoving, unchanging, a poor caricature of the man.

Bulatovich sent the others back, slung the body across his saddle, and stayed there awhile, staring at the grass where it had lain. Already the grass was springing back; soon it would stand straight as if nothing had ever lain there, as if there had never been a man named Smolyannikov.

With that empty form on his saddle, Bulatovich rode back alone that day of triumph.

14

Greater Hsing-An Mountains, Manchuria, August 24, 1900

That night Bulatovich prayed as he hadn't prayed since his sister Lilia had died. He lay prone on the ground in his tent, beneath the icon of Christ, and prayed as he had as a small boy at Lutsikovka when he, Lilia, and Meta shared the same bedroom with their German nurse. His bed had been behind a screen. The wall over his bed was covered with icons and pictures of saints and scenes from the Bible. When everyone else was asleep and the nurse's candle had burned out, he knelt there behind the screen whispering prayers.

He now prayed, as he had then, with the fervor of a young boy who believes implicitly in the power of prayer. He was careful to name every name, to name them in the right order and with the right solemnity.

First he repeated the Lord's Prayer and the Creed. Then he prayed for his father in Heaven, for Lilia and Meta, for his mother, for his great-aunt Elizaveta, for the Tsar, the royal family, the Holy Synod; for his companions Old Hrisko the huntsman and Mihailovo the coachman; for his dogs Usman and Ryabchik. He prayed for everyone he knew and cared for, and for all the people of Russia and of the world. He prayed to God the Father, to Jesus

Christ His Only Son, to the Holy Virgin, to St. John, to St. Anthony, to St. Alexander Nevsky . . .

His child's ritual had evolved night after night from imitation of the prayers his mother had the children say each morning by the bed of their great-aunt. The evening ritual, his ritual, had become a private series of acts and words, with all the rigidity of a holy ceremony handed down through the centuries. And he prayed with the fervor that comes from the belief that any deviation from his self-set rules, any omission, especially the omission of a name, could bring harm instead of blessing to the person forgotten or slighted.

He prayed to confess his sins, to ask forgiveness. Each night he confessed the day's tally of petty crimes, of which there was always an abundance, for he was an independent boy, forever disobeying his mother, treating her with insufficient respect, running off to hunt with the coachman and the huntsman when his mother had said he shouldn't, always bickering and arguing with his sister Lilia. He was an evil little boy. His mother had convinced him of that. He vaguely sensed in the matriarchal household that he was guilty of the primordial sin of being born a boy and becoming a man. He sensed that some women are self-sacrificing and saintly and other women are evil; but that all men are basically evil, however they may act, for they have evil thoughts and evil secret wishes, even when they outwardly behave.

It was confusing, because certainly his father, who was now in heaven, was not evil. And he thought of God and God's only Son Jesus Christ as men, not to mention St. Anthony, and a multitude of other saints. Even soldiers, men like Alexander Nevsky, for whom he was named, could be saints.

By night, he prayed for strength against evil thoughts, for understanding, and for forgiveness. By day, he disobeyed his mother and hid from his governess; he went hunting and riding and played soldier and fought and enjoyed himself. Sometimes, with Old Hrisko and Mihailovo, he'd disappear for weeks at a time; then after he returned to the interminable scolding of his mother, his prayers would last long into the night.

He couldn't say why he was praying now in Manchuria. He simply had to, repeating all the childhood phrases, all the names

of those he had wanted blessed, so many of them dead now—
Lilia, Elizaveta, Mihailovo, Old Hrisko, Usman, and Ryabchik.
Prayer hadn't saved them, nor had it brought them back, not his
prayer. Maybe his soul wasn't strong enough, hadn't been tested
enough for his prayer to have power. Just because his prayer didn't
work at that time didn't mean that all prayer was useless. Just
because God didn't listen to him didn't mean that there was no
God. He felt so small, insignificant, powerless.

He prayed, "Thy kingdom come, Thy will be done on earth
as it is in heaven . . ." But he didn't want God's will to be done,
whatever it was. He wanted his own will done. That was the
point; that was why he prayed. What was the point in praying for
things to happen as they would anyway? He prayed for things to
change or to stay the same. He prayed for what he hoped for. He
wasn't just going to suspend judgment, step back, and accept
whatever life threw his way. If it was God's will that these people
should die, there was something wrong with God's will. And as
he lay there on the ground in his tent, he cursed God as he had
when Lilia died.

He was tired and weak and the ground was hard and unyielding. His back could not blend with the ground as Smolyannikov's
had. He derived no strength from the earth as Smolyannikov had.
Reality was an obstacle to be overcome by will or by prayer. He
prayed for strength of will, for the strength to believe that death
was not final, that life had some meaning.

He needed strength. He needed Asalafetch. Sonya had given
him dreams, but Asalafetch had given him strength.

Sonya had stimulated his imagination—the way she saw the
world and the way she made him see it—as romantic, exciting,
exotic, full of interest and adventure. She was largely responsible
for his going to Ethiopia in the first place and for his wanting to
return there. She made him believe that there was or could be
some special destiny for Ethiopia, that in all the world it was
unique and important. He had found the facts that fit the belief,
but she had made him want to believe it even before he had ever
been there.

By the time he met Asalafetch he was ready for her. Sonya
had stirred yearnings and expectations of some almost mystical
and sensuous relationship. She had primed the well of his imag-

ination to its brink. It took but a touch from Asalafetch to make the water flow.

When Asalafetch held him and touched him, she gave him new strength. She made him forget his individual weakness, insignificance, and mortality. She made him feel like the power of nature was his power—that he was in fact a god who could do anything.

No need to fear blindness or death. She touched him, and their life force joined. They lay on the earth—that potent black jungle earth—and the strength of the earth was their strength.

One night she said, "Possess me, I am the earth and the jungle, and you are my king." He would have answered, but she silenced him with her tongue.

That night they reached new heights of sensation, for she had ventured beyond the realm of touch. Now she was arousing not just his body, as she had before, and not just his imagination, as Sonya had before, but both at once. He should have realized that she was using him or hoping to use him. But even now he couldn't blame her; he needed her now, as he had needed her then, to reach those heights.

After that night, she no longer mocked him as she had before; she no longer stopped him from telling her he loved her. He felt that they had passed some barrier, that now she accepted him as he was, that they were closer than ever before. Little did he suspect that she had begun to recognize his possible usefulness, or that she felt the time was ripe, that she had to capitalize on her investment before duty required him to leave her.

After that night, word play became a part of their foreplay, and it was she, who had always preferred silence, who initiated it. She called herself his "thigh maid," his servant, his sexual slave. She would say, "You are my King. What is your kingdom, O my King?"

And he'd pick a country at random. "I am the King of France."

"And I am the thigh maid of the King of France. I take away his cares and heighten his joys. I am proud to be the woman of the King of France."

One night he picked "Ethiopia," and her hands tensed, anxiously. "Would my lord and master like to be a king in Ethiopia?"

He laughed, "Why not?"

"Be serious," she insisted. Her touch was deliberate. "The Emperor Menelik trusts you. Whatever you ask of him, he will give you. Ask for a domain of your own. He has given as much to far less useful men than you."

"Are you serious?"

She reverted to the tone of their foreplay. "My lord and master is a great man. He is a king in Ethiopia. He is a great warrior. He has killed many elephants. He wears the earring of a great hunter. He has placed his residence at Lake Tana near the source of the Blue Nile. He rules firmly and wisely and is loved by his people. In all of Ethiopia, there is no finer kingdom than his, and I, Asalafetch, am honored to be his thigh maid. I take away his cares and heighten his joys. I am proud to be his woman."

He knew that Menelik had the power to dispose of his territories as he saw fit, to create new *rases* or princes, new dadyazmaches or governors-general, that he had and would give such honors to foreigners, if he saw fit.

On his first journey to Ethiopia, Bulatovich had met such a man, an adventurer named Leontiev, formerly a lieutenant in the Russian army, who had gained favor with Menelik and been granted the title of dadyazmach. Bulatovich and Leontiev had met under most peculiar circumstances.

Bulatovich was riding ahead on camelback with native guides to get permission from Menelik for the Russian Red Cross mission to proceed to the capital. Without word directly from Menelik, local governors were reluctant to allow the mission to proceed, never having encountered Russians before and suspecting their motives. While crossing the Danakil Desert, Bulatovich and his guides were set upon by bandits and left without any animals or supplies—as good as dead. Then who should chance upon them there in the desert but this Leontiev—probably the only other Russian in the country at that time. It was the sort of incredible luck that is enough to make a man believe in divine providence, to believe that he has some special destiny he is being saved for. That destiny might well be to rule a piece of this ancient country and to make his land a model for the rest of Ethiopia, or the rest of Africa, to follow.

After that day, Asalafetch returned again and again to the idea of a kingdom of his own, while guiding him through their mutual fantasies and sensations.

"My king is a great man," she would say. "He sits high on his throne and dares to say to man and to God, 'Mine is the kingdom and the power and the glory.' And I and all our people worship him as a god."

It was fantasy hovering dangerously close to reality. Sonya fantasized, too. She liked to see people and places in a romantic, exotic light. But for Asalafetch fantasy was a tool, a means to an end. She wanted not the fantasy itself and its accompanying sensations, but the practical results that could come from it.

Basically, she was, as she first told him, antiromantic. She preferred to keep things on strictly a physical basis—pure sensation, unsullied by thought. Her sensations were strong—he could feel how she trembled—but she insisted that she felt no emotion, nothing like what he called "love." When he was incredulous that not just she, but, as she insisted, her whole people were unromantic, she jokingly attributed it to circumcision. As was customary, her inner labia had been trimmed seven days after birth. She told Bulatovich that, in some outlying districts, it was the clitoris that was removed. Both operations were supposedly done to control a woman's sexual appetites. But Bulatovich found it hard to believe that anyone's appetite could be greater than hers.

Later, when she began her subtle manipulation of his imagination, she denied her previous denials. He was different from any other man she had known. She pretended that now she was beginning to understand what he meant by emotion and love.

She began hinting that he needn't return to Russia, at least not for years. He could obtain some official position in Ethiopia, as Leontiev had. He could become a dadyazmach, a governor of a province, and she could continue to be his woman. Marriage and divorce were simple matters in Ethiopia. They could go through a civil ceremony that would make them legally married but that could be dissolved at any time simply by saying a few words in front of two witnesses. That was the nature of most marriages in her country—nothing final and binding; just a convenient arrangement that could be set aside when, eventually, he decided to return to Russia.

He was ready to believe her. He wanted to believe her. By now, Ethiopia was a part of him. If he left, he had to return. He couldn't imagine leaving permanently. This was his land. These were his people.

He had seen enough of unnecessary waste and misery. He wanted to take charge, as Asalafetch suggested, of some small part of the country where he could set an example so powerful that it would change all of Ethiopia. He wanted a domain in the northwestern sector, near the source of the Little Abay for an initial period of ten years. In that time, he would undertake to establish discipline, build a series of forts to protect the region from incursions by the British, train a local army for self-defense, make of this newly conquered and dubiously loyal border territory a strong, efficient, and productive province.

He went so far as to submit a proposal to Vlasov, the Russian special envoy in Addis Ababa, trying to get official Russian approval before approaching Menelik. Vlasov replied that the idea was preposterous. He refused to forward the request to Minister of War Kuropatkin or to Foreign Minister Muraviev and ordered Bulatovich not to write them directly.

Bulatovich hadn't expected such resistance. He reported to Vlasov only occasionally, as a matter of form. Vlasov was only an intermediary, the official route for reports to Muraviev. Bulatovich was largely on his own on this expedition. Menelik had heard of a buildup of British troops in the Sudan, and said he wanted military advice. Bulatovich's proposal was a direct result of that assignment, or so he claimed. The British threat appeared imminent and he wanted to take direct action to deter it rather than simply advise.

As for Asalafetch, he hadn't told her about his request. He wanted to surprise her.

Now he had to decide whether he wanted to defy Vlasov, his titular superior, and take the matter directly to Muraviev and Menelik, both of whom, he suspected, would welcome the suggestion.

The night after he received Vlasov's refusal, Asalafetch and he again played their game, and again he was a king in Ethiopia. And it felt good to be king.

"Tell me your wish, O King. I am your slave."

"My wish . . ." he paused and reflected. "You shall be the mother of my children, the mother of kings."

"I am not enough?" she laughed. "You want children, too?"

"It seems fitting and necessary. This flow of the force of nature must continue. Old generations flow to me and through me to new generations. New kings must come."

She caressed him urgently as she did when she had had enough of talking. Her hands aroused him quickly, but he insisted on an answer. "Will you have my child?"

She rolled aside angrily.

"Will you or won't you?" he persisted.

"No."

"You mean you aren't pregnant yet," he tried to interpret. "It may take time. But you will have my child."

"No. Never!" she yelled back. "Many men have planted their seed in this ground, and nothing has grown. You are no different. It's best. If I thought I could have babies I would do something to stop them. I'm here on this earth for having pleasure and for giving pleasure—here and now. If you want to grow babies, spread your seed in other soil."

They did not make love that night. He dreamed the dream of the elephant hunt and of returning to the scene of the hunt. Only this time nothing had grown. Everything was dead and all was desert, as if some enemy had carefully sown the soil with salt. In his dream, Bulatovich tilled the soil and planted seeds and carried buckets of water from the stream and returned day after day and year after year to do likewise, but nothing grew, not even a weed.

It was an agonizing dream that he continually drifted into and out of through the night. When free of it, he knew it was still there waiting to haunt him yet again. When he woke up in the morning, his first drowsy thought was to blame Asalafetch for having given him that dream. He wanted to hurt her, to make her regret having done that to him. So he said, "I'm going to request permission to return to Russia."

232

She looked up at him with her dull daytime eyes. It was one of the few times he could remember looking into her eyes—and he saw nothing. They reflected nothing. They revealed nothing. She was so common, so uninspiring when looked at calmly and analyzed in the daylight.

She didn't say a word. He repeated himself, and still she didn't answer. Somehow he had expected that she would plead with him to stay, that she would sound so hurt and helpless, that, of course, he'd change his mind and stay and defy Vlasov and become a king. But she simply got up and left. By the next day, she had attached herself to a French soldier of fortune.

He put in his request to return to Petersburg. He had had enough of Ethiopia. Menelik, the Emperor who listened so intently to his advice, listened just as intently to the English and the French, slyly played the one nation against the other, and kept his own counsel. Back in Russia, Muraviev favored involvement in Africa, but Kuropatkin was opposed to all foreign entanglements; and it was Kuropatkin, not Muraviev, who had the ear of Tsar Nicholas. Russia would do nothing of significance to help Ethiopia. Bulatovich's presence there was superfluous. All his work there had been futile.

He requested permission to pass through the Sudan, Egypt, Jerusalem, Kurdistan, and Persia on his return trip, so he could quickly survey the political and military situation in those areas. Muraviev sponsored the request, but Kuropatkin vetoed this attempt by an upstart junior officer to meddle in foreign affairs. When Kuropatkin's answer arrived, Bulatovich immediately wrote back asking for assignment elsewhere in the world, anywhere but Ethiopia, wherever he was needed, somewhere where his actions could make some difference, where his efforts would be supported, away from this total futility.

Even then, he had expected to return to Ethiopia. He had expected and hoped that he would be patted on the back and told how indispensable he was, how important his work was, how much he was appreciated. Kuropatkin would get into a stormy argument with the Tsar and fall into disgrace. Menelik would personally request the return of Bulatovich and would give him whatever he wanted. Asalafetch would come running to his side.

233

Half awake, he heard himself praying, "My kingdom come, my will be done . . ." He realized what he was saying, shook himself, slapped himself in the face, and started praying rapidly and fervently, "Lord Jesus Christ, Son of God, have mercy upon me, poor sinner that I am."

After that third trip, on his way back to Petersburg he stopped off at Lutsikovka to see Vaska. Masha, married now and mother of six, was taking care of him. How matronly and obese Masha looked, sitting there with the little black boy on her lap.

He was in no hurry to see Sonya again. He had been gone for nearly a year, and it had been 2½ years now since they had had a chance to be alone together. Correspondence was difficult. It took a month or more for a letter to travel from Addis Ababa to Petersburg. And after meeting Asalafetch he had stopped writing altogether.

After the experience of Asalafetch, it was difficult to think seriously of Sonya. Besides at twenty-three, Sonya was a woman with social connections and charms, ripe for marriage to some eligible young man with prospects far greater than his. But he felt obliged to meet with her, to make it official that they were going their separate ways.

He didn't recognize her when she got off the train. His eyes were tilted up, aiming a few inches higher than her eyes. He was so used to being with Asalafetch. In fact, he was straining to look over her head looking for her as she walked right up to him and introduced herself.

She was in town supposedly for a shopping trip with friends. They walked up and down Nevsky Prospekt together, looking through shop windows, stopping now and then to buy a hat or gloves so she'd have something to show when she returned. She was very much in control, self-possessed, decisive. This was her world, just as Ethiopia had been his.

She asked him about his latest trip. He was vague in reply, avoiding any reference to Asalafetch.

He carried her packages and she talked about the lectures

she was attending at the free university. Despite her parents' objections that it wasn't ladylike, she was pursuing her interest in African languages and cultures, not for a degree but gathering whatever information she could from the few sources that were available to her.

"I don't expect I'll ever be returning to Ethiopia," he told her as they came out of their third hat shop.

She looked at him somewhat puzzled, then once again led the way down the street saying "You always say that when you first come back."

"Never!" he yelled at her, as Asalafetch had yelled at him under different circumstances. People turned and stared at them.

She looked at him seriously. "But I had hoped that we might . . . You have changed, haven't you?" She stared at him inquisitively, then turned decisively, and once again led the way—this time at a hurried pace, as if she really did have a lot of shopping she had to do. At times he had to rush to keep up with her, feeling rather foolish dodging the other shoppers and strollers and balancing his stack of parcels. But she just plunged ahead absorbed in her own business, as if she were content to have him accompany her but if he should choose not to, she would still do what she wanted to do the way she wanted to do it.

That evening back at Tsarskoye Selo, he immediately went to see the colonel, her father.

"Sir," he asked as calmly as he could, "I have a request to make."

The colonel smiled. "Does it have to do with my daughter?"

"No," replied Bulatovich, somewhat disconcerted. "Manchuria."

"Manchuria?"

"As you know, sir, hostilities have broken out. I believe I could prove useful there."

"So soon? You just got back from Africa. Did you have some argument with Sonya? Some little lover's squabble?"

"No, sir," he looked at the floor, the desk, the quill pen.

"Strange. Most strange. I was under the impression that you and she were quite close. Not that you had given me that impression yourself. But my wife. She certainly took a fancy to you from the start. And maybe it was wishful thinking on our part;

but we, I must confess, always rather hoped that you two would get together."

Bulatovich looked up in surprise. He hadn't realized that it would have been so easy, so perfect.

"I'm sorry, sir, if I ever led you to believe that. I certainly hope that I haven't led Sonya to believe that. I do care for her. She's a lovely girl. We are close friends. But I don't think either of us ever seriously thought of marriage. You see, sir, I grow restless in the city. I need action. I need a challenge. I hope to put this peculiar bent of mine to good use in service to the Tsar. I want to go wherever I can be of most use, in the most active capacity. I understand from the newspapers that there's shortage of officers in Manchuria."

"All right, my boy, all right. I had wished to be able to call you 'son.' But that's an old man's foolishness. Whatever I can do for you, consider it done."

15

Kuan-ch'eng-tzu, Manchuria, September 9, 1900

He was riding on a train—from Odessa to Petersburg? from Petersburg to Chita?—he was always riding on a train. And the train carried him forward regardless of what he understood or didn't understand, regardless of what kind of person he was or was becoming. The train steamed ahead; and when it reached the end of the line, he would have to get off; it was over. Time for others to hop aboard and go for their ride.

But what line was he on? Did it matter? He had thought he had a choice. For four years he had been racing along at full steam, quite proud of himself for the direction he had chosen, for the rapid success and special status he had achieved in Ethiopia. But now, somehow, switches had been thrown, and he found his train was on another track, going in another direction. And he wanted to get off, but he wasn't sure how to get off or what to do once he was off. (Was it ever possible to catch a second train?)

Muraviev was dead. He had died suddenly. The papers claimed it was a heart attack after a stormy interview with the Tsar. Probably an argument over China. It was said that Muraviev was largely responsible for Russian involvement there, and now war had broken out.

So Muraviev was dead. Kuropatkin's influence would predominate all the more in the government. The slim hopes that Bulatovich had entertained of returning to Ethiopia were now gone. The train simply couldn't go there anymore.

Why should he do anything? The train was going where it was going anyway. Why struggle? Why strive? Why not just sit back and let it happen? Read a good book. Eat a satisfying meal. Perhaps try to sleep.

A young Chinese girl entered his compartment. Chinese Sonya. Strakhov's woman.

What was she doing here? If he was on his way to Manchuria, he hadn't even met her yet. He must be dreaming, or maybe he wasn't on his way to Manchuria. Maybe he was leaving.

She smiled at him, stared him boldly in the eye. He averted his glance and looked out the window. She was still staring at him—he could feel it. He wanted a woman badly. Whenever he relaxed, whenever there was no new challenge to meet, he felt the absence of Asalafetch, the absence of her arms and legs pressed about him. He was tempted to find out if this young girl was as willing as she seemed.

"Do you have anarchist tendencies?" she asked.

"What?" It brought him away from the window.

"Pyotr said you said you have anarchist tendencies. Rather, he said he told you he had them, and you said you did, too. Don't get me wrong, now. I don't mean that as a slur against Pyotr. Actually, I respect him for it—for telling me and for having those tendencies. It's an aspect of his character I hadn't detected before. And I pride myself on being able to read people through their eyes. I must admit, these anarchist tendencies frightened me at first, but they made me curious too. I thought, here is a man of 'depth,' a man with impulses and energy that he has to keep under control. I couldn't forget something Pyotr said you had said: 'What's the virtue of a virtuous life if you don't have to struggle to act that way?'

"You don't believe. I can see it from your eyes. You were napping and I woke you. You're wondering 'Who is this girl?' and 'What's she talking about?' Well, my name is Sonya. You may remember when your men rescued me at Hailar. Now I'm engaged to Major Strakhov. Well, not actually engaged. The general won't let us make it official yet. But as good as engaged, because Major Strakhov is a most reliable and responsible man. I think very highly of him. Someday I'll love him; I know I will. But here I am rambling on about my private business. I'm always doing that; not just to anyone, but to people like you. I've heard so much about you that I feel I've known you for years. And when Pyotr told me that you said you had anarchist tendencies too, I just wanted to run over here and tell you that I think none the worse of you for it; that I respect you all the more. And yes, I wanted to meet you. I've wanted to meet you for some time now. And now's the time that I got the urge actually to come up to you and speak to you, and I've done it. Pleased to meet you, sir." And she curtsied.

"Where are we?" he asked, fascinated by the lively good-natured flow of her voice, and the way her eyes, so slightly out of line, caught and held his attention.

"Kuan-ch'eng-tzu."

"Kuan what?"

Sonya laughed. "Yes, you're half asleep, exhausted. Kuan-ch'eng-tzu. Remember? General Orlov sent you to check the road to Harbin, to make contact with the Russians who had taken Harbin. Strakhov told me all about it."

"Harbin . . . yes . . ."

"It was after the Battle of the Hsing-An Mountains. And while you were gone, we met the army of General Rennenkampf at Tsitsihar. Rennenkampf then took command of the cavalry from both armies, leaving Orlov with the infantry, and raced southward toward the city of Kirin."

"Oh, God, yes, Rennenkampf," Bulatovich remembered. "Has he taken Kirin yet?"

"No, not yet. He's such a brave commander. Strakhov speaks highly of him, thinks he's far better than Orlov."

"He would," mumbed Bulatovich, wiping the sleep from his eyes and slowly getting up from the ground.

"But of course. They say that Rennenkampf captured Tsitsihar with less than five hundred Cossacks—and that was a well-fortified city with a garrison of more than nine thousand."

"And nobody's going to beat him to Kirin."

"Certainly not. Strakhov says that would be awful. He's thinking of our future, you see. He understands the ways of the army. It's all very strange to me. But he feels it's very important to be with the army that gets credit for taking Kirin. And he's very pleased that Rennenkampf's in charge now, because Rennenkampf understands how important these details can be. Why, ever since he met up with Orlov and took command of the cavalry regiment, we've been moving at breakneck speed."

"I know. I had to race to catch up with you."

"Yes, Pyotr was telling me. You were off on patrol when the armies met. And you were on the road for nearly two weeks."

"Fine. I'm glad you have some of your facts straight. As for 'anarchist tendencies,' that's a malicious rumor. I'm a Christian and a loyal servant of the Tsar."

"You needn't apologize. There's nothing wrong with being a rebel. Really. To hear Pyotr talk, a person would be less of a person without those tendencies. Like his need for revenge. If he were a true Christian, he would have just accepted his brother's death as God's will; everything that happens is God's will. But he couldn't. Something inside of him rebelled. And he went riding off to revenge. Laperdin explained."

"Look, I'm tired. I want to sleep. What do you want of me?"

"It's a missionary," she said in a loud whisper.

"A what?"

"Some forty miles south of here, a missionary is in trouble. I heard from a Chinese Christian convert who managed to escape. Boxers have surrounded the church. Any day, any hour, when the mood strikes, they will kill him and the converts who are with him."

"What business is that of mine?"

"But you're a hero."

Bulatovich laughed. "Look, young lady, if you want something done, get your Major Strakhov to see to it. I'm just a subordinate here. I'm not some knight-errant with the right to go riding off rescuing everybody in trouble. Tell Strakhov about it; he'll . . ."

"I did. He'll do nothing. Rennenkampf's waiting for the right moment to strike Kirin."

"From what I've heard of him, I'd say he's waiting for the reporters to get here. No point in performing heroics unless it gets proper publicity."

"Well, he is waiting, whatever he's waiting for. I don't under-

stand any of this military business. I'm sure he's a great general
and Strakhov's a great major. But they're not interested in what
happens to a missionary."

"And you are?"

"I was raised by one."

"And why isn't he taking care of you now?"

"Because no one rescued him when he needed it. I was in
Hailar. I saw it with my own eyes. The Boxers surrounded the
church and waited. Three days, four days. I lost count. They must
have been purposely torturing us. By day you couldn't see them
and you couldn't hear them, but you knew they were there, waiting to kill you if you stepped out of the church. By night they set
off firecrackers and shot their guns wildly and made hideous
shrill screams, as if any moment they would attack. Father Ioann
led us in prayer. There were thirty of us. Women and children.
All Chinese Christians. We prayed that a savior would come. But
no one came. On the third day or the fourth day, they attacked.
We had no weapons. Father Ioann didn't want us to fight at all.
He just knelt there in front of the icons and waited. But the
women picked up chairs and boards and metal—one even used
a cross—and swung wildly at the Boxers as they poured through
the doors. One of the women must have hit me by mistake or
fallen on me. When I woke up, the bodies of two women were on
top of me. Everyone was dead, even Father Ioann, even the littlest
children. I cowered in a corner, behind the panels of icons, for
several days. There was water and some wine and bread for the
sacraments. The stench of the dead was sickening, but I daren't
show my face outside for fear of the Boxers. It was one of your
men—Sofronov—who found me there."

"I remember," he replied gently. "But what do you expect of
me now?"

"I expect you to act honorably, like the true hero you are. I
expect you to do what's right simply because it must be done,
because the life of this missionary and the lives of his converts
are at stake. You aren't the kind of man who takes risks only for
publicity and personal advancement."

Bulatovich laughed weakly. "Where did you get this notion?"

"I can tell things. Really I can. I can look into a man's eyes
and know what kind of a man he is. And you are a hero, believe

me. Besides, if you don't do this, you'll just be sitting idly about camp."

"And Kirin?"

"That's Rennenkampf's business and Strakhov's business. That's military politics, not war. They don't need you, and they don't want you. Strakhov told me all about it."

"He did?"

"Yes. He was with Rennenkampf when you and your Mazeppy finally caught up with the regiment. 'Who are those creatures?' asked Rennenkampf. He can be quite haughty when he wants to be. 'Are they some sort of marauding mercenaries? More of those damnable railway guards, with their loose discipline and their foul habits?'

" 'No, Your Excellency,' replied Strakhov. 'I regret to admit that they are part of our regiment.' You see, he doesn't really care much for you. He doesn't understand you the way I do.

" 'Your regiment?' asked Rennenkampf in disbelief.

" 'Yes, perhaps General Orlov mentioned to you a certain Staff-Rotmister Bulatovich?'

" 'The name does sound familiar,' said Rennenkampf.

" 'He's an incorrigible glory hunter, with a tendency to disregard orders.' You see, even Strakhov thinks you're an anarchist. And I haven't said a word to him about it." She quickly shifted back to her Strakhov voice. " 'You know the type, I'm sure, Your Excellency. Unquestionably brave, but far too independent in his thoughts and actions for one so lowly in rank. He's forever trying to upstage his superiors and walk away with all the credit and glory. Unfortunately, this being wartime and what with the shortage of officers, we've had to make use of him. Mostly, we send him off with small patrols, trying to keep him away from the rest of the men. A bad influence.'

" 'Indeed,' answered Rennenkampf. 'I know how to deal with men like that. Forget your patrols. Let him rot in camp.' That's what he said: 'rot in camp.' You won't be going to Kirin. They're going to leave you while they go off to get all the glory. But you don't want that kind of glory, and you don't want to rot. I can see that. Anyone could see that, looking at those eyes of yours."

He pulled down his glasses and looked over them. "How can you tell? These are rather thick lenses to see through."

She smiled back. "You will then? I knew you would."

"Maybe," he laughed. "Just maybe. If what you say is true and they go riding off and leave me here with the Mazeppy, maybe we could slip away for a day or two and nobody would be any the worse for it." His tone became more serious. "Do you think your missionary can wait?"

"I don't think he has any choice. I just pray that he'll still be alive when you get to him."

✿ ✿ ✿

Kuan-ch'eng-tzu, September 22, 1900

Sonya," Bulatovich said softly. "My Sonya."

Sonya Vassilchikova had sent him a letter, at last. It read:

> Dearest Sasha. I love you. I tried to hate you, to forget you, but I can't. It's been dreadful here at Kovno. My mother's forever inviting eligible young men to come and visit. She's determined to marry me off, and Father's washed his hands of the matter. Mother claims she always had a soft spot for you until you went off and voluntccrcd for Manchuria. She took it as a personal affront and talks about it all the time—to me, to all of her friends. She makes it sound like you were a scoundrel, leading me on and then running off to Africa and then to China; like my life was ruined by it; like I'm past my prime already. It's dreadful having to listen to her. I don't think she'll let you past the door when you come back.
>
> But all her talk just reminds me of you, makes me miss you all the more. Please come back. I'm tired of playing the decorous young lady. I've written dozens of letters like this at night and torn them up in the morning. But this time, I'm going to give it to a servant girl and have her run and post it right away, before I have a chance to change my mind. I do love you. What does it matter that my parents will try to keep us apart? We'll run off together— to Africa, to China, to wherever you want to go. I'm yours. Do you understand? I'll do anything to make you happy. Absolutely anything.

I don't know what happened in Africa to change you; you looked and sounded so distant, preoccupied. I only hope that you've been able to sort out your problems since then. We had so little time to get reacquainted.

I do love you. I do so much want to love you. Just come back to me safely. I want you whole and sound to take in my arms . . .

Tears. He could feel her tears. No, rain. It was raining. He awoke, with rain dripping in his face, and rolled over. The letter. He groped quickly in the dawn twilight and found two wet sheets of paper. The ink had run and was indecipherable.

"Sonya!" he exclaimed aloud.

"Are you awake?" he heard.

"Sonya?"

"Yes, it's me." Chinese Sonya turned up the flap. "I hoped you were awake, but I didn't dare wake you. Then I heard you call my name. It was as if you were dreaming . . ."

"Yes, yes," he replied impatiently. "Don't just stand there in the rain."

She ducked and entered his little tent. They touched. He recoiled. She noticed the letter. "Oh, what a shame. I hope it wasn't anything important?"

"What do you want" he asked angrily, as if she were some-how responsible for the loss of the letter.

"Rennenkampf has left for Kirin."

"And Strakhov?"

"He went too."

"Kupferman?"

"He's been feeling poorly, hasn't budged from his tarantass for a week. The doctors go running back and forth. Nobody seems to know what's wrong with him."

"How many men did they take?"

"Just two squadrons."

Bulatovich laughed. "Either he's a fool or a genius. That's a city of over a hundred thousand."

"Strakhov was quite confident. He said 'The fewer the men, the greater the glory.' "

Bulatovich laughed. "So now you want me to save your precious missionary?"

"Yes. Now, you must—while your superiors are gone."

"He's probably dead. It's been nearly two weeks."

"But surely you'll try?"

"It's a risk. We don't even know if there's anyone left to save, and you want us to go risk our lives. I don't think I could ask the Mazeppy to do such a thing. Not now . . ."

"Now? But they're ready. They're waiting. Even Shemelin."

"Shemelin? But he's an invalid."

"He was an invalid. I just came from his tent. He was frantic. 'The boy is gone!' he said. 'What?' I asked. 'The boy. Your orphan boy. Mitya. The boy who led to my rebirth and conversion. He has vanished. Like he had never been here at all.' He was trembling. I looked about and could see no sign of him myself. It certainly was strange for Mitya to take off like that in the rain at night. But you never know with an orphan. Maybe his parents had died on just such a night. Maybe he'll come back when the sun shines.

" 'Relax,' I told Shemelin.

" 'Relax, you tell me. Was he ever here at all?'

" 'He is as real as I am.'

" 'Don't say that. Don't!' And he took hold of me and shook me. When I told him he was hurting me, he stopped and lowered his head in shame. 'I'm sorry,' he said; 'it comes over me sometimes. I get this feeling that there's nobody in the world but me; everybody else is just my dreams and nightmares. Maybe there are other real people, but I have no way of knowing who's real and who isn't. It's like there's just me and God, and God is testing me with all these dreams.'

"I slapped him. 'Now stop this foolishness,' I said to him. 'Rennenkampf has left for Kirin. Bulatovich and the Mazeppy are ready to go rescue the missionary and his converts. God grant that they're still alive. And you're going to go along.'

" 'Me?' he asked. 'But my back. It hurts just to breathe.'

" 'Then just don't breathe.'

" 'But I'm a Christian now, a true Christian. How can I fight?'

" 'How can you not fight?' I asked.

" 'I have to pray,' he whined. 'I have to stay here and pray. You know the little book with the hero without a name—*The Way of the Pilgrim*. It once belonged to your missionary father. You and Sofronov helped explain it to me. I'm trying to learn to pray without ceasing like it says in the Bible, like the hero in the book does. When I pray, the pain stops. When I learn to pray without ceasing, I'll never have pain again.'

" 'Then pray with your saber. Pray with deed, not word.'

"He stared at me, like he didn't know what to make of me. Then he smiled and crawled out of his tent and stood up straight for the first time in a month. Just to look at him you could see he had new faith. It's awful when a man loses faith. He was tired of being an invalid, especially after the novelty had worn off. The crowds had died down and there was nothing left but the pain. The prayer took his mind off the pain and the boy reminded him that his experience of God had been real. Now the boy was gone. But I could see from his face, at least for a moment, that the pain was gone, too. He was ready to take his chances with the world again."

"Then let Shemelin lead them."

"But you're the one they look up to. You're the one they worship."

"Worship?" Bulatovich laughed uneasily, sitting stiffly as far from her as he could in the narrow tent. He couldn't keep from glancing at her soaking-wet tunic that clung to her breasts revealingly. His back, rubbing against the side of the tent, got wet from the rain; but he didn't budge.

She seemed to sense his discomfort. She made no effort to move closer to him and looked at the ground. "Many people look up to you. Why, Pyotr, for one, almost worships you. He said so himself, just the other day. I was asking him about his sweetheart, Nadyezhda. He wears her picture in a locket. A lovely girl. I asked if she had written to him. He was obviously upset by the question. She probably hasn't, or the letters went astray or were ruined, like yours there. I do hope it wasn't important. Not a letter from a sweetheart?" she rambled on, still looking at the ground, not really wanting an answer. "I asked him about Nadyezhda, and he asked me about Strakhov. He doesn't understand what a fine man Strakhov really is. He's the father of my child, you know."

"Your child?"

"My child to be. It's too soon to know for sure. But I feel it; I know it in my own way. And I'm so proud and happy. I had to tell someone; so I told Pyotr, and now I'm telling you. But you mustn't say a word to Strakhov. He might think I was trying to shame him into marrying me, that I was trying to trap him. But he has to marry me out of love alone. Nothing else makes sense if we're to spend a lifetime together."

"Why are you telling me this?"

"Yes. Excuse me. It's my way to talk too much. I just wanted to tell you about Pyotr. He said, 'People have a bit of God in them.' Maybe you'd call it 'soul,' but Pyotr called it 'a bit of God'; and I rather like that. Soul makes me think of something separate and individual. But he meant what makes us one—that special spark. He said that's how he can be both a Christian and an anarchist. 'If a bit of God is in us, then maybe our impulses aren't evil—not all of them, anyway—even when they go counter to the teaching. I don't know. I think that when we care for some-one, it's the God-in-us responding to the God-in-him or the God-in-her.' And he said, 'Other times, I feel like I myself am nothing, but there are gods out there in the world—Bulatovich for one. And I feel honored to serve him.' That's what he said."

Bulatovich took off his glasses and rubbed the lenses on his shirt. "So poor little Pyotr thinks I'm a god, does he? Well, it's a shame that saying and believing don't make things real. Butorin thinks they do. He doesn't know anymore when he's lying and when he's telling the truth. A fine pack of madmen I have about me. And me the worst." He held his head in his hands and rubbed the sleep from his eyes. "That letter. I could imagine it saying all kinds of things. But now I'll never know for sure what I saw and what I imagined; like Shemelin, I'll be plagued with that doubt, because I'm not quite as mad as Butorin." He shook his head sharply. "I'm sorry. I was dreaming. It takes a while to wake up. Especially when a young lady like yourself appears, how am I to know when I'm dreaming?"

"Then get up and go. The missionary may still be alive. But who knows? Maybe they'll kill him and the others with him when the rain stops. Go prove yourself a god or a hero or whatever you like." She looked him straight in the eye.

And he stared back at her as if to say, "Can we really be here at dawn in my tent in the rain saying these things?"

She reached out and took his hand. "Yes, I am real and you are real. And men are in real danger. Be proud of your pride. Use your strength. There's no sin in saving a man. The Mazeppy are waiting." She squeezed his hand and left as suddenly as she had appeared.

Just after she left, it occurred to him that he had more he wanted to tell her. Something she had said reminded him about God. Once in the jungle and once as a child, he had had a sensation. It lasted only a moment. "Light and warmth," he wanted to tell her, "and a feeling of peace, yes, peace with the grass and the ground and the sky. Then it was gone. I think people have called such a feeling 'seeing God,' but I didn't literally see him. Rather, it was as if He were in me. The moment passed so quickly, I wondered if it had really happened or if I had imagined it. But I hoped it meant that God is here in me. And probably in others as well. I felt that to find God I should look inside myself. But I've never had the leisure to explore that possibility. Or I never made the time to do it. Probably, I'm afraid that if I look too hard, I won't see anything at all.

"There have been other times, too," he confessed to himself, "times of extreme and sinful pride, times when I felt that I was not just an ordinary man like other men, when I expected that somehow in my case the laws of nature were or could be suspended, when I thought that I could be stronger than other men or braver than other men or more than man, more than mortal. And maybe when I've pushed myself to the limits of physical endurance, maybe that's what I was testing, asking my body again and again, 'Am I just a mortal? Or can I be a god?' I know it sounds insane. It's only a matter of a moment here and there, a moment of foolish prideful exultation, followed all too quickly by pain and exhaustion. But I have felt that, fool that I am."

With that he shook himself, stood up, and strode toward his horse. It was time to act.

16

Ta-ku-shan, Manchuria, September 29, 1900

Bulatovich came to attention and saluted as smartly as he could. He was rather out of practice with such formalities. "Staff-Rotmister Bulatovich reporting, Your Excellency."

"Yes," mumbled Rennenkampf, glancing up for a moment, then continuing to sort through the papers on his table. He was thin, rather athletic looking for someone in his late forties. The ends of his large black mustache turned up sharply. His gestures were restless and abrupt. He paid only minimal attention to Bulatovich.

"Your Excellency, I request permission to attempt to rescue a missionary."

"Missionary? Another missionary?" He sat up straight now and stared at Bulatovich. "Didn't I already hear something about a missionary? Yes, and an officer named Bulatov, I believe. About a week ago . . ."

"Yes, sir. This is another missionary." He resisted the temptation to brag. The first rescue mission had been easy: they rode up, the Boxers ran away, and that was that.

"Ah yes, Staff-Rotmister Bulatovich. Now I remember. I have

heard a lot about you, but I didn't expect to meet you. Considering the chain of command, I didn't think the necessity would ever arise. Now, this matter that you wish to bring to my attention, did you approach Major Strakhov about it first?"

"Yes, Your Excellency."

"And what did he say? Did he tell you to bring the matter to me?"

"No, Your Excellency, he did not. But . . ."

"Oh, indeed. You don't think very highly of the chain of command, do you? A trifle, you would say. I know your kind."

"But Your Excellency . . ."

"Don't interrupt a superior. I know your kind, I said. You think traditional discipline is outmoded. Railroads and machine guns. We must accommodate ourselves to this new world, you would say. But I say these forces can be disruptive; and unless we hold firm to our traditions and our discipline, all of society will fall apart. Modern inventions provide no basis for any order at all. We must redouble our efforts at obedience and discipline. The modern world makes discipline all the more essential. Give me two well-disciplined squadrons and I'll beat any army of rabble."

"Yes, Your Excellency. I understand you were very successful at Kirin."

" 'Successful.' Just 'successful,' you say? Do you understand that we took a city of 120,000, a provincial capital, and we had no casualties at all? Now, that's discipline."

"I heard that the Dowager Empress or her minister Prince Ch'ing had ordered the governor to suspend hostilities with the Russians."

"Rumors, lying rumors," Rennenkampf retorted angrily. "It was only after we had ridden boldly right up to the governor's palace and had taken charge of the city that the Chinese started spreading that story. The Russian press gave us full credit. They understood the situation. Why are you here, Bulatovich? Why did you defy your superior officer and come to me? Why are you deliberately baiting me?"

"I beg your pardon, Your Excellency," Bulatovich replied calmly and politely. This general, with his Germanic name and Germanic manner, reminded him of his old teacher Lemm. The same authoritarian stance, the same injustice—it was almost refreshing to come up against such a man, to be able to feel righteously indignant. Bulatovich was tired of moral quandaries, of doubts about himself and about God, tired of wondering where his life was going and why. Here was an old familiar challenge to meet. He hadn't expected such luxury. He smiled and smiled still more when he saw Rennenkampf's expected anger.

"Get rid of that stupid smile. That's an order. Do you hear me?" he raised his voice and stared at Bulatovich.

Bulatovich calmly adjusted the corners of his mouth to a serious expression, but his eyes still laughed.

"What did you say you want?"

"I request permission, Your Excellency, to attempt to rescue a missionary."

"Another missionary, is it? I understand you took matters into your own hands in my absence, that you went chasing off on some wild excursion on your own authority while your superiors were away at Kirin. I was willing to overlook that eccentricity of yours. I left the matter up to Major Strakhov. In the wake of our glorious triumph at Kirin, he was inclined to be generous. He let the matter drop and that was that. Now you have another one? Where do you find these missionaries? Maybe this time you hope the story will reach the press: 'Guards officer rescues missionaries.' How charming. Who is it this time?"

"A Frenchman. Lavoisier. Just seventy miles north of here."

" 'Just' seventy miles. And north, too, when we're heading south, toward Mukden. That countryside is still crawling with Boxers and bandits. And for one man, and a Roman Catholic at that, you're willing to risk the lives of Russian soldiers? Let the French take care of the French."

"He is a human being, Your Excellency, and a Christian."

"And what are you?"

"Pardon?"

"What's your religion? A name like Bulatovich—a Polish name, isn't it? And the father's name, Xavier—a Roman Catholic name, isn't it? They tell me you're called 'Mazeppa'—a rebel's name, isn't it? It all adds up. There's no place for troublemakers and rebels in the Tsar's army, and certainly not in the officer corps. You've already disgraced yourself in Petersburg . . ."

"What?"

"Some business with a woman, I understand."

"I don't know what you're talking about."

"Something about the colonel's daughter."

"Who told you these lies?"

"Suffice it to say, I know your kind, Bulatovich. If you want to go glory-hunting to erase a blot from your record, do it in someone else's command. Now get out of here, and don't let me see you again."

"But Your Excellency, a man's life is at stake."

"Then go if you like, but it'll be your life that's at stake. If you're not back here within three days—and I can't guarantee that we'll stay here even that long—I'll consider you absent without leave. And if you do not rejoin the detachment within a week, I'll consider you a deserter and take appropriate action. Is that perfectly clear? Do you still want to go chasing off after your dear Catholic missionary?"

Bulatovich quickly calculated. Three days, seventy miles. At Hsing-An, with four squadrons, he had gone sixty miles over rough terrain in a day and a half. It would be faster going with just a few men. If they met no opposition at all, like on the first rescue mission, they could just make it. "Yes, Your Excellency, I want to go. I'll take seven men, the seven best men in the Russian army; and we'll be back—I stake my career on it—we'll be back in three days." He squinted to emphasize his words.

"Seventy miles out and seventy miles back, through mountainous country, and no telling what resistance you may meet." After a moment of anger, Rennenkampf seemed to relent, having second thoughts about the degree of his harshness. "Don't be a fool, Bulatovich. Stay with us. Follow orders. Who knows, maybe this business will all be forgotten in a month or two. Perhaps you've grown too used to Orlov's lax methods. If you straighten out and do as you're told, you can go back to Petersburg with a clean record."

"As I said, Your Excellency, we'll be back in three days." He smiled, came to attention, and saluted smartly.

🛆 🛆 🛆

The confrontation had lasted no more than five minutes. Bulatovich had reacted automatically—committing himself, trapping himself, it seemed, without the slightest hesitation.

He couldn't help but laugh at the way he had reacted. It was like watching while a doctor tapped his knee and his leg flew up without his willing it. It was like the predictable action of a spring let loose from its restraints.

After long frustrating inactivity, after all his confusion and doubts about what he should do with his life—here was a cause, a quest, a nearly impossible task thrust at him as a challenge; and he jumped at it like a hungry animal. He nearly laughed aloud again, realizing how badly he needed a cause to fight for, to strive for to the limits of his strength. He could already feel a surge of energy coursing through his body. It felt good, physically good. There was no way he could turn back now. He might fail to save the missionary; he might die trying; but he would put his whole self into the effort; he had to or he wouldn't be himself.

Rennenkampf's terms—the noose he had just slipped over his head—only made the situation more interesting. Here he was, defying authority again. It amused him to think that someone might say that his whole life up to now had been preparation for this moment; he was destined to save this priest, despite all obstacles.

At dawn, after riding all day and all night, the Mazeppy reached the Ya-nu-shan Pass. That's what their guide, Pierre, a Chinese Christian, one of Father Lavoisier's helpers called it. The pass was blocked by two dozen mounted Chinese.

"Ready sabers," ordered Bulatovich.

"Stop, sir! Stop!" shouted Butorin. "Those men are bandits, not Boxers. They know how to shoot."

"Then we can't count on them missing. We'll have to duck," laughed Bulatovich. "Charge for the middle. Use your sabers only if you have to. Ride right through them and keep riding. Chances are they're just fighting to defend their territory. If we ride through and away, they won't pursue."

And the enemy parted as the Mazeppy charged, letting them continue on their way, just as Bulatovich had predicted.

Later that morning, they reached the mission, a crude stone structure with a cross on top, enclosed by a stone wall several feet high. It stood on the outskirts of a deserted mud-hut village.

The Boxers who had been hovering about the place dropped out of sight without a shot. Everything was going according to plan, thought Bulatovich.

As the Mazeppy rode through the gate and up to the door of the mission, two Chinese wearing crosses around their necks came running out, laughing and cheering. Bulatovich expected just to pick up the missionary and ride back—a simple matter, as simple as the last rescue mission. It was so easy to play "hero" for little Sonya.

Then Bulatovich walked through the door. There was only one room. It was dark, except for the morning light streaming through the doorway, casting Bulatovich's shadow—a giant stretching across the floor and up the opposite wall. He looked ironically at his own projected stature.

There was a heavy smell of sweat in the air. He would have opened a window, but they were boarded up and barricaded with bits of furniture. "Lavoisier!" he called. But no one answered. "Get your things together," he said in French. "We ride in half an hour." Still no response.

His men crowded at the doorway. Their shadows obliterated his, further darkening the room.

Bulatovich turned aside from the remaining light, groping with his feet and hands. He stumbled against a bed and heard a groan. "Lavoisier?" he asked, softly this time. Still no answer.

He reached out. Someone indeed was lying in bed. Probably a late sleeper, probably the missionary himself. He reached out and rolled the figure over to wake him. Starodubov struck a match. It was a man—gray hair, long gray beard; his eyes were open, but they had a faraway look. Starodubov struck another match and stepped closer. Large dark red spots on the man's face. Quickly, Starodubov knelt close to the man, jostling Bulatovich aside. Starodubov struck another match and pulled aside the filthy yellow sheet. More spots all over the abdomen, sides, and arms.

The match burned down and extinguished itself on his fingers. "Typhus!" he shouted with sudden pain.

"Let's get out of here!" responded Bulatovich. He and Starodubov crawled, scrambled, and finally ran in the wake of the other fleeing Mazeppy. Within a minute they were all once again mounted.

"Are you sure it's typhus?" asked Bulatovich.

"My son died of it. I'll never forget those spots."

"But we can't just leave him, can we?" asked Pyotr. "We came all this way. How can we turn back?"

"Do you want to catch it?" asked Bulatovich.

"No," Pyotr admitted. "But can we just leave him here to die?"

"What would you suggest?"

"Laperdin was a medical student. He told me so. Maybe he would . . ."

Everyone looked at Laperdin, who grimaced. "Yes," he said. "We've come this far. Why not save ourselves a priest? For the good of God and man. What the world really needs is another priest." Despite his irreverent tone, he quickly dismounted and walked back into the mission. After a few minutes he appeared again at the door and addressed the guide. "Pierre, fetch water, plenty of water, and boil it," he ordered in French. "Have those two friends of yours carry him out and put him under that tree over there. Better that he be in the fresh air."

"Is it really typhus?" asked Pyotr anxiously.

"Yes."

"Can you do anything for him?" asked Bulatovich.

"Perhaps."

"Will he live?" asked Starodubov.

"Considering his age, I'd say he has a fifty-fifty chance."

"Pierre!" shouted Bulatovich angrily.

The guide tripped and spilled his bucket of water, then looked up guiltily.

"Was your priest sick when you left him?"

Pierre nodded yes and stared at the ground.

"How long ago was that?" asked Laperdin.

"Nine days, maybe ten."

"And had he been sick for long?"

"Three or four days."

"Why didn't you tell us?" asked Bulatovich, exasperated.

"But you wouldn't have come, sir. I was afraid you wouldn't come."

"How contagious is it?" Bulatovich asked Laperdin.

"If we clean him up and keep him out in the open, we can probably get rid of the lice, and chances of its spreading will be slim—if we haven't caught it already."

"Lice?" asked Trofim, nervously scratching his back.

"Yes, they say that lice spread the disease."

Laperdin grinned as everyone started scratching, except Bulatovich, who felt an uncomfortable itch but felt foolish, sitting there on his horse, as the two Chinese, their pendant crosses swinging, carried Lavoisier out and lay him under the tree. Should they leave? Should they stay? Should he scratch or not scratch? And there was Laperdin, godless Laperdin, bending over the sick priest, stripping the rags from his back, closely examining the dark red spots.

Bulatovich dismounted and, despite or because of his fears, walked up to Laperdin. "Why are you doing this?"

"The man is sick. I was, as Pyotr said, a medical student."

"But he's a priest, and we all know you don't believe in God."

"And I don't believe in Christians either," replied Laperdin. "I've never met a Christian. In Russia, much less here in Manchuria. A Christian would do anything to help his fellow man, regardless of who that man was. A Christian would not fear death, all the more so wouldn't fear it when helping another man; for if he should die in such a godly act, surely he would go to heaven. But I've never met such a man. So why should I assume that this priest is one? Why should I hold it against him that he's a Christian, when he probably isn't, any more than you or I?"

"Then why are you taking this risk?"

"To shock. It amuses me to shock people like you, to make you wonder why you wouldn't do it yourself." He had a look of self-righteous glee on his face. He seemed to relish Bulatovich's discomfort. "Stay away. Really. I advise you to keep your distance. It is quite contagious until we've cleaned him up." Laperdin turned and shouted to Pierre. "Hurry up with that water. I don't care if it's cold. You can heat more later. Let's get this business started."

Bulatovich backed away reluctantly. Pyotr came running up to him. "Are we staying?"

"Laperdin!" Bulatovich shouted, as if suddenly awakened from a dream.

"Yes, sir."

"Can this man be moved? Can we tie him to a horse and bring him with us?"

Laperdin laughed. "If you want to kill him quickly, I can think of no better way."

"Then how long . . ."

"Not long at all. The crisis could come any day now. They say on the average it comes on the fourteenth day. If he isn't dead by then, the fever will drop, and he'll start to recover quickly. It's quite fascinating really. The disease is like a story, with a beginning, a middle, and an end. We came in near the end of the drama—the best part, really. See how dark those spots are on the abdomen? And the coma, with the eyes open and the pupils contracted. Yes, we have here a fine case, a very serious one. One of those rare occasions when the patient will come very close to death, then do a sudden about-face—if he's going to live, that is—as if he doesn't like what he sees in death and comes running back, very un Christian, really."

Bulatovich suddenly turned and vomited.

Pyotr quickly rushed to support him.

"Don't worry," remarked Laperdin, casually. "That's not typhus. Just fear. Plain old fear of death. A good old pagan impulse."

A rumble of thunder from the west. And another rumble. Bulatovich watched the black clouds gather, saw the wind thrashing the trees on the hilltops. There was no point in moving any faster than they were. The horses wouldn't be able to keep up the pace. But the rain, if it was heavy, could make them lose another half day or a full day even, and this was the morning of the fourth day. Bulatovich was already "absent without leave." Another two days and Rennenkampf could call him a deserter.

For a day and a night and a day again, Lavoisier had lain naked in the shade of the acacia tree. Laperdin had shaved his head and would regularly apply cold wet cloths to the bare scalp. Every two hours, day and night, Laperdin would rouse the priest as best he could, with hearty slaps on the face and cold water in the eyes, forcing milk or soup down his throat. Pierre and the other two Chinese did the fetching and the cleaning, but only Laperdin himself touched and nursed the priest.

On the second night the crisis had come. The priest had started sweating heavily. His eyes had lost their glassy look. And for the first time in days, urine streamed from his sick body. They left at dawn the next day, the priest, conscious but weak, tied to the back of a horse.

Again a rumble. Only this time the horse of one of the Chinese reared and the rider fell to the ground. It looked like an accident—an inexperienced rider and a frightened horse. Pierre quickly jumped down to help his friend.

"He's shot!" shouted Pierre. "It's Ya-nu-shan! We're at the Ya-nu-shan Pass. They were waiting for us."

More thunder, this time nearer. And shots continued after the thunder ceased—from the sides, from in front, and from behind. Pierre fell. The road was narrow, the undergrowth thick. The bandits were scattered along the hillsides.

"Don't stop to fight!" shouted Bulatovich. "Charge straight ahead. Let's get out of here!"

Before he had finished speaking, the rain started; and as he glanced up toward the clouds, he saw a boy coming at him, jumping from a tree. Afterward he remembered that face, he couldn't forget that face—a young face filled with hate and fear.

He felt a blade strike him in the side and, with automatic reflex, swung with his own saber, severing his assailant's head, leaving one eye, the nose, a hideously contorted mouth.

In his death throes, the boy grasped Bulatovich by the shoulders, viselike. The warm blood from the split skull gushed out at Bulatovich's face, getting into his eyes and mouth. The two of them fell to the ground, the boy first, breaking the fall; but still the grip held and the blood gushed.

✷ ✷ ✷

The pain was familiar now. He couldn't remember what it was like to be without pain.

Bulatovich was lying on his back, on the ground, in the forest. Someone was leaning over him now. Not the boy he had killed. Another boy, with a worried expression on his face and the beginnings of a beard. Pyotr, he remembered. Pyotr Zabelin.

"Where am I?" Bulatovich mumbled as clearly as he could.

"He's coming to!" shouted Pyotr excitedly. "It'll be all right, sir. You slept a full day, but it'll be all right now."

"What happened?"

"You screamed, sir. I've never heard such a scream. It was worse than Aksyonov, dying on the way back from Urdingi. It was a hideous sight, you lying there on the ground with your face in that bloodly mess and the dead boy still clinging to you. And the scream rose and fell, but it wouldn't end. Butorin started laughing uncontrollably. I don't know how much time passed. We were all frozen there, staring, holding our ears. Then I realized that the thunder had stopped. It was raining hard, but there was no more thunder and there were no more shots. We were all as good as dead until you screamed like that."

"How many casualties?"

"Pierre and that first Chinese who was hit are dead. Aside from them, you were the only one wounded, sir."

"Wounded?" he asked in surprise, then remembered the pain, the familiar pain. When he tried to sit up, it got worse. In his side. "Yes. I forgot. That face, that half a face—it made me forget everything. The priest? How's the priest?"

"Well enough to ride, tied to a horse, says Laperdin. You're the one who can't move."

"What?"

"Laperdin's order."

"Since when does Laperdin give orders?"

"Since you're in no condition to do anything," laughed Pyotr. "Besides, it's Starodubov who's in charge. He pulled that dead boy off of you and slapped you till you stopped screaming and lay there unconscious. The rest of us just sat in our saddles and watched. He was the only one with the presence of mind to do something. He wrapped his shirt around your wound, threw you over his saddle, and led us here."

"Where are we?"

"A good five miles south of Ya-nu-shan. Guards are posted. They don't seem to be following us. I can't say that I blame them.

They'll probably have nightmares for months from that scream of yours."

"But we must get back to Ta-ku-shan. Where is that Laperdin?"

"Here, sir." He was sitting right beside him. "If you like, we can get your corpse to Ta-ku-shan in about a day. But you we couldn't get there."

"Are you serious?"

"I'm never serious, sir," Laperdin smiled. "But your wound is."

"How serious?"

"For a while I thought you were as good as dead. You've lost a lot of blood. At best you'll be weak for quite some time."

"How long before I can travel?"

"I'd let it rest another couple days. We'll fix up a litter, something we can rope between two horses, to take you back in."

17

Ta-ku-shan, Manchuria, October 7, 1900

S taff-Rotmister Bulatovich reporting, sir." He snapped to attention and saluted formally.

Strakhov looked up in anger. "Bulatovich. So you finally decided to come back, did you? And on the ninth day. Did you save your precious priest?"

"Yes, sir."

"And how many men did you lose doing it?"

"Two of the priest's helpers died. One of us was wounded."

"Badly?"

"So I'm told."

"So a Russian soldier was badly wounded trying to save a Roman Catholic priest, and you feel no guilt, no regret?"

"For that? No, sir."

"It's your damnable luck. That's what makes you so callous. I've heard that story from your man Butorin about that general in Africa—how he said you would never know what true courage is until that damnable luck of yours ran out. Well, it's run out now."

"Yes, sir, I'm afraid it has."

"Do I detect a note of humility? Humility from the great Bulatovich? Wonder of wonders. What a pity it comes too late, or rather you come too late. You were under strict orders to return within three days. And if you weren't back within a week, Rennenkampf made it clear that you would be treated as a deserter. I warned you myself. I told you that we would be moving shortly, that we could not disrupt the general plan to go racing off after one missionary. I ordered you not to go to Rennenkampf. You disregarded my order. You went over my head. And Rennenkampf let you indulge yourself, within certain clearly stated limits. Well, your seven days ended two days ago."

"Request permission to speak to General Rennenkampf directly, sir."

"Permission denied. Actually, the request is an impossible one. He left for the south with the main body of troops several days ago.

"The war is over. We won, if you wondered. There are a few minor pockets of resistance, but by and large all of Manchuria is under Russian control.

"The cavalry regiment is under orders to rendezvous with Orlov and return with him to Harbin. The men will be returning to Trans-Baikal in time to help finish up the harvest. We just have a few administrative details to take care of first—you for one. What's wrong with you, man? Can't you stand up straight? You look like you haven't slept for days."

"You're right, sir. I haven't slept much lately."

"Well, then go sleep. Don't just stand around here like a drunken fool. You haven't been drinking, have you?"

"No, sir."

"Then go. Get out of here. Colonel Kupferman and I will consider your case in due order. Go, I said. That's an order."

Strakhov was quite proud of himself. He would enjoy telling this story to Sonya. He had acted decisively, with authority. Bulatovich was obviously cowed, bewildered to see him so strong-willed and in command.

With Kupferman acting strangely, suffering from sudden fits of anxiety, incoherence, and depression, Rennenkampf had relied heavily on Strakhov these past few weeks. And Strakhov had risen to the occasion, always a discreet half step behind his commander, making no attempt to upstage a superior. And Rennen-kampf clearly appreciated his competence and discretion. He had written a letter of commendation for Strakhov's permanent file and had recommended him for the Order of Ann of the Second Degree with Swords for his part in the capture of Kirin. But having such a story to tell Sonya about her precious Bulatovich gave him greater satisfaction than any medal.

In walked Kupferman, beaming with delight. "We've got him now. That magic of his must have worn off. He's just a plain mortal in more trouble than he knows what to do with."

"Indeed, sir. You should have been here, sir, to see him squirm."

"Here? Bulatovich? You mean Bulatovich was here?"

"Just a few minutes ago. He was standing right there at attention. Saluting as smartly as he could. Giving me a 'yes, sir' and a 'no, sir.' I've never seen him so docile. I suppose he knows when he's beaten."

"But that's impossible. I saw him not half an hour ago. On a stretcher. Badly wounded."

"He said that one of them was badly wounded. You probably mistook . . ."

"No mistake. I saw him with my own eyes. They were changing the dressing. A nasty wound in the side. He was pale, like he'd lost a lot of blood. Looked like he hadn't slept in days. I doubt that he could stand up if he wanted to."

"But he did, I tell you," insisted Strakhov. "He stood right here."

"My God!" exclaimed Kupferman, pointing at fresh blood on the ground. "What kind of man is that?"

Strakhov said nothing. He simply stood there, staring at the blood, clenching and unclenching his fists. There was no way he could tell this story to Sonya.

⚜ ⚜ ⚜

"I found him behind Strakhov's tent, face flat on the ground," Kupferman repeated for the tenth time to the small group, mostly Mazeppy, gathered at the hospital tent. They were all nervous, anxious for any news, any explanation regarding Bulatovich.

They kept going over remembered details, trying to find some meaning in them. "Why did he do such a damned fool thing?" asked Kuperman. "Why risk his life to show off to a superior?"

"Pride," answered Trofim. "He's a proud man."

"And he'd die for pride?"

"He'd sell his soul for it," Trofim replied, crossing himself quickly with two fingers.

"But why? Why this chasing after missionaries, this disregard for discipline? Why this infernal pride?"

"He tries to prove something to himself," said Starodubov. "He's not proud, Trofim. He wants to make himself proud."

"He tests himself," offered Shemelin.

Kupferman turned pale, as if he just now realized that Shemelin, this man who had caused him so much trauma was standing right beside him and that he himself, a colonel, was fraternizing with such men, talking with them on an equal basis. "But why?" he asked angrily. "Why does your leader act this way?"

Laperdin turned to Kupferman and lifted his glasses for a moment to stare at him. "That's what he asks himself. That's what fascinates me about the man—he keeps asking himself. He doesn't expect to get answers from anyone else. He acts as if all the answers were inside himself. 'Is there a limit? Where is the limit? Why is there a limit?' "

"The God-in-us," added Pyotr. "He's trying to get in touch with the God-in-us."

"Nonsense," asserted Kupferman.

"It's a matter of soul, sir," suggested Sofronov, in a respectful tone. "He's not just testing his body; he's also testing his will, his spirit, his soul. And not just testing it. He's also making it strong by using it."

"But he has no discipline," insisted Kupferman, once again absorbed in the question at hand, half forgetting who he was and whom he was talking to. "He seems to expect rewards and recognition and advancement as if they were his by merit, by right. But they are only his if they are granted by superiors. I don't care how brave you are, what great deeds you have performed; you must obey. Even if the orders are foolish, you must obey. That's what we have to teach recruits. That's what someone should have taught my father.

"A fine example *he* set," he said aloud to himself. "How

Mother could have loved him, disorderly beggar that he was . . . and she did love him; she still laughs warmly whenever she speaks of him. *I* never made her laugh.

"But Bulatovich, yes, Bulatovich, he's an educated man, an officer. He should set an example. Only by the example of men like him can we hope to instill the proper discipline in these men. From him I expect unswerving discipline. And I expect him to strive for the same from his men. I expect . . ."

Sonya laughed, breaking the seriousness of the moment. She was kneeling by Bulatovich's bedside, wiping his brow with a cold wet cloth. She was paying no attention to Kupferman and the Mazeppy outside the tent. Dr. Volf was joking. Tense with concern, she laughed loudly, even though the joke was a bad one.

Kupferman whirled around as if the laugh had awakened him. "Anna, is that you?" Everyone fell silent. He looked about, bewildered, then embarrassed. Why had he thought of his wife? He thought of her so rarely. And it had been so long since he had last heard her laugh like that. Not since the early days of their marriage, before he had instilled proper habits in her, before she had learned to obey. And then again, she had laughed like that when she was having that affair. He hated to admit it, but he missed that laugh, that joyous look in her eye—youth with all its disorderly hopes and desires.

Why was he standing here, with everyone staring at him? That was Sonya, Strakhov's Sonya who had laughed—lucky Strakhov, so young and she so very, very young. Kupferman found himself turned toward the open tent, staring at her. She was looking back at him smiling, with a touch of pity, pity for the old man who was losing his wits. What was he doing here? Why had he talked so freely with common soldiers? Why was he lingering here for them to stare at him? He longed to stretch out in his old familiar armchair. He longed for his wife. Could she laugh again? he wondered. Would he ever make her laugh?

⚜ ⚜ ⚜

"Your precious Sonya was there," Kupferman told Strakhov.
"Where?"
"At the hospital tent, with Bulatovich."
Strakhov grabbed his hat, as if to go immediately.

265

"He's flat on his back," laughed Kupferman. "Unconscious. No need to be jealous. Not yet." He had never chided Strakhov about his woman before, had never envied him before; maybe because he had never before realized what he himself was missing.

"Sir, that man should be court-martialed for desertion."

"You can't court-martial a man who is unconscious."

"Then we'll wait until he regains consciousness and then court-martial him."

"Such passion, my dear Strakhov. We have our orders, remember. We must rejoin Orlov and proceed to Harbin."

"You yourself said he's dangerous. He has an unnatural effect on people. Even on me, I must say—standing there like that when he's half dead and never letting on that he had been wounded. Only a showman, a rebel would do such a thing. He must be stopped. He must be court-martialed."

"Well, I'll not have his blood on my hands. I'll not play Pontius Pilate to his Christ. Bring him along. Let Orlov deal with him."

"I thought of that, too," replied Strakhov. "But Dr. Stankevich says he can't be moved."

"Then don't move him. Simply leave him here. If he lives, that's the will of God. And if he dies, that's the will of God, too. I'll have nothing to do with it. Nothing, you understand? I'm tired of being responsible for people. People I don't even know. Let them be responsible for themselves. And I'll try to be responsible for myself. I'm going to retire. Yes, retire. And the pension be damned. I'm going home. Yes, home. It's time I went home to my wife. If Bulatovich tries to start a rebellion or whatever he's up to, that's his business, that's his test, his trial. If I try to live peacefully with my wife, that's my trial. God grant us both strength and wisdom."

"I don't understand, sir. I don't understand you at all."

"It's time for me to see to my soul, son. My everlasting soul."

✥ ✥ ✥

Sonya went to Strakhov's tent early that evening. She wanted to be sure to get there before he did. She had been sick again that morning. She felt certain now that she was pregnant, and she wanted to tell him. She wanted to share her joy with him, and even her qualms about forcing him into marriage couldn't restrain her anymore. She simply had to tell him.

She had imagined disrobing and waiting for him naked and giving him great pleasure before she told him. But when she took off her clothes, the ground felt lumpy and hard and cold. She was uncomfortable. Her stomach started bothering her again. Her body was changing at a bewildering pace. She was both excited and frightened by the process taking place in her. She was in a mood just to sit in a corner, at peace with herself, alone.

But Strakhov would be coming back to the tent shortly, and he had come to expect that they would make love as soon as he set foot inside. She smiled at the thought. She did it for pleasure and for the pleasure of giving pleasure. And he enjoyed it, too; she was sure of that. But more than this, he seemed to need it—physically and mentally. She could recollect times when he got no pleasure from it at all—he was so wrapped up in the business of the day—but yet he insisted on doing it. Men were so strange.

As for whatever business of the moment was distracting him, she tried not to meddle in that. After his initial help in seeing to the problems of the Chinese Christians in Hailar, he had put up increasing resistance to similar requests from her. It made him uncomfortable. He felt a conflict of interests, or was afraid that others would construe things that way, especially when he was in a position to make decisions himself. How could anyone expect him to judge a petition fairly, on its merits, when he was living with its chief proponent? She sensed his discomfort and respected it. She never discussed with him the matter of Lavoisier. Thinking she was sparing Strakhov's sensitivities, she had gone straight to Bulatovich—the man most likely actually to carry out the rescue, officially or unofficially. She had intended her silence as a sign of respect for Strakhov, but he seemed to have taken it otherwise. That was why she felt it was all the more important to put him in a good mood before telling him about the baby, to do everything she could imagine him wanting her to do, even if she didn't really feel like it, even if she would rather just be alone.

She was unused to the climate of this hilly region of central

Manchuria. The heavy rains of September had ended abruptly with an October chill in the air. The ground was cold. She wrapped herself up in a blanket and huddled in a corner.

She must have fallen asleep. The next thing she knew, Strakhov was unwrapping her and caressing her rather anxiously, doing all the little things that normally excited her, but doing them impatiently and a little roughly. She was a bit put off that he hadn't spoken to her yet or even kissed her gently on the lips. She still wanted to please him, but her body simply wasn't responding to him. She was tempted to pretend that she was still asleep, half hoping that he would lose interest and leave her alone tonight, half curious about what he would do if he thought she was asleep.

Her lack of response made him still more impatient. His fingers hurt her.

"No, please, stop," she said quietly, and firmly pushed his hand away. "I just don't feel like it tonight. I'm sorry."

He shut her up with an insistent kiss on the mouth, and his hand insinuated itself where it had been before.

"Please." She pushed it away again. And he kissed her hard again, forcing his tongue into her mouth despite her resistance. She pulled her mouth away. "I want to make you happy, dear. Believe me, I do. I'm sorry. I just don't feel like it tonight. But if you feel you have to, then do it quickly, please, just do it."

Much to her surprise, he didn't tenderly cradle her in his arms and tell her that he loved her, that it was only giving her pleasure that gave him pleasure, that he understood, that it was all right. That's what he would have done, what he had done more than once in their first days together. But no, this time he simply went about his business, as if her lack of participation didn't bother him. Perhaps it even inspired him to be a bit more forceful, a bit rougher, as if he were trying to prove his manliness to her or trying to arouse her. She couldn't help but stiffen, looking up into the dark where his face must be, wondering what was going on in his mind.

It seemed to last forever; he seemed to drag it out on purpose. Or was he having trouble getting aroused himself? But finally it was over. And he rolled over and lay there beside her, still breathing heavily, not having uttered a word of endearment.

For a moment, she thought that she should tell him about

the baby now anyway. Maybe he'd understand her moodiness if she told him. But instead, without really thinking, she said, "Bulatovich is quite sick."

"Is that all you can think about—Bulatovich?" he snapped back, sitting up quickly. "You make love to me—if you can call that making love—and the first thing you think of is Bulatovich?"

"Are you jealous, dear?"

"I've got every right to be," he snarled. "You're obsessed with him."

"Oh, you are jealous!" She suddenly hugged him tenderly. "I do love you, you know. You're my man. My only man."

"And Bulatovich?"

"Well, he is sick. Very sick. It turns out he's not only wounded, they think he has typhus, too. Caught it from the missionary he saved."

"Typhus!" Strakhov shouted angrily. "Don't go near him again. That's an order!"

She smiled at this sign that he really cared for her.

But he continued "Don't you realize how infectious typhus is? Why, you could pass it on to me."

Quickly, she opened the tent flap. Campfire light streamed into the tent. She examined his eyes closely. Yes, that was what he was thinking—of himself, just of the danger to himself. At this moment, he was concerned about himself, not her.

She slipped on her clothes and quietly crawled out of the tent.

"Where are you going?"

"To the hospital tent."

"To see Bulatovich?"

"Yes."

"Then don't bother to come back," he replied in a threatening, self-righteous tone, as if he expected her to apologize and crawl back in with him, afraid to lose his love.

"Don't worry. I have no intention of coming back. Ever."

From October 7 to October 12, Strakhov lingered at Ta-ku-shan. Kupferman left on October 8 with the main body of the regiment to rejoin Rennenkampf, but Strakhov stayed behind, ostensibly to clear up some minor administrative matters.

He never once went near the hospital tent. He never again brought up the matter of Bulatovich. The question of court-martialing him or exonerating him or giving him a medal (as the rescued priest insisted he deserved) was never officially resolved. Strakhov simply removed Bulatovich's name and the names of the Mazeppy from his roster. Detachments had met and merged and re-formed and split again. Some would stay until the new status of Manchuria was established by treaty. Perhaps some would be stationed here permanently, and Manchuria would become in fact, if not in name, a part of the Russian Empire. But soon this regiment and many of the other Russian units in Manchuria would dissolve. The troops would all go home. As far as the records were concerned, as of October 12, the Mazeppy were no longer with the regiment. They were no longer Strakhov's responsibility.

As he rode away, it was hard not to look back; but he restrained himself. After all, he had been lucky, he told himself. He could have married her and found out only later that she had grown tired of him and was interested in other men. She was only a child, after all. And promiscuous. From the way she had acted when they first met, he should have known better than to get involved with her. Fortunately, he hadn't written to his fiancée, Olga, for two months; so there was no way she could know about his infidelity to her. He would be coming home a bit of a hero, with at least one medal and a good chance for eventual promotion to lieutenant colonel. It was time he finally got married. Sonya had made him realize that. He would certainly miss her. She could be so titillating when she wanted to be; and those last five nights at Ta-ku-shan had been dreadfully lonely. But he was looking forward to seeing Olga, to seeing her reaction to the new man he was proud to have become. He would marry her—quickly. They had waited long enough. It wouldn't be long before he'd be playing with her some of the same games he had so enjoyed with Sonya.

THE NOT-SO-TENDER TOUCH
OF DEATH

18

Bulatovich was alone in the desert. Dry heat. No water. Where had his servants gone? Where were the camels and mules? Just rock and dry ground in all directions. He must have slept. He must have been exhausted and slept through to noon of the next day. It looked like the Danakil Desert. He'd been here before on his way to Addis Ababa. He was back in Ethiopia. How had he gotten here?

It was like his first time in Ethiopia, when bandits had taken his mules and supplies, leaving him and his guides with no water, nothing. That time Leontiev had chanced on them there in the desert. Incredible luck.

Luck. Bulatovich had always had luck before. He had never even had to wish for it. It simply happened. But now he needed it and knew he needed it. He sensed that there was something different about his situation. He could feel himself sweating heavily, more heavily than heat would warrant—he hadn't exerted himself. This was a sweat of desperation.

A sudden chill went up his back. Then he sweated even more heavily. He couldn't survive for long, losing water at this rate.

He remembered Sonya's words (when had she said them?) "Just come back to me safely. I want you whole and sound to take in my arms. . . ."

He scanned the horizon, hoping to find some clue, some familiar landmark. He felt he had been here before. Maybe there was water near, if he could just remember.

Now he remembered. He had been following the course of a mighty river. There had been two streams to follow, and he had chosen this one in hopes that he would be known as a great explorer, a hero. For a while it had been a great roaring river. But it turned out to be the Awash, not the Nile. It slowed, then died abruptly in the desert.

He must have followed the river to its end, then wandered on aimlessly, frustrated. How long had he been walking? Where had he come from? Could he find his way back? He must go back.

He scanned the horizon, looking for signs of water. He thought he glimpsed it, near the horizon to the east. He raced toward it, despite the heat, despite common sense. He ran. It looked like a lake, not a river, a cool, fresh lake. Maybe the river, his river, the river he had devoted his life's efforts to hadn't died; it had gone underground, to rise again as this beautiful lake, this miracle of nature. He could almost taste the water already. It seemed so close. But it must be huge because it didn't seem to get any closer as he ran.

And mirrored on the lake, so vivid, he saw the face of Sonya, Sophia Vassilchikova. His Sophia.

A chill went up his spine. He blinked. It wasn't there. A mirage. A trick of the imagination. "Sonya. Sonya. Sophia," he tried to shout, but his dried-out tongue stuck to his palate; he could only mutter, barely audibly, "Sonya."

✿ ✿ ✿

Chinese Sonya gently wiped his brow and his freshly shaven head with a cool wet cloth. She turned to Laperdin. "He can't be as sick as you say. Listen. He recognizes me. He calls me by name. He's done that many times."

Laperdin smiled, ironically, "Is your name Sonya Vassilchikova?"

"Vassilchikova?"

"A colonel's daughter. I've heard him say as much. He's completely delirious. He says many things. But you choose to hear only what you want to hear."

She bit her lip, then wiped his brow with redoubled tenderness.

⚜ ⚜ ⚜

The desert—everything was dead and desert. Nothing grew, no matter how much he labored. He kept bringing water again and again, pouring it over the dry cracked earth and over his own sunbaked body; but nothing grew, not even a weed.

Then he felt her touch. He must have been dreaming. He was still not completely awake, but he could feel her touch, her unmistakable touch. Asalafetch—so palpable, so present—restoring his strength as only she could. He was capable of anything. He had no limits. He was more than ordinary man. That touch—he'd recognize it anywhere—lingering now on his brow, his eyes. (Had he come down with the fever again? Was that it? But how did he get back to Ethiopia? He couldn't remember.) The eyes, yes, she was taking the sting of the desert out of his eyes. And soon her hands would slowly descend to the rest of his body. He was recovering. She would sense it and arouse him. She had left her Frenchman. He needed her, and she had come back. She loved him. She would do anything for him. She would have his child, his children. And he would be a prince, complete master in his domain.

The touch. There could be no doubt. Or could there? Something about it. A tenderness, a gentle warmth. The touch of someone who sought to give pleasure, to heal and to soothe, but expected nothing in return. Not Asalafetch. No. She gave pleasure only for the pleasure she would receive and did receive in their mutual sensual play. He had never been touched so tenderly before. Could it be another friend of Asalafetch? And Asalafetch was watching, ready to laugh as she had before when he mistook someone else's touch for hers. Who was it then? He wanted to wake fully and see her. But his eyes wouldn't open, and he knew that it would be dark if he did open them—that was the way of Asalafetch, complete darkness, a prerequisite for complete sensuousness. But why so tender—he would almost say "loving"— why should a stranger touch him so?

"*Sin jelada*," he tried to say. It meant "I love you" in Oromi. But his tongue could only manage, "*Sin.*"

✥ ✥ ✥

"Father, pray for him," Sonya asked Lavoisier. "He is very troubled. Not just his body, but his mind, too. I sense it from his troubled face, his restless shifting. And he keeps saying that word. Did you hear it? The English word 'sin' ."

✥ ✥ ✥

Latin. He could hear the singsong Latin of a Catholic priest. When had he heard that before? What about a Catholic priest? Yes. He had rescued one. Lavoisier. Poor man, suffering from typhus. Good to hear that he's well. That's a strong, healthy voice now. Determined. Quite urgent in his prayer.

Mother preferred to pray silently. She did it aloud for social purposes, to make others happy—for Aunt Elizaveta on her deathbed and for Father at his grave.

Father was Catholic. And when they were in Switzerland, Mother had wanted a Catholic priest to pray over his grave because he would have wanted it so—loudly and pompously.

The priest refused. "The wife Orthodox. The children Orthodox. He was no Catholic. I cannot perform a service for such a man."

She cried and said that his prayers weren't worth anything. But then she went herself to the grave, and repeated over and over again, loudly and solemnly, the Lord's Prayer, the only prayer she knew in Latin.

But if you asked her she'd say she didn't understand why some people prayed aloud. Only silent prayers gave her comfort. Everyone to his own comfort, she'd say, but to her it seemed that

274

God was within, and could only be approached privately and silently.

Bulatovich tried to pray. He tried to, as she had once said, pray till the prayer blotted out all thought, so he could sink deep within himself and find the water of life. He needed water.

He was sinking. He felt himself sinking down a deep well. It was dark and he was falling. But where was the water? Was there any water? Had there ever been any water? It was getting hotter, not cooler, and he kept falling.

He was frightened, nothing to grasp or touch or see—no stench even—just falling. He stopped praying but he didn't stop falling. He was dying. Like Aunt Elizaveta, he had fallen too far to climb back to life. He scrambled and struggled and just fell faster.

As he struck the ground, he screamed, he bellowed, he would not die quietly.

God, if there was a God, was not in here. He screamed as his body was crushed on the dry bottom of the well—louder than a desperate bull elephant, tossing dirt to the sky and roaring angrily at God, wherever God might be, for bringing death.

✿ ✿ ✿

It was late at night. Sonya was alone at his bedside. She had fallen asleep on the ground. She was suddenly awakened by an unearthly noise, not loud, but distinct; she feared it was his death rattle. Laperdin had led her to expect as much. A man that weak from loss of blood and loss of sleep couldn't possibly survive so severe a case of typhus. It was a miracle that he had lasted this long. But the deeper he had sunk into his coma, the more she had redoubled her efforts—cold water to keep the fever down, milk and soup forced down his throat to keep up his strength. Lavoisier and the Mazeppy, Starodubov and Pyotr in particular, had helped her and supported her. But she seemed to be the only one who held out any hope that he would even so much as regain consciousness. There was a strength about him. She could sense it when she touched him to bathe him and to cool his fevered frame. He gave her faith—faith that he could meet this new challenge as he had met so many others, that he would live. She hadn't fantasized beyond that point. She concentrated all her efforts, all her will and prayer on helping him survive.

The tenth day and the eleventh day of the disease had passed. Her hopes had grown stronger. Laperdin had told her that, on the average, the crisis and beginning of recovery came on the fourteenth day. He kept emphasizing that this was a particularly severe case and that with Bulatovich's general weakness, having suffered from insomnia and loss of blood, never having recovered from the wound, "It could be three weeks or four weeks, theoretically. All theoretically. The crisis will never come, do you understand? He will die. You're wasting your effort. Worse, you're getting emotionally involved with a dead man. If you believe in God, then pray. But don't pray for his recovery; pray for his immortal soul, and try to take some consolation from that foolish religion of yours. Use it for what it's worth. I have nothing better to offer. Use whatever you can to pull yourself away from him and back to the world of the living. You're young and very beautiful. You will find other men, other heroes to worship. Go, just go. And don't look back."

But she had stayed, and she maintained her faith by touching his brow, sensing his strength remained. Then she awoke to the sound of his death rattle.

Tears rushed to her eyes and she wanted to scream, but instead she lunged at him and pounded on his chest angrily. "Don't die. Don't leave me here. I love you. Do you understand? Don't leave me. Don't . . ." She collapsed, sobbing, on his chest and listened instinctively for a heartbeat. Laperdin had told her repeatedly that it would be the heart that would fail first. He had had her listen to the heart time and again, demonstrating to her, he thought, that it was getting weaker every day. But she had pressed her head closer and harder to his chest each time, amplifying the beat with the intensity of her attention, convincing herself that it wasn't anywhere near as bad as Laperdin contended.

She heard a beat even now and began to sob convulsively, uncontrollably. It was so cruel for her ears to play tricks on her when it was all over. It was probably the beat of her own heart she was hearing.

But the beat grew stronger, and she could sense her own pulse weakening.

She stood up, frightened as if she had seen a ghost.

She lit a candle and came close.

The eyes were open. But they had an empty, dead, glassy look. She turned aside and vomited convulsively on the ground beside his bed.

Again she came close with the candle. There was no response to the candle in his eyes. The pupils were contracted as they had been throughout the disease.

Then she glanced down. Near his abdomen, the sheet was wet and yellow. In his death throes, he had fouled himself. He hadn't urinated for days. She had been watching for a sudden gush as a sign that he had reached the crisis. But now, cruelly, it had come in death.

She tried to shut the eyes. She couldn't bear to look at them. But they wouldn't shut. So she shielded them gently with a cool cloth she had ready near at hand. Then she bent near, holding the candle close. She saw the square head, the firm jaw, the chin still thrust forward, taut muscles holding it rigid in that position. All through his illness, she had kept the top of his head shaven to keep it cool and his beard trimmed the way he liked it. But his cheeks were sunken, the skin pale and loose, discolored with large dark red spots.

She reached under the cool cloth and gently touched the little red indentation on the bridge of his nose, where his heavy glasses used to rest. She tried to remember him alive and well, trying to gather the strength to give him a parting kiss. She had never kissed him, and she had never kissed a dead man before.

The candle flickered wildly, sending eerie shadows swaying. The large airy hospital tent that Dr. Stankevich had been kind enough to leave them was open on two sides—but it was a clear, still, windless night. She trembled and the shadows swung more wildly. She blew the candle out.

She licked her little finger and held it in front of his nostrils. A breeze. She licked it again. Yes, a distinct breeze. A breath.

She pressed her ear close to his heart. A beat. Yes. A beat. And louder than she had heard for days, or she was going crazy. Crazy and happy. She hugged him, and his body responded—warmly and tenderly, if ever so slightly. She was sure of it.

⚜ ⚜ ⚜

Weeds started to sprout in the desert. Then bushes and trees. In a matter of moments a jungle had sprung up—new life, green and abundant. But it was none of his doing. All those days and years of struggling to make something grow had led to nothing; and now, for no apparent reason, a jungle had grown. And he resented the jungle that he had worked for and prayed for, because it wasn't his jungle; it was beyond his control.

So he took an ax and chopped every tree in sight. If it couldn't be his jungle, the result of his effort, there would be no jungle. With his own sweat and muscle, he would tear it down.

But he soon grew weary and rested; and while he rested, new trees sprouted and grew to full height.

He raised his ax again, then dropped it. He was dreaming. He realized he was dreaming.

He bit his tongue, purposely, to wake himself. He hated that dream. The pain was a small price to pay.

⚜ ⚜ ⚜

He opened his eyes. Half a face, one eye was staring at him, hot blood pouring at him. The dead boy. The boy he killed. The boy who wounded him. Did they call this courage? Killing. Facing death. Manhood. Murder. Nothing more than murder. The face. He shut his eyes, and still he saw the face. He prayed for blindness, a blindness that would erase this image from his mind.

⚜ ⚜ ⚜

He woke up, or did he? Something was missing. The train was on the wrong track, it wouldn't stop, and he didn't know how to get off. But Chinese Sonya was there. He remembered having seen her enter his compartment a few miles back. And then she was gone.

⚜ ⚜ ⚜

He missed a touch. Not the sensuous, selfish touch of Asalafetch, not the provocative, playful stroke of his Sonya—no, a tender, loving hand that comforted and asked nothing in return.

He was curious. He longed for it. He felt incomplete without it. The memory of that touch and the desire to feel such warmth, such love again broke through the nightmare images that plagued him, giving him something to look forward to—looking forward, if nothing else, to the memory, the dream that there could be and in fact was such a person.

⊕ ⊕ ⊕

He awoke. His eyes were open. He knew he hadn't opened them—they were open already—but just now he saw through them clearly. Maybe fuzzy images had been mixed with his dreams, but now he was awake, he was sure of it, because the tent was dull brown and static and the ground, the sheets—everything was less vivid than it would appear in a dream.

"Sonya," he said automatically. Pyotr was the figure standing at his bedside. And Pyotr seemed to wince at the word "Sonya." "Where is she? Where is Sonya? I could have sworn that she was here beside my bed."

"Father, he's awake!" shouted Pyotr, running from the tent anxiously, perhaps to spread the word.

"Good morning," Father Lavoisier greeted him.

"Where is Sonya?" asked Bulatovich.

"Oh, yes. You often asked for her in your delirium. Yes, many times these many days. 'Sonya Vassilchikova,' if I heard correctly. You are in Manchuria. Do you remember? We are at Ta-ku-shan. You were badly wounded. Then you caught typhus on top of that. You caught it from me, having saved my life. You deserve a medal for that, you know. And I'll see that you get it. The French Legion of Honor. Your superiors are such narrow-minded men. But no matter. You're alive, no thanks to them. They simply left you here with me and your Mazeppy. Laperdin was the only one with any medical knowledge. Everyone thought that you would die. It was simply too much punishment for a body to take. Your Shemelin kept saying that it was a test, God testing you. I haven't been able to make any sense out of his beliefs. You were dreadfully sick. Even after the crisis, you were unconscious for three weeks and more. It may be another couple of weeks before you have the strength to walk. But Laperdin would know that better than I."

"Where is Sonya?"

"Yes, Sonya, your Sonya. Like I said, we're in Manchuria. Remember? Your Sonya is back in Petersburg, I believe. Safe and sound, in all likelihood. She'll be there waiting for you, I'm sure, when you get back."

"No. I mean the other Sonya. Chinese Sonya. Where is she? I could have sworn that she was here."

Lavoisier grimaced, then took a deep breath. "It was most unfortunate."

Bulatovich quickly raised himself on his elbows. "What are you saying?"

"She was most devoted to you those two weeks up until the crisis. I must admit that she was the only one who believed that you would live that long. A girl of strong faith and strong will."

"Where is she?" Bulatovich persisted anxiously.

"She took sick. Typhus. You caught it from me. And she caught it from you, while nursing you, apparently."

"And how is she now? Has she passed the crisis?"

"No . . ."

"Then take me to her. Call the Mazeppy. Have them take me to her." Looking up, he noticed that the Mazeppy had gathered near the entrance of the tent and were standing about nervously, looking more at the ground than at him. "What's gotten into you, men? Do I look that bad that you don't want to come near me?" He glanced down and saw his protruding ribs. "I must look a sight. Rather like a ghost. Right, Butorin? Is this what your ghosts look like?" He laughed, but no one laughed with him. "What's wrong?" he shouted and fell back on the bed, suddenly aware that he was, indeed, very weak.

Pyotr stepped forward, went up to his bed, and knelt there. "Like Father Lavoisier said, sir, Sonya took sick."

"Well, take me to her. What are you waiting for? I'm the weak one, not you. You and Starodubov, pick up my bed and take me to her."

Laperdin interjected "You wouldn't want to go where she is."

"Let me tell it," insisted Pyotr.

"Tell what?"

Pyotr hesitated, so Laperdin said simply "She died."

Bulatovich sat up suddenly. "Died? What do you mean, died? Lavoisier's alive. I'm alive. She's a strong young girl, stronger than either of us. She'll pull through. Don't worry. She'll pull through. Just take me to her now. Immediately! That's an order!"

"There were complications," Laperdin interrupted.

"What?"

"It seems she was pregnant," he explained. "And it certainly didn't help that she lost so much sleep nursing you," he added in a burst of bitterness, almost admitting how much he had cared for her, then catching himself short. "The fact is she's dead and buried."

Bulatovich lay back, his muscles taut, his jaw thrust forward, his fists ready, but he said nothing and did nothing. For three days, although he often appeared to be conscious, he didn't move.

♔ ♔ ♔

On the fourth day, he started to talk again, but he only showed interest in his own health, complaining of aches and general weakness, inquiring about the course of his disease and what could be expected next. He showed no inclination to try to get up.

Each day he appeared a little stronger physically, but to hear him talk one would think he were much worse. He seemed to magnify every little pain and discomfort. He seemed overaware of his own frailty, vulnerability, and mortality, and unwilling to take the slightest risk.

Pyotr and Father Lavoisier continued to be solicitous, doing everything they could to make things easier for him, to reduce his pain and anxiety.

But Laperdin soon grew impatient with his patient and began to bait him, much to the consternation of the other Mazeppy. "Why do you want to live?" Laperdin asked. "Or do you want to live? Do you have any idea what you want to do with your life? Or are you just hanging onto it out of habit and out of fear of death?"

"Why do you badger me?"

"Because I hate to see a man watch himself die."

"Has my condition worsened?" he asked anxiously.

"You have begun to die," replied Laperdin firmly, but with an ironic grin.

"How much longer do you think I have to live?" asked Bulatovich, seriously concerned.

"Not long at all, sir. Barring accident, I'd say you have no more than thirty, forty, fifty, maybe sixty or seventy years left."

"What nonsense are you spouting now?" asked Bulatovich, showing the first signs of anger of his convalescence.

"You've stopped living, sir. You stopped living when you stopped having a reason to live, when you no longer believed in anything you'd be willing to risk your life for. You stopped living and began to watch yourself die, just a little bit more each day."

"Take him away! Pyotr! Starodubov! Take this madman away!"

👑 👑 👑

Bulatovich was in no hurry to rebuild his muscles, no hurry to stand or walk or push himself in any way. When he did start walking, it was probably because boredom drove him to it—he was sick of looking at the dark walls of the mud hut they had moved him to when the weather turned wintry.

He soon fell into the habit of strolling to the top of the hill overlooking their campsite and sitting next to the headstone Starodubov had carefully fashioned for Chinese Sonya. From there Bulatovich stared off to the east, where several miles away puffs of steam sometimes arose and sometimes the distant clatter of construction echoed. Repair of the railway apparently was progressing. The way to Port Arthur was open, as was the way back to Russia. But Bulatovich showed no interest in trying to board another train.

It was on that hilltop that the Mazeppy confronted him one crisp mid-December morning.

Pyotr spoke first, "Where are you going to go, sir? What are you going to do?"

"Nowhere. Nothing."

"But you can't, sir. There are people who depend on you and look up to you as a hero. You can't just give up."

"I can do whatever I choose to do and that is nothing."

"But your record, sir," offered Sofronov. "Surely, you want to clear your good name?"

He simply shook his head.

"Sir," Shemelin tried anxiously, "you met the test, the test of life. You risked your career and your life not for glory, not for advancement, but simply to save a fellow human being. You have every reason to feel proud."

"You were wounded," added Butorin. "Isn't that magically supposed to give you true courage?"

"I wish it were that simple," replied Bulatovich.

Starodubov, who had been standing just behind him, suddenly picked up Bulatovich and threw him on the frozen ground.

"What in the name of God?" he said as he picked himself up.

Starodubov grabbed him again and threw him on the ground.

"What are you trying to prove?" Bulatovich asked.

But when he stood up again, Starodubov threw him down again.

"Now look," said Bulatovich, beginning to lose his temper. "This ground is hard, and I'm in no condition to play this kind of game."

His glasses had fallen off. He crawled and groped, but before he reached them, Starodubov bent down, picked up Bulatovich, lifted him over his head, and threw him back to the ground.

The impact stung his back and stunned him for a moment. Bulatovich looked up in amazement at the blurred form of this white-haired giant.

"You, sir, are a coward," said Starodubov.

"What?" asked Bulatovich, without glasses unable to determine the expression on Starodubov's face, uncertain how seriously he should take these strange actions and words.

"You're a coward—that's your true name. All your life you've had this luck. You were so sure of it, you could afford to be careless. You could dare to do anything. And now it's gone. You're nothing but a man, just as vulnerable as the rest of us. And now you're scared. Now you see it's not easy to take chances when you know you can die. All along you were just a lucky coward parading around like a hero. You won't be lucky this time, sir. I'm going to kill you."

Starodubov jumped and landed belly down on top of Bulatovich, grabbed hold of his throat, and started choking him in earnest. Bulatovich broke the grip and scrambled free, only to be caught and wrestled down again.

Lavoisier stepped forward to intervene, but Pyotr stopped him. "Just let them alone. Starodubov knows what he's doing."

Bulatovich struggled, using all the strength he could muster in his still-weakened body, but to no avail. His arms and legs were pinned, his back painfully contorted. It was no contest, hopeless—this man was three times his size. At any moment Starodubov could snap his back like a twig. He sensed that this gentle, awkward giant, so like Old Hrisko, so like a father to him, intended to do just that. He had no idea why Starodubov wanted to kill him. He just knew that he wanted to live, that he had to preserve his life any way he could. He lunged with his head and bit hard and with total abandon, missing the throat, teeth digging into shoulder flesh, desperately.

Starodubov screamed, let loose his hold, and straining his powerful arms, managed to pry loose the jaw, throwing Bulatovich to the ground near the headstone. He stood there ominously above Bulatovich, laughing, yes, laughing like some madman ready to take his final revenge for some imagined wrong or for no reason at all. But instead of attacking, he reached out to pull Bulatovich up off the grave and hugged him warmly. "Yes," he laughed and cried, "yes, you are my son."

Bulatovich hugged him back, with all the surge of energy and strength his sudden danger had given him. It felt good to be alive.

AFTERWORD

Alexander Bulatovich (1870-1919) was a soldier, explorer, and religious leader whose field of action ranged from Tsarist Russia to Ethiopia to Manchuria to Mount Athos. *The Name of Hero* covers his life up through the Manchurian campaign of the Boxer Rebellion in 1900. After Manchuria, Bulatovich returned to Petersburg, became a monk, returned to Ethiopia to try to found a Russian monastery and school there, then went to Mount Athos and became involved in a bitter heresy dispute. He was a chaplain at the front in World War I and survived the Russian Revolution, only to be murdered at his family's estate, Lutsikovka, in December 1919. His story and that of a core of people close to him, such as the Mazeppy and the Ethiopian boy Vaska, will continue in two subsequent volumes—*The Name of Man* and *The Name of God*.

The odd shifts in the career of Bulatovich first drew me to him as a subject for historical novels. I was interested in the man himself—his energy and enthusiasm, and the puzzle of what motivated him. I suspected that he was on some sort of quest, driven by an inner need to push himself to the limits of his capabilities.

I was also drawn by the strangeness of the events—Russian explorers in Ethiopia, the Russian conquest of Manchuria, a heresy battle in the twentieth century. I wanted to understand the man and his time, to get some insight into how the people and circumstances could have interacted to produce such events.

I first discovered Bulatovich in the *London Times* of 1913. I was hunting through microfilms looking for leads for another story when I chanced on an article describing how Russian troops had besieged two monasteries at Mount Athos in Greece and exiled some 880 monks to remote parts of the Russian Empire for believing that "the Name of God was a part of God and, therefore, in itself divine." Bulatovich—former Guards officer and African explorer—was the leader and defender of the monks.

News was a far more leisurely business then than now. The reporter drew an analogy to characters in a novel by Anatole France and drew an interesting sketch of the background and motivations of the main figure. I got the impression of Bulatovich as a restless man, full of energy, chasing from one end of the world to the other in search of the meaning of life. Eventually, he had sought quiet as a monk at Mount Athos, only to find himself once again in the midst of a battle.

I was in the Army then (1970), a reservist stationed in San Angelo, Texas. When I returned to Boston and then to graduate school, I tracked down all available leads, but could uncover very little additional information. There was a poem by Mandelshtam about the heresy. The philosopher Berdyaev had nearly been sent to Siberia for expressing support for the heretics. But that was it. I tried spinning a largely fictional account around these few facts, but never got very far.

Then in the spring of 1972, the "B" volume of the new edition of the *Soviet Encyclopedia* appeared. The previous edition had mentioned an "Alexander" Bulatovich who died about 1910. The Bulatovich in the *Times* article was named "Anthony" and was very much alive in 1913. The new edition made it clear that Alexander and Anthony were the same man. (One changes one's name when one becomes a monk.) The item was signed by I. S. Katsnelson, a professor at the Institute of Oriental Studies in Moscow. I wrote to him and he replied, sending me a copy of a book he had just published—a new edition of two long-out-ofprint books by Bulatovich about his experiences in Ethiopia (1896-98), together with a biographical introduction.

Katsnelson specializes in ancient Egypt and Sudan. He has written several books on ancient Egyptian literature and a major monograph on early Sudan. His interest in Bulatovich's activities in Ethiopia is a sideline.

At any rate, Professor Katsnelson was very helpful, providing me not only with copies of his books but also with the address of Bulatovich's 98-year-old sister, Princess Mary (Mariya or "Meta") Orbeliani, who was then living in British Columbia. From that point on, one lead led to another.

In the summer of 1972, I traveled to Mount Athos and visited the one remaining Russian monastery there. On the way I met a scholar, Popoulidis, in Salonika who was writing a doctoral dissertation on the heresy. And in Athens, at the National Library, I found and photocopied a book Bulatovich had written about the heresy.

At Harvard's Widener Library and at Hellenic College in Brookline, Massachusetts, I found more articles and books by and about Bulatovich and the heresy.

The following summer I visited Mary Orbeliani in Penticton, British Columbia. In long tape-recorded conversations and in letters before and after that visit, she provided me with valuable information about her brother's life and insight into his character. At 99 she was very articulate, lucid, and helpful. She was a remarkable and very memorable person in her own right—at that time still active as a watercolor artist and pianist. (She passed away in 1977 at the age of 103.)

Back in Boston, I tracked down references to Bulatovich's participation in the Manchurian campaign of the Boxer Rebellion. The only work in English dealing with that campaign, *The Russo-Chinese War* by George A. Lensen, mentioned Bulatovich often in the few chapters dealing with battles at Ongun, Hailar, Yakeshi, and the Greater Hsing-An Mountains. The comprehensive bibliography led me to the source materials: two versions of General Orlov's autobiographical account of the campaign, one in book form and one in an historical journal, both available at the Widener Library. Also, at that time, Mary Orbeliani's son, Bulatovich's nephew, André, found and sent me a copy of the handwritten official record of Bulatovich's military career, with many previously unknown details on the Manchurian campaign.

Gradually, the story began to take shape in my mind as a trilogy, with the first volume structured around events in Manchuria in 1900.

For the background, the historical events, and the details of camp life, I stayed very close to my sources. The major events of the campaign and of Bulatovich's life as recorded in this volume are true, to the best of my knowledge. But I wasn't interested in simply presenting a series of historical facts.

I was fascinated by Bulatovich's character. I wanted to work out the puzzle of his motivations, to figure out what could have led to all the shifts and twists of his life story.

Regarding his character and motivation, my sources were incomplete and often contradictory, giving me plenty of room to pick and choose, invent and discover, while remaining consistent with historical probability.

As for the rest of the characters: I had some notion of General Orlov from his writings. He emphasizes the feats of the enlisted men in his command. He praises only one officer—Bulatovich. He quotes Bulatovich's superiors, the commander and assistant commander of the regiment, only to present them in a negative light, as doctrinaire disciplinarians—in contrast to Bulatovich's bravery, initiative, and bold individual style. Although Orlov lists the names of hundreds of enlisted men, he never gives the names of this commander and assistant commander. I invented the names "Kupferman" and "Strakhov" and fleshed out their characters and gave them each a past.

As for the Mazeppy, I knew from Mary Orbeliani that half a dozen men in Bulatovich's command were so devoted to him that when he entered the monastery, they followed him there. I speculated that to be that close they would probably have been in battle together. According to Orlov and the military record, Bulatovich frequently led a small group on scouting missions. And according to Mary Orbeliani, his men called him "Mazeppa." So I chose names from the general roster given by Orlov and dubbed the group "Mazeppy."

Orlov described a fifty-four-year-old, white-haired giant of a Cossack named Starodubov, who received a medal for capturing an enemy flag at the Battle of Ongun. I invented the theft and moved him to Bulatovich's command.

One of Bulatovich's men named Butorin actually did get caught behind enemy lines at Hailar and escaped, very much as described here. (At Hailar, too, the headless bodies of three missing Cossacks were found near a temple. My description of that funeral, however, is fictitious.)

The other enlisted men in Manchuria were invented, as was Chinese Sonya. Onc sparse and disputed account of an affair with an Ethiopian noblewoman was the basis for Asalafetch.

There were rumors of love interest between Bulatovich and Sophia Vassilchikova, but only her name and approximate age can be considered "historical."

The same General Rennenkampf whom Bulatovich confronted in Manchuria was largely responsible for the disastrous Russian defeat at the Battle of Tannenburg at the beginning of World War I (see Barbara Tuchman's *Guns of August* and Alexander Solzhenitsyn's *August 1914*).

There was an unexplained gap in Bulatovich's military record. He did, in fact, rescue a French missionary named Lavesier or Lavoisier and later was named a Chevalier of the French Legion of Honor for having done so. His sister described how he killed the young Chinese boy who attacked and wounded him on the return trip (a horrifying vision that rccurred in his dreams). She also mentioned that he caught typhus from the missionary and that after he recovered he made a short trip to Japan. The military record says nothing about that trip and says that he was never on leave for convalescence from wounds. It just skips from the rescue of the missionary to about four months later when he was with another Russian army in another part of Manchuria. Apparently he had been left behind, considered as good as dead.

For background on Ethiopia, I relied heavily on Bulatovich's own accounts. I also received considerable help from Solomon Kenea, an Oromo from an area of Ethiopia Bulatovich had frequented. While he was a student at Harvard, he tutored my wife and me in Oromo. (At that time, just before the Ethiopian Revolution, we had hoped to be able to travel there.)

Chris Rosenfeld was also very helpful, providing insight into the role of women in Ethiopia. She let me read the manuscript of the biography she was writing about the wife of Menelik II, the Empress Taitu.

Many other people have been very helpful to me over the eleven years it took to make this book. Rex Sexton, Claude Thau, and Mark Saxton provided advice and encouragement, reading and reacting to my various attempts. Bulatovich's nephew, André Orbeliani, read several early versions of the manuscript and set me straight on a number of important details. He also provided me with his uncle's official military record and lent me a copy of the original edition of his uncle's book *With the Armies of Menelik II*, which includes photos that Bulatovich himself had taken in Ethiopia 1897-98.

People who helped me with information, advice, and leads included George Ivask, Yfraim Isaak, Zaude Gabre Sellassie, Cynthia Citron, Greg Moshnin, and Sayers Brown.

People who helped by reading and commenting on the various drafts of the book included Gary Wolfe, Laszlo Tikos, Susan Brownsberger, Sheila Goggin, Howie Rosenof, Vicki Mutascio, Bonnie Keyes, Elynor Harrington, Dan and Julie Horton, Mike Chapman, John Huzzard, Terry Earls, Kathy Pikosky, Ed Trobec, Jeff and Dagmar Barnouw, Karen Harrison, Noreen Webber, Derek White, and my parents.

The advice of my agent, Ashley Grayson, led to some important revisions.

The probing questions and detailed comments of my editor, Janice Gallagher at J. P. Tarcher, Inc., led to substantial final changes and additions that, I believe, vastly improved this novel.

I wish to thank all these people (and others whom I may have neglected to mention) for their help and support.

Above all I wish to thank my wife, Barbara, for the crucial advice and keen insights she has provided time and again.

West Roxbury, Mass.
Feb. 3, 1981